I0763370

# A Queen of Fire and Flame

Book Three of the Fire and Flame Series

K.J. Johnson

K.J. Johnson Books

Copyright © 2024 K.J. Johnson

First published by K.J. Johnson Books 2024

All rights reserved. No part of this publication may be reproduced, stored, or transmitted in any form or by any means, electronic, mechanical, photocopying, recording, scanning, or otherwise without written permission from the publisher. It is illegal to copy this book, post it to a website, or distribute it by any other means without permission.

This novel is entirely a work of fiction. The names, characters, and incidents portrayed in it are the work of the author's imagination. Any resemblance to actual persons, living or dead, events or localities is entirely coincidental. K.J. Johnson asserts the moral right to be identified as the author of this work.

ISBN: 978-1-7636825-4-2

# Contents

# Dedication

This one is for all the dark romance readers who go feral for a fictional man with a penchant for a hand necklace and whispering dirty words as a sign of his adoration.

Now turn the page because Silas is waiting for you...

...That's my good girl.

# Content Warning

This story is intended for mature readers only.

It contains extreme possessiveness by the MMC towards the FMC, explicit sexual content, degradation, sexual assault, profanity, depictions of violence, animal death, and other topics that may be triggering for some readers.

Reader discretion is advised.

# Map of Aetherian

# Pronunciation Guide

- Valoren: Val – or – ren
- Netheran: Neh – thuh - ran
- Pyrithia: Py – ri – thee - ah
- Vidyaa: Vid – ee - ah
- Zarinia: Zah – reen – ee - ah
- Elysara: Eh – lee – sah - rah
- Aetherian: Uh – thir – ee – an
- Cathal: Kah - hal
- Cian: Kee – an
- Cillian: Kill – ee – an
- Fionn: Fee - on
- Misneach: Mish – nahh
- Caolán: Kway – lawn
- Oisín: Uh – sheen
- Rónán: Roh - nawn
- Niamh: Neev
- Fórsa: Fohr – suh
- Grainne: Grawn - yaa
- Saoirse: Seer – sha
- Drakkon: Drak – kahn
- Illiana: Ill – ee – ar - nah

- Rhene: Reen
- Eabha: Ay – va
- Caspan: Cas - pan
- Oonagh: Oo – nuh
- Aodhán: Ay – awn
- Orla: Or – la
- Eoin: O - in
- Maxim: Max – eem

# A Quick Recap...

## A Heart of Fire and Flame

A Heart of Fire and Flame is set in the realm of Aetherian. The citizens of Aetherian are all connected to the realm by the magic it offers, fórsa. Their connection to the realm allows them to enjoy long lives, with those who can manifest fórsa into a weapon, living the longest.

When Harlowe was an infant, the Kingdoms of Pyrithia, Zarinia, and Vidyaa attempted to overthrow her father, the King of Valoren, and conquer her kingdom. The citizens of Valoren were able to wield fórsa more freely than other kingdoms, and many speculated it was because of the land itself.

With help from the Kingdom of Netheran, Harlowe's father was able to hold off the attacks, and peace returned to the realm.

Unbeknownst to Harlowe, the aid her father received from Kieran, the King of Netheran, came at a steep price: her hand in marriage. Since Harlowe was an infant, Kieran hadn't acted on the marriage agreement.

Twenty-five years after the war, Harlowe is yet to come into her power, despite most people being able to manifest fórsa by their twentieth birthday.

As Harlowe's twenty-fifth birthday approaches, a visiting delegation of Cathal (dragon riders) arrives on Harlowe's doorstep. Harlowe is surprised to discover the delegation is from Pyrithia, as the kingdoms have not interacted since the war. Despite her mistrust of the foreigners, Harlowe can't help her growing attraction to the sexy-as-sin General of the Cathal, Silas.

Intrigued by the man who has been invited to reignite the practice of dragon bonding within her kingdom, something that was outlawed centuries prior because of the risks involved, Harlowe grows close to Silas.

Strange occurrences begin to happen around Harlowe, and unknown assailants attack her kingdom. Silas and Harlowe work together to protect her kingdom, which draws them closer together.

Kieran arrives to attend Harlowe's birthday celebrations and disrupts their bonding relationship by announcing his intention to court her.

Harlowe senses Kieran is not the gentleman he pretends to be. Rather than allowing Kieran to court her, she sneaks out of her kingdom, accompanying Silas when he leads the Valoren soldiers in their search for dragons.

Encouraged by her curiosity and her best friend Emmerson, Harlowe sneaks after the soldiers to watch as they seek their potential bond mates.

Silas warned Harlowe and Emmerson not to follow, as it was too dangerous. So when they hear the Cathal flying overhead, they hide out in a nearby cave.

Harlowe and Emmerson realize they are not alone when a dragon, Misneach, speaks to Harlowe, telling her he feels a pull towards her, and that they were destined to meet. Misneach offers his bond to her and Harlowe accepts. They then return to her kingdom with the others.

When they arrive back in Valoren, Kieran shows his true nature, which culminates in him attacking Harlowe at her birthday celebrations and informing her of their betrothal.

Harlowe, injured and feeling betrayed, confronts her parents who confirm Kieran was telling the truth.

Kieran apologizes to Harlowe, and her father insists she fulfills the marriage contract. When she refuses, Harlowe's father locks her in her chambers while they undertake the wedding preparations.

Kieran visits Harlowe in her chambers, revealing his unique powers and confessing to tricking her father into accepting his marriage proposal. Kieran tells Harlowe that he had witches spell the monarchs of Vidyaa and Zarinia to encourage them to invade Valoren. When Netheran offered aid to Valoren, Pyrithia, fearing the outcome of the war and a more powerful Netheran, joined the war to push Kieran back.

Kieran reveals Harlowe was prophesied to wield great power, and he wanted to secure her hand in marriage so he could control her powers.

On the eve of her wedding, Harlowe's mother sneaks into her chambers and gives her the key so she can escape.

Harlowe, Misneach, and Emmerson flee the palace and head towards the Forest of Nightmares, where the last truth-sayer, the Lost Witch, is rumored to be hiding out.

When a group of Cathal spots them, the trio separates, with Misneach serving as a distraction while Harlowe and Emmerson flee.

Inside the forest, the monsters of myth and legend lurk, and Harlowe and Emerson narrowly avoid falling victim to them when Harlowe releases a torrent of flames, decimating the creatures.

Harlowe and Emmerson locate The Lost Witch, and she confirms Kieran has unique abilities that disrupt the balance of power within the realm. To counter this imbalance, the fates created Harlowe and bestowed her with the ability to call upon dragon flames. This allows Harlowe to have a unique bond with all dragons and not just her bond mate.

The Lost Witch also informs Harlowe that her power is the only thing that can stand in the way of Kieran and his nefarious intentions. However, the Lost Witch also warns Harlowe that should she join forces with Kieran, her power will amplify his, and together they would be the ruination of the realm.

Armed with the knowledge they sought, Harlowe and Emmerson make plans to leave the forest. On the way, they reunite with Silas, and his group of Cathal and decide to stay with them for the safety they offer.

However, the next morning, Harlowe wakes to find herself cuffed to the inside of Silas's tent. When she demands to know what's going on, he only tells her he is trying to protect her.

Emmerson discovers that the King of Pyrithia sent Silas and his Cathal to Valoren, pretending they were training the Valoren soldiers. However, their real aim was to abduct Harlowe and bring her back to Pyrithia.

The King of Pyrithia learned of the impending marriage between Harlowe and the King of Netheran, and feared what a stronger alliance between the two kingdoms would mean. He instructed Silas to bring Harlowe to Pyrithia in the hope he could persuade her father to join forces with Pyrithia rather than Netheran.

Upon the group's arrival in Pyrithia, Harlowe discovers Silas is the second-born son of the King and the Prince of Pyrithia.

Silas also learns that his father's plans have changed during his absence. The King now plans to wed Harlowe to his first-born son, Silas's older brother. The King hopes they will produce an heir to strengthen any alliance between the two kingdoms.

Harlowe refuses the match and Silas makes plans to flee with her. However, before they can get away from Silas's father, Kieran arrives and disappears with Harlowe back to Netheran.

# A Daughter of Fire and Flame

Harlowe's abrupt disappearance leaves Silas and his companions reeling, as they struggle to come to terms with the death of Cian.

During the unfolding chaos, Zeke arrives with his dragon, Rónán, and the pair absconds with Emmerson, followed closely by Misneach.

At Cillian's behest, they trail after Emmerson while working on a plan to track down and rescue Harlowe.

Meanwhile, Kieran has forced Harlowe to return with him to the Kingdom of Netheran. While there, Harlowe meets two women, Everly and Lucinda.

Everly, a kind woman, is appointed as Harlowe's chambermaid. She does her best to help Harlowe adjust to her new life in Netheran. However, she is fearful of Kieran's wrath should she step out of line.

Meanwhile, Lucinda makes her contempt for Harlowe known early on, as she perceives her as a threat to winning the title of Queen of Netheran.

While Harlowe has every intention of escaping Kieran and the Kingdom of Netheran, she soon finds out that it will be a much harder task than she originally thought. In large part, this is due to the fact that an enormous maze surrounds the palace. Despite her best efforts, the complex system of twists and turns prevents Harlowe from navigating her way out of the labyrinth.

Meanwhile, Silas, Cillian, Fionn, and Teller catch up with Emmerson and Zeke at an abandoned castle that has fallen into ruin. As they explore the ruins, they sense there is something different about the place, but they can't quite put their finger on it.

Both groups decide it is best if they work together, and agree to start their search for Harlowe in Netheran. Before they can leave, however, Cian's dragon, Saoirse, arrives and bonds with Emmerson.

Back in Netheran, Harlowe is called to attend a gathering where she observes the debauchery of Kieran's court. Harlowe unknowingly consumes wine that Kieran has enhanced with an elixir, dissolving her inhibitions and making her more receptive to his advances.

During the night, Harlowe senses someone watching her and she catches sight of an unknown figure lurking in the shadows. Beneath the man's hood, Harlowe is able to make out the glowing amber eyes of the man before he disappears into the darkness.

The next morning, Harlowe wakes up to find herself inside Kieran's chambers, with a hazy memory of the events from the night before. The pair argue and Kieran offers Harlowe a deal to settle all grievances between them. If Harlowe can guess the source of Kieran's magic, he will release her from the marriage contract her father entered on her behalf. However, if she cannot guess correctly, Harlowe is to submit to Kieran without further contest.

But there's a catch: Harlowe can only make three guesses, and Kieran forbids her from seeking the assistance of his staff.

Determined to escape Kieran's clutches, Harlowe turns to the only source of knowledge she has access to: Kieran's impressive collection of ancient tomes.

However, the library fails to provide Harlowe with any insights into Kieran's abilities. Despite this setback, Harlowe comes across a passage detailing the Aurora Stone. Harlowe learns the stone was used to set the wards around the Forest of Nightmares and that is why the creatures cannot venture into the rest of the realm.

Frustrated at her lack of progress, Harlowe returns to the maze, intent on mapping the twists and turns, hoping to find a way through. As she travels through the maze, Harlowe senses she is not alone and is attacked by the golden-eyed man from the party. Harlowe escapes the struggle but is injured.

Everly tends to Harlowe in the following days, where she learns Harlowe is the prophesied Daughter of Fire and Flame. Everly agrees to help Harlowe escape and tells her the source of Kieran's powers: the Original Witch.

When Harlowe informs Kieran of her guess, he becomes enraged and immediately suspects that someone helped her. He mistakenly assumes Lucinda is the culprit, believing she did it in an effort to remove Harlowe from Netheran. Kieran kills Lucinda by snapping her neck and Harlowe confesses she was not responsible.

Kieran presses Harlowe to reveal who helped her, but she refuses. However, she inadvertently reveals Everly's involvement when she glances in her direction.

Kieran threatens to kill Everly, and Harlowe makes a trade for Everly's life. Harlowe agrees to stay with Kieran if he lets Everly go. Kieran agrees and Everly departs Netheran.

Once Everly is free and no longer at risk of harm, Harlowe enters the maze in the hope of finally making it to the end. Once she crosses the threshold into the maze, Harlowe senses that something is different and follows a low humming sound, which brings her to the end of the maze. Harlowe crosses through a magic barrier and flees Netheran.

Once Harlowe is free of Kieran's magic, Misneach is able to sense Harlowe and he abandons the others in search of her. The rest of the group quickly follow and they are all reunited when Misneach locates her. It is during this moment that Harlowe realizes she can communicate with all the dragons.

Harlowe insists they must find Everly, so the group spends the next few days searching Netheran until they eventually find her.

Unsure where to go and who to trust, the group returns to the castle ruins. Harlowe senses something is amiss and is pulled into the void: a plane between worlds, where she meets the Original Witch.

The Original Witch reveals the fates gifted her powers but cautioned her against using them for malicious purposes, as the magic would become unstable and dangerous. The magic gifted to the Original Witch was passed down from mother to daughter and the realm prospered with the help of the witches.

However, some witches became dissatisfied with their advisory roles and sought to overthrow the monarchs they served. In response, the kingdoms cast out all witches, whether or not they shared this view, triggering the War of the Witches.

After being defeated and feeling bitter about being cast aside despite only ever serving the monarchs, the Original Witch passed on her powers to Kieran from the void. Kieran sought retribution for what his kingdom lost during the war and the Original Witch saw this as an opportunity for her own retribution.

Following her encounter with the Original Witch, Harlowe is pulled into a dream with Kieran. Kieran informs Harlowe that she has the choice to either return willingly and serve him at his side or he will have to hunt her down and eliminate her, as she poses a significant risk to his plans.

Harlowe, Emmerson, Zeke, and Everly decide to remain with Silas and his men until they can determine what their next steps should be.

Harlowe remains suspicious of Silas and his intentions, but agrees to work with him to continue her training. During one such training session, the group is attacked by Viddyan warriors and their roc. To save Silas, Harlowe uses her fire powers, exposing her secret.

Once Silas learns about Harlowe's powers, he insists she must train with them. However, when Harlowe tries to wield her flames again, nothing happens.

When the group is unable to assist Harlowe in coaxing out her powers, the dragons suggest she travel to the Mountains of Dragonia to visit the Ancient Dragon. Misneach is against the idea because he can't go with her, and the journey is filled with dangers. Despite this, Harlowe goes to seek answers and Silas volunteers to go with her.

Silas and Harlowe experience a few setbacks along the way, but they eventually find the Ancient Dragon, Drakkon. During this meeting, Drakkon explains to Harlowe how she came to be connected to Kieran. When the Original Witch gifted her powers to Kieran, it created an imbalance in the realm. As the beings responsible for maintaining the balance, the fates created Harlowe to counteract the imbalance Kieran's immense power posed.

The only force strong enough to overcome the power of the Original Witch is dragon flames. So, the fates asked Drakkon for an offering. As the first dragon, all dragons within Aetherian are born from the power that Drakkon houses. Since Harlowe was created from the same source, she shares a connection with all dragons, and Drakkon reveals that this is why she can communicate with them.

Drakkon further explains that Misneach was created specifically to be Harlowe's bonded dragon. As Harlowe is human, she was never supposed to house such power. As a result, she is at risk of drawing too much power, which could have deadly consequences. To counteract this, the fates created Misneach to be an anchor for Harlowe. If Harlowe ever draws too much, Misneach can sense it and help pull her back.

Harlowe also learns that the reason she cannot access her powers at will is because she is blocking herself. Drakkon helps Harlowe understand her fears about succumbing to the connection she feels to Kieran and informs her he is not her twin flame, as she had feared. Harlowe then realizes that Silas is her twin flame.

Armed with this knowledge, Harlowe returns to the group and she learns to command her powers at will. Now that Harlowe has greater control over her flames, the group sets out for Silas's family manor house, where they can determine what to do about Kieran in relative safety.

Before they reach the manor house, however, the group is attacked. Leading the attacking force is the man with the glowing amber eyes. Outnumbered and without the aid of their dragons who had departed on a hunting trip, the group is forced to defend themselves.

During the fighting, Teller is fatally wounded protecting Fionn, and Harlowe is also severely injured by the man with the golden eyes. He reveals he was sent to hunt down Harlowe, so she doesn't get the chance to side with Kieran.

Just as the man is about to deliver a killing blow, Silas kills him, saving Harlowe's life. It is then that the group realizes the unknown assailant who had been hunting Harlowe was, in fact, the Crown Prince of Vidyaa.

The group retreats to Silas's manor house, where Harlowe recovers from her injuries. Kieran once again dream-walks with Harlowe and informs her he plans to conquer the realm. As Harlowe refuses to join him, Kieran releases Harlowe from the dream after declaring that he is coming for her.

The group makes plans to seek alliances with the other kingdoms in the hope of thwarting Kieran's ambitions.

# Chapter One

"Silas," I moaned as pleasure built inside me.

"That's it Little Menace, give in to me," he said roughly.

His hard chest pressed against my back as he threw his leg over my waist, deepening his reach. My body moved in sync with his as he plunged inside me. His slow, languid thrusts had me seeing stars as he hit that delicious spot that had me on the verge of unraveling.

"Oh gods," I gasped, as I reached around the back of his head, pulling him closer. Silas buried his face in the crook of my neck, nipping and kissing his way to the shell of my ear.

"Shatter for me, Little Menace," he commanded, and my body had no choice but to obey.

My orgasm tore through me and I cried out, his name falling from my lips as I came undone.

With a low growl, Silas increased his pace as he chased his own release while I came down from the one he had given me.

A loud banging on the door pulled me from my lust-induced haze before I was ready, and Silas snarled behind me.

"Fuck off," he bellowed as his movements became jerky.

"I wish I could, Brother, but we have a problem," Cillian said from behind the door.

"Fuck," Silas hissed as his body trembled. Seconds later, his hot come filled me, spilling down the inside of my thighs.

Silas withdrew from my body hurriedly, and I mourned the loss of him and the way he stretched me.

In the dark room, Silas fumbled for his pants, colliding with furniture, and cursing softly.

As he reached for the door, he swung it open with such force that I was surprised he didn't rip it from its hinges.

"What is it, Cill?" he asked.

The light from the hallway illuminated the ripple of muscles along his shoulders and back, making my mouth water as I took him in.

As if sensing my eyes on him, Silas glanced behind him, a sly smirk gracing his perfect lips. Desire stirred low in my belly despite my recent orgasm.

"Will you two stop eye-fucking each other?" Cillian scowled, redirecting our attention. "Kieran is here."

Cillian's words doused any lingering heat between us.

"What do you mean, he's here?" Silas demanded as he stalked back into the room to retrieve his tunic and boots.

"He's outside the fucking manor," Cillian said, gesturing towards the window.

I sat bolt upright, gripping the sheet to my chest to conceal my nakedness.

Silas stormed to the window and peered outside.

"Motherfucker," he hissed before making his way back to me, collecting my clothing from the floor as he went.

"Why the fuck is he just standing there?" Silas asked.

"Little Bride," Kieran called, the sound eerie in the stillness of the night. "Come out, come out, wherever you are."

My shoulders stiffened and goosebumps erupted down my spine at the sound.

Silas growled as he pulled my tunic over my head. I let the sheet fall as I pushed my arms through the sleeves before pulling on my pants. Silas passed me my boots, and I'd nearly finished tying my laces as more figures rushed inside the room.

"He's alone," Emmerson said as she walked to stand beside Cillian. Despite it being the middle of the night, she was dressed for battle and armed to her teeth.

"Did you check the northern edge of the property?" Cillian asked and Emmerson glared at him. "Sorry, Little Viper," he said sheepishly before he placed a chaste kiss on her temple.

"Why would he come alone?" Fionn asked.

"Because he knows he's strong enough to win," I mumbled to myself.

"You have such little faith," Silas teased, but I could hear the worry in his tone.

"What's the plan?" Zeke asked.

"He's here for me," I said as I strode toward the table where my daggers lay and began re-sheathing them.

"Don't even think about it," Silas snarled, at the same time Misneach said, **"I will incinerate him before you take a single step towards him, Fire Heart."**

"We will do this together," Emmerson added, leaving Cillian's side in favor of mine.

They were right, of course. I didn't stand a chance against Kieran on my own. However, my need to protect those who stood in the room was a powerful motivator.

"We're not ready," I whispered, meeting Emmerson's eyes only to find her steely resolve reflected in her gaze.

She wouldn't sit this one out, no matter what I said.

"If tonight is the night we fall, then we fall together," she said as she reached out and grabbed my hand, giving it a gentle squeeze.

My gaze flicked to Silas, and I found his dark eyes appraising me. Whatever he saw had him nodding his head in approval. He marched towards me and fastened my short swords over my shoulders.

"Nobody is dying tonight," he declared as he tugged on the leather to ensure it was secure. "Don't get any ideas, Little Menace. We fight until we can't, and then we flee."

I opened my mouth to argue, but closed it when Silas's narrowed gaze bore into me.

"Alright," I agreed.

As I looked around the room, I noticed someone was missing.

"Where's Everly?"

"I told her to stay in her room and not come out," Zeke informed me.

"Thank you," I said as I let out a relieved breath.

I wouldn't forgive myself if something happened to Everly. She was too gentle to be caught up in the impending confrontation. I also wouldn't put it past Kieran to lash out at her for helping me in Netheran.

"Last chance, Little Bride. Then I'm coming in to find you," Kieran taunted.

"This fucker," Emmerson muttered.

"And Harlowe, I will spare no one if you force my hand."

I swallowed the lump forming in my throat as I approached the window.

"Little Menace," Silas growled. His hand snaked around my forearm to stop me from moving any closer. "What are you doing?"

"I'm only going to show my face, I promise." Silas studied me for a moment before he released me and nodded.

I felt the warmth of his body as he pressed into my back. He wouldn't let me do this alone, it seemed.

When I pulled the curtain aside, my eyes collided with cruel blue ones I knew all too well. A smirk pulled up the corner of Kieran's mouth before his upper lip curled in disgust.

I didn't need to turn around to know who Kieran was glaring at.

"What do you want, Kieran?" I asked, drawing his attention back to me.

"You know what I want, Little Bride, now come down here and play with me."

Shadows formed around Kieran's hands before slowly climbing their way up his arms.

My eyes remained locked with his as I searched for any weakness hidden there. As if he could hear my thoughts, Kieran barked out a laugh, throwing his head back as he did so.

"You should know better than that, Bride," he purred.

Fuck.

*Did he know my thoughts? Was that one more mutation of his powers?*

Kieran curled his fingers in a come hither motion and I retreated from the window.

Turning, I studied every face standing before me. "Remember what Silas said. We fight until we can't, and then we flee. I'm not losing anyone else tonight."

Heads bobbed around the room as everyone acknowledged my words.

**"Misneach?"**

**"Yes, Fire Heart?"**

**"Are you ready?"** Misneach scoffed, not bothering to answer my question.

The thunderous sound of beating wings disrupted the silence of the room as the dragons moved into position.

Kieran's unhinged laughter followed as we made our way downstairs.

# Chapter Two

I took a steadying breath as I gripped the door handle, trying to still my trembling hands.

I wasn't afraid of dying.

I understood it was entirely possible that Kieran would end my life before I got the chance to see another sunrise.

What left me shaking in terror was the knowledge that he could easily take someone else I loved from me as well. It had only been a handful of weeks since we lost Teller, and the pain was still so raw.

I couldn't lose anyone else.

I wouldn't lose anyone else.

Determination straightened my spine, and I summoned my flames. They responded immediately, and I felt their warmth as they licked a path up my arms.

"Ready?" I asked as I cast a glance over my shoulder.

Small orbs of energy pierced the darkness as everyone prepared for battle.

As I threw open the door, I pulled up my shield and spread it wide until it encircled those behind me.

Kieran's face lit up with a wide grin that reached his eyes. "Now that, Little Bride, is impressive," he said.

I could hear the awe that filled his tone.

Kieran ran his eyes down the length of my body, his eyes darkening as he did so. "Power suits you," he said huskily.

A threatening growl sounded behind me, and Silas stepped further into my back.

Kieran smirked. "Think you have what it takes, boy?" he taunted.

"I know I do," Silas retorted. "You and I have a few things to settle."

"I'm right here," Kieran said, throwing his arms wide.

"Silas," Cillian warned, sensing the promise of violence emanating from his friend.

A low rumbling sound erupted in the open space moments before blazing heat ripped past my barrier.

I jerked my head to the side and saw Misneach unleash a torrent of red-hot flames, sending them sailing through the air toward Kieran.

Kieran's fingers unfurled and dark shadowy tendrils coated his palms before they surged forward to meet the violent inferno. As if they devoured the very essence of the dragon's flames, Kieran's shadows smothered the fiery blaze burning a path towards him.

Mischief sparkled in Kieran's eyes as he said, "You'll need to do better than that."

"Now!" I bellowed as I lowered my shield, needing to make the most of Kieran's distraction.

Flashes of light darted past my head as, one by one, those behind me sent fòrsa straight for Kieran in a coordinated assault. When the last ball of light flickered in my peripheral vision, I pulled my shield back into place, locking it down before Kieran could retaliate.

Dark tentacles curled and danced in the distance as Kieran's shadows deftly deflected each blow. A frustrated growl sounded to my left and the unmistakable sound of steel being pulled free quickly followed.

"No one leaves this shield," I barked, anticipating the next move of whoever sought to take matters into their own hands.

It was either Silas or Emmerson, and I wasn't about to let either one of them loose.

"Is that all you've got?" Kieran laughed.

"Harlowe," Silas growled.

"No!" I gritted out in response, knowing exactly what he was demanding of me.

"If we get in close, his shadows will be less of an advantage," Silas murmured. "We can overwhelm him and end this fight right here and now."

Before I could answer, an unnatural darkness covered us, blocking out all traces of light and blinding us to the world beyond my shield.

"What the fuck?" Emmerson muttered.

Small jolts of lightning cracked along the exterior of my shield, pulsing and probing as Kieran's shadows tried to find a way inside. The darkness began to twist and writhe, as if alive and with a malevolent will of its own. My breaths grew heavy as I watched, almost transfixed, as the shadows crept across the surface of my shield. Every move was calculated and precise. The air sparked with tension and I watched in horror as my flames recoiled from the power relentlessly pursuing them.

"Draw your weapons," I hissed, not knowing if my shield would withstand whatever Kieran had to throw at me. If he broke through, the others needed to be ready.

The sound of scraping steel dominated the small space, and I sucked in a sharp breath.

The darkness ebbed as the shadows slowly receded, and I gasped in surprise as cerulean blue eyes met mine from the other side of the barrier. Kieran now stood less than a foot in front of me, his head tilted to the side as he studied me.

"Very impressive indeed," Kieran murmured.

An involuntary shudder crept down my spine as his gaze locked with mine and I saw the mania dancing there.

Kieran's shadows darted forward again, spreading over my shield and hammering the fiery barrier as they attempted to pass through.

This time, each blow felt as if someone delivered them straight to my body, battering and bruising it into submission. I gritted my teeth as I pushed my palms forward, sending all my strength outward to keep my shield in place.

"Harlowe," Silas and Emmerson said in unison, their panic clear in their tone, alerting me to the fact that I was doing a poor job of concealing my struggle.

Flames exploded around the edges of my vision as the dragons fought their own battle beyond the barrier. I breathed a sigh of relief, knowing they had all arrived.

Kieran's gaze never strayed from mine as he studied me, assessing me for any sign of weakness.

A pained cry sounded from behind him and my eyes moved of their own volition, seeking the source of the disturbance.

A solid wall of shadows protected Kieran's back while dark tentacles surged forward, attacking the dragons as they fought to bring him down.

**"Misneach?"** I called out as my eyes darted around in panic.

**"Grainne!"** he snarled, and my gaze found the amber dragon as she thrashed against the thick band of shadows tightening around her throat.

"NO!" I roared as an amused smirk spread across Kieran's lips.

Another pained moan sounded from the dragon followed by a sickening crack that echoed around us moments before Grainne's lifeless body went sailing towards the ground. The land vibrated beneath my feet as the dragon's enormous form collided with the earth.

A string of furious roars tore through the ringing in my ears as the dragons all darted towards Kieran like an army of winged death ready to deliver his reckoning.

A sob made its way past my lips and my shoulders shook as reality slammed into me.

"Lower the shield," Silas screamed, drawing me back to the present.

"I can't," I whispered. "He's too strong."

"Lower the fucking shield, Harlowe!" Silas yelled again.

As much as I understood Silas's need to exact revenge on Kieran, I also knew that if I removed the only barrier standing between him and us, none of us would walk away from this night.

The sound of Misneach's murderous snarl pulled my focus, and a lump formed in my throat as he sped towards Kieran.

**"Misneach, no,"** I begged as panic threatened to drown me.

A knowing glint mingled with the mania sparkling in Kieran's eyes as another thread of shadows darted back, racing to meet Misneach head-on.

The others hollered behind me as they desperately tried to get me to lower my shield. Their voices were swallowed by the deafening roar of the dragons as they fought against the onslaught of shadows in their bid to bring Kieran down.

I blocked it all out as I focused on the man before me.

Pressing one hand to my shield and sending the other behind me, I pushed the others back towards the manor house, creating a barrier around them. I could faintly make out their pleas for me to stop, but I ignored them.

**"Caolán, pull the dragons back. Get everyone out of here,"** I begged.

**"Fire Heart!"** Misneach roared as he realized I was facing Kieran alone.

**"Get ready,"** I commanded, and he darted to the side, dodging Kieran's shadowy projectile as he registered my intentions.

**"Hold on, Little One,"** Caolán said. **"Prepare to drop your shield."**

My arms trembled with the effort of holding both shields in place as Kieran continued to assault the one surrounding me.

**"NOW!"** Caolán roared, and I lowered the shield protecting the others.

I never took my eyes off Kieran's and he narrowed his gaze at me as he pushed even harder against my flames. A small wince escaped my lips despite my best efforts to avoid revealing just how much he was getting to me.

My blood pounded in my ears and the sound of shouting and wingbeats became so loud that the sensory overload made my skull feel as though it was about to split wide open.

Even so, I still heard the small gasp that sounded from behind me and the whisper of my name in the darkness.

And Kieran heard it too.

A cruel smile twisted his lips as he turned to face Everly.

# Chapter Three

Everything happened so fast, and yet, it felt as though time stood still around me, keeping me captive and unable to move.

One moment, Kieran stood before me; his taunting expression revealed his intentions. And the next moment, he was across the grounds, his hand wrapped firmly around Everly's throat.

"Kieran, no!" I cried, as I lowered my shield and sprinted towards them.

"HARLOWE!" Silas roared from somewhere nearby, but I didn't falter in my attempt to reach Everly.

"Every decision has a cost, Bride," Kieran called out. "You best make sure you're willing to pay it."

My footsteps fumbled, and I almost toppled over when Kieran pulled his hand away from Everly's throat.

Everly gasped as she tried to suck in air, but the gurgling sound that echoed in the space between us told me her efforts were futile.

Blood trickled down Kieran's forearm and glistened in the moonlight. My stomach roiled as my gaze fixed on the gaping hole in Everly's throat.

Kieran tossed the mangled flesh he had ripped from Everly aside, as if ending her life was of little consequence.

Everly's wide eyes clashed with mine and I saw the moment her body gave up its fight. Her eyes rolled to the back of her head just as her body crashed to the ground.

"NO!" I screamed and attempted to get my feet moving again so that I could get to her.

Strong arms wrapped around my waist, and I was pulled against a hard chest. My arms flailed, and I kicked my legs as I tried to free myself from the iron grip that held me in place.

"Harlowe, please. Stop fighting me," Silas begged, but I barely registered his words.

My body moved without conscious thought as my fear and anguish drove me forward.

A sense of weightlessness washed over me and it took a moment for me to realize that I was airborne.

"No, Silas! Put me down. We can't leave her. FUCKING PUT ME DOWN!"

"I'm sorry, Harlowe," he whispered, not bothering to hide his own pain. "I can't do that."

"Silas, please," I begged. Tears clogged my throat as I spoke, making my words sound muffled as they left me.

"Hold on to me tightly, Harlowe," he commanded, even though I was secure in his arms.

The reason for his instructions became clear a moment later when we began free-falling. I let out an involuntary scream, but it was quickly cut off as I collided with a hard surface and all the air left my lungs.

My gaze darted upward, and I saw the green and grey tones of Caolán's underbelly. As I glanced down, I recognized the indigo hues that decorated the dark coloring of Misneach's wings.

Caolán just dropped us.

That realization was enough to extinguish what little fight I had left in me.

A heavy weight settled in my chest and I gripped the front of Silas's tunic like my life depended on it. As I buried my face in the soft fabric, I let the tears flow.

My body trembled as my violent sobs rent the night air, and Silas pulled me closer as he smoothed my hair.

"Shh, Harlowe. I've got you," he promised.

It wasn't enough to stem the onslaught of emotions as wave after wave of grief crashed into me. Images of Everly's brutalized body danced across my vision before morphing into Teller, lying bloodied on the battlefield. Teller's anguished face was quickly replaced by Cian's, his head lolling to the side with his neck sitting at an unnatural angle. Then Grainne's pain-filled cries assaulted my senses, and it all became too much as my heart hammered wildly in my chest.

I struggled to draw in oxygen as my throat closed over between each wretched sob. My head spun, and I knew if I didn't calm down, I would lose consciousness.

Tiny black spots clouded my vision and just as I thought my body was going to betray me, a gentle voice soothed my soul.

**"Breathe with me, Fire Heart,"** Misneach said. **"I am here. I am with you. Your pain is my pain. Let me carry the weight of your agony until you are strong enough to bear it once more."**

I sucked in heaving breaths as my starved lungs expanded and inflated once again. Each inhale burned like I'd swallowed hundreds of fiery embers. When the pain began to ebb, I sagged against Silas, no longer able to support myself.

**"That's it Fire Heart, just breathe."**

**"Thank you, Misneach. Thank you for always being exactly what I need."**

**"Always, Fire Heart. Always."**

"Where are we going?" I asked Silas when I was sure I could trust my voice again.

"To the other manor house. I don't know how Kieran tracked us, but it is far enough away to put some distance between us."

I nodded my head, glad to have Silas take charge. The gods knew I wasn't in any state to be making decisions at that moment.

I must have drifted off to sleep because I woke with a start when Misneach's landing jolted me forward. We stopped in front of another vast manor house that was not dissimilar to the one we had just fled.

Silas gripped my hips as he slid from Misneach's back, pulling me down with him.

"Thank you," I breathed.

Concern swirled in Silas's brown depths as he studied me. His calloused fingers brushed my cheek as he tucked a stray lock of hair behind my ear.

"There was nothing you could have done, Harlowe," he murmured.

"Let's get inside," I said, a bit more harshly than I had intended as I moved around him.

**"He is right, Fire Heart. You cannot blame yourself. Not for this."**

I didn't know what to say, so I said nothing.

Emmerson met me halfway and pulled me into a tight hug as she whispered promises of retribution.

My throat tightened and I could only nod my head as I hugged her back just as fiercely. Zeke joined us a moment later and threw his arms around both of us as if his protective embrace would keep us safe.

We said nothing as all three of us walked hand-in-hand into the manor house.

We stopped mid-stride, realizing we didn't know where we were going, and waited for Silas to lead the way.

"That way," Silas said, pointing to the left. We let him pass before falling into step behind him.

# Chapter Four

We sat at a large dining table, the eerie silence deafening as we all struggled to comprehend what had just happened.

"We should have attacked. Overwhelming him with our numbers. One of us could have reached him," Silas said, breaking the heavy silence.

"Silas," Cillian warned, but I was already moving.

My chair scraped across the wooden floor and toppled over as I jumped to my feet. I reached Silas in three strides and bunched my fists in the collar of his tunic, pulling him from his seat.

"You would have died," I growled through gritted teeth.

"It would have ended the threat against you and —"

I didn't let him finish his sentence as my palm sailed through the air and connected with his cheek.

My hand throbbed, and a shocked gasp sounded from behind me.

Silas just stared at me in shock, his mouth hanging open as he continued to gape at me. A red hue colored his cheek in the distinct shape of a handprint.

"Don't you ever speak of sacrificing yourself for me again," I seethed.

"Harlowe, I —"

But I hadn't finished yet. My hands curled into fists and I shoved against Silas's chest hard, forcing him back a few steps.

"I am done," I said through gritted teeth.

"I am done losing those I care about," I added, as I pushed him again.

"You think you are protecting me by sacrificing yourself? Think again," I scoffed.

"If I lose one more person in this room, then those hunting me will no longer need to worry about what I might become because I will gladly embrace the monster they fear lurks inside me. I will burn this entire fucking realm to the ground with Kieran and everyone else right along with me."

My chest was heaving, and my whole body trembled as I glared at Silas.

"Do you fucking understand me, Silas?" I snapped.

When he just continued to gape at me, I pummeled my fists into his chest as I let loose an anguished scream.

That seemed to snap him out of whatever daze held him captive, and he wrapped his thick arms around me, crushing me against his chest. His hand snaked into my hair and he rocked me back and forth as sobs wracked my body.

"I'm sorry, Harlowe. I'm so sorry," Silas muttered against my hair. He continued to repeat the words as if they alone had the power to quell the pain tearing my body apart from the inside.

I vaguely registered the sound of scraping chairs as the others left the room, giving us some privacy.

**"Fire Heart,"** Misneach breathed, letting me know he was there, should I need him.

It could have been minutes or hours that we stood like that; with me curled against Silas, the unrelenting cascade of tears soaking his tunic. All the while, he whispered words of reassurance, never letting me go.

When I had no more tears left to cry and my body felt as though it was on the verge of giving out, I lifted my swollen, puffy eyes and locked my gaze with his.

"Promise me," I said with a rasp. "Promise me you will never sacrifice yourself for me."

His chocolate-brown eyes searched mine for a long moment. He released a resigned sigh and nodded his head in acquiescence.

"Say the words, Silas," I demanded.

"I promise, Little Menace. I promise."

Silas lowered his lips to mine and kissed me tenderly.

His kiss was an apology.

A vow.

A declaration of his love.

The sound of a throat clearing drew our attention, and we broke apart. Cillian stood in the doorway, his hand rubbing the back of his neck as he glanced between us.

"Is it safe to come back in?" he asked, his eyes lingering on me for a moment before darting back to Silas.

My neck flushed with heat as I thought about the show I must have put on for everyone. As if sensing my unease, Silas's arm tightened around me.

Emmerson barged past Cillian, muttering something about him being a coward as she stalked toward me.

She pulled me free of Silas's tight grip and embraced me in a bone-crushing hug.

"Are you all right?" she whispered against my ear.

"No," I answered honestly, "but I will be."

Emmerson stepped back so she could look at me. Her hands framed my face as she studied me, needing to reassure herself that I would be okay.

"I have you, Harlowe. I'll always have you," she promised. Leaning in, she added, "If you need help keeping Silas in line, all you have to do is ask."

I barked out a laugh as we broke apart.

"What's so funny?" Silas asked with a furrowed brow.

"Nothing you need to concern yourself with," Emmerson replied, grinning.

Silas and Cillian shared a look, but it didn't seem like either of them was any wiser.

A moment later, Fionn and Zeke re-entered the hall and took their seats at the dining table.

Once everyone had settled in again, Silas focused his gaze on me. "Can you tell us what happened out there tonight, Harlowe?" he asked gently.

I blew out a breath.

"He's too strong," I admitted. "I was barely holding my own against Kieran tonight and he was only playing with me, testing my strength and abilities."

"What do you mean?" Cillian interjected.

"I don't think he intended to kill me. When he used his powers against me, he was only assessing me, looking to see how far he could push me. I'm not sure why he didn't just kill me. Morbid curiosity perhaps, but he was holding back tonight."

Cillian cursed under his breath and a flash of rage crossed Silas's features.

"Did your shield hold?" Emmerson asked.

"Yes, but it was a struggle," I confessed.

"You felt it, didn't you?" she pressed.

"Felt what?"

"I saw you wince, Harlowe. When Kieran was hammering your shield with his shadows, you felt those hits, didn't you?"

I flinched, and that was all the confirmation Emmerson needed.

"Why didn't you drop your shield? You can't protect us at the cost of yourself," she chided.

"Emmerson, if I had dropped my shield, none of us would be sitting here right now. Kieran would have murdered us all. Just like Everly." I didn't mean to say the last part out loud, but when Silas threaded his fingers with mine and squeezed gently, I realized my mistake.

"That wasn't your fault, Harlowe," Emmerson murmured.

"I know," I said, cutting her off. I didn't want to speak about Everly, and I could see Emmerson readying herself to convince me of her words.

"So, what do we do now?" Fionn asked, redirecting the conversation.

I glanced in his direction, and he gave me a subtle nod. He understood what it was like to bear the weight of someone's death, and he understood my need to distance myself from it, at least for now.

I smiled back at him in gratitude.

"The plan remains the same," Silas said. "We need allies, but we need to be cautious. I don't know how Kieran found us, but we can't take any more unnecessary risks."

"He's too strong," I said again.

"He has had centuries to learn how to control his powers, Harlowe. You can't expect to be on the same level as him," Silas said, to comfort me.

I tuned out the others as they debated what to do among themselves.

I needed to even the odds. To bridge the gap between us somehow.

"What do you expect her to do, Cillian? She can't just amplify her powers until she is strong enough to beat him," Emmerson hissed, drawing me back into the discussion.

Amplify my powers?

*The true power of the stone lies in its ability to amplify the power of the individual who possesses the stone.*

"That's exactly what I'll do," I murmured.

"What?" Emmerson asked.

"I said, that's exactly what I'll do."

"I know what you said, Harlowe. I just don't understand what you mean."

"I'm going to retrieve the Aurora Stone."

# Chapter Five

"The Aurora Stone?" Silas asked, his confusion etched into the furrow between his brows.

"While in Netheran, I discovered an old tome in the library," I answered. I licked my lips nervously as I prepared to divulge the details of what I had learned, or more specifically, where the stone was located.

"The tome spoke of the Aurora Stone. It was believed that this stone could amplify the powers of whoever wielded it."

"I've never heard of such a thing," Cillian muttered to himself.

"It pre-dates the War of Witches," I added. "If I could retrieve the stone, then I might be able to use it to amplify my powers and overcome the centuries of experience Kieran has over me. I might be able to defeat him."

Silas narrowed his eyes at me. "What aren't you telling us, Harlowe?"

Damn him and his perceptive gaze.

"Well… it's believed the stone was lost within the Forest of Nightmares," I admitted sheepishly.

"Oh, for fuck's sake," Emmerson grumbled.

I couldn't argue with her. I didn't relish the idea of venturing back through the forest, either.

"Oh no," Silas said, as he rose from his chair. "We aren't heading back inside that forest. We barely escaped with our lives last time."

"Are you telling me you're scared, Silas?" I teased.

"Nice try, Little Menace," he retorted. "I'm not risking your life on some legend."

"Hear me out," I pleaded, raising my hands in a placating gesture.

Silas glared at me, but it was Cillian who encouraged me to go on. "What do you know, Harlowe?" he asked.

Silas's harsh gaze shifted to Cillian, but he remained unperturbed.

"I don't know a lot, but what I read suggested the stone had the power to deflect negative or harmful energy." I paused, searching the recesses of my memory. "At least I think that's how it was described," I mumbled.

Silas made an exasperated sound, and I rushed to continue before he could interject. "From what I understand, the stone was used to create some sort of barrier around the forest to keep the creatures lurking within the forest trapped inside."

"What will happen if we remove the stone?" Fionn asked, a slight edge to his tone.

I winced. I'd hoped no one would identify that pitfall in my plan. Well, not until I had their agreement, at least.

"Honestly, I don't know," I answered. "The text only recounted that a witch entered the forest to lay the stone, but she never re-emerged."

"The Lost Witch?" Emmerson asked, her thoughts going to the same place mine had.

"I don't think so. Everything I heard about the Lost Witch suggested she entered the forest after the witches were defeated in the war. The barrier surrounding the forest was already set by then."

"Just so I understand what you're asking," Silas said. "You want to return to the Forest of Nightmares to retrieve a mythical stone? The same stone that is the only thing keeping the monsters contained, on the off chance that it might help you strengthen your powers?"

I bristled at Silas's tone. "I'm only stating my concerns, Little Menace. You need to understand what you're asking here."

I deflated a little. He was right. Racing off into the unknown without careful planning would be foolish and dangerous.

"All right Silas. I admit there are holes in my plan, but it's better than nothing, right? We can't defeat Kieran like this," I said, gesturing around the room. "He was only toying with us tonight, and he almost broke us. If we don't do something drastic, then I'm not sure we can win against him," I confessed.

"We have a plan, Harlowe. We can rally allies."

"Will that be enough, though? I honestly don't know the answer to that question. I'm willing to take the risk if it means we have a stronger chance of defeating him."

Silas blew out a long breath.

"If we were to do this, and that's a big *if*, where would we even look for the stone?" Silas asked.

I glanced towards Emmerson and found her already looking at me with a knowing grin.

"The Lost Witch," I said confidently. "She has lived inside the forest for..." I trailed off. I didn't know how long she had called the forest home. "I'm not certain how long she's lived there, but it's been a long time. If anyone knows where the stone is, it's her."

"Would she help us?" Cillian asked.

My eyes darted to Emmerson once again. She raised her shoulder in a half-shrug.

"I'd hope so," I said hesitantly. "She helped me once before."

"Your confidence is overwhelming, Harlowe. Maybe try to temper it a little," Zeke drawled.

Emmerson raised her hand and swatted him over his ear. "Ow," Zeke hissed. "What was that for?"

"Your attitude," Emmerson barked, and Zeke had the good grace to look suitably chastised.

"Sorry Harlowe," he muttered.

"That still leaves us with the problem of unleashing the monsters of legend," Fionn interrupted, that same edge to his tone that now bordered on hysteria.

The room fell quiet. I had no suggestions for how we would overcome that bump in my plans. It seemed no one else did either.

"We need to speak with Arabella," Silas said, slicing through the tension.

"Is she familiar with such magic?" I asked, not wanting to get my hopes up.

"I don't know," he replied, "but I see no better option at present."

Silas glanced around the room, waiting to see if anyone would argue. When no one did, he nodded his head and rose from his seat.

"Let's all get some rest. Tomorrow, we will return home to Pyrithia."

He walked to my side and held out his hand for me. I placed my palm in his and let him lead me out of the dining hall.

Tomorrow, we would return to the place where everything had gone awry.

Would Silas's father listen to us? Would he lend us his support in the war that was coming faster than any of us were ready for?

Or would he seek to cage me once again?

Silas seemed to sense the direction my agonized thoughts were leading me.

"Don't worry, Harlowe. I promise no harm will come to you inside my home. If I have to stand against my father to protect you, then so be it. This I vow to you."

Silas sealed his vow by placing a soft kiss on my temple.

# Chapter Six

I couldn't stem the unease roiling and twisting inside my gut as I readied myself for bed. It had to be close to dawn by now, and as exhausted as I was, I doubted sleep would claim me. Everly's death weighed heavy on my heart. It replayed in my mind over and over, trying to drag me down into the darkest depths of my grief.

A soft kiss on my bare shoulder startled me, and I peered behind me to see Silas's intense gaze scrutinizing me. He kissed a path up my neck until his scorching lips met the shell of my ear.

"I can see your mind twisting you in knots, Little Menace," he whispered huskily. "Let me distract you, even if only for a moment."

A shiver ran through me at his words, and I couldn't stifle the moan that escaped me when Silas tugged my pebbled nipple between his thumb and forefinger.

"Silas," I said with a breathy moan.

His other hand snaked around my waist, gliding down my stomach until he reached the juncture of my thighs. My hand moved behind me as I gripped his hard length in my palm and stroked firmly.

Silas groaned, and a satisfied smile curled the corners of my mouth.

I spun in place as I turned to face him. He closed his beautiful brown eyes and tilted his head toward the heavens, getting lost in his pleasure.

"You really will have to marry me now, Harlowe. No woman could compare to the way you make me feel with just a touch."

I pressed onto my toes and chuckled as I whispered in his ear. "No need for flattery, Silas. When my palm is already gripping your cock, it's a done deal."

Silas's eyes flew open, and he gripped the sides of my face. "I'm serious Little Menace. You're it for me. You're all I want."

I swallowed roughly, emotion clogging my throat as I thought about everyone else I still had left to lose. I wasn't aware that I was crying until Silas gathered the moisture with the pad of his thumb.

He said nothing as he held me tight, kissing away the tears as they fell.

"Better?" he asked, once all my tears had dried up.

"For now."

Silas captured my lips with his own and I angled my head to the side, deepening the kiss. I craved this man intensely, and the firm pressure against my stomach suggested Silas desired me just as much.

Silas pushed me backward as he moved me towards the bed. He lowered me down onto the mattress and then climbed on top of me. Lacing his fingers with mine, he placed our joined hands on either side of my head.

His kisses were tender, sweet, and very unlike Silas.

"What are you doing, Silas?"

"Am I not allowed to worship your body, Harlowe?" he said, his tone sounding almost uncertain.

"Of course you can. I'm just not used to you being so... gentle."

"There is a time and a place for brutality in sex, Little Menace. Tonight, however, I want to make love to my woman."

My lips parted, but no words escaped me.

Silas took that as his cue and lined up his hips with mine, pushing inside me. The sensation of his length filling me never ceased to steal my breath. It was overwhelmingly pleasurable and yet, it provided a sense of comfort that I had never experienced before.

Silas rolled his hips, seating himself deeper inside me. When he pulled out to the tip, I whimpered at the loss of him. He swallowed my protests with a searing kiss before his hips thrust forward and he entered me once more.

Silas maintained his rhythm, rocking back and forth. With each roll of his hips, he made me see stars as my pleasure consumed me.

"Silas, I'm going to come."

"Then come with me," he whispered against my ear before catching my earlobe between his teeth.

That was all the stimulation I needed to fall over the edge, into oblivion. Silas quickened his pace, his movements becoming jerky before he spilled himself inside me.

We lay like that for the longest time, Silas still sheathed inside me, while he cocooned me within the protective warmth of his arms.

"We should try to get some sleep," he mumbled, disturbing the peace we had found.

"Do you think your father will support us?" I asked, giving voice to the fears that had been plaguing me.

Silas sighed and rolled off me, pulling me with him until I lay atop his broad chest. He drew lazy circles over my spine as he considered his response.

"I'm not sure, but even if he doesn't, there will be others ready to join us. Many of our people remember the Skirmish of Power and they will not want to sit idly by as history repeats itself."

"And August?" I asked hesitantly.

"Should he make a play for you, I will end his life with my bare hands, brother or not. You are what matters to me, Little Menace. I know I have given you reason to question my loyalty in the past, but I hope you can trust my words now. I'd sooner die before allowing any harm to come to you."

"I know you would, Silas," I soothed. "And I'm not questioning your loyalty. I only want to ensure you're ready for whatever we will face in Pyrithia."

Silas lifted my palm to his mouth and placed a soft kiss there, to reassure me.

"To be honest, Harlowe, I don't know what kind of reception we will get when we reach Pyrithia." He paused, contemplating his next words. "But whatever it is, we will face it together."

I nodded my head against his chest, acknowledging his promise.

"Now sleep. I know that you're exhausted and I don't want Misneach to burn me alive for depriving you of your respite."

I laughed, but it quickly turned into a yawn.

My eyes had a will of their own as they shuttered closed, pulling me into darkness.

# Chapter Seven

Silas

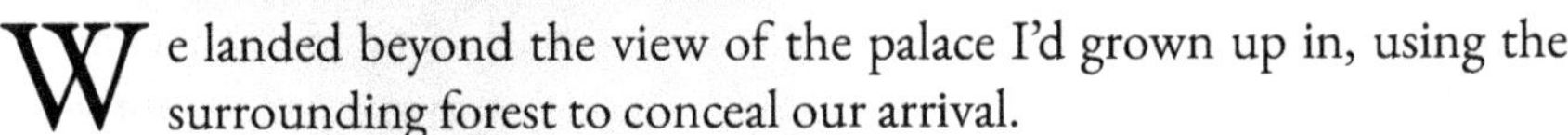

We landed beyond the view of the palace I'd grown up in, using the surrounding forest to conceal our arrival.

After taking a day to recuperate, we'd left the manor house early in the morning, so the sun hadn't reached its zenith yet. My body had been tight with tension and I'd hardly spoken a word the whole journey. While I hoped my father would welcome us, I wouldn't risk Harlowe if he didn't.

Dismounting Caolán, I made my way over to her and Misneach. The enormous dragon watched me approach intently. Harlowe slid down his flank, meeting me halfway.

"You remember the plan?" I asked as I cupped her cheeks.

Harlowe's palms rose to cover my own. "I'm to stay put while you get the lay of things," she said with an adorable pout that had the corner of my mouth twitching as I fought to contain my smirk.

I placed a gentle kiss on her lips. "Trust me, you'd be the first one I'd want beside me in a fight, Little Menace," I teased. "But I'm hoping we can avoid burning down my childhood home."

Harlowe pushed me away and the smirk that had threatened to surface earlier broke out into a wide grin.

"Will you be all right?" she asked, all traces of teasing vanishing from her features.

"Worried about me, Little Menace?" I asked, cocking a brow.

She elbowed me in the ribs, not indulging my attempt at humor.

"You know I am. Please try to take this seriously. What are we to do if things go awry?"

"You're right, I'm sorry," I said, placing a quick kiss on her temple. "I'll send word to Caolán. Don't make any moves unless he says so."

Harlowe nodded once, and I turned my gaze to my dragon.

**"We will protect her. You don't even have to ask,"** he said, sensing my thoughts. I gave a curt nod, acknowledging his promise.

"Cillian, you're with me," I said, flicking my head to the side.

My second-in-command turned and whispered something in Emmerson's ear before kissing her briefly. He strode towards me, determination straightening his spine.

"Harlowe has command. You Listen to her as you would me," I said, but there was little need. Zeke and Emmerson *only* listened to Harlowe, and Fionn had become close to her ever since Teller died.

I forced myself to push all thoughts of my fallen brother out of my mind. I had a task to complete and Harlowe was relying on me to do it well.

Fionn nodded, acknowledging my command. Emmerson, however, looked offended that I would even hint she might behave otherwise.

I would never admit this to the Little Viper, but I admired her dedication to Harlowe. Knowing Emmerson was with Harlowe helped ease the fear coiling tight in my chest at leaving her unguarded.

Caolán snorted, letting me know exactly how he felt about my observations.

"Let's go," I said to Cillian before my dragon could berate me.

Cillian and I both raised the hoods of our cloaks, obscuring our identities from anyone we might encounter.

"What's the plan?" Cillian asked as we headed towards the palace grounds.

"You remember Link the stable hand?"

"Yes. He's a damn drunk and an awful gossip," my friend huffed.

"Exactly," I grinned. "We'll test the waters with him to see how my father feels about my recent... escapades."

"Good idea," Cillian grunted.

We found Link right where I thought we would. Asleep on the hay bale he was supposed to have shoveled by now. Everyone knew that the man enjoyed a late-night drink and seldom woke up before midday.

I kicked his boot with my own, eliciting a startled yelp from Link.

"Whoa... what's..." he trailed off, looking up at me as if he'd seen a ghost. "Your Majesty," he muttered as he scrambled to his feet.

I barked out a harsh laugh. "Since when have you bothered with titles, Link?"

The man's eyes darted around the stables, and he shifted nervously on his feet.

"What's wrong?" I asked as unease crept up my spine.

Link lifted his eyes until his gaze met my own. Dread, sorrow, and fear looked back at me.

"What's happened?" I pressed.

"Do you really not know?" he whispered.

"Spit it out, man," Cillian snarled.

"I'm sorry to be the one to tell you this, my Lord. It's… it's the King. He… well, he's dead."

The weight of his words hit me straight in the chest, knocking the breath out of me.

"Silas?" Cillian asked, his hand outstretched as if ready to catch me should I fall.

I took a step back, bracing myself with one hand on the stable door.

"When?" I breathed. "How?"

Link shifted nervously again, and I knew the worst was yet to come.

The silence of the stables was deafening, and I heard Link swallow roughly.

"It was your brother, my Lord. He… he overthrew him, and…" Link trailed off, or I stopped listening. I couldn't tell which over the sound of my blood pounding in my ears.

"Silas," Cillian repeated, trying to gain my attention. His gaze darted around, as if sensing an unknown threat lurking just out of sight.

"And," my voice came out raspy. Clearing my throat, I tried again. "And my brother, where is he now?"

Link looked at me in confusion, unsure of what to say next.

"My brother?" I urged, gripping the front of the man's tunic in my fist.

"Easy, Silas," Cillian muttered from beside me.

"He… he's…"

"He what, Link?" I gritted out, impatience blanketing me with a suffocating force.

"He's the King, my Lord," he whispered, his whole body trembling under my grip.

I released him with unwarranted roughness and took several steps back.

My brother had killed our father, for what? A throne that was already his by birthright? It made little sense. Why would August kill our father when he knew it was only a matter of time before he stepped aside, allowing him to take his place as king? Gods, my father was preparing to do just that when he thought he could coerce Harlowe into marrying August.

Unless August grew tired of waiting.

That single thought sent rage shooting through my body, coiling my muscles tight and balling my hands into fists. I clenched my jaw so tight that I was surprised I didn't hear my teeth crack.

"Silas, whatever you're thinking right now, we need to take a moment to process this news," Cillian said, his hands coming up in a placating gesture. "It does nobody any good for you to go off on your own and declare a one-man war against your brother. Think this through," Cillian warned.

Not a one-man war.

It was time for my brother to feel the full fury of my Little Menace.

And it was long overdue.

# Chapter Eight

I paced the length of the tree line as I waited for Silas to return. I hadn't been enthusiastic about staying behind while he took all the risks, but I had to have faith that Silas's father wouldn't harm his own son.

**"He will be all right,"** Caolán soothed. **"His father cares a great deal for him, even if he doesn't always show it."**

I nodded my head in agreement, even though I was far from convinced by Caolán's words.

The quiet chuckle that came from the dragon had me wincing, knowing that he was well aware of my internal musings.

**"Sorry,"** I mumbled, feeling my cheeks heat.

A scurrying sound through the thicket caught our attention and everyone froze, our hands going to our weapons on instinct.

A moment later, Silas stepped through the shrubbery. His expression was inscrutable, yet his body was vibrating with tension. Cillian followed behind him, worry and concern marring his features.

"What happened?" I asked, striding towards the pair.

Silas's jaw clenched and his hands balled into fists as he stared at me. His eyes hardened, and he furrowed his brow as if he was assessing me.

My steps faltered for a moment, unease coursing through me as Silas continued to watch me.

Misneach, having sensed my mounting discomfort, bristled and stretched out his wings as he moved to stand behind me.

**"It is not what you think, Misneach,"** Caolán snapped.

**"If anyone else gave her that look, they wouldn't be alive to talk**

**about it, Caolán,"** Misneach growled.

I closed the distance between me and Silas, and gripped his forearms as I waited for him to speak.

The furrow in Silas's brow deepened, and he tilted his head to the side. "What are Caolán and Misneach arguing about?"

"Ignore them. What happened?"

Silas stiffened, and then both of his palms landed on my hips, drawing me against him. He buried his nose in my hair, inhaling deeply. I could feel the rapid beat of his heart under my cheek and my unease grew.

Whatever had happened, it wasn't good.

Silas took a deep breath, his resolve strengthening. He took a step back, and our gazes locked.

"How would you feel about a little retribution?" he asked, his eyes darting between mine as he waited for me to answer.

"I don't understand what you are asking of me?"

Silas lifted his head so that he had everyone in his sight. His hands dropped away from my sides and he reached down, intertwining our fingers.

"My father is dead. My brother killed him," he said simply.

Silence filled the space surrounding us as everyone struggled to comprehend what he had said.

My gaze darted to Cillian, who gave me a small nod in confirmation.

"I'm so sorry, Silas," I said, returning my attention to him.

"August has declared himself king. I intend to remove him from my father's throne."

"Anything you need, just ask it," I said.

Silas gave me a brittle smile. "I don't believe he has the support of the people. They love... loved... my father, and I don't think they will stand in my way if I seek to challenge him."

I didn't miss the way his words caught in his throat, or the slight tremble in his hands. Silas had narrowed his attention to a singular focus; removing his brother. That didn't mean he wasn't hurting, however. The time would come when he fell apart, and I would be there to hold his pieces together.

"We may need your protection to get us to that point," Silas said sheepishly, his gaze softening as he looked at me.

"Of course, Silas. You have it." He gave my hand a gentle squeeze, the only flicker of emotion he would allow himself in this moment.

"We go in as quietly as we can and we keep a tight unit," Silas commanded. Turning to Emmerson and Zeke, he said, "This isn't your fight. I won't begrudge you if you sit this one out."

Emmerson scoffed. "When have you ever known me to step aside in a fight?" she said, drawing her short swords over her shoulders.

The corner of Silas's mouth lifted in a smirk. "I was hoping you would say that. Zeke?"

"I've nothing better to do," he said with a shrug. I couldn't help the snort that escaped me with his response.

Silas shook his head before turning his attention to the dragons. "Stay back and remain hidden until I give the signal."

**"That is not happening,"** Misneach growled.

"It's only until we breach the palace," Silas said, as if aware of Misneach's objection. "If you are detected before then, we'll lose the element of surprise. I also need you to surround the palace once we've made it inside to prevent my brother from escaping, should he try."

**"His plan makes sense, Misneach,"** I muttered.

**"I don't care if it makes sense,"** he huffed. **"I care about protecting you at all times."**

**"Have a little faith, Misneach. I can protect myself."**

**"And who will protect you from yourself?"** he challenged. **"You lose all sense of self-preservation whenever those you love are in danger."**

It was pointless to argue with him. I would sooner throw myself into a fiery pit than abandon those I cared about.

**"You see,"** Misneach said knowingly.

Sighing, I said, **"That changes nothing, Misneach. Silas is right."**

"What's wrong?" Silas mumbled next to me.

"Misneach doesn't trust me to not act foolishly if I am out of his sight."

"He has a point," Silas muttered to himself.

I jabbed my elbow into his ribs and he jolted back, rubbing the spot I had connected with.

"What was that for?" he asked indignantly.

"I heard you," I gritted out.

Silas flashed me a broad grin and winked. Turning towards Misneach, he said, "I promise I will return her to you safe and unharmed."

Misneach only snorted, his claws raking across the dirt in agitation. **"The fool has a short memory,"** Misneach snapped.

**"Misneach, please, be reasonable,"** I begged.

After a brief pause, he huffed out a breath, and warm air coated my cheeks.

**"Fine, but if there is even a hint of trouble, I'm coming to get you.**

**I don't care if I have to destroy the palace to get inside, I will,"** he promised.

I had no doubt he would be true to his words.

I acknowledged him with a nod and turned back to Silas.

"We're ready."

# Chapter Nine

We huddled against a wall on the southern side of the palace, waiting for the guard rotation.

"Once the bell tolls, the guards will be relieved of their post and we will have about five minutes to get inside and concealed from view before their replacements arrive," Silas whispered.

Silas's intimate knowledge of the palace and their protective measures was certainly useful in this situation.

"Once inside, we head straight to the kitchens. No hesitation and no delays," he added.

The tension was thick as we waited, and everyone was eager to move. Adrenaline flooded my veins and there was no outlet for it as we held our position.

**"I can't even begin to imagine how that must feel,"** Misneach grumbled.

**"Not helping,"** I hissed back.

The piercing sound of the bell toll interrupted our bickering, startling me.

"You all right?" Silas whispered so only I could hear.

"I'm fine. I was caught off guard, is all." Silas nodded and returned his gaze to the two men as they moved out of sight.

We waited a painstakingly long minute before Silas tipped his head, instructing us to move.

My palms tingled with a familiar heat as I readied myself to draw upon my flames, should I need to.

To my surprise, the short hallway leading into the back entrance of the kitchens was empty. No servants were scurrying around and no soldiers patrolled the corridors beyond, as one might expect.

With silent footfalls, we reached the kitchen door and darted inside. No one noticed our arrival as they continued to work, putting the finishing touches on the midday meal and scrubbing the mountain of dishes by the sink.

We were only a hair's breadth away from a rotund woman with greying hair pulled into a tight bun atop her head when she finally noticed our presence.

"By the gods," the woman breathed, her hand fluttering to her chest as she spoke.

Before anyone could move, she spun around, waving her wooden spoon in the air as if it were a sword.

"Not a word, you hear me?" she hissed.

The woman glared at the workers until they each nodded their heads in compliance.

Turning back to us, her hardened gaze softened, and she reached out, cupping Silas's cheeks in her palms.

"Let me get a good look at you."

Silas grinned and pulled the woman into a tight hug. "It's nice to see you too, Adelle."

When Adelle pulled away from Silas, her cheeks were damp with tears and more filled her eyes, threatening to spill over.

"I'm sorry about your father," she sniffed.

Silas clenched his jaw. "That is why we have come, Adelle. My brother and I have things we need to discuss."

"Please don't do anything foolish," Adelle pleaded. "He has been cruel and unforgiving to anyone who questions his right to sit on your father's throne. All of your father's personal guards were executed, along with most of his advisors."

"Don't worry, I don't intend to die at my brother's hands," Silas rumbled.

"I am serious, Silas," the woman breathed. "You can't underestimate him. He is no longer the sweet boy you grew up with."

I doubted August was ever *sweet,* but I kept that thought to myself.

"I don't intend to. I have a secret weapon," he said, his gaze turning to me. "Adelle, I would like you to meet Harlowe," Silas said, as he pulled me close to his side.

"The Princess of Valoren," Adelle whispered as she ran her hands over her skirt to smooth it.

"Please, just Harlowe," I said, offering what I hoped was a reassuring smile.

"You must be careful, child. The King has not forgotten you. He sent men out looking for you not long after he took the throne."

A menacing growl sounded behind me. "Why?" Silas barked, making Adelle flinch at his tone.

"I'd also like to know that," Emmerson said in a lethal tone right next to my ear, making me jump. I hadn't even heard her approach. My attention had been wholly fixed on Silas and Adelle.

"Don't do that, Emmerson," I hissed, my heart still pounding rapidly, as if trying to escape my chest.

Emmerson just smirked.

Smirked.

My nerves were frayed, and we needed to get moving before we lost our advantage.

"Where is August now?" I asked, directing my question to Adelle.

"He is in the throne room." Her gaze darted to Silas for a moment before she continued. "He has called in all dues to the court, and summoned anyone with outstanding debts to the palace to explain themselves."

Silas swore under his breath and Cillian sidled up next to Emmerson.

"What is he planning?" Cillian asked. "Why is he gathering funds?"

Adelle hesitated. "Adelle," Silas said in warning.

"I don't know all the details, but there have been rumors circling the palace that he intends to make an offer for the Princess." Adelle glanced in my direction and my spine stiffened.

"An offer?" I asked in confusion.

Silas growled again, low and dangerous. "He thinks he can buy you from your father," he said through gritted teeth.

I reeled back at the same time Emmerson snarled, "Not fucking likely."

I felt Zeke step close to my back as he and Emmerson surrounded me. To my surprise, Fionn had joined them.

"I don't understand why he would want me. He has already taken his father's throne. What purpose do I serve at this point?"

"I imagine he didn't take too kindly to your sudden disappearance," Cillian said. "He saw you as a way to hurt Silas, and I doubt he realizes that you two are together."

"Of course he does. That's the whole point," Silas snapped.

Cillian sighed, exasperated. "I meant he doesn't realize you two have reunited, let alone that you are both here in Pyrithia. He's the type to try to steal Harlowe away when he thinks you're not around to her. Which begs the question, do we proceed with your plan, Silas? Things have changed beyond what we anticipated."

Silas hesitated, so I answered for him. "The plan hasn't changed. We came for allies, but instead found a usurper. You owe it to these people, Silas. You can't abandon them when they need you most."

**"Fire Heart,"** Misneach warned.

**"Trust me, Misneach."**

"I would, if it meant protecting you," Silas murmured, drawing my attention back to the discussion at hand.

I placed my palm on the side of his cheek, and he leaned into my touch. "You can't protect me, Silas," I whispered, and he stiffened. I went on before he could argue. "I am being hunted by Kieran and Vidyaa. I will always be at risk. The only way we get ahead of those threats is to keep moving forward. We stick to the plan, and while we're here, we get of your brother."

Silas studied me, then a wide grin appeared on his face. "Gods woman, I love you," he groaned. "My very own, bloodthirsty, vicious, Little Menace." Silas cupped my cheeks with both of his palms and kissed me passionately.

"Did he just say he, ow," Emmerson hissed.

"Let them have their moment," Zeke chastised.

"You didn't have to deploy physical violence to get your point across, Zeke," Emmerson grumbled.

"Seriously Emmerson? You are the very first one to use violence to make your point."

Breaking our kiss, I turned to face our friends.

"Who's ready to reclaim a kingdom?"

The broad grins that answered me told me that we were about to unleash hell.

August had no idea what was coming for him.

# Chapter Ten

"Get ready," Silas murmured. He withdrew his sword and gripped it between his palms.

The twin daggers I gripped in my hands glowed faintly from the flames warming them.

As we rounded the corner, all eyes fell on us. Four guards stood sentinel at the throne room doors and they appeared momentarily stunned as they gazed upon Silas. They glanced around, seemingly unsure of what to do.

"Your Highness," one guard said, stepping forward. I didn't miss the way his hand drifted to the pommel of his sword.

"I don't want to harm any of you," Silas said, cutting him off. "But make no mistake, I will."

A tense moment passed between us before the guard cleared his throat. "I am afraid I am not allowed to permit you entry, my Lord."

"Good thing I wasn't asking your permission," Silas seethed.

Silas moved before the guard could collect himself. He swept his leg low, pulling the man's feet out from underneath him. He fell to the floor with a loud *clang* and Silas drove the pommel of his sword into the side of the man's head, rendering him unconscious.

Silas stood from the ground in one graceful motion before approaching the remaining guards, Cillian and Fionn flanking him.

Silas stared at the three men, his eyes narrowed with menace. "Run," he growled, and all three guards abandoned their posts, fleeing the intensity of Silas's glare.

"Damn," Emmerson whispered next to me. "That was kind of hot."

Cillian whipped around to glare at her while Silas chuckled to himself.

"What?" Emmerson asked nonchalantly. "Fear and violence get me going," she said, wiggling her eyebrows at Cillian.

"Time for your grand homecoming," I said as I walked to Silas's side, redirecting Cillian's attention.

"Thank you," Emmerson mouthed over his shoulder, and my lips twitched as I tried to hide my smirk.

Without preamble, Silas swung the doors to the throne room wide, and those standing at the back turned to look at the newcomers. Their mouths fell open when Silas crossed the threshold; their nervousness was evident in the slight shuffle of feet and subtle glances toward the dais.

Silas ignored it all, marching through the crowd with purpose as he approached the front of the room.

An elderly man was chittering about his recent harvest, unaware of the mounting tension as the room fell silent behind him.

A small bead of sweat ran down my spine as my eyes flew around the room, searching out any hidden threat lurking in the shadows.

"Silas," a woman gasped, and my head snapped in her direction.

Sienna sat in an elegant chair off to the side of the dais. It wasn't as grand as the throne occupied by August, but it was clear that she held a position of influence in his court. When her eyes flicked to me, a sneer pulled up her lip, and I smiled back at her. Next to me, Emmerson gave her a little wave, the sardonic intent not lost on me.

"Brother," a deep masculine voice sounded ahead of me, drawing my attention.

August sat on his father's throne, a large crown decorated with a multitude of jewels atop his head.

Honestly, it was garish and difficult to look at.

I had no idea if it was the same crown Silas's father had donned while he ruled over his kingdom, but if it was, I could understand why he hadn't worn it much.

"And I see you've returned my bride. How considerate," August cooed.

My gaze darted back to Sienna, and I noticed the absence of a crown on her head.

"Seize her," August commanded, and a single guard stepped toward me.

Silas raised his sword, the blade meeting the tender flesh of the man's throat as he swallowed roughly.

"I would think *very* carefully about your next move, because if you lay a single finger on my wife, your throat will kiss my blade," Silas said. There was no mistaking the lethal promise in his tone.

Emmerson's eyebrows shot up into her hairline as she gaped at me. "Wife?" she mouthed, stunned.

I groaned. "I'm not his... never mind," I said, narrowing my eyes at Silas. He just smirked, unfazed by the awkward silence enveloping us.

"Your wife?" August scoffed.

"Yes August, *mine*," Silas growled.

August tilted his head, observing us. I straightened my shoulders, not letting this prick see how much his gaze unsettled me.

With a small flick of his head, August commanded his guards to seize us all.

I summoned my flames, throwing up my shield before any of them could take a step toward us.

Unfortunately, the man standing at the end of Silas's blade got caught in the crossfire. The acrid smell of burned flesh assaulted my nostrils as the man wailed and thrashed. He fell to the floor, rolling around as he tried to extinguish the flames slowly consuming his life essence.

With a final shudder, the man stopped moving, and I knew he never would again.

"I wouldn't come any closer if I were you," I said, directing my comment to the remaining guards, who stood frozen in terror.

A quiet gasp pierced the silence and whispered conversations erupted within the chamber.

"That's very impressive," August said from the dais. "It appears you will be more useful than simply warming my bed, Princess."

"This man is fucking delusional," Emmerson muttered.

"Why don't you come closer and see for yourself?" I taunted, lowering my shield.

No one made a move towards us.

"You fucking whore," Sienna seethed, rising from her chair. "First Silas and now August!"

"Trust me, there is no competition for August," Emmerson snickered.

"What are you even doing here? You're supposed to be in Netheran," Sienna hissed.

"Ah, so it was you. I had my suspicions, but thank you for confirming it," I said.

Silas's head turned to me. "What do you mean?"

"Someone within these walls had to alert Kieran of my whereabouts. He didn't stumble upon me by luck," I said.

"You told him?" Silas snarled.

"Silas," Sienna pleaded, her voice softening and taking on a seductive lilt. "She was in our way. Don't you see she has only brought us trouble? I did what I had to do. I did it to protect you."

"You did it to protect me," Silas scoffed. "You have only ever been interested in what benefited you, Sienna. You did it to protect yourself and the delusion that you would ever sit on a throne. From the looks of it, not even August wants you by his side, and you and he are cut from the same cloth. So tell me, Sienna, why would I ever want someone as manipulative and vile as you?"

Sienna released an animalistic snarl as she darted forward, the glint of metal flashing in her hand as she pulled a dagger from her thigh.

Before I could retrieve my own dagger, something flew past my head, a small brush of wind kissing my cheek as the object sped through the air. A slight *thud* echoed around the chamber, followed by a barely audible gasp.

It took my mind a moment to realize what I was seeing.

Sienna stopped abruptly, inhaling a sharp breath. I couldn't quite figure out what halted her movements until I noticed the crimson liquid slowly spreading out from the center of her chest; the hilt of a dagger standing proudly.

As I spun around, my eyes fell on Emmerson, her arm still suspended in mid-air after she had hurled her dagger across the room, piercing Sienna's heart.

Emmerson lowered her arm. "What?" she shrugged. "She was annoying. You were going to have to kill her anyway. I just spared us all the nauseating whining."

Silence once again engulfed the entire room.

A harsh laugh sliced through the tension and I glanced at Zeke, who was rapidly losing himself to hysterics. His shoulders were shaking from the effort of trying to contain his laughter and he bent at the waist, placing his hands on his knees.

"I'm sorry," he wheezed. "But fuck, if that wasn't the most warped iteration of Emmerson logic I have ever heard. She just killed a woman to spare us from her *whining*."

Emmerson smirked smugly and even Cillian fought to contain his grin.

"SEIZE THEM!" August roared, sobering us immediately.

The guards hesitated, their gazes darting between Silas and August.

"This man murdered your King," Silas spat. "And you have done nothing to avenge him."

"He is the heir," one guard mumbled.

"He is not worthy of the throne he stole. His presence atop it tarnishes the memory of my father, your King. And you all allowed it!" Silas's chest was heaving with the fury behind his words. His whole body was trembling with rage as he stared the guards down.

"Is this how you repay the man who protected you, cared for you, treated you as his equal? You should be ashamed of yourselves."

The men shuffled their feet and lowered their gazes, no longer able to meet Silas's wrath.

A tense moment passed before one man took a tentative step toward Silas and I stiffened. Taking a knee, he placed his sword at Silas's feet.

"I have failed my King and my kingdom," he said, his head bowed. "I am no longer worthy of carrying this sword." He rose from his feet, moving backward until he blended into the crowd.

One by one, the other guards followed until there was no longer anyone left to oppose Silas.

"Cowards," August barked. "I guess I will just have to do it myself."

August prowled toward Silas with a confidence he had no business possessing, given the pampered life he had led.

When August reached Silas, he thrust his finger into Silas's chest. "I am the heir. The throne is mine by birthright."

Silas gripped August's wrist, bending it at an odd angle until his brother cried out in agony.

"You gave up that right the moment you ended our father's life," Silas hissed, as he applied more pressure, forcing August to his knees.

"But fear not, Brother, for I am merciful."

The grin twisting Silas's lips suggested he was anything but.

"I challenge you to a battle of ascendance."

# Chapter Eleven

"What the hell is a battle of ascendance, Silas?" I demanded as we made our way down a long tunnel that led into some kind of arena.

"Exactly as it sounds," he said with a shrug.

"I wouldn't have asked if I understood the meaning," I gritted out.

Silas stopped walking, and I had to backtrack a few steps to meet him.

"You don't need to worry about me, Little Menace," Silas said gently as he laced our fingers together.

"That doesn't answer my question, Silas," I responded, pulling my hand from his.

Sighing, Silas ran a hand through his hair. He tugged on the short strands as if he needed the pain to ground himself. When he turned back to me, his gaze softened, and he reached for my hand again.

"The battle of ascendance is an ancient Pyrithian tradition used to dispense with traitors," he explained. "It is a battle to the death. The accused traitor would battle the Monarch's chosen warrior, and if they won, all crimes were forgiven."

"And if they lost?" I asked.

"They ascend to the planes of the gods."

"Silas, do you think this is wise?" I pressed, worry swirling in my gut.

Silas raised a single brow. "Do you doubt my skills, Little Menace?" he teased.

"You know I don't. But I also do not trust your brother to fight fair. I know you're capable, Silas, but I can't shake the sense of dread tugging at me."

Silas pulled me to him, one hand resting on my lower back while the other lay against the back of my head, crushing me to his broad chest. "I have trained for battle my entire life, Harlowe. In all that time, August has shown no interest in the blade. I do not expect this to be a challenge," he said, soothing me.

My body relaxed under his firm embrace, the tension leaving my muscles as a resigned sigh escaped me. I felt Silas's lips brush against my hair. It never ceased to amaze me how one small touch from this man was enough to turn my core molten, forcing me to squeeze my thighs together.

"Little Menace," Silas growled. "Keep that up and I'll be compelled to take you against this wall. And while I wouldn't mind the deviation, I doubt the people currently filling the arena are feeling particularly patient."

The reminder of what Silas was about to do cooled the rising desire flooding my veins.

Silas adjusted himself in the front of his pants before stepping away, taking my hand in his. "Come on, let's get this over with."

Silas led me into an open-air arena, the echo of dirt crunching beneath our boots as we marched to the center of the space, was the only sound that greeted me. All around me, rows and rows of seats spanned the length of the arena, all filled with silent spectators, seemingly unsure if they should be excited or concerned.

At our approach, whispers flittered down to me from above, but I heard none of it. My full attention had been captured by the man standing at the far end of the arena.

Dressed in polished armor that shone so brightly, I doubted it had ever seen a day of use, stood August. Every inch of him was covered, and I had to wonder if there were any weak points in his defenses.

The most unnerving thing about his appearance, however, was the slight tilt of his head and the greedy smirk playing along his lips.

He looked like a man who had already won.

A shiver raced down my spine as our gazes locked, and his smirk split his face into a wide grin. My earlier unease returned tenfold.

A thunderous symphony of beating wings broke through the tension, and my eyes darted to the sky.

I watched as the dragons descended, perching around the top of the arena, silent sentinels to the impending violence. Rubble crumbled underneath their iron grip as they found purchase in the masonry; a testament to the sheer power they possessed.

Misneach was the last to arrive. The enormous expanse of his grey wings created a windstorm of dirt and debris inside the arena with each mighty beat. Each indigo hue that streaked his scales was vibrant and mesmerizing in the afternoon sun.

He landed with a *thud* beside me and the ground quaked under his footfalls. The impact sent vibrations through the earth in a powerful wave, as if the land struggled to accommodate his colossal presence.

It was a primal display of dominance. Nature bending to the will of the majestic beast beside me.

Misneach shook out his wings, causing some in the stands to cough and splutter as more dirt and debris were swept their way.

**"Why aren't you up there with the other dragons?"** I asked, pointing to where they had perched.

**"I'm exactly where I should be,"** he replied.

My body instinctively sought the comfort and protection of his much larger frame as I nestled myself against Misneach's flank.

**"What troubles you, Fire Heart?"** Misneach asked.

**"I don't know exactly. Something just feels... off. August appears too confident for a man who has hardly trained a day in his life. I do not trust it."**

**"Hmm, trust your instincts, Fire Heart. If something feels wrong, it usually is. Have you spoken with the General?"**

**"Yes, but he asked me to trust him,"** I said.

Misneach rolled his eyes. **"The man's ego will get him killed one day,"** he muttered.

**"Stop,"** I chided.

**"You know I speak true. All the same, I will remain vigilant, Fire Heart. You can trust in that."**

I had to admit I felt better knowing Misneach was close by, ever watchful.

"Are you ready?" Cillian asked Silas, bringing my attention back to the man readying to end the life of his brother.

"Almost," he said as he tightened the buckle on his leather vest.

"Why aren't you wearing armor, Silas?" I asked, my panic returning.

"It is too restrictive, and it's unnecessary against August."

**"See,"** Misneach huffed.

I elbowed him before refocusing on Silas. "Please be careful," I said, reaching for a dagger from Cillian's outstretched hand and placing it in Silas's thigh sheath.

He pulled me in for a quick kiss and then whispered in my ear, "Always."

"Oh, Brother," August called from the far side of the arena. "Are we going to play, or are you frightened I'll dispense with you as I did our father?" he taunted.

Silas's jaw clenched and all traces of humor and softness bled out of him, only to be replaced by ruthless determination.

Cillian walked up to Silas, sword in hand, and clasped his forearm. "Make him answer to the gods," he said, his tone deadly. Silas gave him a curt nod before turning back in my direction.

When he turned, however, he didn't look at me. Rather, he looked at Misneach, their gazes locked as they stared at each other with an intensity that had me shifting uncomfortably on my feet. After a moment, Misneach inclined his head, and Silas bowed at the waist before turning on his heels and stalking towards his brother.

**"What the hell was that?"** I asked.

**"An agreement between the General and me,"** he replied.

**"You can't communicate. How can you have an agreement?"**

**"Not all communication requires words, Fire Heart,"** Misneach chided.

**"Spare me, Misneach,"** I grumbled, and a low chuckle filled my mind as I watched Silas head toward his tribulation.

# Chapter Twelve

August stood proudly, his hand resting on the pommel of his sword as though it were an ornament.

Every muscle in my body tensed upon seeing him and the condescending smirk he wore. His grin faltered as I walked towards him, stepping over the roughly drawn line in the dirt that was supposed to serve as our starting point.

I continued to approach August until I invaded his space, our noses a hair's breadth from touching.

"Tell me why," I demanded.

August stumbled and took a step back before regaining his composure. "Why what?" he spat.

"You know exactly what I'm talking about, August. Why did you murder our father? Tell. Me. Why!"

"He was never going to step down once your *wife*," — he spewed the word as if it left a vile taste in his mouth — "fled."

"So you just murdered him!" I bellowed.

"Yes," he hissed. "I was never enough for him. No matter what I did, he always favored you, and I wasn't about to take the chance that he would give my throne to you. It was mine by birthright, so I took it."

August squared his shoulders as though the poison he just driveled justified patricide.

I threw my head back and barked out a rough laugh. When I returned my gaze to August, all that remained was rage.

Pure, unadulterated rage.

"I do not want the crown, August. I never have. Had you come to me and conveyed your fears, you would have known this."

"Oh, because we have such a close relationship, Brother," August mocked.

"And whose fault is that?" I gritted out.

Some emotion flickered across August's face, but it was gone too quickly for me to register.

"I grow tired of your tirade, Brother. Let's finish this," August said.

Regret clenched around my heart like a vise, and I allowed myself to sink into it for the briefest moment. Then I yanked myself out with the fury of a storm and made peace with the fact that I was about to kill my own brother.

"So be it."

The feel of my sword against the rough callouses on my palm was a welcome sensation. It centered me, allowing me to block out everything else around me, narrowing my vision to a single focus; August.

I waited for August to make the first move. I had seen plenty of battles in my life and there was one lesson that resonated with me above all others; never be eager to die.

August raised his sword and lunged for me, slashing his blade through the air between us. I side-stepped his advance and August spun, sending the steel of his vambrace smashing into my nose.

The metallic taste of my blood coated my tongue, and I turned to spit the crimson liquid onto the ground.

August smirked down at me.

"You underestimated me, Brother."

"It appears I did," I said, swiping at the blood trickling from my nose. "I won't make that mistake again."

Without hesitation, I thrust my sword toward him and the sound of steel meeting steel reverberated around the arena. I leaned into the strike, my added weight weakening August's resistance. He pulled away, his sword grating against mine as he withdrew.

Sweat dripped from his forehead, and he panted heavily.

I began circling him, and he raised his sword again, doing the same. Our eyes locked, and the tension mounted. With a sudden burst of energy, I charged forward, our swords clashing once more, the sound ringing out to fill the air surrounding us.

Small sparks flew between us as metal bit into metal. August thrust, I parried, and he dodged, each movement fluid and artful.

"You've been practicing, Brother," I grinned.

"You're not the only one who is capable, Silas, despite what you and our father may have thought."

The reminder of my father and what my brother had done was enough to dissolve the momentary lightness I had fallen prey to.

I feigned left, and August followed. Spinning towards him, I gripped August's forearm and delivered a hard strike to the side of his head with the pommel of my sword.

August faltered, plummeting towards the ground as he did so. Sprawled out before me, I stalked toward him, kicking his sword out of his grip while he struggled to reorient himself. Leaning down, I wrapped my hand over the top of his breastplate, pulling him close to me.

"Was it worth it?" I growled. "You were King for a mere moment, Brother. Now you will be eradicated from history, like the pathetic worm you have proven yourself to be."

August thrashed in my hold, trying to get free, but my grip only tightened.

"You lived a life of excess and indulgence, you had your every whim catered to, and you wanted for nothing. Our father placed no expectations on you in return. You should have been content with your lot in life, but instead, you let your greed guide you, and now, you will pay for your sins with your life."

A sharp stinging sensation erupted in my side, and I peered down to see the hilt of a dagger protruding from my flesh. As I turned back to August, he grinned.

"It will take more than a scratch to claim me, Brother," I said in a sardonic tone.

August only grinned wider.

A faint tingling sensation crept over me as I stared down at my brother; his features distorting and blurring in front of me.

"What's wrong, Silas? You don't look too well," he crooned.

I stumbled back, my legs buckling beneath the burden of my failing limbs and pressing weight. My back hit the ground, and the impact robbed the oxygen from my lungs.

"What did you do, August?" I slurred.

My brother's face came into view; the look of victory reflected in his features.

"I am not an idiot, Silas. I know I am at a disadvantage when it comes to brute strength. After all, you're an animal, the beast our father trotted out to inspire fear in the hearts of his enemies," August scoffed. "So I took the liberty of evening the odds."

Sweat coated my entire body and I could feel my limbs begin to tremble.

"The dagger," I said roughly. "It was poisoned, wasn't it?"

"Very good, little Brother."

My stomach roiled, and nausea threatened to spill the contents of my fragile stomach.

Somewhere in the distance, as if I was hearing it from underwater, the sound of Harlowe's desperate cries filled my ears.

"Get up, Silas. Fight, damn you. Fight!" she commanded.

August reached down and gripped the hilt of the dagger, pulling it from my body with agonizing slowness. Pain scorched my side, and it took everything in me not to vomit.

**"You must fight, a chara. If not for you, then for her,"** Caolán pleaded. **"Don't make me break my oath to you. I promised not to interfere, but I will not lose you."**

**"I've got this Caolán."**

**"I am glad to hear you say that because from up here, you appear to be losing. Now get up!"**

I rolled to my side, using my palms to push myself upwards. Thick arms wrapped around my throat, and I instinctively clawed at them.

"I want your *wife* to watch as I slit your throat," August sneered.

My gaze darted to where I had left Harlowe. Cillian clutched her in his arms as she thrashed wildly, trying to get to me. I could not let her down. I could not add to the unbearable pain she had already endured.

With a snarl, I grabbed the back of August's head and pushed all of my remaining strength into pulling his body over the top of mine. When his back collided with the ground, I straddled his waist, reaching down to grip his head between my hands. With one hand on his chin and the other on the top of his head, I twisted August's neck violently.

A sharp crack echoed in the silence of the arena.

The only other sound was my ragged breathing as I fought the rising darkness that was trying to claim me.

August's limp body slipped from my grip and my limbs gave up their fight, sending me careening to the ground beside him.

Dark spots crept along my vision and I tried to blink them away, but they only spread further.

Soft hands cupped my face, and I breathed a sigh of relief when Harlowe's delicate scent filled my nostrils.

"Silas! Silas, what's happening? Where are you injured?" she cried, emotion clogging her throat.

“Poison,” I rasped, brushing my hand over the wound on my side.

“Arabella,” Harlowe screamed, and it was the last thing I heard before the darkness claimed me.

# Chapter Thirteen

The faint echo of pain clung to my limbs as I pried my eyes open. The room was dark, save for the pale light spilling from the bathing chambers. As I shifted to a sitting position, a wave of dizziness momentarily disoriented me. When the sensation passed, I pulled back the covers and slipped out of bed.

A quick glance around the room revealed I was inside my chambers. Although, I couldn't recall making it out of the arena.

I remembered fighting August, and the poisoned blade, but everything after that was unclear.

August.

Guilt and grief collided inside me, and I had to steady myself on the bedpost. August and I had hardly been close, but he was still my brother, and I had killed him.

A soft gasp drew my attention and my gaze flicked to the open door of the bathing chamber. Harlowe stood in the doorframe, her creamy legs on full display beneath her tiny nightgown. She had just finished washing, and I tracked a small droplet of water as it made its way down her throat and settled between her breasts that were pushed up and on display.

The front of my loose sleeping pants began to tent as my cock swelled at the sight of her.

Completely unaware of the effect she was having on me, Harlowe darted forward, her hands cupping my face as she looked me over.

"What are you doing out of bed, Silas? You need to rest," she chided. "Get back beneath the covers before Arabella has my head."

I chuckled lightly. Although I couldn't blame her for being apprehensive. Arabella was a tiny woman, kind and nurturing by nature. But she had a fierce temper when upset, and nothing upset Arabella like an uncooperative patient.

"I'm fine, Harlowe," I said to reassure her, but she didn't listen as she continued to push me back towards the bed.

I placed my palms on her shoulders to halt her efforts, and when her eyes met mine, they were brimming with tears, her fear and concern clear for me to see.

"Hey," I soothed. "It's all right, Harlowe. I'm all right."

Her body trembled in my hold, and I rubbed my hands up and down her back until she regained her composure.

"I thought you were going to die, Silas," she mumbled against my chest.

"Such little faith," I teased, and she shoved me, making me fall back onto the bed.

I barked out a laugh. "You're so vicious, Little Menace."

"Shit, did I hurt you?" she asked as she climbed over the top of me.

I took the opportunity to pull her flush against my body and roll us so that she was trapped beneath me.

"Silas," she warned.

I grinned down at her and then placed a gentle kiss on her lips. Harlowe melted against me, her arms snaking around my neck as she tugged me closer. Then she pushed at my chest, remembering that I was supposed to be resting.

"Nice try," she scoffed.

"You can hardly blame me, Little Menace. Have you seen what you're wearing?" I asked as I ran my finger along the hem of her nightgown.

She caught my wrist, putting an end to my exploration.

"Are you sure you're all right?" she asked.

"I'm a little sore, but nothing beyond that."

Harlowe released a breath. "Arabella is quite the healer," she mused.

"What happened after I lost consciousness?" I asked, eager to fill the holes in my memory.

"Cillian carried you inside to your chambers and Arabella removed the poison."

"When you say removed..." I trailed off, not sure what she meant.

"I mean, she sucked it from your body. It was disgusting, and I had to fight the urge to vomit, but she assured me it was the fastest way to expel it. She could have given you a tonic that would help your body fight the effects, but we couldn't rouse you enough to swallow it."

My stomach rolled as Harlowe explained what Arabella had done to save me and I wasn't ashamed to admit that I was relieved to have been unconscious during it all.

"After she had removed all the poison, she applied a balm to the wound and wrapped it. She's confident it will be healed by morning."

"How long have I been out?"

"Not long," Harlowe said. "Around six or seven hours."

"You and I have different definitions of 'not long', Little Menace."

"Compared to an entire week, a few hours didn't seem like long," she retorted with a raised brow.

Fair point.

"And August..." I cleared my throat, trying again. "Where is August?"

Harlowe shifted uncomfortably.

"I know I killed him, Little Menace," I blurted. "I just meant what was done with his body?"

Harlowe visibly relaxed. "Cillian arranged for his body to be sent to the healers. He wasn't sure what you would want to do... for his burial... but he wanted it to be your choice." I nodded as I swallowed past the lump forming in my throat.

"It's all right to be upset, Silas," Harlowe said gently. "He was still your brother, despite everything."

"I should feel overjoyed that I avenged the death of my father," I said. "Not this... this..."

"Grief," Harlowe finished for me.

She reached out and took my hand in hers, entwining our fingers.

"It's more than that," I whispered. "I feel betrayed by August and not only because he killed our father. I feel betrayed because he forced me to do the same to him."

I inhaled a sharp breath, my shoulders trembling as the full weight of my words hit me.

"He was my brother," I choked. "We couldn't stand each other in the end, but there was a time when that wasn't so. I used to look up to him growing up. I wanted to be just like him. There was nothing he wouldn't do for me. He was my protector, my first friend, and today he forced me to end his life."

Harlowe's soft fingers brushed along my cheek and it was then that I realized I was crying. I tried to stand, to get away before I could make an even bigger fool of myself, but Harlowe's forceful tug on my hand pulled me back into place.

Harlowe stood from the bed and stepped between my legs. She cupped my cheeks between her palms and tilted my head until our gazes locked.

"There is nothing wrong with feeling, Silas," she whispered. Then she brought her mouth to mine in a soft kiss.

I never realized how much I could need someone until that moment.

Wrapping my arms around her waist, I pulled her to me, and she guided my head to her chest. The sound of her beating heart was the only thing I could hear. The only thing I could feel.

Until it wasn't.

A traitorous howl tore free of me and all of my pain, all of my suffering, was laid bare for her to see as I came undone.

Harlowe held me through it all, gently stroking my hair and humming quietly to herself.

This woman was my anchor, and I would worship at her altar for eternity.

In this life and the next.

# Chapter Fourteen

Silas hardly slept throughout the night. He tossed and turned relentlessly, his limbs getting tangled in the sheets until the darkness of the night began to soften and fade, yielding to the violet hues that signaled the sun would soon rise to claim the day.

When he finally rose from bed and announced he was going for a walk, I was relieved. The thought of some much-needed respite was a welcome change.

I should have known better.

The man that stood before me now was not Silas. He was a vessel for his rage.

Silas's whole body was charged with an intensity that had me swallowing roughly. From fear or anticipation, I could not tell.

He wore loose sleeping trousers and nothing else. His chiseled torso was on full display, the sweat coating his skin only enhancing the allure of his tattoos.

"Is everything all right?" I asked, drawing his attention.

He barked out a harsh laugh. "Not really."

I rose from the bed and went to him, my hands gliding over the corded muscles of his forearms.

"Where have you been?" I asked.

"Training."

"Talk to me, Silas," I begged.

"I don't want to talk," he snapped. His jaw was set in a hard line, and he ground his teeth together as he worked to contain his mounting fury.

I leaned forward, balancing my weight on the tip of my toes as I placed a kiss to the pulse point hammering at the base of his throat.

"Fine, we won't talk."

"Harlowe," he growled. "My head is not right this morning. I don't want to hurt you." His tone was almost pleading.

"I think you and I both know that I like it when you do," I purred.

Silas groaned, and in the next moment, his large, calloused hand darted out and gripped me by my throat.

"Tell me to stop," he snarled.

"Never."

Silas squeezed my throat tighter, cutting off my air before loosening his hold.

"Get on your knees," he commanded.

He didn't release his hold on my throat as I sank to the floor.

"Good fucking girl," he praised. "Now take off your nightgown. Show me everything that belongs to me."

Liquid fire drenched my core as I slid the thin strap of my nightgown down my shoulder and then did the same with the other. The silken fabric pooled below my navel, exposing my breasts to his hungry gaze.

"All the way off," he demanded.

It was awkward to maneuver with his hand still clutching my throat, but when I rid my body of the last vestige of clothing, I was rewarded with Silas's sharp inhale of breath.

"No panties," he rumbled.

Silas released my throat and pushed his pants down his hips. His cock sprang free, standing proudly against his lower abdomen, and he gripped it tightly, stroking his hand up and down his length.

I watched him hungrily, not bothering to hide the need simmering beneath my skin.

"Is this what you want?" he asked as he pumped his cock harder. I nodded, and Silas chuckled darkly.

"You want to be my dirty little whore that I use to find my pleasure?" A shiver raced down my spine at his filthy words, and I licked my lips.

"I'm going to claim you, Harlowe. I'm going to fill you with my come until you're overflowing with it and your pussy weeps for me."

Silas stalked towards me, his fist still wrapped around his cock. He stopped in front of me and tipped my chin up with his finger until our gazes locked.

"Open," he commanded.

I parted my lips, opening my mouth for him. Silas leaned down and spat into my mouth.

"Swallow," he growled.

And I did.

Fucking hell! Why was that so hot?

I rubbed my thighs together to ease the throbbing need making itself known in my core.

"You like that, Little Menace?" Silas tittered. "Of course you do. You're a wanton little thing, aren't you?"

"Open," he repeated, tapping my cheek with his fingers.

I obeyed without hesitation.

Silas wasn't gentle when he thrust his hard cock into my waiting mouth. He wasn't gentle when he thrust so deep, I gagged around his length. And he certainly wasn't gentle when he pushed the back of my head until my face was flush against his hips, cutting off my oxygen as drool spilled from my mouth and tears streaked down my face.

Silas was anything but gentle.

And I fucking loved it.

"That's it Little Menace, choke on my cock," he panted as he continued to thrust into my mouth.

Just before he was about to find his release, Silas pulled back, his cock slipping past my lips as I sucked in a lungful of air.

"Get on the bed and spread your legs for me."

I scrambled to my feet and climbed onto the bed. Despite all the times we had come together just like this in the past, I couldn't fight the small blush that heated my cheeks as I spread my legs wide for him.

"Touch yourself," he demanded.

Silas stood at the foot of the bed, his eyes glued to my center that I was certain glistened with my arousal.

My fingers slid down my stomach, past my lower abdomen, until they circled my tight bundle of nerves. A small moan escaped me as pleasure tightened my stomach and I closed my eyes as I let the ecstasy roll through me.

I yelped and pulled my hand back when Silas delivered a sharp slap to my pussy.

"Eyes on me, Little Menace," he growled.

"Silas, wha—" I didn't get to finish my sentence when he delivered another slap to my aching core.

"You do as I say, no question."

I nodded my head as my pussy clenched with need.

"Good girl," Silas cooed. "Now make yourself come with your dainty little fingers while I watch you."

This time, when I lowered my fingers to my clit, I didn't drop my gaze from Silas's. He reached down and fisted his cock, pumping himself in time with my strokes.

Pleasure coiled tight inside me, my toes curling as my impending orgasm built to a crescendo.

Only, it never came.

Silas ripped my hand away, tearing my orgasm from me as I stood at the edge of oblivion.

"What the fuck, Silas?" I hissed, but the feral look in his eyes silenced my protests.

"Turn over," he barked. "Get on your knees and point your ass in the air."

I swallowed, but did as he said. Silas climbed onto the bed behind me and fisted my hair in his hand. I cried out at the sudden burst of pain as he pulled me to him by my copper strands. My back was flush with his hard chest, and I felt his hot breath fan against the shell of my ear.

"If I were you, Little Menace, I'd grab a hold of that bedpost and hold on tight because I am about to destroy your pussy."

Without warning, he thrust me forward, and I fumbled to grip the bedpost. I had one hand planted on the mattress and one arm clutching the post when Silas entered me with a ferocity I had never experienced with him before.

His thickened cock filled me to bursting, and I struggled to adjust as he pounded into me. The sound of a sharp slap echoed around the room, followed quickly by a stinging sensation on my ass.

I didn't have time to complain, as a loud moan left me without permission.

"Don't you dare come, Harlowe," Silas sneered. "Not until I say you can."

"Silas," I whimpered, "please."

"You beg so pretty, Little Menace," he chuckled.

Silas gripped my hips with a bruising force and all I could do was hold on as he unleashed on me. His movements became jerky and with one last thrust, Silas groaned out his release.

He pulled out of me and I felt the sudden loss of him to my soul. But he quickly replaced his cock with his fingers, two at first, followed by a third. He fucked his come back inside me as a string of incoherent words left me.

"That's it Little Menace, now you can come."

Silas pressed his thumb over my swollen nub and I unraveled. Pleasure like I had never experienced before crashed over me with the force of a tidal wave. My arms gave way, no longer able to hold me up, and I collapsed atop the mattress.

A moment later, the mattress dipped beside me, and powerful arms lifted me as Silas placed me over his chest. My heart beat furiously against the confines of my ribcage, and I panted as I tried to regain control of my breathing.

Silas stroked my hair with a gentility I wasn't aware he possessed, and I sighed in contentment.

"Are you all right, Little Menace?" he asked. "Was that too much for you?"

I could hear the concern in his words, but I was too exhausted to meet his gaze.

"Too much," I snorted. "That may have been the best sex of my life."

Silas's chest rumbled with laughter and he said, "Best sex of your life, you say?"

"Don't let it go to your head."

"Oh, Little Menace, we are way past that point."

My lips tugged up in a grin, knowing full well I would regret ever uttering those words.

# Chapter Fifteen

Whispered conversations followed us as we walked through the palace toward the main dining hall. The servants were nervous, unsure of what awaited the future of their kingdom.

"Why are they all acting so strangely?" Silas asked, as he waved his hand around. "Is it because I killed my brother?"

"Silas," I said carefully. "The people are anxious to learn what your court will bring."

"My court?" he repeated with a furrowed brow.

"They are awaiting the address of their King."

Silas stopped walking, his body rooted in place as all the color drained from his face.

"I am not their King," he whispered hoarsely.

"You are the last living heir to the throne, Silas. The crown falls to you."

"No, that's..." Silas trailed off as realization hit him. "No, no, no, no... this wasn't supposed to happen. I am the second-born son. I was never meant to rule."

Silas tugged on the strands of his hair and I ushered him into a nearby alcove to prevent anyone from overhearing his distress.

His pleading eyes met mine, and I nearly chuckled at the sheer horror in his gaze.

Silas began pacing the small area, his discomfort growing by the second. "I loathe people, Harlowe. It's why my father arranged for me to enter the military. I excel at what I do and people respect me for it. I don't have to waste my time feigning interest in their lives for them to listen to me. Everyone knows exactly what they're getting with me. They don't bother me with trivial squabbles. They don't expect me to host grand events and spend the whole evening listening to them speak utter nonsense in the hope of winning my good graces. Court politics are not my forte. There is a reason I prefer dragons over people, Harlowe."

I couldn't contain my laughter any longer. It burst free of me with a very undignified snort, and Silas turned towards me, his eyes narrowed in aggravation.

"What's so funny?" Silas hissed.

When I finally got myself under control, I replied, "All of it."

"Little Menace," Silas growled.

"Just take a breath, will you?" I said, raising my palms and planting them firmly on his chest.

"Breathe."

Silas rolled his eyes, but did as I instructed.

"Being respected is not contingent on being sociable or likable. I think you'll find being king makes people listen to you in any case."

"What about other kingdoms?" he pressed. "Other monarchs have no incentive to heed my demands. How am I supposed to maintain the relationships my father has built over centuries?"

"I would suggest not having Caolán burn their kingdoms to the ground for a start," I teased.

Silas, however, was not in the mood.

"I can't do this, Little Menace."

"Of course you can, Silas. You're a natural leader, and you're pretty charismatic when you put your mind to it. You'll figure it out."

"Charismatic, you say?" Silas said as a small smirk fought to break free. "Tell me more about this charisma you speak of."

I rolled my eyes. "That's what you focused on, out of everything I just said?"

"It seemed the most pressing," he chuckled, pulling me against him.

I pushed him away playfully, unable to hide my grin. "Come, your kingdom awaits."

"Fuck," Silas muttered. "I'm the King."

"You are. Now get to it!"

"Thank you, Little Menace," Silas said as he pressed a kiss to my temple.

"You're welcome, Silas."

We walked in companionable silence until we reached the doors leading into the dining hall. Silas pulled them open, and loud cheers immediately greeted us. Cillian, Emmerson, Zeke, Fionn, and others I didn't recognize gathered around a table. As we approached, they all stood.

Well, except Emmerson and Zeke, who carried on as if nothing had changed.

Cillian reached us first and pulled Silas into a tight hug as he thumped his back with his fist.

"I'm sorry for your loss, Brother," he said, placing his large hands on either side of Silas's throat. "But I am glad it is you who lives to fight another day."

Silas acknowledged Cillian's words with a nod and the two men pressed their foreheads together for the briefest moment. When Cillian released Silas, both men's eyes were misted.

Clearing his throat, Silas said, "I appreciate the loyalty you have all shown me and I will not forget those who stood at my back during my darkest hour."

Turning towards me, Silas placed a quick kiss on the side of my head. "I'd also like to introduce you to —"

"Your wife, we heard," a tall, broad man with brown, wavy hair called out, and the table erupted with another round of cheers.

"About that," Emmerson said, as she stood from her chair and strode towards me. I didn't miss the way the men's gazes followed her.

From the look on Cillian's face, he didn't miss it either.

"What the fuck, Harlowe?"

I rubbed a hand over my face and groaned. "We are not married," I said, pointing my finger between Silas and me. "He keeps asking, and I keep saying no."

The table erupted in howling laughter, and Silas scowled at them.

"Good, because you need to remember that best friend privileges are attached to all major life events. Specifically, you can't undertake them without me," she huffed, crossing her arms over her chest.

I laughed at the seriousness in Emmerson's tone. When she raised an expectant brow, I realized she was waiting for a response.

"I vow not to exclude you from any major life events," I promised, my hand over my heart.

"Good," Emmerson grunted.

"Same goes for you."

"He should be so lucky," Emmerson scoffed as she flicked her braid over her shoulder.

Cillian growled low in his throat and marched up to Emmerson, pulling her in for a heated kiss.

I had the sneaking suspicion Cillian was less worried about Emmerson's comment and more worried about how the eager men watching her may interpret her dismissal.

Because Cillian didn't just kiss Emmerson. He claimed her with his kiss.

When they finally came up for air, Emmerson appeared a little stunned; a rare feat. Cillian pulled her close and glared at the men, confirming my suspicions.

**"The hellcat is outraged for the wrong reasons,"** Misneach chimed in. **"She should be asking if your chosen is a worthy mate before worrying about being excluded from trivial events."**

**"Misneach,"** I grumbled.

**"I'm not saying he is unworthy."**

**"Actually, you say it all the time."**

**"Yes, well, I just think he needs to prove himself. Only then will I give him my blessing."**

**"Yes, Father,"** I teased.

Before Misneach could retort, a disheveled-looking man burst into the dining hall, drawing my attention. The sound of steel grating against steel filled the chamber, but everyone was already re-sheathing their blades when I glanced behind me.

The man was elderly, his hair a light grey, and he had eyebrows that had overtaken his forehead. His long, black robe *swished* around his ankles as he hurried toward us, clutching an oversized book in his hands.

"Your Majesty," he panted, bowing low at the waist as he addressed Silas.

"The Master of Ceremonies," Silas muttered so only I could hear.

"I am pleased to see you have recovered," the man gasped. "We have much to discuss."

Silas raised a brow, waiting for the man to continue.

"Your coronation."

"Ah, no," Silas said, raising a finger. "That's not going to happen."

"My Lord?"

"Do what's necessary to make it official, but I depart Pyrithia in one day. War is coming, and we need to be prepared," Silas said.

"War!" the man exclaimed.

"Do not repeat that," Silas said sternly. "Consider it a royal decree or something."

The Master of Ceremonies only gaped at Silas, but he had already shifted his attention to the others.

The man left the dining hall, muttering to himself as he went.

"Maxim," Silas said to the man who had teased him earlier. "Find Arabella." Maxim nodded and stood from the table.

"And bring Eoin too."

# Chapter Sixteen

We spent the rest of our time in Pyrithia making arrangements for Silas's absence. Eoin, the former King's personal advisor, took on the role of Regent, and Silas assigned Maxim the responsibility of preparing his forces for war.

War.

I knew it was coming, but it was still sobering to see preparations underway for the inevitable conflict.

It had taken some work to convince Arabella to accompany us into the Forest of Nightmares, but she eventually relented once we'd explained what we needed from her.

Silas had also taken the time to lay his brother to rest, and I was glad for it, if only for the closure it brought him.

The most challenging task, however, had been meeting with Kingsley, Teller's sister, to inform her of his death. She had been inconsolable, and the gaping hole his absence had left inside my chest was ripped wide open again. I was forced to excuse myself, unable to bear the weight of her grief too.

Now, however, as I stood at the edge of the Forest of Nightmares peering up at the towering tree line, I had to wonder just how much harder things were going to get from here on out.

The air was heavy with an eerie stillness, broken only by the occasional rustle of leaves that swayed alongside the wind. The forest was dark beyond the rows of trees, their gnarled limbs and skeletal branches weaving together into a macabre snare, ready to ambush unsuspecting travelers.

An involuntary shiver escaped me as I recalled the last time I had ventured into this forest.

**"You don't have to do this, Fire Heart,"** Misneach said.

**"I do, Misneach. It's the only way we will stand a chance against Kieran."**

**"Stop babying her,"** Rónán said with a roll of his eyes.

**"Rónán,"** Saoirse warned at the same time Misneach lunged for the other dragon.

Rónán darted back, not an easy feat for a creature of his size, barely escaping the snap of Misneach's jaws.

**"I was only teasing,"** Rónán said, aghast. **"You threatened my pretty head for a jest?"**

Misneach growled low in his throat, the threat clear.

**"Evidently, it is not appreciated,"** Niamh interjected, before things could escalate further.

**"Misneach,"** I chastised. **"You can't go around killing everyone who disagrees with you."**

**"You should listen to your Cathal!"** Rónán huffed indignantly.

**"I can try,"** Misneach said with a flick of his tail, ignoring Rónán's antics.

This time, Rónán failed to avoid Misneach's hit, and the end of Misneach's tail connected with the side of his colossal head.

**"Always a delight, Misneach,"** Rónán grumbled, and Misneach huffed.

Gods above, we could not get this over with fast enough.

**"On this, we agree,"** Misneach added.

My gaze returned to the unending thicket before me.

The forest seemed alive, its pulse echoing mine. Shadows danced and twisted, deceiving my eyes into believing every bush and underbrush was a monster lying in wait and ready to pounce. Yet, despite my fear and the chill creeping up my spine, there was an allure to the forest. A primal fascination that drew me in, calling me home.

Silas's large palm settled on the small of my back, breaking my reverie.

"Are you ready to go?" he asked, his warm breath a caress against the shell of my ear.

I shivered, and this time it was for an entirely different reason.

I nodded my head in agreement, not trusting my voice not to give away my current state of arousal.

The corner of Silas's mouth tipped up, letting me know he knew exactly what my traitorous body was thinking.

"So we track east if we're heading for the Lost Witch?" Silas asked as he unrolled a map.

"That's what we did last time. But honestly, we more or less stumbled across her cottage. Emmerson did the best she could to navigate us through the forest, but in the end, she sort of found us," I finished sheepishly.

"Harlowe," Silas growled as he dragged a hand over his face. "You said you could lead us to her."

"I am well aware, Silas," I hissed, my spine straightening with my growing anger. "I said I would, and I meant it. Besides, Emmerson will help guide me."

"We've got this," said the woman herself as she sauntered over to join our conversation. "We are the only ones who have ever located her if you recall," Emmerson added. She arched a brow in Silas's direction, daring him to contradict her.

He considered her for a moment before huffing out, "Fine, but if anything goes awry in there, I'm pulling everyone out. I won't risk my men for an uncertainty."

Emmerson beamed at him as she rested her elbow on my shoulder. "Yes, General," she said, giving him an exaggerated salute.

Silas shook his head and sighed. "I'm going to finalize our plans with Caolán and then we head out." Silas marched in his dragon's direction and my eyes followed him without my permission.

Emmerson dropped her elbow from my shoulder and turned towards me. "Let's hope we can stumble our way through the forest that convincingly," she muttered, "because I can't remember a damn thing about how we got to her cottage."

I groaned. "Neither do I. It's all hazy. I think our only focus at that point was not dying."

Emmerson chuckled. "Fun times."

I cast an incredulous look in her direction. "No! Not fun times. We almost died, if you recall."

"Exactly!" she beamed. With mirth twinkling in her eyes, Emerson spun on her heels and headed towards Cillian.

**"I know you care deeply for the hellcat, Fire Heart, but have you ever considered she might just be insane?"** Misneach mused.

**"More than once,"** I admitted.

Misneach chortled, and I stepped between his forelegs, reveling in the safety he offered.

**"If anything happens in there, Fire Heart, promise me you will call**

**for me,"** he pleaded.

**"I'm unsure how the forest will impact our bond,"** I admitted, finally voicing my fears.

**"You are stronger than you were before. Believe in yourself as I believe in you."**

**"What would I do without you, Misneach?"**

**"The more important question is, what would I do without *you*, Fire Heart?"**

Misneach lowered his forehead to mine, and I drew strength from his imposing presence.

**"Promise you will burn the entire forest down if you must, Fire Heart."**

**"I promise."**

Someone cleared their throat behind us, and we pulled apart.

I turned and met the soulful brown eyes of the man I trusted to watch my back, just as I watched his. Determination shone from his chocolate depths, and I squared my shoulders, matching his energy.

"It's time."

# Chapter Seventeen

The moment I crossed the threshold into the Forest of Nightmares, I felt the shift in the atmosphere surrounding me.

It was subtle at first.

The air thickened, weighed down by the growing unease tugging at my senses. A cold sweat broke out over my skin and my heartbeat escalated until it felt like it would beat its way out of my chest.

That familiar feeling of dread settled in the pit of my stomach screaming at me to run, to turn around, that only danger lingered inside this place. The feeling intensified until it was almost suffocating. It was as if a clamp had shut tight around my chest, making it hard to breathe.

My eyes darted around, my senses on full alert as every shadow seemed to elongate, taking on a sinister form as if preparing to attack. With every rustle of the leaves and the crunch of dirt under boots, fear flooded my system, making my body jolt in response.

I fucking hated this place.

"I hate this fucking forest," Emmerson muttered, echoing my thoughts.

"That... was unpleasant," Zeke added.

**"Fire Heart, are you all right?"**

**"I can hear you,"** I said, breathing a sigh of relief.

**"As I said you would."**

I rolled my eyes. **"You didn't say that, Misneach. You said I needed to believe in myself as you believe in me."**

**"It's the same thing,"** he huffed.

**"Not quite."**

**"Just be quick about your business, Fire Heart. I do not relish the separation."**

I peeked back over my shoulder and saw my dragon pacing the edge of the forest. My gaze slid to Caolán, who gave me a slight nod, letting me know he would watch over my friend.

Returning my attention to the task at hand, I straightened my pack on my shoulders and headed further into the forest.

A small hand slipped into mine, and I glanced down to find Emmerson's fingers entwined with my own.

"We can do this, Harlowe. We survived once before, we will survive again." She gave my hand a gentle squeeze before releasing me.

Silas and Cillian stepped up beside me and Emmerson, flanking us. "This is roughly where you think we're headed?" Silas asked, gesturing to a spot on his map that I had pointed out earlier.

Emmerson and I shared a glance before I answered. "Yes, that is where we're headed. It will take two, maybe three, days."

Silas nodded and then flicked his head to the side, indicating for Cillian to move closer. I caught pieces of their muttered conversation and deduced they were making plans for our campgrounds later tonight.

Zeke, Fionn, and Arabella brought up the tail end of our group and my chest swelled with pride when I saw my friend trying to ease Arabella's burdens. He had taken her pack and carried it alongside his own, while he tried to reassure her she had nothing to worry about despite never having stepped foot inside the forest himself.

Arabella attempted to appear brave, but I noticed her trembling hands tightly clutching her pants, as she worked to suppress the shaking.

We never should have brought her to this place.

"You know we had to, Harlowe. She is a powerful witch and we may need her help to retrieve the stone."

I hadn't realized I had expressed my disquiet out loud until Emmerson's voice broke through my musings.

"I know. I just feel terrible that she is here, scared out of her wits."

"Aren't we all," Emmerson snorted.

I glanced at my best friend from the corner of my eye. "Are you telling me you're afraid, Emmerson?" I teased.

"Of course I am. I'd be foolish not to be," she shrugged. "The last time we were here, you had literal chunks taken out of you. Then you exploded into a raging inferno and almost got crushed by a giant wyrm. Oh, and don't forget how we were hunted through the forest by a horde of vicious-looking minotaurs."

She had a point.

"All of those things are about me, Em. Tell me what you're afraid of." I probed.

"I fear losing you, Harlowe. That's what I'm afraid of."

My throat constricted as I fought the emotion clogging it. I didn't deserve a best friend like Emmerson, but I thanked the gods for her all the same.

"I love you, Emmerson. You know that, right?"

"Of course I do, Harlowe. But stop talking like we aren't going to make it out of here, because I for one, plan on meeting that bastard Kieran on the battlefield," she grinned, lightening the mood.

We walked in companionable silence as the day wore on, but all too soon, the night made its presence known.

"Fionn," Silas called.

The young Cathal jogged over to Silas's side.

"Go ahead and find a place to set up camp." Fionn nodded and darted out of sight.

"Is it a good idea to send him off on his own?" I asked, unable to hide my concern for my friend.

"Fionn knows what he's doing, Harlowe. I trust him to be careful."

"You know," Arabella's sweet voice traveled over the group. "I thought, with this place being called the Forest of Nightmares, that we would have seen more monsters by now."

A collective groan sounded in response to Arabella's words and her eyes widened in surprise and perhaps a little fear.

"What? What is it?" she asked.

"When things are going smoothly, *never* question it. Especially when you're doing something dangerous. You may just tempt the fates," Zeke answered.

"Do you mean to tell me you are all superstitious?" she asked, incredulous.

"You're a witch," Emmerson pointed out. "Shouldn't you be the most superstitious one here?"

Fionn emerged on the trail up ahead, cutting off Arabella's response.

"There's something you need to see," he told Silas.

"What is it?" Silas demanded.

"It's... just come and see," Fionn said as he jogged back in the direction he'd come.

Everyone turned to glance at Arabella.

"What? I certainly didn't do anything?" she huffed.

"The fates," Zeke murmured.

"Oh please," Arabella scoffed, but there was a forced casualness in her tone.

We all followed Fionn as he led us further into the forest. When we broke through the tree line to a small clearing, I sucked in a ragged breath.

Behind me, someone gasped, and the noise was quickly followed by the telltale sounds of retching.

My eyes took in the scene before me and the feeling of dread I had carried with me since stepping into the forest, amplified, clawing at my chest until I thought my heart would give out.

"What, in the name of the gods, could have done that?"

# Chapter Eighteen

The stench of decay assaulted my senses, and I fought the urge to follow in the footsteps of my companion as my stomach twisted and roiled.

I will not vomit. I will not vomit. I will not vomit.

I tried breathing through my mouth, but that only made the nausea worse.

The mutilated remains of countless bodies littered the clearing and judging by the green tinge to their skin, a vast majority of them were minotaurs. Some of the corpses were little more than tattered scraps of flesh and bone, their bodies bearing distinct teeth impressions where something gnawed at their limbs.

Insects buzzed around the field of death, drawn in by the promise of rotting flesh. Rivers of blood painted the ground, although it had lost its crimson hue, taking on a muted brown color.

At least the massacre wasn't fresh. Whatever could do that to a group of minotaurs was not a creature I wanted to cross paths with.

"Please tell me whatever ate their remains was just some wild animal and not whatever tore them to shreds," I pleaded.

Silas grimaced, and my stomach swirled in response.

"By the looks of it, they were attacked by ghouls."

"Ghouls?" I questioned.

"They are grotesque, monstrous creatures that eat the flesh of the dead, or as in this case, they tear it from a living victim," Silas supplied.

A violent tremor wracked my body at the image Silas's words conjured, and I wrapped my arms around myself in a protective embrace.

"How could they overpower such a large group of minotaurs?" I asked, barely above a whisper.

"They are cunning creatures. They hunt at night, lurking in the shadows and striking when their victims are at their most vulnerable."

"When they're sleeping?" I asked.

Silas nodded his head in confirmation. "They are also said to possess supernatural abilities, but we haven't been able to confirm that."

"How do you know so much about them?"

"The Cathal keeps records of any creatures encountered in this forest during the trial of monsters."

A cold sweat broke out on my forehead at the thought of children entering this forest just so they could prove themselves worthy of joining the ranks of the Cathal.

"Over here," Cillian called out.

My eyes scanned the clearing, finding Cillian crouched down beside one of the bodies. I followed Silas as he made his way over to him.

"You see that?" Cillian asked, pointing to a bite mark.

Silas nodded his head, and I studied the area, trying to figure out what they were seeing. Judging by the impressions left behind, the ghoul possessed a mouth full of razor-sharp teeth. There were rows upon rows of needle-point fangs that could easily tear and shred flesh from bone.

"And this one," Cillian added, pointing to another set of bite marks.

"What are you both seeing?" I asked, unable to distinguish one bite mark from the next.

"Come here," Silas said, pulling me down next to him. "You see these tiny indentations here?" he asked, pointing to one bite mark and then another.

"Yes."

"What do you see?"

I narrowed my eyes, focusing in on the minute details. "They're slightly different."

"That's right. Cillian has identified around a dozen different bite marks, which explains how they overpowered such a large group of minotaurs."

Silas stood abruptly, taking my hand and pulling me up with him. "I want to put as much distance between us and this clearing as possible. You never know when they might wander back for their next meal."

"Cheery," Emmerson muttered next to me as she made her way towards Cillian.

Ready to be done with this place, I headed to the edge of the clearing where Zeke and Fionn stood with Arabella. She had been intermittently emptying her stomach, while Zeke rubbed her back and held her hair out of the way.

"Sorry. This is all new to me," she said sheepishly, gesturing around the clearing.

"Don't be. It's new to me too." I leaned in to whisper so only she would hear. "You're not the first one to heave in front of this lot, and I doubt you'll be the last. Trust me, they're used to it."

Arabella gave me a tentative smile, which I returned.

"Let's go," Silas called from across the clearing. We skirted around the edge of the massacre, not wanting to get any closer than necessary, until we met up with him, Cillian, and Emmerson.

It was a few hours later when Silas mercifully declared we'd make camp. The light of the day had long since faded into the darkness of night, and I was eager to get behind the protection of the concealment spell.

Arabella set to work laying the protective ward. She placed small crystals around the perimeter of our camp and explained that she had infused the crystals with her magic, which acted as a barrier, preventing negative energies from crossing into our camp.

Arabella's magic was truly impressive, and I was reminded of everything that had been lost to us during the War of Witches.

"All set," Arabella announced.

We opted not to set up the tents we had brought with us considering the lack of light, and instead unfolded our bedrolls around the fire we lit in the center. Unsurprisingly, no one was hungry for meat of any variety, so we ate a simple dinner of bread and cheese.

"Should we put out the fire?" I asked, feeling more nervous the closer we came to sleep. I knew Arabella's wards were in place, but I couldn't shake the feeling of unseen eyes watching us.

"It's fine, Harlowe. The concealment spell hides the flames. To any creature passing by, this —" Silas gestured to the makeshift camp we had laid out — "is an empty forest floor. Now try to get some sleep. We have another long day ahead of us tomorrow."

Silas pulled me flush against his body and placed a chaste kiss on my temple.

Try as I might, my mind didn't allow my body to succumb to the darkness of sleep.

It didn't help that our wailing companion from our last foray into this forest had made their presence known the moment my eyes shuttered closed.

**"Misneach?"**

**"I am here, Fire Heart."**

The sound of his deep, masculine voice was a reassurance I didn't realize I needed.

**"Will you tell me what troubles you?"** he asked.

**"I worry it won't be enough. I'm scared that even if we retrieve the stone and it amplifies my powers, it still won't be enough to beat Kieran,"** I admitted.

**"You are not in this fight alone, Fire Heart,"** Misneach soothed. **"Flawed as he may be, the General is now a king. He commands an army ready to stand at your side, and others will follow his lead."**

**"Tell me again about the unbonded dragons,"** I pressed.

Misneach hesitated briefly. **"As I said, they will recognize you as one of our own, and they will follow you."**

**"What aren't you telling me, Misneach?"**

**"Well,"** my dragon said. **"There is a faction amongst our kind that does not believe dragons should bond with humans. They believe humans to be unworthy and do not involve themselves in their conflict."**

**"When you say there is a faction..."** I asked, trailing off.

**"It is mostly the unbonded dragons living in the Mountains of Dragonia. Those willing to bond tend to live in the mountains bordering the kingdoms."**

**"Misneach,"** I growled. **"That's a very different sentiment from the last time we discussed this."**

**"I am confident that they will follow you, Fire Heart. They just need to meet you and they will know your intentions are honorable."**

I sighed, hoping he was right. We would need all the allies we could get.

**"Try to get some rest, Fire Heart,"** Misneach said.

**"Don't think I don't recognize your attempt to redirect this discussion."**

**"Is it working?"** Misneach asked, humor lacing his tone.

Before I could answer, a rustle in the bushes caught my attention.

**"What is it?"** Misneach asked, sensing the change in my demeanor.

**"I don't know,"** I answered, as I strained my eyes to see beyond the darkness. **"I'm going to have a look."**

**"Do not, under any circumstances, leave that protective ward, Fire**

**Heart,"** Misneach ordered.

**"I won't go far. I'll just scan the perimeter."**

**"Fire Heart,"** Misneach growled, but I was already moving.

Plucking my dagger from the ground beside me, I crept to the edge of the ward. I remained rooted in place, barely breathing as I listened intently, waiting to hear the noise again.

Nothing happened.

**"Must have been an —"** my words died on my lips as sickening green eyes that seemed to glow in the moonlight, locked with mine.

**"Fire Heart?"** Misneach demanded.

**"Ghoul,"** I breathed.

# Chapter Nineteen

All around me, glowing green eyes appeared throughout the shrubbery surrounding the camp. I stepped back, ensuring I was well within the boundaries of the concealment spell.

And yet, that first set of eyes remained locked on me. It was as though it could see through the wards that were supposed to mask our presence here.

Bile rose in my throat and I swallowed it down as I took another step back.

"Silas," I called. "Emmerson. Everyone, wake up."

Murmurs sounded from behind me as my companions grumbled about being woken. "What is it, Harlowe? What's wrong?" Silas asked, his voice still thick with sleep.

"In the bushes," I whispered. "Look."

Silas was at my side with his blade drawn before I had a chance to blink. "Circle formation," he barked. "Arabella, in the center."

Everyone snapped to attention, creating a protective barrier around Arabella, who stood in the middle of our group trembling violently.

"Are they what I think they are?" Emmerson murmured.

"If you think they are ghouls, then yes," Cillian confirmed.

"This fucking forest," she seethed.

"What the fuck?" Zeke whispered.

My gaze darted in the direction he was staring, mouth agape. The sight that greeted me sent my stomach roiling for what had to be the dozenth time today.

A creature stumbled out of the bushes, its rotted skin hanging loosely from its skeletal frame. Lesions covered the grotesque pallor of its flesh, giving it a mottled appearance.

It mirrored the embodiment of death.

Its sunken eyes made the glowing green irises even more sickening, and an involuntary shudder crept down my spine. Blood dripped from the rows of sharp, jagged teeth, and a small chunk of flesh hung from the corner of its mouth.

My gaze darted away from the grizzly reminder that these creatures, quite literally, ate their kills, and landed on the razor-sharp claws adorning its fingertips.

It was no wonder the bodies of the minotaurs had been so viciously mutilated.

The elongated tips were crafted for tearing and shredding flesh, which they were clearly adept at judging by the remains we'd found.

I ran my gaze over the rest of the ghouls emerging from the brush. Their gaunt frames were contorted and twisted, and their limbs were wiry, giving them a disturbingly unnatural form. Some had long, tangled strands of hair that hung in greasy clumps around their faces, while others were completely bald.

They looked feral, yet deadly.

"They can't get inside, right?" Fionn asked nervously.

"They can't cross the wards," Arabella confirmed, although her voice quivered as she spoke.

"Aren't the wards supposed to conceal us from them?" Cillian asked. "They're looking right at us."

"Be prepared to defend yourselves," Silas commanded.

My grip tightened on my dagger as I bent down to retrieve another from my boot.

"Try to avoid using your flames, Little Menace. We don't want to alert any other creatures to our presence here," Silas said.

"What a comforting thought," Zeke muttered.

"Come on Zeke," Emmerson crooned. "Where's your sense of adventure?"

"I'm not insane, Emmerson," he hissed. "I saw what they did to the minotaurs."

"Focus," Silas snapped.

"Unlike you, Silas, I can do more than one thing at a time," Emmerson retorted in a saccharine tone.

**"Fire Heart?"**

**"Not right now, Misneach. I'm sort of busy."**

**"Busy doing what? What did you see in the bushes?"**

**"I already told you, a ghoul. Now please be quiet so I can concentrate."**

**"What the hell is a ghoul?"**

**"Misneach,"** I snapped.

**"Splitting her attention will get her killed, Misneach. You need to calm down and stay quiet,"** Caolán said.

Misneach growled, but he didn't interrupt again.

"It's crossing the ward," Fionn said, pointing to a ghoul that stepped over the crystal, signifying the edge of the barrier.

"Fuck," Silas snarled. "ATTACK!"

When we moved towards the ghouls, everything changed.

Their slow, languid movements disappeared, only to be replaced with a speed and agility that stood in stark contrast to their skeletal forms.

"Holy fuck they're fast!" Emmerson breathed.

I didn't have time to even peer over my shoulder at my friend. A ghoul towered over me, its sharp teeth bared in a snarl as saliva dripped from its mouth. I didn't hesitate. I danced forward, thrusting my dagger into its gut before retreating out of reach.

I expected a howl of pain, for the creature to double over in agony, or the rapid spread of crimson over its abdomen.

Instead, there was... nothing.

Only a slight wound marred the ghoul's stomach where my blade had pierced its flesh. No blood colored the site and if the creature felt the blow, it showed no sign of it.

Swallowing, I gripped my daggers in my hands and tried again. This time, I came in close, pivoting at the last moment, and raked my daggers across the ghoul's back.

Once more, the creature seemed impervious to the slice of my blades. No blood flowed in a torrent from the wound and the ghoul just stood there, unperturbed. When I faced it again, an eerie smile spread across its face.

"Our blades don't work against them," I called out.

"Yes, I was just figuring that out," Emmerson called back.

The ghoul in front of me moved with lightning speed as it sprang forward, gripping my throat. Its claws sank into the side of my neck and I most certainly felt the trickle of blood escaping from the site.

It lowered its face towards my neck, as if intending to kiss it. I thrashed in its grip, certain a kiss was the furthest thing from its mind.

"Flames, Harlowe," Silas shouted.

"I thought you said no flames?"

"Fucking ignite the creature," he hollered back.

I felt the sharp press of its teeth against my skin and pulled my flames around me. The ghoul dropped me as it desperately sought to extinguish the fire now consuming it.

Blasts of white light drew my attention to the battle unfolding around me as fórsa went sailing through the air toward the ghouls.

I scanned my surroundings, and my gaze landed on Cillian. A ghoul stood in front of him, his sword hanging loosely at his side, and he made no move to defend himself as the ghoul moved closer.

What the hell was he doing?

The creature lifted its claws, the pointed tips reflecting the shimmering moonlight. With a burst of speed, the ghoul plunged its claws into Cillian's side as he stood by idly, allowing the creature to overpower him.

"Cillian," I screamed, but he didn't move. He just stood there, awaiting the next blow.

I rushed forward, reaching them as the ghoul lowered its mouth to Cillian's shoulder. The sound of flesh tearing from bone met my ears, and I leaped into the air with a battle cry, landing on the creature's back.

My hands gripped the ghoul's head, and I pushed my flames into its skull. It reared back, releasing Cillian and knocking me to the side. Not wasting another second, I engulfed the ghoul in a flood of flames. Only after the creature turned to ash did I release my hold. The remnants of its body drifted to the ground, where it was carried away by the wind.

I darted to Cillian's side, and the sight before me sent me spiraling. Cillian lay on the ground, his mouth parted and blood covering his lips. His palm rested on his side, covering the wound from the ghoul's claws.

"Cillian," I breathed, cupping his head between my hands. "Cillian, open your eyes."

Hazel irises peered up at me, glazed and unfocused.

"What," he spluttered. "What happened?"

"Shh, don't talk. Arabella!" I yelled, scanning the area for the witch.

"I'm here," she said from my other side, startling me.

"Help him!"

Arabella set about assessing Cillian's injuries, muttering to herself as she went.

"Emmerson," I called, scanning the battlefield for my best friend.

When her eyes locked with mine, she paled, seeing the prone form lying before me. She sprinted toward us, dropping to her knees beside me.

"Cill?" she cried, shaking his shoulders roughly.

"Gods, woman. I'm injured. Stop shaking me."

Emmerson released a choked sound before burying her face in Cillian's tunic.

"It's good to know you care about me," Cillian chuckled and then winced.

"Shut up," Emmerson said, the sound muffled by Cillian's tunic. "It's battle fatigue. It doesn't count."

A flurry of white light filled my peripheral vision before Silas, Zeke, and Fionn joined us.

"What happened?" Silas panted.

"He was stabbed and bitten by one of the ghouls," I said.

"Brother, that's very unlike you," Silas chuckled, but it sounded forced.

"I don't know what came over me. One minute I was in the fight, and the next, it was like a dull cloud descended and all I could see was fog."

"Ghouls are hypnotics," Arabella chirped from her crouched position as she tended to Cillian's wounds.

"What?" Silas asked.

Arabella paused, looking up at us. "Ghouls are hypnotics," she repeated. "They can trap your mind so you don't fight them."

"This information would have been useful to share," Silas gritted out.

"I thought you knew," Arabella said, shrugging. "I need you to step back, Emmerson."

I pulled my best friend to my side so Arabella could work.

"It's not as bad as it looks," she muttered.

"Feels pretty fucking bad," Cillian grumbled.

"Here." Arabella cupped the back of Cillian's head and raised a vial to his lips.

He grimaced as he swallowed the amber liquid.

"We need to get out of here," Silas said. "Fionn, Zeke, can you give me a hand to pack up?"

Both men nodded and followed Silas.

"There, all done," Arabella said. "It should only take a moment and then you'll be good to go."

Getting to her feet, Arabella packed up her supplies and wandered off to do the same with the rest of her belongings.

"Come here, Little Viper," Cillian muttered, and Emmerson slid up his long, muscled frame.

He cupped the back of her neck with his palm and pulled her mouth to his in a scorching kiss.

"I'm just… I'm going to go," I muttered, not wanting to be a voyeur in their moment. Neither one of them heard me.

**"Fire Heart?"**

**"I'm all right, Misneach."**

**"Thank the gods,"** he breathed.

"Time to go, Little Menace," Silas said, passing me my pack.

I nodded my head in agreement. "Definitely."

# Chapter Twenty

"Can you be more specific than *east*?" Cillian growled.

"No, Cillian, I cannot," Emmerson spat.

"So much for taking it easy on me while I recover."

"I heard that," Emmerson scolded.

"I said you are my guiding light, Em. My true north, my —"

"You can knock it off now," Emmerson grumbled.

Cillian met my gaze over Emmerson's head and winked.

"Harlowe, help me out here," Emmerson said. "You," — she pointed a finger at Cillian — "can go away."

"Good luck," Cillian whispered as he passed me the map.

Emmerson and I pretended to study it thoughtfully. "Any idea what we should tell them?" she muttered.

"None," I replied.

"So we just keep saying east?"

"Heading east worked well enough last time." I wasn't sure if I was trying to convince Emmerson or myself.

"Fine, but don't let them find out that's the extent of our knowledge. I don't want to listen to them whine."

"What do I say if they ask?" Silas was most certainly going to ask.

"Tell them we know exactly where we're going and we don't have to justify our every move," Emmerson said. "Add a little haughtiness for effect."

"But we don't know where we are going," I whispered.

"They don't need to know that," Emmerson chided.

"You don't know where you're going, do you?"

We both jumped at the sound of Zeke's voice coming from behind us. I whipped around, clutching the map to my chest, as I willed my heart rate to calm down.

"You are so busted," he grinned. "You get this wild look in your eyes whenever you try to deceive, Harlowe."

"You really ought to work on that," Emmerson mumbled.

"Spill," Zeke demanded, crossing his arms over his chest.

"We know roughly where we're going," I answered vaguely.

"Bullshit."

"Zeke," I huffed like a misbehaving child. I had to fight the urge to stomp my foot. "When we sought the Lost Witch before, we knew her cottage stood on the forest's eastern border."

"Well, that's not entirely true. We were only following rumors and speculation. We didn't know for sure."

"Not helping, Emmerson," I said through gritted teeth. "Anyway," I drawled, turning back to Zeke. "We got a little lost, but we found our way, eventually."

"What Harlowe doesn't want to say is that we didn't find the Lost Witch. We stumbled through the forest until she took pity on us and revealed herself."

"Emmerson!"

"What, he already knows, why not give him the full account?" she shrugged.

"Are you fucking kidding me?" Zeke said, pinching the bridge of his nose. "We are wandering aimlessly inside a forest full of creatures trying to kill us, and what, hoping for the best? Is that what you're telling me?"

"That's exactly what I said the last time," Emmerson chimed in, pointing in Zeke's direction.

"Harlowe?" Zeke pressed.

"Well, I wouldn't say aimlessly..." I trailed off, unsure how to finish that sentence.

"For fuck's sake, you two," Zeke muttered to himself.

"What are you looking so chuffed about?" I asked Emmerson when I caught sight of her broad grin.

"Zeke's about to lie for us," she said cheerily.

Zeke arched a quizzical brow. "Oh, really?"

Emmerson nodded. Before Zeke could press her further, Silas joined us.

"What's going on?" he asked.

"Harlowe and Emmerson were just giving me a rundown of the route," Zeke lied. "We're almost ready."

"Make it quick. I don't want to lose too much light."

Zeke nodded, and Silas gave us another hard look before he turned and headed back to Cillian.

"Told you," Emmerson purred.

"Yes, well, Harlowe will be my Queen one day. I can hardly go against her word."

Emmerson grinned wider, but let it go.

"So... east?" Zeke questioned.

"East," Emmerson and I confirmed.

I rolled up the map and rejoined the rest of the group. When I informed Silas we were ready, he simply waved his hand in front of him, gesturing for me to lead on.

We continued tracking east until nightfall once again pushed down on us.

"We'll camp here for the night," Silas said, calling us to a halt.

He leaned in close to me and asked, "Is everything all right?"

"Fine," I answered, careful not to meet his eye.

"I don't think we should set up the tents," Silas said as he removed his pack. "We still don't know how the ghouls got through Arabella's concealment spell, so it's safest to stay in the open where we can see what's coming for us."

"I agree."

Growling sliced through the night air around us, and everyone reached for their weapons. My palms heated as I called forth my flames, ready to throw my shield up before another monster could slip past our defenses.

Yellow eyes peered back at us from the darkness of the night as the growling intensified.

Silas grabbed my wrist and pulled me behind him.

"Wait," I yelled, stepping back beside Silas. "I know these creatures."

"Harlowe," Silas barked as I let my flames recede and took a step in their direction.

"Do you remember me?" I cooed. My footsteps faulted when the closest creature snapped its jaws in my direction.

I peeked over my shoulder and saw that everyone had their weapons raised.

"Lower your weapons," I hissed. Returning my gaze to the yellow eyes tracking my every move. I put my hand out, palm turned up, and waited.

Slowly, the first wolf stepped forward. It trundled up to me and sniffed my palm before licking it. The others quickly followed, crowding me and nipping playfully at one another as they each vied for my attention.

"Those are fucking dire wolves," Cillian said. "They are some of the most vicious creatures in the realm."

Emmerson snorted. "They look vicious too, what, with all the licking and attention seeking they're doing."

"Your friend is right," a feminine voice sounded behind us. "They are lethal creatures, but only when provoked."

I turned my head towards the woman. She wore the same black dress she had been wearing the last time we met, and her long brown hair flowed over her shoulders.

The dire wolves trotted over to her, standing at her side as her silent sentinels.

"Queen of Fire," the Lost Witch hummed. "I thought I made myself clear the last time we spoke. Only death awaits you here. So tell me, what are you doing inside my forest?"

# Chapter Twenty-One

Silas's head whipped in my direction and I fought the urge to shrink away under the intensity of his piercing gaze as he glared at me.

So, I might have forgotten to tell him about the Lost Witch's warning.

"Harlowe," he snarled.

"We need your help," I said, cutting him off.

"That much I had gathered for myself," the Lost Witch snorted.

"We seek the Aurora Stone."

"No," she hissed.

"No?" I asked, confused. "No, what?"

"No, I will not help you."

I jogged towards her, closing the distance between us. "You don't understand," I said desperately.

"Oh, I understand perfectly, child. It is you who has failed to grasp the enormity of what you ask."

"Please, just hear me out."

The dire wolves began to whine as they pawed at the ground. Their glowing yellow eyes were full of pleading as they gazed upon the Lost Witch.

Were they begging on my behalf?

One wolf stood, shook out its fur, and then moved to stand beside me. One by one, the others followed.

The Lost Witch rolled her eyes and sighed. "Fine. I'll listen, Queen of Fire, but you won't change my mind."

I grinned and ran my palm over the thick coat of the dire wolf next to me. With a wave of her hand, the forest surrounding us shimmered, and a sense of déjà vu washed over me. The Lost Witch's cottage materialized before our eyes and it was no less unsettling the second time around.

"Come," she barked, and the dire wolves trotted off after her.

"As pleasant as always," Emmerson muttered beside me. I chuckled and took her hand as I followed the Lost Witch.

The brownstone cottage was just as I remembered it. The worn wooden door and the tiled roof gave it a homely quality. That changed the moment you stepped across the threshold, however. The entryway was dimly lit, giving the cottage a dark, lifeless feel, but the elegant taste of the Lost Witch still shone through with her blue velvet settee and plush cream rug.

The five enormous dire wolves looked almost comical as they sprawled their massive bodies out on the rug.

I moved past them and entered the kitchen. The others followed behind me, leaving plenty of room between them and the dire wolves relaxing on the ground.

The Lost Witch stood leaning against her kitchen sink, her arms folded over her chest, as she glared at me.

"Speak," she snapped.

"May I?" I asked, pointing to one of the chairs around her table.

She gave a curt nod, and I pulled out the chair to sit down. Emmerson took the seat beside me and the others all filed in behind us, shifting uncomfortably.

The Lost Witch raked her gaze over our group, then stopped abruptly, narrowing in on someone. When I peeked over my shoulder, I saw Arabella swallow.

"You," she jutted her chin towards Arabella. "You are a witch, yes?"

Arabella nodded in confirmation.

"You're powerful. I can feel it from across the room, but you don't embrace it."

"I only practice the art of healing," Arabella confirmed.

"But you know defensive magic, correct?"

"Some," Arabella admitted. "My mother was a practitioner, and she taught me when I was younger. However, that was centuries ago and I haven't practiced since."

"Why?"

"After the War of Witches, it was safer for a witch to remain anonymous.

Practicing that kind of magic tends to draw attention to oneself."

The Lost Witch tsked. "Fools, the lot of them."

"Speak Queen of Fire. I do not have all day," she barked, making me jump in my seat.

It hit me then that I didn't know the woman's given name. "Forgive me, I seemed to have forgotten my manners. I never asked your name the last time I visited."

The Lost Witch hesitated for a moment. "Illiana."

"Well, Illiana, I have learned much since we last spoke," I said. "I know my destiny is to stand against Kieran. I know where he sourced his powers and why. I also know he has had centuries to grow in strength and master his control, and I know I cannot defeat him without the Aurora Stone."

Illiana scoffed. "You house dragon flames, child. Your magic is deadly. Of course you can defeat him. It is why the fates created you, after all."

"That may be true," I hummed, "with time. And time is something we are lacking. Kieran has brought war to our doorstep. He knows I'm not ready to face him, and he is pushing his advantage. He hunts me as we speak, and he has already found me once. We barely escaped with our lives."

I sucked in a sharp breath against the prickle of tears I felt forming in the corner of my eyes. "Some of us were not so fortunate," I mumbled.

The room was deathly silent, but I wasn't done. "I read about the Aurora Stone when I was being held captive by Kieran. I know it wards off negative energies and amplifies the power of the one wielding it. I need to level the battlefield, Illiana. I need the Aurora Stone. Without it, we don't stand a chance. I have felt his power firsthand, and I am no match for him."

Illiana studied me for a long time. So long that I couldn't help but fidget in my seat.

"That stone has brought me nothing but trouble," she mumbled to herself.

I straightened in my seat. "You know where it is?"

"Of course I do," she scoffed.

Emmerson and I shared a glance. "You set it in place, didn't you?" I asked.

"I did," she confirmed.

"I knew it," Emmerson said, pumping her fist into the air.

Illiana smirked. "They all thought the inhabitants of this forest destroyed me, and I was happy to let them continue believing that."

"And no one realized who you were during the War of Witches?" I asked.

"Evidently not," she preened. "If they had any idea, they wouldn't have recorded me as two separate women in the sagas."

Emmerson burst out laughing and Illiana and I both stared at her, waiting for her to regain her composure.

"Sorry," she wheezed. "It's just, it never ceases to amaze me how stupid people can be."

"So, will you help us?" Silas asked from behind me.

"It's not that simple. The stone is a double-edged sword," Illiana said, her gaze boring into me. "Whoever wields the stone must do so with caution and the utmost respect for the power bestowed upon them. Deviating from that path would have disastrous consequences. Mishandling the power of the stone or using it for impure purposes, well, let's just say you wouldn't need to worry about what the King of Serpents might unleash upon the realm."

An icy shiver raced down my spine, and my palms grew clammy with sweat.

"And even if I was willing to help you retrieve the stone," Illiana continued, "I am not strong enough on my own to reseal the wards to keep the monsters contained." Her gaze drifted to Arabella. "I would need someone who could match my strength to help me restore them. It takes a lot of power and skill, some of which lean into forbidden magic."

Arabella visibly paled at Illiana's words.

"Oh, thank the gods," Fionn breathed, clearly relieved that the monsters within the forest would not be released upon the realm.

"What do you say witchling, are you ready to embrace your full potential?" Illiana asked.

Arabella swallowed audibly, her eyes wide with fear.

"You won't be forced to do anything against your will, Arabella. You have the freedom to choose."

"Then you will never retrieve the stone," Illiana said.

Arabella closed her eyes and tipped her head towards the ceiling. She remained like that for a full minute. I saw the exact moment her resolve strengthened. She squared her shoulders and returned her gaze to Illiana.

"I will do whatever is necessary," she said confidently.

"That is not all," Illiana said, returning her hardened gaze to me. "If we try to remove the stone, the forest will do whatever it must to stop us."

Illiana smiled, but it lacked any semblance of warmth or kindness.

"There is a reason I told you only death awaits you here, Queen of Fire."

# Chapter Twenty-Two

Illiana's cottage was far larger than I had first surmised. When she led us down the darkened corridor off her sitting area, I barely stifled my surprise when it… just kept going.

An endless number of rooms lined the walls, and Illiana waved her hand around casually as she told us to pick one. She didn't so much as glance back in our direction as she continued down the hall, all five dire wolves trotting behind her.

I slipped past the door I'd watched Silas retreat behind moments earlier and gasped.

The room was stunning.

A magnificent four-poster bed sat on an elevated platform in the center of the space, with the softest bedding I had ever felt, and a plethora of cushions that almost resembled a cloud, beckoning me to sink into its soft embrace.

And I desperately wanted to dive in.

However, the brooding man radiating fury behind me was unlikely to allow that.

I turned from the bed, regret seeping into the very marrow of my bones as I pulled my eyes away from the pillows, and faced Silas.

He was standing in front of a closed door, which I assumed was a bathing chamber. His corded arms were folded across his broad chest, and he wore a menacing scowl on his face.

Sighing, I moved to the settee at the edge of the rug and sat down. I sensed this would not be a pleasant discussion.

"Say what you have to say, Silas."

Silas scoffed. "How about we start with the fact that you lied to me."

"I didn't lie to you. I just didn't tell you everything."

"A lie by omission is still a lie, Little Menace," he growled.

"What do you want me to say?" I asked, throwing my hands in the air.

"The fucking truth!" he shouted.

Silas took a deep breath and raked his hand through his hair.

"You demand my trust, but you show me none in return," he said, the hurt cutting through his anger.

Ouch. That fucking stung.

"You're right," I said, sighing. "I wasn't completely honest with you."

Silas relaxed his stance a little and released a controlled breath.

"What did Illiana tell you about death waiting for you inside this forest?"

"Just what she repeated in the kitchen. She said only death awaited me here, but she gave me no other information. I assumed she meant that if I stayed in the Forest of Nightmares, the creatures within would eventually find me and kill me. Honestly, Silas, I had no idea removing the stone would trigger any sort of attack. I know as much as you do."

Silas sighed before walking over to where I sat and joining me on the settee. He pulled me into his lap and buried his nose in my hair.

"I'm sorry I lost my temper," he said. "I can't bear the thought of something happening to you."

"I know. I feel the same," I whispered, nuzzling his neck.

"Where does that leave us?" he asked. "Do we move forward with our plan?"

"I don't think we have much of a choice, Silas."

"I feared you might say that," he chuckled without mirth.

"I suppose it's a good thing we know to expect trouble."

Silas grunted. "I'm not sure that's much of an advantage given we have no idea what we'll be facing, Little Menace."

"I was trying to be optimistic," I said, hitting his chest.

"Come on," Silas said, lifting me into his arms. "You need rest."

Silas carried me over to the bed and nestled me beneath the covers. A moment later, he extinguished the flame from the lantern, shrouding the room in darkness.

The mattress dipped as he slid in behind me. Silas's large palm landed on my stomach and he pulled me flush against his muscled chest. I could feel his erection pressing into me and I wiggled my ass against it.

"Later," he growled. "Sleep first, Little Menace."

I pouted, and he laughed as if he could see me clearly in the darkness.

Despite my silent protest, sleep quickly claimed me.

I was restless.

The sheets were damp beneath me from the sweat coating my skin.

My body felt as if it were on fire and no matter how much I tried, I couldn't get cool.

I pulled the covers off me and got out of bed.

My eyes darted around the darkened room, and I froze.

Even though I couldn't see much, I knew something was wrong.

I peered back at the rumpled bed.

Silas was gone.

Not only that, but the bed was completely different. It was still an elegant four-post frame, but much larger, more grand, and most importantly, black.

I swallowed thickly.

"I see you've realized your predicament," a sinister, masculine voice sounded from across the room.

I spun around, my eyes searching the shadows for... *him*.

Kieran lounged in his chair, one arm lazily slung over the back. He wore loose sleeping pants and nothing else.

He flexed the muscles of his bare chest, and my gaze raked over his torso without my permission. His chiseled abdomen was a work of art, and his tattoos only enhanced the comparison.

Kieran tsked. "It's rude to stare, Bride," he said huskily. "Regretting the choices you've made, perhaps?"

My eyes snapped to Kieran's ice-blue ones, his cockiness plain to see.

"You killed Everly and Grainne," I said in a hoarse whisper. "I could never choose you, Kieran, even if I wanted to."

I didn't want Kieran. I was more certain of that than anything else in my life at this point. But I still felt the strange pull towards him. The connection of our warring powers drawing us in.

Kieran moved quicker than I could blink. One minute he was lazing in his armchair, and the next, he was standing in front of me.

His large hand collared my throat, and he forced me backward until my back collided with the wall.

"You forced my hand, Little Bride," he hissed. "You are just as much to blame for their deaths as I am."

"That's where you're wrong, Kieran. You chose to kill them. No one forced you to do it. I would never choose to kill innocent people to further my own agenda," I panted, fighting for each breath as his rough grip cut off my airway.

Kieran invaded my space and snarled. "You are young and naïve, Harlowe. You have yet to see how power corrupts even the most noble of intentions."

"Why do you care what I think, Kieran? Why have you brought me here? Why haven't you killed me already?"

"Don't tempt me, Bride. I'm not one for idle threats."

"Don't play with me, Kieran. You keep telling me I will die by your hands and yet, every time you have me at your mercy, you let me live. Why is that?"

"That's an excellent question, Harlowe," he said, loosening his grip. "It's something I have asked myself more than once."

My eyes widened in surprise.

"You can't do it, can you? Kill me I mean."

"I wouldn't say I can't. You and I both know I am capable of doing terrible things. It's more like I don't want to. Not yet, anyway."

"Why?" I pressed.

"I haven't had my fill of you."

"What do you mean?"

Kieran chuckled darkly and the heat banking in his eyes had my cheeks burning red hot.

"One taste wasn't enough to sate the monster lurking inside me. We both want more. We want to feel the way your tight pussy takes my cock. We want to watch your perfect little tits bounce up and down as you ride me. We want to hear your unabashed moans as you beg me to fuck you deeper, harder, without restraint. But most of all, we want to watch as the life leaves your pretty green eyes while I pound into you, my hand firmly wrapped around your throat."

"What the fuck is wrong with you?" I spat.

"A great many things I'd suspect," he laughed.

Without warning, Kieran spun me, my cheek pressing against the wall as he gripped the back of my neck harshly.

"Let's see what's under this tiny scrap of fabric, shall we?" Kieran hummed.

I looked down to see a tiny nightgown that I had most certainly not worn to bed barely covering my body.

"Do you intend to rape me and kill me, Kieran?" I jeered. "How heroic of you. Are you afraid to face me on the battlefield, is that it? Your mother must be so proud," I taunted.

Kieran stiffened behind me and I knew I'd hit my mark.

"I don't plan on killing you, Harlowe. Not yet anyway. As I said, I have plans for your death, and they will be so much sweeter in reality. For now, though, it doesn't hurt to take a peek at what awaits me when I eventually catch up with you."

Kieran's rough palm ran up the outside of my thigh. When he reached the hem of my nightgown, he fisted the material in his hand and yanked it above my waist.

"No panties," he growled. "Is that your imagination or mine?"

"What are you talking about?"

Kieran didn't answer me. Instead, he palmed my ass before delivering a hard smack to my exposed flesh. A moan escaped me involuntarily, and Kieran chuckled darkly.

"Look at you," Kieran taunted. "Eager to get your fill of me, aren't you, Bride?"

"Fuck you," I seethed.

"Oh, I plan on doing more than that. Tell me, are you wet for me?"

I pursed my lips, refusing to play his game.

"Let's see, shall we?"

Kieran's fingers traveled down my side, over my stomach, and cupped my bare pussy. A shiver wracked my body, and I bit my tongue to stifle my reaction.

It's just our power calling to one another.

It means nothing.

You're not attracted to this psycho.

Fight the pull. Fight it!

But I couldn't fight it. Not when his fingers dipped inside me, curling against the spot that had stars exploding behind my eyelids.

"You're dripping wet for me, Bride. Your pussy is just begging to be filled by me, isn't it?"

An incoherent sound escaped my lips, and I bit down on my tongue, hard, until the taste of copper filled my mouth.

"Don't fight it, Harlowe. Don't fight me. Let me in," Kieran said, almost pleading.

"Harlowe!" Silas's panicked tone filled my head, cutting through the lust-induced mania I was trapped in.

I scanned the room wildly, but I couldn't find him.

"Stay with me, Harlowe," Kieran begged, his fingers pumping in and out of me with desperation. "Please," he whispered.

"Harlowe, wake up!" Silas's voice commanded.

"Silas?" I croaked.

Kieran growled behind me. "Why can't you forget about him? You were never meant to be his. You were always destined to be mine, and he stole you from me. I'll kill him. The next time I see him, I'll fucking kill him, Harlowe. And then I'll fuck you on his corpse so you will always remember to whom you belong."

Kieran was unraveling.

He took his desperation out on my body as he fucked me ruthlessly with his fingers.

"Harlowe, come back to me," Silas said.

I was reaching the peak. My orgasm built inside me until it was almost painful.

But I wouldn't let myself fall.

This was not the man whose touch I craved.

Kieran was not the man I chose.

I reared back, slamming my head into Kieran's face, and the satisfying sound of bone-crunching filled the room.

Kieran stumbled back, his hands clutching his nose.

"I was never your destiny, Kieran," I hissed. "I was never yours to steal. I am my own woman," I shouted, pounding my fist against my chest. "I choose who I give myself to, and I choose him."

Kieran let out a feral snarl.

But before he could lunge for me, the room shifted, and darkness took its place.

# Chapter Twenty-Three

I sucked in a ragged breath.

**"Fire Heart,"** Misneach barked.

"Fucking hell, Harlowe," Silas breathed and pulled me to his chest.

My body quivered uncontrollably, overwhelmed by the shock of two worlds colliding.

**"I'm alright, Misneach, but one conversation at a time,"** I pleaded.

**"You and I have very different understandings of the word, Fire Heart. Something we will need to rectify,"** he grumbled.

"What happened?" I mumbled against Silas's tunic.

"You were thrashing and murmuring in your sleep," Silas said. "You looked like you were in pain. I was afraid..." he trailed off.

Silas cleared his throat and tried again. "I was afraid Kieran had found you in your dreams," he said.

"How did you do that?" Illiana's voice startled me and I swung my head toward the other side of the room where she stood.

Where she and everyone else stood, watching me.

My cheeks heated under their scrutiny and I thanked the gods I had gone to bed fully clothed.

"Why are you all in here?" I asked nervously.

"Silas was screaming the place down and we all came running thinking you were being murdered in your sleep," Emmerson said and then grimaced. "Were you? Being murdered in your sleep, I mean?"

I shook my head. "Kieran pulled me into a dream, but he was only taunting me."

I decided not to disclose the full extent of my experience to everyone, at least not yet.

"Thank the gods," Emmerson said as she relaxed into Cillian's embrace.

"Tell me how you did it?" Illiana demanded, her arms folded over her chest as she studied me.

"Did what?"

"Pull yourself out of the dream."

"I..." I swallowed thickly. "I don't know. I heard Silas calling to me and I followed his voice, I guess." Silas's grip on me tightened possessively.

"You guess?" Illiana raised a brow as if I was being purposefully evasive.

"Honestly, I have no idea how it happened."

"It takes great power to thwart dark magic," she murmured, eyeing me.

"Dark magic?" I asked with a note of panic in my tone.

"Quite," Illiana said, pushing off the wall. "It's an invasive ability, and considering one can be harmed inside the dreamscape... well, it goes against the fates intentions when they bestowed their power upon the Original Witch."

When Illiana reached me, she crouched before me and thrust a chain in my direction. On the end of the chain hung a small crystal, a light pink color which caught the beams of light emanating from the lantern.

"What is it?"

"It's a talisman. Wear it at all times. It won't prevent the Serpent King from pulling you into another dream, but he won't be able to harm you while inside the dreamscape."

Illiana glanced over her shoulder towards Arabella. "You should have already been wearing one," she sneered, and Arabella bowed her head.

"Don't blame Arabella. She didn't know," I said curtly.

Illiana said nothing as she studied me with narrowed eyes. She seemed displeased with what she found because she snorted indignantly and stormed towards the door.

"Get some rest. All of you. Tomorrow will be a trying day," she threw over her shoulder as she marched from the room.

I spent the next few minutes convincing everyone I was all right and they could, in fact, leave me unguarded and return to their own much-needed slumber.

One by one, everyone left. Silas and I had to reassure Arabella several more times that it wasn't her fault before she relented and left the room.

**"About time,"** Misneach huffed.

**"You too, Misneach. I don't need coddling, I need sleep!"**

**"You are incredibly ungrateful at times, Fire Heart."**

**"I love you too, Misneach,"** I said with a grin.

**"Love,"** he scoffed. **"Sometimes I feel as though I want to throttle you. If that's love, may the gods help us."**

I couldn't help but laugh.

"What's so funny?" Silas asked, looking very concerned for my mental well-being.

"Misneach," I said in answer and Silas nodded in understanding.

"Tell me what happened in there?" he asked, tapping my forehead with his finger.

I didn't want to divulge what had happened between Kieran and me.

Not yet.

What I wanted to do was replace his touch with Silas's.

"I have a better idea," I purred, climbing into his lap.

Silas went stone cold, seeing straight through me.

"Did he touch you?" he growled.

"Silas," I said, sighing.

"Did he lay his hands on what's mine?" he demanded.

In one smooth motion, Silas flipped our positions and pinned me beneath him.

"Tell me what he did," he said in a menacing tone, that sent a bolt of lightning straight to my core.

When I didn't answer him, Silas gripped my hands above my head, pinning them in place with one hand, while the other collared my throat.

My hips jerked forward, and I shamelessly rubbed myself against him.

"Do not move your hands," he warned.

When I made no move to disobey him, Silas ran his hand down my arm until he reached the front of my tunic. His other hand left my throat and a tearing sound filled the room.

The chilly night air kissed my exposed breasts, and I shivered.

Silas's warm mouth engulfed my breast, sucking and tugging on my puckered nipple before he turned his attention to its twin.

I let out a breathy moan.

"Did he touch you here?" Silas asked against my flesh.

"No," I panted.

"No?" he repeated, leaving a trail of fervent kisses down my stomach.

I drove my fingers into Silas's hair, needing to touch him. A moment later, a sharp stinging sensation erupted over my breast, startling me.

"I told you not to move your hands, Little Menace."

Silas stood and leaned down to retrieve something from the floor. My throat bobbed when I saw what he was holding.

The leather of his belt was pulled taut between his fists and a wicked smirk pulled up the corner of his lips.

Silas climbed on top of me, grabbing one wrist, and then the other, as he bound my hands together. Reaching above me, Silas secured my bindings to the headboard.

"Is that too tight?" he asked.

I pulled on my bindings. They were tight, a little uncomfortable even.

"A little."

"Good," he purred.

Silas's fingers dipped into the waistband of my pants and he tugged them down roughly. Discarding them on the floor, he placed his hands on my knees and spread my legs.

Heat crept up my neck and settled on my cheeks as he stared down at me, open and laid bare for him.

Silas dragged his finger along the length of my slit. "And what about here, Little Menace? Did he touch you here?"

My breathing grew rapid as he touched me, but I didn't answer him. Silas dipped a finger inside me, stroking leisurely as he explored me.

It wasn't enough, though. I needed more. My legs squeezed tight, desperately seeking friction.

Silas chuckled darkly before withdrawing his finger.

A needy whine escaped my lips before I could prevent it.

"You want me to touch you, Harlowe?" he asked, his tone low and full of gravel.

I nodded my head eagerly.

"You want me to fuck you with my fingers until you shatter for me?"

Yes! I thought I'd made that pretty fucking clear.

I nodded again.

Silas's hand darted forward, gripping my throat. "Then you'll answer my fucking question," he snarled. "Did he touch my pussy?"

"Yes," I panted.

Silas clenched his jaw, and he looked ready to unleash every monster in this forest if it would bring Kieran to him, right here, right now. "With what?" he demanded.

At first I was confused, not understanding Silas's question. Then realization struck me.

"His fingers."

Silas growled low in his throat, the sound both terrifying and arousing. "Do you want me to take away his touch?" Silas asked huskily. "Replace it with my own?"

"Yes! Gods yes, Silas."

"Hmm, that's my good girl," Silas growled. He leaned down, his lips catching mine in a brutal kiss.

He thrust two fingers inside me, and my lips parted on a moan. Silas seized the opportunity and plunged his tongue into my mouth, conquering me with each stroke.

Silas was going to war on my body, and the thought made heat coil tight in my belly.

"That's it Little Menace, fucking come undone for me," he snarled.

And I did. I came so hard, that violent tremors wracked my body.

Silas withdrew his fingers, the digits glistening with the evidence of my release.

With his eyes locked on mine, Silas lifted his fingers to his lips.

"Mine," he growled, before pushing his fingers inside his mouth, licking them clean.

"Yours," I breathed, heat banking in my core once again.

Silas reached up and untied my wrists, then pulled me onto his chest. "One day, Harlowe. One day, he'll pay for everything he's done to you."

My eyelids grew heavy as the euphoria of my orgasm waned. As I was drifting off to sleep, cocooned in Silas's safe embrace, I heard his final promise.

"Soon."

# Chapter Twenty-Four

Illiana's mood had not improved the following morning when we left the cottage. She kept muttering to herself while eyeing me with suspicion. The dire wolves flanked her every step, whining as we went.

By the time we stopped for our first break, I was tense and on edge, unable to take it anymore.

"What's wrong, Illiana?" I snapped and then winced. By the sharp narrowing of her eyes, she didn't miss the bite in my tone.

Illiana pursed her lips and folded her arms over her chest. Her gaze raked over me; assessing.

I wanted to fidget under her scrutiny, scream in frustration, or shake some sense into her.

I did none of those things.

Instead, I lifted my chin, straightened my spine, and waited.

"You are immensely powerful, yet you insist you need the Aurora Stone..." she trailed off, letting me draw my own conclusions.

I ground my teeth together. I didn't come this far to fail.

"I have already explained the situation to you, Illiana."

"Yes, yes, the King of Snakes is too powerful," she said with condescension.

Did she truly not believe me?

The wolves' whining intensified.

"Hush," Illiana murmured, scratching one wolf behind its pointed ear.

"What do you think is going on here?" Silas demanded as he came to stand beside me.

"I think she lies," she answered, pointing to me.

"Lady, you're itching for a blade," Emmerson started, but I put my hand up to silence her.

"No, Emmerson. Let's hear her out."

Illiana smirked. "I think someone powerful enough to pull themselves free from the dreamscape is also powerful enough to defend themselves, no matter the opponent."

I took a deep breath to steady my growing frustration. "Kieran has centuries of experience to draw upon," I gritted out. "Even if I matched his strength, he possesses superior control over his power, and time is not on our side. That is why we need the stone."

"Or," Illiana said.

"Or?" I pressed.

"Or maybe you're working with the Serpent King, and this entire thing is a ruse."

I heard Emmerson cursing Illiana, and the sound of steel grating against steel as the others drew their weapons.

But the noise was muted.

The thunderous pounding of my blood in my ears drowned out the surrounding sounds.

My anger roiled inside me.

After everything I had been through, and everything I had sacrificed, this woman stood before me and questioned my integrity.

My palms tingled, and I looked down to see my hands were alight with blistering flames. Something was different, however. My flames felt more... potent.

**"I'm coming, Fire Heart."**

**"No need, Misneach. I have this handled."**

**"You're drawing too much power,"** he protested.

**"I'm only getting started."**

As I glanced at the group again, Illiana's eyes met mine, and her lips curved into a satisfied smirk.

I let my flames consume me until my entire body was ablaze.

Lifting my hand, I let a torrent of flames free from my palm. They engulfed my friends, shielding them and pushing them away from the conflict.

I could hear them shouting at me, telling me to drop my shield, to let them free, but I ignored all of it.

"Kieran has hurt me, shackled me, tried to take away my freedom, and killed those I cared about. I would never, *never*, side with him," I seethed.

The wolves whined louder as they shuffled away from the intensity of the scorching heat.

"I know what I'm doing," Illiana snapped.

I furrowed my brows, unsure who she was talking to.

"I don't believe you. I think you spent your time in Netheran... getting to know your enemy," she said suggestively.

Red coated my vision as fury decimated me from within at her suggestion. My flames grew, the blistering heat intensifying with my rage.

The surrounding shrubbery caught alight, and I realized with alarm that if I didn't pull myself together, this entire forest would quickly become an uncontrollable wildfire.

**"Fire Heart!"** Misneach howled, the panic lacing his tone enough to center me.

I took a deep, steadying breath as I recalled my flames to me. Little by little, the glowing embers died out, leaving charred remains in their wake.

Silas rushed to my side as soon as my shield dropped. Cupping my face, he brought his forehead to my own as his breathing settled.

"Don't you ever do that again," he growled. "When we fight, we fight together."

"I'm with him," Emmerson said, glowering at me one moment, before she pulled me away from Silas and hugged me the next.

**"I am forced to agree with the General, Fire Heart,"** Misneach grumbled. **"And that physically pains me to admit."**

**"He's a king now, you know,"** I said absentmindedly as I considered how quickly I had let Illiana get under my skin.

Was I losing control of my powers?

**"I do not care,"** Misneach huffed.

"You are quite the vision when you are angry, Queen of Fire," Illiana preened.

My head snapped in her direction, my anger returning to the surface when I saw the wide grin on her face.

"What are you playing at?" Emmerson demanded.

"I needed to see for myself," Illiana said, shrugging.

"See what?" I snapped.

"What you are capable of."

"What I am capable of?" I repeated slowly.

"Yes, a test of your power, if you will," Illiana said. "And of your control," she added.

"Explain yourself," Silas growled.

"I just did," Illiana said dismissively.

"Do it again," he gritted out.

"I needed to witness the Queen of Fire's power firsthand," she said, as though her methods were entirely justified.

"So you antagonized her to trick her into a demonstration?" Zeke asked.

"Yes," Illiana said cheerfully.

**"Oh, I like this one,"** Rónán chuckled.

**"She just risked all of their lives, your Cathal included,"** Oisín scowled.

**"I know! Isn't she fun,"** Rónán beamed.

"She could have burned down the entire forest," Cillian said incredulously, echoing his dragon.

"Ah, but therein lies the second test." When we all continued to look at her expectantly, Illiana sighed and said, "Control."

"Control?" Fionn repeated as if he was testing how the word sounded.

"Yes, control," Illiana said, sounding exasperated. "It is not enough for the Queen of Fire to simply wield great power. She also needs to control it, pull it back if necessary." Illiana turned her gaze on me. "If she cannot control it, it will control her. And if that happens, well, let's just say that the realm is not ready for that kind of power to be unleashed."

"Are you saying that the Aurora Stone will try to manipulate me? Make me wield it in a way I do not intend?"

"That's exactly what I'm saying, Queen of Fire." My breath caught in my throat as unease washed over me.

Illiana stalked past the burnt remains of the shrubbery and continued in the direction we had been traveling.

"You best be prepared, Queen of Fire," she called over her shoulder.

"For what?" I asked, dread sitting heavy in my stomach.

"For the creatures that guard the stone."

# Chapter Twenty-Five

Illiana's warning weighed heavily on the group as we continued our journey through the forest. While Illiana knew *something* guarded the stone, she could offer us no further insight.

Everyone was on edge, unease permeating the air surrounding us. It was suffocating, and the tension grew with every step we took towards the unknown.

To distract myself, I wandered over to Illiana to ask her the one question she could answer.

"Were you talking to the dire wolves earlier?" I asked.

Illiana raised a questioning brow. "When you were riling me up," I explained. "You were conversing with... someone or something... you said you had everything under control."

Recognition crossed Illiana's petite features. "Ah yes."

"Yes, you were talking to the dire wolves or yes, you know the comment I am referencing?"

Illiana rolled her eyes. "Yes, I was talking with the dire wolves," she confirmed. "They were worried about my methods. They are quite fond of you and did not wish for me to upset you."

"So, the dire wolves can speak?" I asked.

"Not exactly," she said as she patted the enormous wolf closest to her. "The dire wolves are my familiars."

"What does that mean?"

"We share a bond. It is much like the bond you share with your dragon. They are a conduit for my magic and they connect me to the spiritual planes."

"By spiritual planes you mean..."

"The void," she confirmed. "But they also tether me to the fates."

"The fates?" I asked, not sure I was following.

"Yes. I am a truth-sayer after all. Where do you think my knowledge comes from?" she said with a pointed look.

Honestly, I had never thought about it enough to ask the question.

"The dire wolves guide me in the direction set forth by the fates, and the link we share enhances my magic. It also grants them their own power. They are stronger, faster, and more lethal than any other creature I have encountered inside this forest. Your friend is right to fear them," she said smugly.

"So you can speak with them inside your head?" I clarified.

"The bond is telepathic, yes."

I glanced towards the five dire wolves flanking Illiana. "They have never been threatening towards me," I mused. "In fact, they are all very sweet." I leaned down to stroke the fur of the one nudging my palm for attention as if trying to prove my point.

"That is because they like you. And also because your power calls to them. Had circumstances been different, you'd see a whole other side to them, I assure you."

I had no doubt the enormous wolves could be deadly when warranted. I was just thankful that they didn't direct their wrath towards me.

Illiana's steps slowed, and I shortened my stride to match hers.

"We're here," she said, all casualness leaving her tone.

I glanced around my surroundings, but all I saw was the unending forest.

The high treetops that hovered above us and blocked out the sun which cast the forest in an ominous darkness.

The gnarled roots that curved and twisted around, ready to catch the unsuspecting and drag them to the forest floor, where they would be vulnerable and easy prey for the monsters who called this place home.

The thick underbrush that made every step a challenge, as it pulled and tugged on your boots while concealing all manner of threats lying in wait for the perfect opportunity to strike.

The Aurora Stone, however, was noticeably absent.

"Here, where?" I asked.

Illiana gripped the low-hanging branch beside her and pulled it back. A glint of light caught my attention, and I stepped forward.

Amongst the towering trees sat an old, weathered altar. Carved from stone, it stood defiant and imposing. Although its edges had become rough and chipped from the countless centuries of exposure to the elements.

As I stepped closer, I could just make out the runes etched into its surface, barely visible beneath the layers of moss and lichen.

The surrounding trees seemed to lean in towards the altar, their looming shadows creating a dark ring around its base. Even so, glimmers of sunlight broke through the dense canopy above, illuminating the stone and giving it an ethereal glow.

It was as if nature itself was bowing in reverence to the altar.

No, not the altar.

The primordial power of the forest bowed before the Aurora Stone.

Sitting atop the weathered structure was a stone, about the size of my palm, with iridescent colors dancing across its translucent surface. Brilliant hues of blue, green, yellow, and purple shifted and swayed in the sunlight as if beckoning me closer.

"Beautiful, isn't it?" a soft voice said from beside me.

I jumped and barely concealed a yelp as I turned to face Illiana. I had been so caught up in the mesmerizing display, I had forgotten I wasn't alone.

"Quite," I whispered.

The sound of shuffling feet drew my attention, and I turned to see the others crowding in behind me.

"Is that it?" Silas asked, inclining his head towards the stone.

"It is," Illiana confirmed.

"Are you going to take it?" he pressed, seemingly confused by the delay.

"It isn't that straightforward," Illiana said.

"Of course it isn't," Emmerson muttered.

Illiana rounded on Arabella. "It is time to embrace your power," she said cooly, and Arabella swallowed nervously. Zeke gave her elbow a gentle squeeze, encouraging her to step forward.

"Do you know how to perform a linking spell?"

"Y-yes," Arabella stuttered.

"Good. You will lend me your power, and I will cast the spell to break the wards around the stone."

Turning to look at me, Illiana continued, "Then it is all on you, Queen of Fire."

"All on me? What do you mean?" I asked, nervous tension coiling my body tight.

"Once we break the wards, the guardians of the stone will awaken. I'm unsure of the creatures we'll face, but they'll keep attacking until you get the fates to release the stone."

"What do you mean, release the stone? Speak plainly Illiana!" I snapped as panic gripped me.

"When you lay your hand upon the stone, it will transport you to the void," she said.

**"Fire Heart,"** Misneach growled.

"You said nothing about entering the void," Silas snarled.

"Fucking witches," Emmerson hissed and then smiled apologetically to Arabella. "I meant the tricky kind."

"Stop," I said, raising my hand. "Let her finish. What will happen in the void, Illiana?"

"Inside the void, you will meet the fates. They will decide if you are worthy of the stone."

"And if they decide I'm not worthy?"

"Then you won't be leaving the void," Illiana said casually, as if she wasn't speaking of my impending demise.

Everyone spoke at once.

"What game are you playing at, witch?" Silas spat venomously.

"You led us this far, only to drop this on us now?" Zeke asked incredulously, with Cillian and Fionn grunting in agreement.

"Harlowe, this isn't worth the risk. We'll find another way," Emmerson pleaded.

**"I agree with the hellcat,"** Misneach growled. **"I'm coming to get you."**

"Everyone, calm down," I hissed.

**"Calm down!"** Misneach balked. **"She just said you might not survive."**

**"Misneach, this is Harlowe's decision,"** Caolán said.

**"Do not try to get between me and my Cathal, Caolán,"** Misneach barked.

**"When I said everyone calm down, that included you, Misneach."**

**"Fire Heart,"** he growled again.

**"No!"** I yelled. Taking a deep breath, I added, **"Trust me, Misneach."**

"Illiana," I said, drawing everyone's attention. "What do I need to do to prove I'm worthy?"

"That, I cannot tell you. Only the fates can decide."

"I'll go instead," Silas chimed in.

Illiana snorted. "You're definitely not worthy."

Silas growled, but before he could let his anger get the best of him, I pressed on. "I am the one who will wield the stone. Therefore, I must be the one to face judgment."

"Harlowe," Silas breathed. "This isn't a good idea."

I smiled gently. "We have little choice, Silas."

Silas clenched his jaw, but nodded. He would let me make this decision myself.

Emmerson rushed to my side, gripping my hands in hers. "Please don't do this. I don't care if Kieran conquers the entire realm and we have to live in hiding for the rest of our lives in some dank cave that isn't big enough for everyone. I would rather have that future than one without you in it."

"I know you would, Em. My safety has always been your priority. Now it's my turn to protect you for once. I couldn't bear it if anything happened to you. And let's face it, Kieran would never allow us to live out our days in hiding. He would hunt us down until we all perished. I honestly don't know if I'll be able to change that fate, but I have to try."

Emmerson's eyes filled with tears, but she nodded her head and pulled me against her. "I would have traded places with you if I could," she whispered.

"I know."

**"Fire Heart,"** Misneach tried again.

**"Misneach, please. I can't do this and be at odds with you. I need you to trust my judgment on this,"** I begged.

There was a brief pause before Misneach released a resigned breath. **"I trust you, Fire Heart. You are the strongest creature I have ever met. If anyone can succeed here, it is you."**

**"Creature?"** I asked playfully, lightening the mood.

**"You know what I mean,"** he grumbled.

Pulling away from Emmerson, I straightened my tunic and squared my shoulders.

"I'm ready," I said with a confidence I didn't feel.

"Good. Everyone else, prepare your weapons. Be ready to face whatever monsters lurk just beyond the veil," Illiana barked.

Pointing to Arabella, she said, "You, child, come here."

Arabella rushed towards Illiana and placed her hands in her upturned palms.

"Ready?" Illiana asked.

Arabella nodded, and then both women lowered their heads and began chanting.

# Chapter Twenty-Six

The temperature dropped without warning, turning the cool air freezing in an instant. My teeth began to chatter, and I wrapped my arms around myself to conserve what little warmth my body could offer me.

Silas strode towards me, taking his place at my back and sharing his body heat with me.

"Be careful in there, Little Menace," he whispered. "I can't lose you, not again." He said the last part so quietly I wasn't sure he meant for me to hear it.

"You too, Silas. No playing hero," I warned.

"Harlowe," Zeke said as he approached me. "Take this."

I looked at his proffered hand and saw the dagger my father had gifted him in his outstretched palm.

My throat tightened with emotion. I knew how much that dagger meant to him. My gaze flicked to Emmerson, and she looked as though she was in pain as she stared at the dagger with longing.

"I can't take that, Zeke," I said. "It's precious to you, and besides, I have no idea if it will be of any use to me once I'm inside the void," I said.

"All the same," he said, thrusting the dagger towards me.

I reached out a hand tentatively and picked up the dagger. "Thank you, Zeke. This means a lot."

He nodded once and then returned to his place beside Emmerson and Cillian.

"You have loyal friends," Silas said with approval.

"Indeed, I do."

I sheathed the dagger on my thigh and returned my attention to Arabella and Illiana. They were still chanting quietly, their heads bowed as they worked.

A shiver of unease worked its way up my spine and I knew they were close.

"Get ready," Silas commanded, sensing the same thing I had.

Illiana's head snapped up, her eyes glowing a blinding white as her voice deepened to the masculine baritone I had heard the first time we met.

"It is time, Queen of Fire."

Arabella gasped and stumbled back, breaking their connection. The light in Illiana's eyes dulled and then receded, leaving her panting as she fought to catch her breath.

My gaze darted around, scanning every inch of our surroundings.

"Did it work?" I asked when I found nothing.

"It worked," Illiana said, her voice returning to her usual feminine tone.

Arabella returned to Zeke's side, and he reached into his boot and retrieved a dagger for her. She eyed the blade cautiously before taking it in her small hand.

An unnatural wind swept through our small group, stirring the air with a sense of foreboding. The howls and wails that followed had my small hairs standing to attention.

"Well, that's not ominous or anything," Emmerson muttered.

The trees began to sway, bending at odd angles as the moaning intensified. Debris flittered in the air, whipping at my face as they danced chaotically on the wind.

I could hear muttered ramblings, but no matter how hard I strained to listen, I couldn't make out what the voices were trying to say. "Can anyone hear that?"

"It sounds like someone is being tortured," Fionn murmured in reply.

My heart battered the inside of my chest, ramming against my ribcage as the sense of dread intensified. My skin prickled as if unseen eyes were watching me from hidden depths and I scanned our surroundings wildly.

"What is it?" I asked, giving voice to my rising panic.

"I'm not sure," Illiana mumbled, never taking her eyes away from the darkened shadows surrounding the altar.

Something moved in my peripheral vision and I spun to see what appeared to be a tattered cloak darting past us.

"Oh, perfect," Illiana groaned.

"What is it?" I hissed as another figure passed us on the other side.

"Wraiths," Illiana snarled. "You may as well lower your weapons. They won't do you any good."

"Why not?"

"Wraiths are malevolent spirits. They can't be killed because, well, they're already dead."

"Fuck," Silas seethed.

"How do we fight them?" Cillian asked.

"I hope you can all summon fòrsa because that's the only thing that will keep you alive long enough for the Queen of Fire to reach the stone."

No sooner had Illiana uttered the words than a wall of shadowy figures descended upon us. A blood-curdling screeching filled the silence, and I instinctively covered my ears.

A bone-chilling cold settled on the nape of my neck and traveled down my body as I stood frozen in place. A sense of utter despair filled me, and the need to lie down and surrender myself to the mercy of the forest became so overwhelming that my knees buckled.

I compelled myself to turn around and found myself staring into chilling blue eyes. A wraith stood before me, their face obscured by the hood of their weathered cloak. Despite the darkness, I could see their blue-tinged skin and the chilling gaze that paralyzed me.

The wraith parted its blue lips and exposed a long, forked tongue that tasted the air around me. An involuntary shiver wracked my body as the wraith inhaled a deep breath.

The feeling of despair amplified, and I bent over my knees as I sobbed without restraint. It was as if my world lost all color, leaving only grey. I lost my will to fight and wondered why I'd pushed so hard to reach this point.

Bursts of light flared around me, but I had no desire to join my companions. All I wanted to do was give in, relinquish all my suffering, and embrace the nothingness surrounding me.

Someone called my name, but it barely registered. I sank to my knees, hugging myself as I rocked back and forth.

In the next moment, everything changed. Air filled my lungs to the point of pain, and every one of my senses sparked to life as the world around me shifted and reformed.

I gasped as something hard slammed into my chest. When I peered down, however, there was nothing there.

A sound caught my attention, and I realized with alarm Illiana was calling my name. The shock of hearing her use my given name instead of the title she had insisted on ever since I met her was enough to regain my senses.

"What? What is it?" I asked.

"Are you all right?" she said, and I got the impression it was not the first time she'd tried to gain my attention.

"I... I think so. What happened?"

"Wraiths are soul-wrenchers," she said. "That one almost took yours."

My shock must have been clear on my face because Illiana slapped my cheek, the burning pain drawing me upright.

"Pull yourself together and get to that stone!" she yelled.

I glanced around, seeing everyone locked in battle with the wraiths. Emmerson raised her hand and struck one in the head with a glowing white orb. The wraith dropped to the ground before reanimating and coming at her again.

My eyes scanned the area for Silas and when they landed on him, I watched in horror as he battled two wraiths, unleashing blast after blast of his power. Sweat beaded on his forehead and his arms trembled slightly as he fought to push them back.

A quick scan of the others told me they were fairing no better.

They were using too much fórsa and wouldn't last much longer.

"Go!" Illiana commanded, and I scrambled to my feet.

I ran headfirst into the thick of the battle, dodging and weaving my way through the wraiths as they attacked my friends relentlessly.

Guilt tightened around my chest and I had to remind myself I wasn't leaving them to fend for themselves. I knew retrieving the stone was the only way this would end. Pumping my arms harder, I pushed myself forward, every step closing the distance between me and our salvation.

I was close. So close I could almost touch it.

My hand reached out, my fingers a hair's breadth away from brushing the stone.

Ghostly fingers wrapped around my wrist and that familiar bone-chilling cold spread up my arm. I shook my head to clear the intrusive thoughts trying to pierce through my consciousness, pleading with me to yield.

My lips parted and an animalistic roar escaped past my lips as I raised my other hand and sent flames spiraling towards the wraith. Its cloak caught fire and an ear-splitting scream cut through the cries of battle.

I didn't waste another second. I lunged forward, my fingers circling the stone as I gripped it in my hand.

My stomach dipped as a sense of weightlessness crashed over me and darkness closed in around me.

The last thing I heard was the sound of Silas calling my name.

And then I was falling.

# Chapter Twenty-Seven

I landed with a *thud* on the cold forest floor.

Peering around, I saw a reflection of the world I'd left behind. Only I was alone when I surveyed my surroundings.

No, not alone.

I could *feel* the unseen eyes watching me, assessing me, as I waited. I fought the shiver that tried to work its way down my spine and squared my shoulders. Lifting my chin, I let determination settle deep into my bones.

"I know you're there," I called out.

The crunching of leaves underfoot was my only warning before three women stepped out from behind a thick tree trunk.

The first woman, young in appearance, with curly brown hair and a kind smile, waved at me as she stepped closer.

The second woman appeared to be older. Somewhere in her middle years, if I had to guess. Her brown hair sat atop her head in a tight bun, and she held herself with a level of authority that reminded me of the Matron of the Kitchens, Adelle, in Pyrithia.

The third woman was much older. She had rounded shoulders that left her hunched over, and she walked with the support of a cane. Her light grey hair was almost white, and it hung to her waist limply. The crooked grin plastered on her face put me at ease in an instant.

"Welcome, Queen of Fire and Flame," the second woman said. "My name is Rhene." She turned towards the younger woman and continued, "This is

Oonagh, and this is Eabha," she finished, gesturing towards the older woman. "We've waited a long time to meet you."

"Are you the fates?" I asked, shifting uncomfortably.

These women held the power to grant me the stone.

Or...

*They could end your life here and now,* my inner voice taunted.

Rhene smirked. "We are known by many names. That is but one of them."

"I have come seeking the Aurora Stone," I said hesitantly.

"We are aware of why you have entered the void, child," Eabha said.

"Come, sit with us," Rhene added.

All three women positioned themselves on the ground, arranging their skirts around them until they were satisfied. Then, three pairs of eyes locked onto me.

I stepped forward, unsure of how to act given these women were... what? Were they gods?

Oonagh chuckled. "We don't bite. Come, join us." She waved me over, her broad smile reassuring and friendly.

I sank to the ground, crossing my legs in front of me, and waited.

"You must have many questions," Rhene said.

"Not really."

Shit!

Was I supposed to be more inquisitive? Was this part of the test?

"Relax," Rhene said. "I can see your mind working itself into a frenzy."

"It's just that I have already spoken with Drakkon. He answered all of my questions and shed some light on my purpose in the world," I blurted.

"Ah, Drakkon," Eabha sighed. "It has been some time since I have seen my old friend. Did he tell you about us?"

"He, ah, said you created me to counter the imbalance of power within the realm when the Original Witch gifted her powers to Kieran, and that he provided you with his flames, which is the source of my powers."

"Very good," Oonagh said, clapping her hands.

"What did he tell you about our role in the realm?" Rhene pressed.

"He said that the fates maintained the balance within the realm and fostered free will."

Eabha snorted. "Yes, free will. That's what you call it when you guide the child through the labyrinth, right Rhene?"

Rhene cut Eabha a glare that would have had me curling in on myself.

"She could have navigated the maze alone. I was only pushing things along," she snapped.

The older woman cackled and mischief twinkled in her eyes. Oonagh covered her mouth to conceal her own grin.

Wait. The maze? Were they talking about... surely they didn't?

"Are you talking about the maze in Netheran?" I asked.

"The very same," Eabha grinned. "Our dear Rhene felt you were taking too long to reach the end, so she gave you a little push in the right direction."

When I entered the maze that final day, I had sensed something was different.

Now I understood why.

Rhene scowled, but the old woman laughed even harder.

"Let me tell you a story, Queen of Fire and Flame," Rhene said, returning her attention to me.

Oonagh sat up straighter, her smile wide and endearing as she readied herself to hear what Rhene was about to say.

"We have a distinct role to play within the universe," Rhene said. "And that is to oversee the weaving of each thread of life. We lay the thread, and then let destiny run its course."

"That doesn't mean every life is predetermined, however," Rhene said. "We set every being on their path, but it is their own free will that determines their true trajectory."

Oonagh nodded her head enthusiastically and Eabha added, "Of course, there are times we must correct a misstep or intervene if the situation calls for it."

"Precisely," Rhene agreed. "We are also responsible for maintaining the balance. Too much power in one being and the entire realm can collapse."

"That doesn't sound like free will," I muttered.

"Well, it's free-ish," Rhene mumbled, causing Eabha to howl with laughter again.

"The point of the story is this," Rhene continued, again redirecting the conversation. "In your realm, a true imbalance of power emerged many centuries ago, and as the beings responsible for maintaining the balance, we plucked a thread here and pulled a thread there to get everything back on the proper path."

"The War of Witches," I said.

"Yes," Rhene confirmed. "As I am sure you are aware, we weren't entirely successful in our endeavors to restore the balance."

"You didn't predict that the Original Witch would gift her powers to

Kieran," I surmised.

"We did not," Rhene confirmed. "That is why we created you."

Rhene's gaze bore into me, making me feel as though every secret, every vulnerability I had ever experienced was exposed and laid bare for her perusal.

"We gifted you with enough power to overcome the imbalance the Serpent King created."

"And yet, you seek the Aurora Stone," Eabha mused.

The intensity of their scrutiny made my palms clammy with sweat, and I swallowed roughly.

"I do not seek the stone to create a further imbalance of power."

My mouth felt suddenly dry and my tongue darted out to wet my lips.

"Kieran has had centuries to grow his power and learn to control it. This leaves me at a significant disadvantage, and Kieran knows it. It's why he is hunting me. He seeks to end the threat I pose to him before I can grow and learn as he has. I seek the stone to overcome the weakness of my inexperience."

"You could learn, with time," Eabha countered.

"That's true. However, I fear time is not on my side. Kieran has brought the war to our doorstep. Now we must do everything we can to ensure we are victorious."

I hoped I was making a compelling argument because it was more than my life on the line should I fail.

The three women studied me before turning their backs on me and murmuring among themselves.

When they faced me once more, I had to fight the whole body tremor that sought to ravish me.

"We will give you the stone, Queen of Fire and Flame," Rhene said, and I exhaled a shaky breath. "But know this; should you fail, your entire realm will perish, and we will allow it. We will wipe the slate clean and start anew."

A lump formed in my throat, and the weight of responsibility threatened to crush me.

"Do you accept our terms, Queen of Fire and Flame?" Eabha asked.

I hesitated for a moment before nodding. "I do."

"So be it," Rhene said.

All three women stood and peered down at me.

"The fate of Aetherian now rests with you," Rhene said solemnly. "May the gods favor you."

Rhene waved her hand, and the world around me shifted.

And then I was falling once more.

# Chapter Twenty-Eight

My eyes snapped open, and I sat bolt upright as I peered around me. Flashes of white light momentarily disoriented me and when I realized they were orbs of fórsa, panic seized my chest in a stranglehold.

The fates had given me the stone, so why were the wraiths still attacking?

As if to remind me of this, the stone grew cold in my palm and I looked down to see the iridescent colors swirling and shimmering as they leaped across its surface.

Someone grunted nearby, and I jerked my head upward to see Silas bent at the waist, his palms flat against his knees, as he struggled to steady his breathing.

I jumped to my feet and rushed to him.

"What's wrong, Silas?"

My jaw dropped to the forest floor when I registered what was happening.

One by one, the wraiths froze in place.

The unnatural wind from earlier returned with a vengeance, blowing through the area, and bringing with it a mist that coiled and danced around our legs. Tortured screams cut through the silence and I shivered violently.

Once the mist dispersed, no evidence of the wraiths remained.

"Are you all right?" Silas asked, drawing my attention back to him.

"I'm fine. Tell me what's wrong with you."

"Just winded," he said breathlessly.

Silas straightened, cupping my face with his calloused palms. His gaze roamed over me with an intensity that had my toes curling in my boots before he slammed his lips to mine. The kiss was rough and demanding; fueled by the desperate need to hold on to one another and never let go.

When Silas broke our kiss, he lowered his forehead to mine and closed his eyes. "You did it, Little Menace," he whispered, and then a broad grin split his gorgeous face.

His enthusiasm was infectious, and I found myself grinning widely in return.

A cacophony of inhuman sounds emanated from deep within the forest, breaking through the moment. All around us, creatures howled, screeched, and cried out in agony as the steady beat of drums set a demanding rhythm.

"What the hell is that?" I whispered, afraid of giving voice to the fear swimming inside my head.

"Ah," Illiana said hesitantly. "I may have omitted one more detail." Her sheepish expression told me I would not like whatever came next.

"Speak woman," Silas snarled.

"So, when Harlowe removed the stone, its power was unlocked, and that triggered a pulse of magic to burst forth, sweeping throughout the entire forest," Illiana said in a rush.

"The creatures would have felt that surge of power, and well, they're reacting to it, as you can see," she added as she gestured towards the forest.

Silas growled, and I heard Cillian swear under his breath.

"Arabella and I will need to set the wards back in place before we can leave, however..." Illiana trailed off, seemingly unwilling to finish her sentence.

"However," Silas pressed.

"It is likely every creature inside this forest is now converging on this spot to identify the source of the power surge," Illiana finished with a wince.

I stared at Illiana in disbelief, and from the silence permeating the space around me, everyone else was doing the same.

And then utter chaos erupted.

"What the fuck do you mean they are converging on us?" Silas rumbled.

"For fuck's sake Illiana! I'm all for keeping your secrets close to your chest, but this is taking it a little far, don't you think?" Emmerson said incredulously.

"Little Viper, I want you out of here NOW!" Cillian roared. "I'll cover you, now run."

"Gods, just stop for a minute," Zeke yelled over the escalating noise, to no avail.

**"That's it. Send up a signal right now, Fire Heart. I am getting you out of there,"** Misneach demanded.

"It's like you know nothing about me, Cillian," Emmerson scoffed.

**"They all need to leave,"** Oisín added, a hint of panic lacing the usually stoic dragon's tone.

"ENOUGH!" I bellowed.

"Illiana, what do you need?" I asked.

"Time. Buy us enough time to lay the wards."

"Forget the wards, let's get out of here," Fionn exclaimed.

"We can't, Fionn. If we don't set the wards, we will unleash these creatures on the entire realm. Pyrithia is the closest kingdom to the Forest of Nightmares, need I remind you?" I said pointedly.

Fionn's gaze darted around, but when his eyes landed back on me, he nodded in agreement.

"Arabella, help Illiana with whatever she needs. The rest of you form a circle around them. We protect them at all costs," I commanded.

Everyone moved into place, Silas taking the spot next to me. "You're fucking hot when you get all bossy," he purred.

I slowly turned my head to stare at him. "Now Silas? Really?"

He just shrugged. "I can't help it if you get my dick hard at inopportune moments."

"You're unbelievable," I muttered.

"Unbelievably turned on," he smirked.

"If you two are done?" Zeke said, clearing his throat.

**"The General is an idiot,"** Misneach groaned.

**"Try to see if you can narrow down our location through our bond, Misneach. I can't afford to send any kind of signal in case the creatures don't know our precise location,"** I said, ignoring his jab.

**"Already ahead of you, Fire Heart."**

**"Good. Once you've located us, check for any clearings or riverbanks nearby where you can meet us. It's going to be a rolling extraction."**

**"Life is never dull with you, Queen of Fire and Flames,"** Rónán said cheerfully.

**"Not you too,"** I moaned. **"Enough with the queen talk."**

**"Never,"** Rónán said, aghast. **"Misneach would burn me alive."**

**"Trust me, Rónán, if I could, I would have done so already,"** Misneach growled.

**"Rónán, enough!"** Caolán snapped. **"Everyone is to locate their**

**Cathal, and then find a suitable landing spot."**

**"On it,"** Saoirse said. **"Niamh, with me."**

"Over there," Zeke shouted, pointing towards the forest.

I caught sight of an unnatural shade of green, barely visible between the thick forest trees, about two hundred yards away.

Glancing over my shoulder, I saw Illiana and Arabella crouched on the ground, hands locked together, as they chanted rapidly.

"I don't mean to rush you or anything," I said, my voice coming out at a higher pitch than I intended. "But it'd be a good idea to hurry things along."

A roar pulled my attention back towards the tree line just as the earth trembled under my feet.

The nightmares of the forest were coming.

# Chapter Twenty-Nine

The competing sounds of the drums, the rumble of the creatures' footfalls, and their primal battle cries as they ran toward us overwhelmed my senses.

Taking a deep breath, I let the cool, crisp air fill my lungs before exhaling, releasing the fear threatening to immobilize me.

With each inhale, I felt my body calming, determination flowing through me like a soothing balm for my frayed nerves.

My mind cleared, and my focus sharpened. I blocked out the sounds of impending bloodshed until they became muted and distant. In this moment of stillness, I fortified my resolve, allowing the steady thrum of my heartbeat to anchor me.

I sheathed my daggers and tore my bow free. Plucking an arrow from my quiver, I knocked it against the string of my bow and pulled it taut.

My gaze locked onto my first target, and I took aim, narrowing my eyes in concentration. I released a controlled breath and let the arrow loose. It flew through the air with a satisfying *twang* and landed in the center of a minotaur's chest with a resounding *thud*.

I didn't hesitate as I reached over my shoulder and withdrew another arrow. I drew the string of my bow tight once more and released another deadly projectile.

My hand moved instinctively, my fingers tousling the feathered ends of my arrows as I sent one after another streaking through the air until they found purchase in the flesh of our enemies.

Out of my periphery, I saw more arrows unleashed on the horde; the others following my lead.

"Conserve your energy," I yelled without looking back when I saw a brilliant white orb sail through the air past me. "You'll need it before we are done."

Arrows continued to cut through the space surrounding me, swift and fluid, each shot executed with precision.

It wasn't enough, though.

The horde of beasts, led by the minotaurs, were undeterred as they rushed towards us. An axe came hurtling through the air and I ducked to avoid being struck by the weapon.

"Prepare to defend yourselves," I called out, throwing up my shield.

**"Misneach, how far away are you?"**

**"We are above you,"** he said, but I didn't dare take my eyes off the monsters closing the distance between us to look.

**"Over there,"** Niamh shouted. **"There's a small clearing."**

**"That's not a clearing,"** Oisín scoffed. **"More like the remnants of a terrible storm. A few toppled trees will hardly be enough space to land."**

**"Look around you, Oisín,"** Saoirse seethed. **"That is our only option if you intend for your Cathal to live long enough to see the moonlight."**

**"We'll make do,"** Caolán said, cutting off any argument.

**"Misneach, what are you all looking at?"**

**"West of your position, there is a slight break in the treetop. A few trees have been upturned, but it's only big enough for one dragon to go in at a time. It's not large enough to land, so we'll only be able to lower ourselves enough for you to jump the remaining distance."**

**"How far away?"** I asked.

**"A thousand yards."**

**"A thousand yards!"** I repeated, hysteria breaking through my resolve.

At that moment, the first wave of creatures collided with my shield. Green skin, mottled fur, and thick scales hissed and burned before the monsters ignited into a blazing inferno.

Wails and howls sliced through the forest as the creatures unleashed their agony. The smell of their burning flesh assaulted me and I had to swallow the bile trying to force its way up my throat.

Unable to halt their strides in time, the second wave of creatures followed suit.

The third wave pulled up short, examining my shield's fiery exterior with both reverence and disdain.

"Illiana?" I called.

"Almost done," she gritted out.

"Silas?"

"I'm here, Harlowe."

A minotaur bared its teeth at me as it pounded its axe against the wall of flames. The steel burned red-hot before melting under the intense heat. When it realized it couldn't get through my shield, the creature leaped back, another snarl escaping its twisted muzzle.

The dire wolves moved to stand at my sides, growling and snapping their jaws at the horde on the other side of the barrier.

"Silas," I said again. "The dragons can only extract one person at a time."

"I know. Caolán relayed the conversation, and the other dragons did the same."

"We will need to stagger our retreat," I panted, the strain of holding my shield in place beginning to wear me down.

"How would we do that? You would need to drop your shield to allow the others to escape."

I didn't miss the way he omitted himself from those plans.

"When I drop the shield, attack with fórsa. Hopefully, it will be enough to hold their attention."

"Done," Illiana shouted.

She rose from her feet, pulling Arabella with her. Both women were sweating, exhaustion etched into their features as they struggled to remain upright.

"Are you able to leave the forest or are you trapped inside like the monsters?" I asked Illiana, the thought just occurring to me.

Illiana scoffed. "You think I'd lay a ward that would trap me here?"

We didn't have time for this.

"Just answer the question, Illiana," I hissed.

"Of course I can," she huffed.

"And the dire wolves?"

The thought of abandoning the wolves made my chest ache.

"We share a bond and that allows them to go where I go," she said.

"How do you think they would feel about a flying lesson?"

The wolves whined in answer to my question.

"There is no need. The wolves and I can outrun the beasts," Illiana said confidently.

"Are you certain?"

"I am," she confirmed.

"Great," Emmerson interjected. "Now that's settled, let's get this escape moving. Harlowe can't hold on much longer," she said with a knowing look.

"Zeke, take Arabella, and you and Fionn, go first," I ordered.

Zeke nodded, gripping Arabella by her elbow, and giving her a reassuring smile.

"Cillian," Emmerson barked. "Get over here and help Harlowe!"

"You know where you're going?" I asked Zeke.

"Yes, and I'll see you there," he said pointedly.

On the other side of the barrier, the creatures stood motionless as they studied us.

They couldn't have heard our discussion from where they stood. Yet, they sensed a shift had occurred.

"NOW!" I roared as I dropped my shield.

The others sent fórsa racing past me, the orbs landing with sickening accuracy. Bodies were ripped apart, and the forest floor was soaked with torrents of blood.

"Clear!" Silas yelled, and I slammed my shield back in place.

I was panting hard, my arms beginning to tremble from the exertion.

A shrewd-looking minotaur assessed our group anew, its red eyes sparking with fury. It stepped closer, sniffing the air in our direction.

"They're escaping," it snarled.

"Fuck me!" Emmerson said. "Is anyone else surprised they can talk?"

"GO!" I bellowed, needing to exploit the monsters' momentary stun before they could recover and stifle our escape. "Cillian, get Emmerson out of here! Illiana, run!"

**"Misneach, cover Emmerson and Cillian. They will have company."**

**"I have them, Fire Heart, now get yourself out of there!"**

I heard Emmerson protesting as Cillian pulled her away.

"I'm right behind you, Em. Now run!"

I threw flaming balls of fire at the creatures while I waited for the others to clear the threshold of where my barrier had stood. White orbs of energy joined my flames, and I realized Silas hadn't heeded my demands.

"Get out of here, Silas!" I shouted.

"Not on your life, Little Menace. It's you and me, or nothing at all!"

I didn't have the energy to argue with him.

A small group of trees, five feet to my right, ignited in flames, and I caught the hint of indigo through the canopy above me. My eyes tracked the burning inferno as Misneach stalled those trying to pursue the others.

Heaving, I snapped the shield back in place, needing a moment to breathe.

**"What are you doing, Fire Heart? Get out of there,"** Misneach growled.

**"If we don't stagger our escape, Misneach, we'll be left vulnerable at the extraction point."**

My dragon roared in fury, leaving no uncertainty as to his feelings on the matter.

Sweat covered every inch of my flesh and soaked through my tunic until it stuck to my body like a second skin.

"Any idea how to use that stone?" Silas panted from beside me.

"None."

The creatures recovered quicker this time. They fanned out, circling my shield, which was growing weaker by the second.

"Fuck," Silas spat.

**"A chara?"** Caolán said, the concern in his voice an indication of just how fucked we were.

Silas withdrew his sword, rolling it between his palms as he readied himself to take on the entire Forest of Nightmares alone.

A quick glance around confirmed that would be a losing battle.

"Put it away, Silas," I said. "You'll need your hands free."

Silas chuckled darkly. "I'm not sure if you're seeing what I'm seeing, Little Menace, but we're going to have to fight our way out of here."

"That won't work," I replied.

The minotaur from earlier whispered something to its companion, who nodded and signaled for the others to press forward.

Its red-eyed gaze scanned me from head to foot while it remained in place, seemingly not prepared to take any risks itself.

"If you think I'm going to allow them to lay a single finger on you, Harlowe, then you have severely underestimated what I'm prepared to do to keep you breathing."

"That's not what I meant."

Silas raised a brow, waiting for me to continue. "I'm going to push my shield out like I do when I'm trying to cover you and the others," I said. "However, this time, I'm going to try to burn them with the expanded exterior instead of bringing them inside."

"Try?" Silas asked skeptically.

"Do you have a better plan, Silas?" I hissed.

Silas raised his hands in surrender and then returned his sword to its scabbard.

"All right, Harlowe. Then what?"

"We make a run for it. It'll only startle them for a moment, so be ready to move."

Silas gave a curt nod, his determination lending me the strength I needed to execute this.

"Ready?" I asked.

"I'll bring up the rear," Silas said.

I opened my mouth to argue, but one look from Silas silenced my protests.

**"Misneach, are you in place?"**

**"I will follow you from the sky. Should you need me, I'll be there."**

I took a deep breath and sent all of my remaining energy into pushing my shield outward. The creatures lining the other side shuffled nervously.

With a battle cry of my own, I pushed harder, sending a wave of flames out around me and catching the monsters in its crosshairs before they could retreat.

"Run!"

Silas didn't hesitate. He grabbed my hand and sprinted forward.

My legs shook and my footsteps faltered as I struggled to keep myself moving.

I felt completely drained as my body protested against my demands to run faster.

I could hear the thunderous sound of the horde giving chase and I didn't know at that moment If I could do it.

**"Don't you dare give up, Fire Heart!"** Misneach shouted.

Spurred on by the desperation of my bond mate, I pumped my arms harder, pleading with my body to hold on just a little longer.

I was vaguely aware of Silas sending blasts of fórsa over his shoulder in an effort to slow down the advancing masses.

**"You're almost there, Fire Heart,"** Misneach breathed.

Silas's large hand pushed against my head, forcing me to the ground just as a flurry of knives and axes flew by.

He pulled me to my feet a moment later, dragging me alongside him.

As we broke through the tree line to the tiny clearing, Silas's hands gripped my waist and he flung me into the air a moment before he took a running leap from a fallen log.

I gasped in shock as the feeling of weightlessness washed over me, only to be followed by the visceral sensation of falling.

Before I could scream, a sudden jolt wracked my body, jerking me from one side to the other before leveling out.

As I glanced up, I saw a familiar indigo hue, and a sob tore free of my throat without permission.

**"I have you, Fire Heart,"** Misneach soothed. **"I'll always have you."**

# Chapter Thirty

Misneach lowered me to the ground before landing next to me and shaking out his wings. I'd flown out of the Forest of Nightmares in the clutches of his enormous claws and it was an experience I was not eager to repeat.

Of course, Silas had somehow managed to take his seat between Caolán's broad wings and he looked no worse for wear as he slid gracefully from his dragon's back and strode towards me.

It was Emmerson, however, who reached me first.

"I'm right behind you!" she scoffed before pulling me into a vigorous hug that sent us both tumbling to the ground.

Laughter fought its way free from my chest as I marveled at the fact that we had made it.

We survived the Forest of Nightmares... again.

Hysteria took over and Emmerson joined me as we cackled like maniacs while lying on the soft grass.

Zeke came into view above us, his hands on his hips, and a wide grin on his face as he peered down at us.

"Have you two finally cracked?" he teased.

Emmerson grabbed his hand and pulled him down alongside us before he could resist.

"Ow, Emmerson! Was that your elbow?"

"If you can complain, then you survived, and that is something worth celebrating, Z."

"I could have done without the bruised ribs," he grumbled.

Silas shook his head as he sat down on the grass beside me. "You saved us back there," he remarked with a hint of reverence.

A flush crept up my neck and I glanced around to escape the intensity of his gaze.

Then I noticed someone was missing.

"Where's Illiana?" I asked, staggering to my feet.

Everyone avoided my gaze, but I caught Arabella's eye before she could lower her head. "Arabella?" I pressed.

"She hasn't returned yet," she mumbled.

"Fuck!"

I knew I should have made her leave with the dragons.

**"Misneach, can you search the area to see if you can spot her?"**

**"No need."**

Before I could question my dragon, a low howl rent the air and another echoed the call a moment later. Then, one after the other, more wolves added their voices to the symphony until the sounds mixed, wrapping around us in a primal call that reverberated throughout the wildness of the forest.

I held my breath as I waited.

Seconds passed. The tension built as the sounds drew nearer.

A flash of red caught my attention through the thicket, but it was moving too fast to determine what it was.

Another soul-stirring howl cut through the tension, and I feared the worst.

A mass of black fur bundled through the tree line, heading straight for me. When the wolf sank its paws into the dirt to slow its pace, its amber eyes scanned our surroundings for any lingering threats.

The dire wolf lowered itself to the ground and Illiana slid from its back.

"Well, that was exciting," she said as she dusted her hands off on her skirts.

I released a shaky breath and rushed towards the woman, throwing my arms around her in a hug not dissimilar to the one Emmerson had inflicted upon me.

Illiana stiffened and then rigidly patted my back. "There, there," she said, clearly uncomfortable with the display of affection.

I chuckled, but released her.

She gave me a tight smile that looked more like a grimace.

The woman had been alone, with only her wolves as companions, for too long.

"I am grateful for everything you have done for us, Illiana," I said, emotion lacing my tone. "And I am thankful you survived."

Illiana cleared her throat. "Very good," she said as she shifted her weight from foot to foot. "Now what?"

My gaze flittered to Silas, and he stepped forward.

"We return to Pyrithia."

We descended on the open courtyard in front of the palace and the subjects of Pyrithia murmured amongst themselves as they waited to catch a glimpse of their new king.

Some eyed Misneach warily, reminding me of the last time we had landed in this spot. He curled his lips back, baring his teeth.

**"Misneach,"** I scolded.

**"A little fear is a healthy thing, Fire Heart,"** he replied.

Mothers pulled their children behind them while their broods peeked out from beneath their skirts to grin at my cantankerous dragon.

**"See. The hatchlings are building their courage as we speak."**

**"Children, Misneach. We call them children."**

My dragon rolled his eyes.

Silas caught my eye and tilted his head towards the palace steps.

**"Does he think you're some kind of dog? Ready to jump at his every command,"** Misneach grumbled.

Not bothering to respond to Misneach, I folded my arms and raised a single brow at Silas in a challenge.

A smirk pulled up the corner of his lips. He bent low at his waist, dipping into an exaggerated bow as he waved a hand for me to proceed him.

**"That's more like it,"** Misneach snorted, the seriousness in his tone reinforced by the feelings creeping up the bond.

I shook my head, unable to hide the smile spreading across my lips.

Small gasps broke through our private communication and the crowd parted to let Illiana and her five very large and very lethal-looking dire wolves through. People gaped open-mouthed as they watched the colossal beasts with both apprehension and astonishment.

Illiana smirked. "I must admit, it's quite refreshing to be gazed upon with fear once more," she said, as if the anxiety gripping the crowd was as pleasant as a warm embrace.

**"See, Fire Heart. She understands,"** Misneach said as he bumped my shoulder with his maw.

"Illiana, has anyone ever mentioned that you're slightly unhinged?" Emmerson asked. "And that's coming from me," she added, pointing a finger toward her chest.

Illiana shrugged, unperturbed by the comment.

Cillian snorted and then ducked just in time to avoid Emmerson's backhand.

"Woman, your affinity for violence is grating on my last nerve."

"And your propensity for stupidity is grating on mine," Emmerson retorted.

"All right," Silas interjected. "Let's not frighten my subjects." Turning to me, he said, "After you, Harlowe."

I headed towards him and he placed his hand on the small of my back as he led me into the palace.

"My King, my King," the Master of ceremonies called as soon as he caught sight of us.

"That will take some getting used to," Silas muttered, and I chuckled at his discomfort.

"I'm not opposed to bending you over the banister and spanking you, Little Menace," Silas whispered against my ear, and my cheeks heated. His hand slipped from the small of my back and snaked around my waist as he pulled me against him in a possessive hold. My skin warmed, and I trembled under his touch.

"That's more like it," Silas growled as he nipped my earlobe with his teeth.

"Thank the gods you have returned," the Master of Ceremonies babbled, wrenching me from my lust-induced haze.

"I left Eoin in charge for a reason, Conrad," Silas said with annoyance.

"Yes, well, he is not the most agreeable man to work with," the man, Conrad, muttered.

Silas cocked a brow. "I'm sure it was all one-sided."

"Of course," Conrad said, missing Silas's jab. "My only interest is to serve my King."

"That man needs a hobby," Emmerson muttered, and I caught Cillian stifling his laughter behind his fist.

"Whatever it is, it will have to wait," Silas said.

"But my King," Conrad protested.

Silas held up his hand, cutting him off. "We have had quite the journey and my Queen and I need to discuss a few things with our guests before we all get some much-needed rest."

"Silas!" I hissed, and Misneach echoed my sentiment with a growl.

"Your… q-queen?" Conrad spluttered before he dropped to his knees and bowed so low his head met the cold, tiled floor. "My apologies, my Queen," Conrad said. "I did not know."

I rushed towards the man and pulled him to his feet. "Never mind him, Conrad," I said, dusting the elderly man's cloak. "Your King is quite delusional."

Silas only smirked as he watched me fussing over the old man. Snickers sounded behind me and I turned to glare at my friends.

"I am so glad you find all of this so entertaining," I seethed.

"Harlowe, if you could see your face right now, you'd think so too," Emmerson chuckled.

"Stop molesting the poor man," Zeke laughed.

Horrified, I pulled my hands away from Conrad and retreated a few steps to create some distance between us.

There was a moment of silence before everyone erupted with raucous laughter, enjoying my unease.

"I hate each and every one of you," I snarled before storming away from them.

"Harlowe," Silas called after me, but I didn't slow my steps.

"The throne room is in the other direction," he said, amused.

Cursing the gods for my poor taste in men, I pivoted on my feet and stalked down the opposite hall with the sounds of laughter haunting my every step.

# Chapter Thirty-One

Silas sat atop a large obsidian throne, with delicate carvings that were a stark contrast to the towering backrest and wide frame that made the occupant appear formidable and commanding.

It suited him, not that I'd ever tell him that, given the size of his existing ego.

The only ones present inside the throne room were those who had ventured into the Forest of Nightmares, with Silas having dismissed all remaining soldiers, affording us the privacy to speak freely.

"Now that we have the stone, what do we do with it?" Fionn asked.

"Harlowe," Illiana said, and I turned to look at her.

Only she wasn't looking at me. Her gaze was trained on Fionn.

"What's that?" he asked, confused.

"Harlowe," Illiana repeated. "Harlowe has the stone. The fates entrusted it to her, and her alone."

Emmerson huffed. "That's not what he meant, Illiana," she said, coming to Fionn's defense.

"All the same," Illiana replied. "It is best we set clear boundaries at the outset, no?"

Her gaze flicked to mine, and my skin prickled under the weight of responsibility.

"As I was saying," Fionn said. "Now what?"

"Now," Illiana drawled. "The Queen of Fire must master the stone."

All eyes turned to me, and I fought the urge to shrink away from their scrutiny.

"Who will train her?" Silas asked.

"No one here can," Illiana said with a casual shrug.

Emmerson closed her eyes and pinched the bridge of her nose. "We need to work on your communication skills, Illiana."

"Can you at least help her?" Zeke asked.

"I cannot," Illiana replied curtly.

"Illiana," I groaned, reaching the limit of my patience. "Speak plainly. What is it I need to do?"

Illiana opened her mouth to answer me, but I cut her off. "Exactly," I pressed.

Illiana scowled. "The stone reacts differently for everyone. I cannot tell you how to wield it because I simply do not know how it will respond to you."

"What do you mean?" I asked.

"I mean," she snapped. "You need to figure out how to activate the stone."

"I already activated the stone when I removed it from the altar... didn't I?"

Illiana's lips twisted into an impish smirk. "That doesn't mean the stone won't continue to test you. I believe I already mentioned it has a will of its own."

I groaned. This discussion was not helping. "So what, trial and error?"

Illiana shrugged, and I sensed Emmerson's excitement from where she stood behind me.

"All right, everyone out!" Silas barked, putting a halt to the discussion.

"I am not your subject, Silas, King of the mighty Pyrithia," Emmerson scowled.

"Of course, Emmerson, where are my manners? May I please have a moment alone with Harlowe?"

Emmerson muttered something under her breath, but before she could retort, Cillian placed a hand on the small of her back and guided her towards the door. "Let's get you something to eat," he said. "You must be starving."

One by one, the others left the throne room.

Silas relaxed back into his chair, his shoulders slumping as he propped an elbow on the armrest and rested his chin against his fist.

"What are you up to?" I asked.

A wicked grin split his gorgeous face, and he curled his fingers in a come hither motion.

I surveyed him a moment longer before moving towards him. When I was within arm's reach, Silas grabbed my wrist and spread his legs wide until I was standing between his powerful thighs.

"I have been thinking of nothing other than my pussy since you got all commanding on the battlefield," he said gruffly.

To emphasize his point, Silas's large hand released my wrist and snaked down my stomach until he cupped me between my thighs.

A bolt of pleasure shot up my spine at the contact.

"Is that right?" I asked breathlessly.

Without warning, Silas spun me and pulled me down into his lap. One hand slid across my stomach, holding me in place, while the other hand collared my throat. I could feel the hard outline of his erection against my ass as he thrust his hips upward.

"Do you feel what you do to me, Little Menace?" he purred.

When I didn't answer him straight away, Silas tightened his hold on my throat, squeezing gently.

"Yes," I breathed.

Calloused fingers brushed against my collarbone before dipping beneath my tunic and gripping my breast roughly. A moan slipped past my lips without permission, and Silas chuckled darkly.

"You're wearing too many layers, Little Menace."

"Then do something about it."

There was a silent pause before a tearing sound filled the room. When I looked down, I saw my tunic had been torn down the front, exposing my breasts. My nipples hardened when the bite of cold air assaulted them.

"Silas," I hissed. "I didn't mean for you to destroy my clothing, you asshole!"

"You should know better than to challenge me, Harlowe. Now, do you want to take your pants off yourself, or would you like me to do it for you?"

I slid from Silas's lap, pulling my boots off and slipping my pants past my hips until they reached the floor.

Turning to face Silas, I saw him reach behind his back, yanking his tunic over his head as his muscles tensed and flexed with the movement.

I bit my bottom lip, enjoying the pulse of desire that washed over me as I watched him. Silas reached beneath his leathers and freed his cock as he wrenched his pants down, kicking his boots off in the process. Fisting himself in his hand, he stroked his length leisurely, a masculine smirk gracing his sensual lips when he saw me watching him, transfixed.

"Are you going to be a good girl and climb on my cock?" he said, quirking a brow.

It wasn't even a question. My feet moved of their own volition.

Silas lifted his hand and made a circular motion with his index finger, indicating I should turn around, and I complied.

Rough palms gripped my hips, and he pulled me into his lap once more. Silas's hands slid down my body, reaching between my inner thighs where he spread my legs wide open.

My breath hitched, and I glanced toward the doors. "Anyone could walk in and see every inch of me right now."

"Does that concern you or excite you, Little Menace?" he asked, his tongue darting out to flick the shell of my ear.

"Both."

"You're a naughty little minx," he teased. "I didn't take you for an exhibitionist, Little Menace."

His fingers caressed my entrance, and I bucked my hips, chasing the contact.

"Of course, if anyone laid eyes on what's fucking mine, I'd be forced to remove them." Silas sank a finger inside me and my eyes fluttered closed as my head tilted back against his shoulder.

"It wouldn't be their fault," I panted as he thrust another finger inside me.

"And I wouldn't fucking care," he growled. "No one gets to see you like this but me."

Silas brushed his thumb over my sensitive nub, and I moaned.

"Your greedy fucking pussy is trying to swallow my fingers, Little Menace."

"You have… such a dirty… mouth… Silas," I gasped.

"A mouth that has tasted every inch of you."

Silas brushed his lips over my shoulder before biting down on the flesh. I cried out in both pleasure and pain as Silas fucked me mercilessly.

"That's my good girl. Fucking scream for me."

Silas's other hand cupped my breast, squeezing and tugging on my nipple while I rode his hand. The roughened skin of his palm caused a delicious friction that had me seeing stars.

"Come for me, Little Menace," he demanded.

And I did.

A low groan worked its way up my throat as I shattered around him. Silas gripped my hips when my movements became erratic, guiding me through my orgasm until it receded.

"Now I am going to fuck you on this throne, so every time I am forced to oversee petty squabbles, I'll remember how good it feels to come inside you."

Silas pumped his erect cock once, twice, before he plunged inside me all the way to the hilt. I inhaled a sharp breath as my body stretched around him.

"You were made to take my cock, Little Menace. Now fucking take it," he growled.

"You say the sweetest things to me, Silas."

"You love it," he taunted.

"Mmm," I moaned as he rocked his hips against my ass.

"You love it when I degrade you," he said, thrusting deeper. "You love it when I hurt you." This time, his thrust was accompanied by a sharp slap to my breast, and I cried out, unable to deny him.

"You love it when I take away your control." A shiver raced down my spine, and I clenched around him.

Silas groaned, the sound deep and throaty. "And you love it when I own you."

He grabbed my throat, and I placed my palms on his thick, muscular thighs as I met him thrust for thrust.

"What would our subjects think if they saw just how much of a glutton their Queen is for my cock," Silas mocked.

"I'm not their Queen," I hissed, as I continued grinding myself against him.

The pressure on my throat increased as Silas squeezed tighter. "I could be fucking the heir into your womb right now, Little Menace."

I barked out a laugh. "I hope that hasn't been your plan all along, Silas, because I take the yearly fertility tonic."

"Maybe I just like to see my come dripping from your tight little pussy. Tell me, how wet are you for me right now, Little Menace?" Silas asked, his voice coarse with the same lust raging through my body.

"Soaking," I moaned.

Silas snarled, pumping his hips harder and faster as he fucked me without restraint. His grip around my throat tightened and the edges of my vision darkened.

"Fuck!" Silas growled. "Your pussy is choking my cock."

I tried to pull air into my starving lungs but couldn't. "Give in to me, Little Menace. Come all over my cock while I own your sweet pussy."

The first hint of my orgasm sent tingles dancing along my spine and Silas loosened his grip, allowing me to suck in a ragged breath. Then a wave of pleasure so strong crashed into me, sending violent tremors throughout my body. Silas continued to hold me against him as he chased his release.

With a grunt, Silas came, filling me with his come, just as he'd promised. We both panted heavily as we tried to steady our breathing.

Silas pressed soft, gentle kisses against the column of my throat as he nipped his way to my ear.

"I will never get enough of you, Little Menace," he whispered reverently. "You were made for me. You take my depravity and wear it like a fucking crown... the perfect woman," he hummed.

"You are far too easily impressed, Silas," I chuckled.

Strong fingers gripped my chin and Silas turned my head until I faced him.

"I mean it, Harlowe," he said, his brown eyes searching mine intently.

"I know," I said, reassuring him.

"Then why do you fight me?" I could see the hurt he fought so hard to conceal.

I knew what he was referring to; my reluctance to accept his proposal, the fact that I had never told him I loved him, even though I did.

"Because when I give in to you, I want it to be on my terms. No war looming over the horizon, or the threat of death shadowing our every move. Just you and me," I said, placing a hand over his wildly beating heart.

Silas lifted my palm to his lips and kissed it tenderly. "I can live with that."

"Good, because you're not getting it any other way."

A sharp slap rang out around me, and it took me a moment to register the bite of pain emanating from my ass cheek.

"Silas!" I shouted, jumping out of his lap. "That hurt."

"Good, because that was my intention," he said as he stood to his full height, his lips pulling up into a sinful smirk.

Silas gripped his semi-hard cock and stroked it. "Better run, Little Menace, because I'm not done with you yet."

Silas crouched low, and a yelp tore free of my throat as I turned to run.

My core turned molten in a second.

It seemed like I wasn't done with him either.

# Chapter Thirty-Two

Silas had brought me to a wide, open field covered in lush, green grass that swayed gently with the breeze. The small white and yellow flowers that peeked out from beneath the greenery made the space feel welcoming and serene.

I hoped I didn't destroy its enticing beauty by the end of this training session.

Illiana strode towards me, clutching a small object shrouded in a white cloth.

The Aurora Stone.

"Ready?" she asked as she removed the covering.

The iridescent colors of the stone captured the sunlight, sending flashes of red, green, and violet dancing across its smooth surface.

My gaze flicked upwards, taking in the outline of the palace turrets in the distance.

**"We are far enough away, Fire Heart,"** Misneach said, having sensed my hesitation. **"You have nothing to fear."**

**"We can't be sure though, can we, Misneach? We don't know what kind of power we are about to unleash."**

**"Trust that I will anchor you, Fire Heart. I won't let you draw so much power that you pose a threat to anyone."**

I took a steadying breath and reached for the stone.

As soon as my fingers grazed its smooth exterior, an electrifying surge of energy coursed throughout my body. A tingling sensation started at my fingertips before it intensified into a pulsing wave that raced up my arm. It was a vibrant, almost buzzing warmth, and my heart beat in rhythm with each pulse of the stone.

My breath quickened, and my muscles tensed at the sudden influx of power.

**"Are you all right, Fire Heart?"**

**"I'm fine,"** I said. **"Just a little taken aback is all."**

The pulsing energy continued to ravish my body, clearing my mind and leaving behind an alertness like I had never experienced before. My senses sharpened, colors became more vivid, and the sounds around me became crisper. It was like I was seeing the world for the first time.

It was a heady feeling.

I felt as though I held the power to conquer the entire realm.

**"Easy, Fire Heart,"** Misneach warned.

At Misneach's reminder, I reigned myself in.

The power of the stone was intoxicating, which made it even more dangerous.

**"There,"** Misneach breathed. **"Better?"**

**"Much. Thank you, Misneach."**

**"Always, Fire Heart."**

I turned to glance over my shoulder at where my dragon stood, and he dipped his head in acknowledgment.

"You've unlocked the power of the stone," Illiana said with surprise.

"I did. Although, I thought it would be harder," I mused.

At my words, my palm heated, and a blast of fiery hot flames erupted from my hand.

Illiana and I both dropped to the ground on instinct.

An unstoppable energy surged forward as the explosion of power rushed outward. As the flames roared, the air hummed with an almost tangible vibration, decimating everything in its path. The wave of heat that followed rippled and trembled in its wake, creating a raw, visceral force that could be felt to the very core of my being.

As the embers died and the world settled once more, I tentatively rose to my feet.

I groaned when I saw the scorched earth, and ruined flowers left behind.

When I glanced back over my shoulder, my eyes locked with Misneach's. **"So much for anchoring me, Misneach,"** I chided.

**"Don't look at me like that,"** he growled. **"You're the one who tempted the fates by claiming it was too easy."**

**"I never said it was easy. I said I thought it would be harder,"** I mumbled.

**"And the difference is?"** Misneach asked with an expression that had to be the dragon equivalent of a raised brow.

**"All right! No need to be smug."**

"Did you see that?" Emmerson cheered from behind me.

"I don't think there is a single citizen of Pyrithia who didn't," Cillian responded.

I scrubbed a hand down my face. That was exactly what I had hoped to avoid.

A hand gripped my waist and turned me, tugging me close until I was flush against a hard, muscular chest. My eyes clashed with rich brown ones and I released a shaky breath within the confines of Silas's embrace. Leaning forward, I rested my forehead on his shoulder.

Silas gripped my braid, pulling my head back until our gazes locked once again. He leaned down and placed a tender kiss on my lips.

"I can see your mind working to convince you not to use the stone. That it's too dangerous and you'll do more harm than good," he said.

Sometimes I hated how well he could read me.

"But," he said.

"But?" I pressed.

"The fates chose you for a reason, Harlowe. Your intentions are pure and you hold more strength in your little finger than most men hold in their entire bodies. You can do this," he said, sounding more confident than I felt.

"Now, put your big girl boots on, and get it done," he added with a smirk.

Silas stepped back, a wicked gleam in his eye.

"Silas," I said in warning, but before I could stop him, he darted forward and landed a hard smack on my ass.

The sound of laughter filled my ears, and my cheeks reddened.

"You're a fucking prick," I mumbled.

"Don't make me come back and do it again," he said as he marched back to the others, a swagger in his step as he went.

**"I'm going to burn him alive,"** Misneach snarled.

**"You can't protect her from everything,"** Caolán interjected. **"Besides, I get the impression she rather enjoys his antics."**

**"For the love of the gods, we are not doing this again!"** I growled.

**"Why not?"** Rónán said. **"It's not like we don't already know what you and the General get up to when you're alone."**

**"Males,"** Saoirse snorted. **"They're the same in every species."**

Niamh grumbled in agreement.

**"For once in your life Rónán,"** Oisín said, sounding as exasperated as I felt. **"Do shut up."**

**"It might do you some good to let go of all that self-righteousness for once in *your* life, Oisín,"** Rónán taunted. **"You never know, you may enjoy yourself."**

I blew out a long breath as I worked to clear my mind until only one bond remained.

**"Let's do this, Misneach."**

A rumble of approval was my only answer.

# Chapter Thirty-Three

**"Six against one doesn't seem fair,"** I said, feeling a little uneasy.

**"Please, Fire Heart! You could take all of them blindfolded,"** Misneach said, puffing out his chest.

**"Hardly,"** I scoffed. **"Have you seen the size of you lot?"**

After some initial success wielding the stone with Misneach's help, the dragons, encouraged by Rónán, thought it would be a fantastic idea to test the limits of my control by battling all of them... at once.

To say I was not enthusiastic would be an understatement.

Emmerson, however, was delighted and pushed me to agree for reasons I am sure included her own entertainment.

"Come on, Harlowe!" Zeke hollered. "You've got this."

"If it's so easy, why don't you do it?"

"No fire power, Princess. Besides, you'll look a hell of a lot hotter doing it than I would."

A low growl followed Zeke's teasing.

"Simmer down, Silas," Emmerson chided. "He's only teasing." I could almost hear the roll of her eyes in her tone.

**"Size does not matter in battle, Fire Heart,"** Misneach said, drawing my attention away from my friends. **"The power you possess and the courage to wield it will determine the outcome. And you, Fire Heart, have plenty of both."**

**"All right, all right. I can do this."**

I shook out my hands and reached into my pocket to withdraw the stone.

That same surge of energy crackled across my skin, delving into every corner of my body and eliminating every weakness until only absolute power remained.

I turned in a slow circle, marking every enemy and calling my power forward. The warmth of my flames caressed me like an old lover, as they made their way up my body until I was ablaze.

"Holy shit, look at her eyes," someone called, but I ignored them.

My focus had narrowed to the threats circling me.

**"Eviscerate them, Fire Heart,"** Misneach growled.

**"You realize you are one of *them* in this exercise, right, Misneach?"**

My dragon huffed. **"Not even if my life depended on it. It's you and me, Fire Heart."**

**"Wait, what?"** I asked, confused.

**"Focus!"** Misneach snapped as Niamh lunged towards me.

I skittered back, falling to my back as I sent a blazing inferno in her direction. Scrambling to my feet, I threw up a shield to protect myself.

**"Misneach,"** I hissed.

**"I will never fight against you, Fire Heart. Not even in practice. I will, however, assess your performance, so stay vigilant."**

**"It would have helped if you told me this *before* we started,"** I muttered under my breath.

**"I heard that!"** Misneach scowled.

I didn't have time to respond as Niamh and Saoirse came at me in tandem. Dropping my shield, I spread my arms wide, my fingers splayed as I channeled my power.

The flames emanating from my fingertips were reflected in the dark, serpentine eyes of the dragons opposite me. Their scales shimmered against the fiery backdrop I had created and the sight was so beautiful, I was stuck in a captivating trance as I watched them.

I was pulled from my musings when the dragons opened their maws, showcasing their rows of razor-sharp teeth, and the deep glowing embers making their way up their throats.

Saoirse released her flames first, forcing me to duck and roll over my shoulder into a crouch to avoid being hit. I hurled a blazing orb at her and she deftly deflected it with a beat of her massive wings, sending it flying in the opposite direction.

Niamh used my distraction to her advantage as she crept up on my other side. I caught sight of her just before she unleashed a torrent of flames and I thrust my hands out, creating a massive wall of fire meeting her head-on.

Sweat beaded along my hairline as I stood beneath the fiery wall. On shaky limbs, I raised myself up until I was standing. I searched for Saoirse out of the corner of my eye as the collision of our two burning forces sent sparks flying in all directions.

The dragons could not hold their flames for as long as I could, as I didn't need to hold my breath while wielding them. Eventually, Niamh would relent, and I knew Saoirse would be waiting for me.

When I felt the push of Niamh's flames receding, I dropped my wall of fire and spun to face my new enemy.

It wasn't Saoirse who met me, though.

It was Oisín.

And judging by the grin, if one could call it that, he was looking forward to this.

**"Well, would you look at that,"** Rónán cooed. **"Oisín is smiling. I never thought I would live to see the day."**

**"Oisín,"** Misneach warned.

**"Calm down, Misneach. I would never harm your Cathal. I only seek to guide her in her training,"** Oisín said.

We circled each other and thankfully, the other dragons remained on the sidelines. I had a feeling that I would need every advantage I could get if Oisín was anything like his Cathal.

Oisín lowered himself to the ground, his wings tucked tightly behind him, and I bent my knees, mirroring his stance. We stared at each other for a moment, and then Oisín charged forward. His mouth was open wide, but no sparks or embers were chasing across his tongue to signify he was about to unleash his flames.

I leaped into the air and spun, landing on Oisín's back just as his jaws snapped closed with a deafening crunch.

A furious roar sounded nearby and Misneach pawed at the ground as if preparing to attack, but Caolán stepped in front of him.

**"Fuck, Oisín! I thought you said you wouldn't hurt me."**

**"And I didn't,"** he said simply.

**"You tried to eat me!"** I said incredulously.

**"Have more faith in my control, woman. I was only testing your reflexes, and they are outstanding. Well done! Now, get off my back before I throw you off."**

I slid down Oisín's foreleg, somewhat dazed, as I tried to reconcile how close I came to death.

**"You can't let every near-death experience rattle you,"** Oisín said. **"You must always be ready to continue the battle. Later, you will have time to contemplate what went wrong, but first, you must survive."**

He was right.

Shaking out my limbs, I took my stance and watched as Oisín launched himself into the sky.

I drew my flames around me and moved my hands in rapid succession, creating an enormous swirling inferno I sent sailing through the air towards Oisín, who was circling me from above. Oisín dipped his wings and narrowly avoided the hit before correcting and coming straight for me.

With a roar, I threw up my shield and pushed it out until Oisín collided with the impenetrable force. The intensity of the collision vibrated across my shield, sending shock waves dancing down my arms.

I gritted my teeth and dug my heels into the dirt until Oisín relented, flying backward away from my shield.

My arms trembled as I lowered them, and my breaths were now coming in heaving pants. Sweat coated my entire body, and I didn't know how much longer I could last. While using the stone enhanced my power, it also drained me that much quicker.

There was no time to worry about that now though, as Oisín came hurtling back towards me with Rónán in tow.

**"You didn't think I would miss out on all the fun now, did you?"** Rónán teased, but I didn't have the energy to engage with his banter.

The two dragons parted, taking up positions across from one another as they sought to ensnare me.

An idea popped into my head. One I had never tried before, but I was willing to give it my all.

I closed my eyes as I visualized my weapon of choice.

**"Open your eyes, Fire Heart!"** Misneach ordered, panic lacing his tone. **"They are coming!"**

**"Shh, Misneach, let's see what she can do,"** Caolán said.

When I opened my eyes again, I saw Oisín and Rónán barreling straight for me. With a flick of my wrist, I let my power flow through me until a long tendril of fire shot forward from each palm.

The tendrils snaked through the sky, twisting and turning as they sought their targets. As they reached the dragons, it was too late for them to pull out of their respective dives. My fiery tendrils wrapped around their throats and I pulled them taught.

The dragons thrashed wildly as they fought against my tightening hold, and the strain on my arms was almost too much. I could feel my body weakening as they tugged against my bonds, my feet lifting from the ground as the mighty beasts sought to reclaim their dominance.

But then I felt it.

The grounding force that kept me anchored to the earth beneath my feet.

**"Misneach,"** I breathed.

**"I've got you, Fire Heart,"** he said, although I could feel the strain behind his efforts on my behalf.

With renewed vigor, I yanked on the blazing tendrils as Misneach and I worked together to bring the two dragons down. I lifted my head to the heavens and screamed through the burning in my limbs, and just when I thought I couldn't take it anymore, the tension snapped, and both dragons came careening toward the ground.

"Oh, thank the gods," I muttered to myself as I released my power and bent over, resting my hands on my knees.

Loud cheering and clapping erupted all around, but I could barely hear it through the blood pounding in my ears.

I took large, gulping breaths as I fought to calm my breathing. An enormous figure loomed over me, blocking out the sun and casting my vision in shadows. As I tipped my head up, I saw Oisín looking down at me.

He studied me for a long moment. **"You are worthy, Queen of Fire and Flame,"** he said with conviction.

The ground vibrated beneath me, and a moment later Rónán joined us. **"That was incredible!"** he beamed. **"Let's do it again!"**

The other dragons stepped forward... all of them... and began to circle me.

**"Oh, come on!"** I said, throwing my arms up in the air.

**"We can't risk pushing her too far,"** Misneach snapped.

**"That's why you are here, Misneach,"** Caolán said.

Through the smoke and dying embers now encasing the field, I watched as blue, red, green, grey, and black scales flickered and merged as the dragons surrounded me.

A low growl sounded from the dragon at my back and I whipped around, coming face to face with Saoirse. The obsidian scales on her snout glowed as the churning flames within her prepared to unleash their devastating power.

Another low rumble sounded to my left, and I flicked my gaze to meet

Caolán's sleek, serpentine eyes that glinted with cunning intelligence. His head tilted at an unnatural angle as he assessed me, his gaze calculating and cold as he prepared to strike.

Niamh scraped at the ground, her long, elongated claws tearing chunks of the earth free as she readied herself to charge.

Rónán unfurled his wings, shaking them out and creating small gusts of wind that fanned the embers floating in the heated air, before tucking them against his back.

The harsh smell of burnt shrubbery hit my nostrils in the wake of Rónán's movements, making my eyes water. I scrubbed my forearm over my face to clear my vision and watched as Oisín moved into position.

Caolán roared, a thunderous call to battle, and then they all charged, descending on me in unison. Flames licked at the edges of the dragons' maws as they opened their jaws wide and released columns of destructive flames directly at me.

I dug my heels into the dirt beneath my feet and raised my arms. Adrenaline flooded my veins, and I pulled up my shield, locking it in place just as the first kiss of flames would have reached me.

As the flames collided, the air crackled with power, and sparks flew in every direction. The ground quaked beneath me from the force of the impact and I gritted my teeth to keep myself from giving in to the allure of surrender.

The sound of the combined flames was deafening; a cacophony of raw, elemental fury. I inhaled sharply and forced myself to push back, drawing on the strength Misneach offered me.

With a desperate cry, I summoned every remaining ounce of power within me and released it outward, generating an intense wave of fire that had the dragons recoiling. Not wasting my advantage, I spun in a tight circle as I continued to push the dragons back until they eventually retreated, the last embers of their fire dying on their tongues.

Tremors wracked my entire body, and I was panting heavily as I lowered my shield and recalled my flames.

The dragons studied me with a mixture of awe and admiration before they all lowered to their forelegs, dipping into a bow.

**"Here stands our Queen,"** Caolán called out as he rose from the ground. **"All Hail the Queen of Fire and Flame!"**

**"Long live the Queen!"** the other dragons repeated before turning their heads heavenward and releasing a stream of burning flames.

Pride swelled inside Misneach, and it saturated the bond.

**"They would have killed for you before, Fire Heart, but now, they will die for you,"** Misneach murmured.

# Chapter Thirty-Four

I didn't have a chance to dwell on Misneach's words as someone wrapped their arms around me and lifted me off the ground.

"I can't believe what I just saw, Harlowe!" Emmerson squealed. "You were amazing."

"Yes, well, I can barely hold myself upright now, so be careful when you put me down," I chuckled.

"Oh, right," Emmerson said, as she lowered me to my feet.

My legs faltered under my weight and I almost went to the ground until another set of arms encircled me.

"Easy," Silas said as he guided me to a sitting position.

"Very impressive," Zeke beamed from above me.

"But did you see her eyes?" Fionn asked.

"What about my eyes?"

Fionn's face split into a massive grin. "They were on fire!"

"Doesn't that always happen?" I asked, somewhat confused.

"Not like that," he grinned. "Well, I mean, you catch fire or glow with flames, or, I don't know... whatever you do when you use your powers, but your eyes are still the same."

"And this time they weren't?" I clarified.

"No. Your eyes blazed with flames."

"I'm not sure I follow," I admitted.

"What our articulate friend here is trying to convey," Emmerson teased, "is that you had flames where your eyes should have been. It was quite exciting!"

"I'll have to take your word for it," I shrugged. "It's probably a side effect of the stone."

"Likely," Illiana said, joining the discussion. "You exceeded my expectations, Queen of Fire."

"I aim to please, Illiana," I laughed as I retrieved the stone and handed it to her.

She placed it back in the cloth and stowed it in her skirt. "Arabella," she barked over her shoulder.

"Yes?" the younger woman said tentatively.

"It is time for your training."

Arabella's face paled, yet she still followed Illiana as she led her away from the group.

"That's our cue," Silas said.

"For what?" I asked.

"Training," he smirked.

"I couldn't lift my arms for all the power in the realm right now."

Silas chuckled. "Not you, Little Menace. You rest."

He leaned down and placed a soft kiss on my forehead. My eyes fluttered closed and I let my exhaustion pull me to the ground.

"Good," I mumbled, as I stretched out my arms.

I didn't even hear the first sounds of training before I was asleep.

Darkness surrounded me when I woke.

Rubbing my eyes, I tried to clear my vision but couldn't make anything out beyond the shadows dancing in my periphery.

"How long have I been asleep?" I muttered to myself. "And why didn't anyone wake me?"

"You were not awakened since you remain asleep," a voice from the darkness said, startling me.

A very familiar voice.

"Kieran," I hissed, jumping to my feet.

"Aww, are you not happy to see me, Bride?" he taunted.

"I can't see you now. Where are you?"

Kieran chuckled menacingly, but it sounded like it was coming from all around me instead of a single direction.

The small hairs on the back of my neck stood alert, recognizing the danger stalking me.

"What? You're not afraid to face me, are you?" I said, trying to provoke him into revealing his whereabouts.

"Cute," he chuckled.

Damn it.

I reached for the necklace around my throat and let out a soft sigh when my fingers grazed it. Illiana had given me the talisman to protect me from Kieran within the dreamscape, and right now, I prayed to any god listening that it worked.

"You made a mistake not choosing me," Kieran continued.

He sounded so close.

Spinning in place, I strained to see through the thick shadows surrounding me. My heart was beating wildly as it fought to break free of my chest. Fear and adrenaline flooded my body as I struggled to steady my breathing.

"So you've told me," I said, sounding far stronger than I felt.

"And now you've left me with no choice," Kieran snarled.

"Again, so you've told me."

Taunting Kieran into action was undoubtedly a bad idea. Especially since he could very well kill me, but I had no other plan.

"You would throw your life away for what?" Kieran growled. "A realm undeserving of such a sacrifice. You had the potential to be a queen as powerful as the gods."

"But we're not gods, Kieran," I said. "We're only mortals. Our humanity is what separates us."

"All the same," Kieran replied. "The realm must be held accountable for what it has taken from me."

"What about the things you've taken from others? Are you to answer for your sins?" I challenged.

"Oh, I have no doubt," Kieran chuckled. "But not before I have achieved everything I set out to accomplish."

"Kieran," I said, softening my tone. "None of this will bring your mother back. She is gone. This is not the life she would have imagined for her son. From what you've told me, she loved you very much."

A heavy silence settled around me, and the air grew thick with tension as

I waited for Kieran's response.

But it never came.

"Kieran?" I called out into the darkness.

Only silence greeted me.

"Kieran," I tried again, a sliver of panic seeping into my tone.

What would happen if he abandoned me here? Would I wake up? Would I remain trapped in the dreamscape?

Apprehension gnawed at me from the recesses of my mind, taunting me that not everything here was what it seemed.

I wandered blindly through the darkness, my hands outstretched as I desperately sought a connection to... something... anything... I didn't know what.

As I stumbled through the dreamscape, I *felt* more than heard his approach. A sense of awareness coated me like a second skin, making goosebumps appear on my flesh.

"You should not speak of things you know nothing about," Kieran hissed against my ear.

Before I could turn to face him, a sharp stinging sensation erupted at the base of my spine. The pain was so raw, so intense, I gasped in shock as I sucked in a jagged breath.

Fiery agony spread up my spine and I stumbled forward, landing on my hands and knees. My breathing became labored, and I struggled to draw in breath as the pain overwhelmed me.

"W-what... what did you do?" I gasped as I collapsed onto my elbows.

The pain was so severe, I didn't think I would remain conscious for much longer.

"What I had to," Kieran murmured.

I couldn't get enough air into my lungs. Breathing was too painful, and I lay down on the ground as I succumbed to whatever injury Kieran had inflicted on me.

There was a wet, gurgling sound that accompanied my every inhale.

Was that sound coming from me?

The taste of copper coated the back of my tongue and, to my horror, I realized I was choking on my own blood.

Oh gods, he'd done it. He'd finally done it.

I guess the talisman was useless after all.

I closed my eyes, no longer in any shape to fight the inevitable.

Just as the darkness consumed me, I thought I heard what would be

Kieran's last words to me…
"I'm sorry, Little Bride."

# Chapter Thirty-Five

Screaming rang out around me.

The noise was so loud I instinctively covered my ears to drown it out.

If this was the afterlife, it was truly disappointing.

The screaming continued, and I gritted my teeth against the pain it generated in my skull.

And that was another thing. If I had died, why did I still feel pain?

**"You aren't dead, Fire Heart."**

Whether he was real or the work of my imagination, Misneach's presence brought me comfort in my last moments.

**"For the love of the gods, woman, open your eyes,"** he snapped.

Even if he was rude.

A low growl rumbled from beside me. **"If you do not open your eyes and stop making that gods-forsaken sound, I will pick you up and toss you in the lake!"**

**"Why do you want me to open my eyes? I'm not sure I'm ready to see what my death looks like."**

**"So you will realize you are not, in fact, dead,"** he gritted out.

My eyes snapped open, but all I could see was a blinding white light.

**"I thought you said I wasn't dead."**

**"May the gods have mercy,"** he muttered. **"Perhaps try blinking."**

I opened and closed my eyes in quick succession. With every movement, the world around me grew clearer.

**"Better?"** Misneach asked.

I whipped my head around to face him, and then immediately pulled back.

He was a little closer than I had expected.

**"Have you ever heard of personal space, Misneach?"**

My dragon shook his head, and I flung myself towards him, landing somewhat awkwardly on his snout.

**"I thought I died,"** I confessed.

**"I gathered that from all the screaming,"** he chuckled.

**"The screaming? That was me?"**

**"Indeed it was. It sounded like you were being murdered."**

That's because I was, I thought.

**"You gave everyone quite the fright,"** he added.

My hands flew to the base of my spine where Kieran had struck me.

But there was nothing there.

No gaping wound, no blood, no pain.

"Oh gods," I breathed. "It worked."

"What worked?" Silas asked from behind me.

I slid from Misneach's snout and turned around. My cheeks heated when I saw everyone staring at me. Their expressions varied from terrified, bewildered, and amused.

"The talisman," I said, answering Silas's question. "Illiana just saved my life."

"What happened?" he demanded.

"It was Kieran," I said. "He... stabbed me, I think. It felt so real."

"He fucking stabbed you?" Emmerson shouted, rising to her feet.

"Fuck!" Silas spat. "Are you sure you're all right? Let Arabella look at you."

"I'm fine," I said, waving him off, but Arabella had already moved behind me.

"Where did he stab you, Harlowe?" she asked softly.

"At the base of my spine."

"May I?" she asked, tugging at my tunic. I nodded my head, giving her permission.

Gentle fingers traced over the exact spot where I first felt the searing pain.

"It was only a dream, right?" I asked, growing concerned. When she didn't answer me, I barked, "Arabella."

"Hmm, yes. You should be all right," she said absentmindedly.

"Should be?" Emmerson and Silas said in unison.

"Illiana, can you please look at this?" Arabella said, ignoring them both.

"Look at what? What is it?"

"Just give them a moment," Zeke said, giving me a reassuring smile.

It was hard to settle, though, with Silas wearing a path into the dirt beside me.

"How odd," Illiana mumbled.

"Someone better tell me what the hell you're looking at!" I snapped.

"It's some kind of marking," Illiana mused. "Mostly indistinguishable. If I had to guess, I'd say it was a shadow."

Icy fear slid up my spine, and I shivered.

"Tell me what happened inside the dreamscape," Illiana demanded.

"I... I woke up surrounded by darkness. I thought I had woken in the field only hours later."

My tongue darted out to wet my lips as my brain worked to piece it all together.

"Then Kieran spoke, and I knew I was dreaming."

Silas growled again as he continued pacing.

"He told me I made a mistake not choosing him. We argued and then I..." I trailed off.

I couldn't explain why, but I didn't want to reveal what happened to Kieran's mother. It felt too raw, too personal, too... intimate.

"I made some comments about his mother. He did not take kindly to that, and that's when he stabbed me."

The agony I had felt at that moment was something I wouldn't forget soon.

"The pain was so intense that I fell to the ground, and that was when I realized I was dying. I started to choke on my blood and then... then I passed out or woke up. I'm not sure."

"Hmm," Illiana hummed.

"Hmm? What does hmm mean?" I pressed.

"It means I don't know," Illiana said as she rose from her spot behind me.

"But you always have the answers," I spluttered.

"If only child. Whatever that mark is," she said, pointing at my back. "I am certain of one thing."

"Which is?"

"The fates aren't done with you yet."

I struggled to shed my unease in the days that followed my encounter with Kieran in the dreamscape. Not knowing what the new marking meant wasn't making it any easier.

"I think we should keep moving... continue building our allies," I said as I traced idle circles over Silas's muscular chest. "Kieran doesn't know that he failed to kill me so we have a window of opportunity to make our moves undetected."

Until he found out, at least.

"Maxim is satisfied with the progress our troops are making and our stockpiles are almost complete," Silas responded. "I need a few more days to ensure everything is in place in Pyrithia before I can leave again."

Guilt gnawed at my chest. Silas was a king now. He had duties here, and I was keeping him from his obligations.

"Silas," I said cautiously.

"Yes, Little Menace."

"Maybe you should stay here, in Pyrithia."

Silas growled as he sat upright to look at me.

"Just long enough to solidify your rule. You've barely been here since you took the crown. Your people need you more than I do right now."

"Harlowe," he said, the single word a warning.

"I don't mean forever, Silas. Just a couple of weeks at most. Your people need to know that you will do whatever it takes to protect them and your kingdom. They're not stupid. They know something is coming."

Silas gripped my chin and angled my face so I could not escape the intensity of his penetrating gaze. "Listen to me very carefully, Little Menace," Silas said in a low, deadly voice.

It was the tone of voice that had my nipples puckering and my core clenching.

"I would surrender the crown, and this kingdom tomorrow, if it meant I would never have to spend a single moment without you. There is no title, no treasure, nor land that could ever come close to taking your place. You are my home and wherever you go, I will follow. If I have to set the heavens ablaze and watch the stars fall to keep you safe, and by my side, then I'd do it without hesitation. There is no force in this life or the next that could keep me from you. So, no, I will not stay behind. My place is at your side, and that is where I will be."

Tears pricked the back of my eyes as I studied him. There was no doubt in my mind that he meant it. Silas was never careless with his words. Every choice was deliberate and saturated with intent.

"All right, Silas," I said with a ragged exhale. "We'll wait."

His gaze raked over me once more before he leaned in and placed a gentle kiss on my lips.

"Now that's settled," he said, pulling away. "Where are we headed next?"

I took a deep breath. I had been thinking about this a lot over the preceding days. We needed to approach Elysara and the unbonded dragons, but there was one more place I had to go before finalizing our plans.

Exhaling, I said, "It's time for me to go home."

# Chapter Thirty-Six

Nerves raced throughout my body the closer we came to Valoren. Sweat coated my palms, making it difficult to hold my place on Misneach's back. The slight tremor coursing through my fingers didn't help, either.

**"What is it that has you so concerned, Fire Heart?"** Misneach asked.

**"They sold me to Kieran like chattel, Misneach."**

The thought sprang free before I could stop it. I could not deny that even after everything I had experienced, everything I had endured, this was the one thing that still hurt me the most.

**"You and I both know that's not the entire truth, Fire Heart,"** Misneach said.

**"I know,"** I sighed. **"Sometimes it is easier to hold on to the pain than examine the reasoning behind their decisions, no matter how flawed."**

**"Are you forgetting your mother aided your escape, Fire Heart?"** Misneach pointed out.

I let out another long sigh. **"I know. I am being unfair."**

The beat of Misneach's wings against the faint hum of the wind helped settle my mind and clear my thoughts.

**"It is all right to be upset about the choices they made, Fire Heart. Just don't let that color your judgment."**

**"When did you get so wise, Misneach?"** I joked.

**"I've always been wise, Fire Heart. You simply refuse to heed my counsel."**

I snorted. **"When have I ever ignored your advice, Misneach?"**

**"When I told you to keep the General at arm's length,"** he said knowingly.

My cheeks heated, and I shifted in my seat.

**"Exactly!"**

**"It worked out all right in the end,"** I mumbled.

**"We'll see."**

We settled into a companionable silence as Misneach cut through the clouds with each masterful stroke of his colossal wings. The rhythmic beating was a balm to my nervous energy, and I got lost in the magnificent display of strength and grace.

"Prepare to descend," Silas called out.

**"Well, this is it,"** I said, steeling myself against my warring emotions.

**"Everything will work out as it should, Fire Heart."**

The turrets were the first glimpse I got of the palace. The place I had called home for twenty-five years.

My heart pounded like a drum inside my chest the closer we came. Masses of people scurried about below us, trying to get out of the way of the impending arrivals.

Misneach landed with a *thud* and shook out his massive wings. Onlookers stared open-mouthed, still not accustomed to the majestic creatures that had long been feared within the lands of Valoren.

I slid from Misneach's back and made my way toward the stairs leading into the palace. Emmerson and Zeke flanked me, and I was grateful for their support.

"We've got you," Emmerson whispered as she took my hand.

"It's going to be all right, Harlowe," Zeke added.

As I climbed the steps, my father appeared at the threshold of the entryway.

"Harlowe," he breathed.

When I reached the top, I paused, leaving a few paces between us.

My father's gaze darted behind me. "Ah, General," he said, having spotted Silas. "I see you have returned my daughter to me."

Silas moved around me until he was standing in front of my father. He peered over his shoulder at me with a sexy-as-sin smirk gracing his lips. Turning back to face my father, he crossed his corded arms over his chest.

"Not exactly," he said.

My father's eyebrows narrowed in confusion, but before he could say anything further, a choked sob sounded from behind the wall of soldiers standing at my father's back.

"Harlowe," my mother cried as she pushed her way through the throng of bodies.

When our eyes locked, she pulled herself up short, her delicate hand fluttering to the base of her throat. Tears filled her eyes and she let out a guttural noise as she rushed toward me.

And just like that, all of my pain, fears, and hurt dissolved, as though they had never existed to begin with.

Her arms wrapped around me in a tight hug, and I held onto her just as fiercely. My mother buried her face in my hair, sobbing uncontrollably.

"I was so worried," she blubbered. "I had no idea where you were or if you were safe."

I rubbed my hands up and down her back to soothe her.

"I'm all right Mother," I said. "I made it home."

She continued to hold me as though she feared I would disappear if she let me go.

My father cleared his throat and said, "Perhaps we should take this to my study."

Reluctantly, my mother let her arms fall to her sides. When her sky-blue eyes met mine again, she smiled and laughed before pulling me back in for another quick hug.

"Come," she said, taking my hand in hers. "I want to hear everything that has happened since we last spoke."

I glanced over my shoulder to ensure Emmerson, Zeke, and Silas had followed, but there was no need. They were all there.

When we reached my father's study, he pushed open the heavy wooden door and stepped inside. My mother followed, pulling me along with her.

Inside the room, Samuel stood hunched over my father's desk, examining a piece of parchment. At our arrival, he raised his head, taking us all in. His eyes darted behind me and from the sheer relief I saw cross his face, I knew exactly who he had seen.

"Emmerson," he whispered, straightening to his full height.

"Father," she replied, sounding hoarse.

"By the gods, you're here," he said, disbelief clear in his tone. "You're really here."

Samuel raced around the edge of my father's desk and barreled towards his daughter. When he was within arm's reach, he scooped her up and pulled her against his chest, murmuring something only she could hear. Emmerson nodded her head and the tension he had been holding in his shoulders faded.

Samuel placed Emmerson back on her feet and held her at arm's length. "Let me look at you."

His gaze raked over her body, checking to make sure she was unharmed, no doubt.

"Father, I'm fine," she laughed.

"I'll be the judge of that," he grumbled.

Apparently satisfied with his assessment, he pulled her back against his chest, tucking her head under his chin just like he had done when we were children.

"Gods, I missed you," he said.

"I missed you too, Father," Emmerson replied.

As if remembering they had an audience, Samuel released his daughter and cleared his throat.

"Harlowe, are you well?" he asked.

"I am," I answered with a wide smile. "In no small part, that is thanks to Emmerson."

"Please, you should see the tricks this one has learned since we've been gone. You'd be proud, Father," Emmerson scoffed.

Heat scorched my cheeks at her praise.

"I have no doubt," he said in earnest.

Emmerson shifted from her father's side and came to stand next to Cillian. Samuel's eyes narrowed at their closeness.

"And who is this young man?" he asked, as he crossed his arms over his chest.

A wicked gleam entered Emmerson's eyes as she curled into Cillian's side, placing a hand over his chest. "This is Cillian. You met him at Harlowe's ball, remember?"

"Perhaps you should introduce us again."

Samuel's narrowed gaze appraised Cillian, and the stoic Cathal swallowed roughly.

"He is one of the Cathal from Pyrithia. He is Silas's second-in-command. Or is it Captain of the King's guard now?" she asked innocently.

"What?" my father barked.

Silas stepped forward. "My father is no longer with us," he said solemnly. "Nor is my brother, August," he added, wincing. "I am now the ruling monarch of Pyrithia."

My parents gasped.

"You're Leith's son?" my father asked at the same time my mother said, "What happened?"

"It is a story for another time. We have come with more pressing concerns," Silas deflected.

"Before we move on," Samuel said, his gaze flicking back to Emmerson. "Who is Cillian to you, Emmerson?"

Cillian's throat bobbed, and I had to admit, I was enjoying his discomfort more than I should.

Zeke snickered behind me, echoing my thoughts.

"He is my betrothed," Emmerson said, as she fluttered her eyelashes. Mischief sparkled in her eyes and I got the distinct impression she was enjoying Cillian's discomfort just as much as the rest of us.

"What did you say?" Samuel asked in a low tone, stepping closer to the pair.

"My betrothed," she repeated.

Out of the corner of my eye, I saw Silas biting his lower lip as if to stifle a laugh.

Cillian shifted uncomfortably, his hand reaching around his head as he gripped the back of his neck.

"I, ah, well," Cillian stuttered.

"You, ah, well, what?" Samuel demanded.

When Cillian opened and closed his mouth a few times with no words coming out, Emmerson took pity on him. "I am only kidding, Father," she chuckled. "He wishes he was that lucky."

Cillian let out a nervous laugh and Samuel scowled at him.

"But you are spending time together, are you not?"

"Something like that," Emmerson purred. The color drained from Cillian's face as he went as still as a statue.

"You and I," — Samuel said, pointing a finger between him and Cillian — "will have words."

Cillian nodded his head but said nothing.

"So back to the matter at hand," my father said, failing to hide his amusement. "Will someone tell me what the hell is going on?"

# Chapter Thirty-Seven

We all took a seat, and I laid out everything that had occurred since I left Valoren.

"That's a lot to take in," my mother said as she released a shaky breath.

Her eyes pivoted to me and she studied me as if she was seeing me for the first time. "A fire wielder," she said in disbelief. "And multiple dragon bonds."

**"One dragon bond,"** Misneach interjected. **"The others only share a connection, not a bond."**

I ignored the interruption and gave a curt nod, uncomfortable with all the attention trained on me.

"You should see her," Zeke said. "She's incredible."

My mother's face split into a wide grin. "Oh, I can imagine."

My father cleared his throat as his gaze settled on me. I could see the guilt etched into his features, and my heart squeezed painfully in response.

"Kieran really tried to kill you?" he whispered.

"He did," I confirmed, and Silas growled next to me. I placed a hand on his knee to calm him and he took it in his.

My parents' gazes zeroed in on the movement, but they said nothing.

"Harlowe," my father said hesitantly, his gaze flicking around the room. "I owe you an apology."

I straightened in my seat as I waited for his next words.

"We both do," my mother added, taking his hand, and my father gave her a grateful smile.

"I thought I was doing what was best for our kingdom. I did not know Kieran had set the whole thing up." My father swallowed thickly.

"I should have listened to you when you came to me after he..." he trailed off, unable to finish his sentence.

Rising from my seat, I moved towards my father, who stood at my approach. "I forgive you," I said before hugging him.

"I love you, Harlowe. And I am so proud of you," he said so only I could hear.

"I love you too, Father."

My father trembled in my embrace and I squeezed him tighter. When he had composed himself, he stepped back and looked down at me.

"You met the fates?" he asked, wonder coloring his tone.

"I did. They were... interesting," I replied, unsure how to describe my brief encounter with the women.

"Amazing," he hummed. "Well, I, for one, would like to see this power of yours."

When I groaned, the room broke out with quiet laughter.

I left the study with my parents at my side and the rest of our group trailing close behind us. When we reached the entryway to the palace, my mother gasped at the sight before her.

At the bottom of the stairs leading into the palace, the dragons lined up on either side, creating a small pathway. At our approach, they lowered themselves into a bow.

"Ignore them. They can be rather dramatic when they feel like it," I mumbled.

**"They are not being dramatic, Fire Heart. They are showing you the respect you deserve,"** Misneach chastised.

I hunched my shoulders, feeling appropriately admonished. **"Sorry. It still feels strange to me. That's all."**

**"Well then, I suggest you get used to it,"** Misneach retorted.

**"Helpful,"** I drawled.

**"You're welcome, Fire Heart."**

I resisted the urge to roll my eyes. That would only encourage him.

Once we had reached the courtyard in front of the palace, the dragons lifted to their full height. There was a smattering of gasps and shuffling feet as the onlookers took a step back.

I understood their reactions. They could be intimidating if you were not used to their presence.

**"As it should be,"** Saoirse snorted.

**"Play nice, Saoirse. These are my people, and one day, I will be their queen."**

She lifted her shoulder in a shrug before spreading her wings wide and shaking them out. The movement created a small windstorm, picking up dirt and debris, and spreading it around until everyone had to cover their mouths to avoid choking.

**"Show off,"** I grumbled, and she grinned, displaying rows of razor-sharp teeth that had my people retreating further.

Caolán chuckled. **"Our Little One is right. There is no need to scare the poor people."**

**"There is always a need,"** Saoirse countered.

Caolán huffed out a breath and gave me an exasperated look.

As I stepped away from my mother, I said, "I need you all to move back and give me some space to work."

Everyone moved away, creating a wide circle around me.

I took a deep breath to steady myself.

Closing my eyes, I pulled my flames to me. The familiar warmth spread throughout my body, leaving no corner untouched.

A ripple of gasps followed, and I didn't need to open my eyes to know that my entire body was ablaze.

I pushed outward and extended my shield until a small ring of flames surrounded me.

"Incredible," my mother murmured. "And it's stronger than fórsa?"

"It is," Zeke confirmed. "Emmerson made me train with Harlowe and it was certainly an experience."

My mother chuckled, and I opened my eyes. "Did you forget you outrank her?"

"Have you ever tried to argue against Emmerson?" Zeke asked with a raised brow.

"Good point," my mother laughed.

She took a tentative step towards me, and then another until she was standing in front of me.

"Stop!" I shouted when she tried to touch my shield, and she flinched back.

"Sorry," I winced. "If you touch it, you will injure yourself."

"Don't we know it?" Emmerson said to Cillian with a knowing smile. He grumbled something indistinguishable, and I laughed.

"Do you trust me?" I asked, returning my attention to my mother.

"Yes," she said without hesitation.

"Stay still and let me bring you inside my shield."

My mother nodded her head, and I forced my shield further out until it encompassed her. Once inside my shield, she gasped again, her mouth wide as she took it all in.

"This is something else," she said.

"You can touch it now."

With trembling fingers, my mother raised her hand to the fiery dome. When no burning pain met her, she returned her gaze to mine.

"You, Daughter, are magnificent. You will change the course of our future and I couldn't be more proud to call you mine."

Tears pricked my eyes as I smiled at her. I dropped my shield and pulled her into another tight hug.

"I echo the sentiment," my father said as he stepped up beside us. He leaned down and placed a soft kiss on my head.

My eyes darted around me until they locked with dark brown ones. Silas was beaming. He tilted his head in acknowledgment and I smiled back at him.

"I have something to say," my father called out and everyone gathered around fell silent.

"You have all seen what my daughter can do," he said as he peered down at me, pride shining in his eyes.

"She is powerful, she is steadfast, and the fates themselves have chosen her to lead our people. Valoren has been truly blessed by the gods."

Cheers erupted at his words, and I straightened my spine, feeling the weight of them.

My father reached for the small circlet that sat atop his head and I inhaled a sharp breath. When he settled it in my hair, he lowered himself to one knee.

A moment later, everyone else followed.

I spun in a tight circle, trying to convince myself this wasn't happening. But then I caught Silas's eye. He stared at me for a long moment before giving me an encouraging nod.

That slight gesture was enough to calm my wildly beating heart.

When I looked back at my parents, all I saw was unyielding love and a promise that they would stand at my side, no matter what lay ahead.

I swallowed thickly and then nodded.

"May your light guide you, and your courage shield you, Queen Harlowe of Valoren."

My father's words echoed around me before another chorus of cheers sounded.

My gaze darted back to where the dragons stood, tall and proud. When our eyes met, they dipped their chins in acknowledgment.

**"We are with you, Queen of Fire and Flame."**

# Chapter Thirty-Eight

My father insisted on an impromptu celebration following my very unorthodox coronation, and despite being given little notice, the kitchens prepared an impressive feast.

There was also drinking, dancing, and entertainment, but what caught and held my attention was the intense discussion between Samuel and Cillian.

Oh, to be a fly on that wall.

I had no doubt Emmerson was enjoying herself immensely.

"You look tired. Do you want to call it a night?" Silas asked when I yawned for what had to be the dozenth time.

"Yes," I groaned.

After saying goodnight to my parents, Silas and I made a quick exit from the ballroom and headed towards my chambers.

"How does it feel to be queen?" he asked.

"Strange, and yet… not," I mused.

"Very precise, Little Menace," he chuckled.

"I have been preparing for this moment all my life and now that it is here, it feels… I don't know exactly… premature."

Silas nodded his head in understanding. "I can relate somewhat, as I never intended to wear the crown."

"Thank you for being here, Silas."

"I wouldn't be anywhere else," he said, taking my hand and pulling me to him.

By the time we made it to my chambers, I was so exhausted, I fell onto the bed and lay there unmoving.

"The idea is to get under the covers, Little Menace."

"Too tired," I said although, my pillow muffled my words.

Silas tugged on my boot, and I raised my head to watch as he removed them. Next, he pulled off my pants before he made me roll onto my back so he could remove my tunic.

Left only in my undergarments, Silas meandered over to my dresser and withdrew a pale blue nightdress.

"Arms up," he commanded, and I complied.

Once dressed for bed, Silas pulled the covers back and tucked me in before removing his own clothing.

I drew my bottom lip into my mouth as I watched him.

"Don't look at me like that, Little Menace," he said, tossing his tunic to the ground. "You are far too exhausted for the things that look awakens."

"What things?" I asked huskily.

Silas growled. "Things that would keep you up all night."

I pouted, and Silas chuckled darkly. "You are very tempting when you sulk, Little Menace."

"Not tempting enough," I grumbled.

Silas slipped into bed behind me and pulled me flush against his muscled chest.

"Sleep, Little Menace. Tomorrow we can play."

With the promise of pleasure on the horizon, I drifted off to sleep cocooned in Silas's warm embrace.

A mixture of scents bombarded my senses, some sweet, and some a little spicy. Distinct floral aromas danced with fruity, citrus undertones, while the occasional hint of something crisp, almost sour floated on the breeze.

As I sat up and looked around, I noticed the feel of the soft grass beneath my palms.

I was sitting in the most beautiful garden I had ever seen, bursting with life and vibrant colors.

Inhaling deeply, I let the various scents fill my lungs, and I exhaled a contended sigh.

"Little Menace?" a deep, masculine voice rumbled.

I glanced around and saw Silas perched on a bench nestled within the flowerbed. He wore the same sleep pants he had gone to bed in.

Looking down, I noticed I was wearing the same nightdress I had fallen asleep in.

"Where are we?" I asked, looking around.

"This is my mother's garden."

"How are we here?"

"I have no idea. I'm pretty sure I was dreaming and then you just... showed up."

My brows furrowed in confusion.

"Maybe I dreamed you into existence," he said, wiggling his eyebrows at me.

"Well, now that you have," I purred, "what do you plan to do with me?"

"Oh, Little Menace, a great many things," he growled as he stood from the bench.

Silas prowled towards me, every inch the predator getting ready to claim his prey.

When he reached me, he lowered himself over my body, his corded forearms caging me in as he rested his elbows on either side of my head.

"Do you feel what you do to me, Little Menace?" he asked, grinding his hard length against my center.

A moan slipped free, and Silas groaned.

"Even in my dreams, there is no escape from the incessant need I have for you."

Silas nipped the pulse point at the base of my throat before sucking it into his mouth. When he released it, he began kissing his way toward my breasts, licking and biting as he went.

His mouth settled over the material covering my breast, and he sucked on my puckered nipple. Without breaking contact, he reached up and pulled down the strap of my nightdress, exposing my breast to his warm mouth.

Silas bit down on the swollen flesh, and I arched my back off the ground, pushing myself further into his touch.

"You like it when I mark you, don't you, Little Menace," Silas taunted. He reached his other hand up to pull the remaining strap down and freed my other breast.

"You know I do," I breathed.

"Good," he rumbled as he bit down again.

The pain mixed with pleasure, and I rubbed my thighs together to ease the mounting tension.

Silas's rough hands gripped my knees, and he wrenched them apart.

"I'm the only one who will pleasure you, Little Menace," he growled. "So if there is something you need, ask for it."

"Silas, please," I begged.

"Please what, Little Menace?"

"Please make me come," I panted.

"See, that wasn't so hard now, was it?"

Silas settled between my thighs, his nose pressed to my core as he inhaled deeply.

"I love the smell of you, Little Menace," he rumbled.

I was too far gone to be embarrassed by his actions.

Silas curled a finger around the edge of my panties and tore them from my body. I jerked at the movement and my heartbeat thrummed madly.

Why was that so hot?

"You're fucking soaked," Silas groaned, as if he were in pain.

Before I could say anything, Silas dipped his head. His tongue found my entrance as he licked the length of me.

A violent tremor wracked my body and pleasure sparked along my spine.

"Oh gods," I moaned.

"No, Little Menace. Not the gods, me. Now say my name," Silas demanded.

"Silas," I panted.

He made a sound of approval before pressing his tongue flat against my core once again. Silas licked and sucked, nipped, and nibbled until I couldn't take it anymore.

"Not yet, Little Menace," he said as he withdrew his tongue.

"Fuck. Silas," I growled, and wicked laughter filled my ears.

"Not yet," he repeated.

Silas used his tongue to bring me to the brink repeatedly, only to deny me each time.

"Silas please," I pleaded. "I can't take it anymore."

"No?" he asked, the cocky tone of his voice making me wild with... something... anger, arousal. I didn't know anymore.

"Beg for it," he commanded.

"I've been begging," I barked in frustration.

"Then it should be easy for you. Tell me how much you need me. Tell me how much you want me to make you come."

"I need you, Silas," I said, the sound so desperate I barely recognized my own voice. "I need you to make me come. Please."

Silas snarled. The noise sounded feral and unhinged.

Then he pushed two fingers inside me, pumping in and out of my drenched core as his tongue lapped at my bundle of nerves, setting me ablaze. When he curled his fingers, pressing against that spot deep within me, I exploded.

My vision blurred, and I cried out, Silas's name falling from my lips like a prayer.

I whispered incoherent words of adoration while Silas continued to thrust into me as I rode out the wave of pleasure.

When I came down from my high, I was a panting, sweating mess.

Silas climbed up my body, capturing my mouth in a bruising kiss. He parted my lips, forcing his way inside as our tongues battled for dominance.

"Do you taste yourself on my tongue?"

"Yes," I said with a shuttered breath.

"You are so fucking beautiful when you come apart under my touch," he said with a hint of desperation in his voice. "Now it's my turn."

Silas took both of my hands in one of his and held them above my head. With his other hand, he reached into his pants and freed his cock.

A bead of moisture glistened on the tip as he stroked himself. I watched with rapt attention as he grew impossibly hard, the thick vein on the underside of his cock throbbing wildly.

"Let me touch you," I pleaded.

"You'd like that, wouldn't you, Little Menace?"

I nodded my head.

"Well, unfortunately for you, you're going to watch as I make myself come all over these gorgeous tits of yours," he snarled.

Silas pumped his length harder, his breathing becoming labored as he did so.

"I'm going to smear my come all over you," he gritted out. "I'm going to make a mess of your perfect porcelain skin."

His movements became jerky as he gripped his cock with vigor.

"I am going to ruin you, Little Menace, because you belong to me, and only me."

Hot ropes of come landed on my chest as Silas continued to stroke himself above me. He didn't stop until he had drained every drop from his softening cock. Once he was satisfied, he reached down and smeared his come across my breasts, my chest, and my throat, just as he had promised.

"There," he said, masculine pride pouring out of him in waves. Silas settled his large palm against the base of my throat and lowered his head until our lips were almost touching.

"I'll claim you time and time again, Harlowe," he breathed. "Because there is nothing in this realm that will keep me from taking what's mine."

Then he crashed his lips against mine, sealing his vow.

# Chapter Thirty-Nine

I woke with a start, my body covered in sweat and my chest heaving as I tried to settle my breathing.

Next to me, Silas fared no better.

"Harlowe, are you all right?"

"Yes, I..." My hand flew to the base of my neck, where my pulse hammered wildly. "I had a strange dream."

"Me too," he groaned as he adjusted himself.

An uneasy feeling washed over me.

"Silas?" I asked tentatively. "What was your dream about?"

He threw me a mischievous grin. "You were in it. It was very, *very* hot."

My core turned molten at the memory. It absolutely was.

"Did this dream take place in your mother's garden, by any chance?" I asked.

Silas stiffened before turning his whole body to face me. "How did you know that?"

"I think we had the same dream," I said quietly.

"How would that even be possible?"

"I don't know, but I think we should speak with Illiana."

Without waiting for his agreement, I rose from the bed and started for the door.

"Little Menace," Silas barked.

"Yes," I said impatiently, as my hand hovered over the door handle.

"Are you planning to go out wearing that?" he asked, scrubbing a hand down his face.

My gaze dipped to my nightdress, and I shivered. "No, I don't think I will."

Silas reached me a moment later and wrapped a satin nightgown around my shoulders.

When I assessed the thin cotton sleeping pants he was wearing, I raised a brow. "Are *you* planning to go out wearing that?"

His eyes flicked to his pants. "What's wrong with my pants?" he asked.

"Nothing. But what about the rest of you?" I said, gesturing to his bare chest.

A slow grin spread across his lips. "Are you concerned someone will see my naked chest, Little Menace?"

"Concerned isn't the word I would use. I'm more questioning if it's appropriate," I muttered.

"I practice without my tunic all the time," he challenged.

My cheeks grew warm, and I averted my gaze.

Silas barked out a laugh. "Are you perhaps jealous, Little Menace?"

"Just put your damn tunic on," I hissed.

Silas chuckled, but did as I asked.

"I quite like how jealousy looks on you, Little Menace," he said as we made our way down the hall towards the guest chambers. "It brings out the pink in your cheeks."

"Fuck off, Silas," I growled, pushing him away from me.

"You wound me, Little Menace," he retorted, clutching his heart.

"I will if you don't knock it off," I ground out.

"Fine, fine," he said, lifting his hands in surrender. "I meant what I said, though."

"About what?"

"That jealousy looks good on you. I like it when you stake your claim," he growled as he pulled me in for a quick kiss.

I couldn't help but laugh. Of course that would please him.

When we arrived at Illiana's door, I knocked lightly, and a low whine greeted me.

"She brought the dire wolves inside?" Silas asked incredulously.

I shrugged. "Where else was she supposed to house them?"

"Literally anywhere else," he muttered.

"Are you, perhaps, scared of the dire wolves, Silas?" I purred.

Silas stiffened. "Of course not."

"Ah-huh."

An irritated Illiana interrupted our banter when she ripped the door open. "Is there a reason you are disturbing my sleep at this ungodly hour of the morning?" she snapped.

"It's important, I promise," I said as I fought to contain my smile. "Can we come in?"

"By all means," she grumbled.

Once I crossed the threshold, all five dire wolves bounded over to me. Their wet tongues lapped at my palms as they vied for my attention. They gave Silas a cursory glance and then ignored his presence altogether.

"Well?" Illiana demanded, as she crossed her arms over her chest.

"Right," I said, extracting myself from the wolves. "I think I may have dream-walked with Silas tonight."

Illiana's eyes widened. "Why do you think that?"

"We shared a dream and then woke up together as soon as it ended," I answered.

"What was the dream about?" she asked.

I averted my gaze, and Silas grinned.

"Forget I asked," Illiana mumbled. "And you're sure it was the same dream?"

"Yes. It took place in Silas's mother's garden and I've never even seen it before."

Illiana hummed. "Turn around," she commanded. "Let me see your back."

I did as she instructed and she lifted the hem of my nightdress.

"Cute panties," she remarked, and Silas tried to stifle a laugh.

"Shut up," I hissed at him.

"The mark is darker," she said, as if she was speaking to herself.

The base of my spine tingled in response to Illiana's scrutiny.

"I guess that solves that mystery," she mused.

"Care to enlighten the rest of us?" Silas asked.

"The mark on her back," Illiana said as she lowered my nightdress. "It symbolizes the transition of power."

"What power?" Silas and I asked in unison.

"The power to enter the dreamscape. I don't know how, but whatever happened in your last encounter with the King of Snakes, he inadvertently transferred some of his power to you."

"How is that even possible?" I asked.

"Didn't I just say I don't know the specifics?" Illiana said with a raised brow. "Although it likely had something to do with the talisman I gave you."

My hand moved to the chain wrapped around my throat.

"The talisman prevented any harm inflicted by the Serpent King in the dreamscape from crossing over into the waking world. But it seems it may have taken something from him in return."

"So what does it all mean? Can Kieran no longer enter the dreamscape?" I asked.

"I'm not sure," Illiana sighed. "He may have gifted you that power, or he may have simply shared it with you. It's impossible to know which."

The room fell silent as we all contemplated this new development.

"However," Illiana said, her brown eyes flicking over me in assessment.

"However?" Silas pressed.

"We may be able to use this to our advantage."

"How so?" Silas asked as he crossed his corded arms over his broad chest. The General in him had taken over.

"Perhaps the Queen of Fire could use this newfound talent to spy on the Serpent King," she answered.

"Would it be dangerous?" Silas asked. "What if he discovered her?"

"So long as she continued to wear the talisman, she'd be safe," Illiana said. "Well, as safe as she has been until this point."

"What does that mean?" Silas demanded.

"We can't prevent the Serpent King from harming her inside the dreamscape." Illiana's gaze flicked to me and regret flashed across her features before she blinked it away. "We can only ensure that whatever harm he may inflict dissolves once she wakes."

The thought of enduring my death again at Kieran's hands did not sit well with me. The agony had been all too real.

Silas closed the distance between us, and he rubbed his large, calloused hands up and down my arms.

"This is your decision, Harlowe. You're not obligated to do anything you don't want to. Just say the word and this goes no further."

I studied Silas's dark brown eyes, which held so much emotion. His fear for me was evident, but he wouldn't stop me.

That thought settled my nerves.

Taking a deep breath, I let the cool night air fill my lungs, clearing my mind. "I'll do it."

# Chapter Forty

The following morning, I sat with my parents to discuss preparations for the inevitable war that was headed our way.

"Silas has already made arrangements for Pyrithia to ready their forces, and they have stockpiled weaponry and other resources," I informed them. "We need to do the same here."

"We have always had a strong contingent of soldiers and with the reintroduction of the Cathal to our ranks, we'll be ready to march whenever you are," my father said.

"How are they progressing?" Silas asked.

"Very well," my father said. "You are a very capable instructor."

Silas dipped his chin, acknowledging the praise.

"Did the remaining soldiers ever travel to the Mountains of Dragonia?" he asked.

"No," my father said sheepishly. "After Harlowe disappeared, I diverted our resources."

"Ah," was all Silas said in response.

"So," I said, redirecting the conversation. "We have the support of Valoren and Pyrithia. The next step in our plan is to make a personal appeal to Elysara."

"Elysara?" my father asked.

"Yes," Silas answered. "They are some of the most capable warriors in the realm."

"This is true," my mother added. "Yet, they have always remained neutral in past conflicts."

"We haven't faced a threat like Kieran before though either," Silas said, echoing his words from months prior.

"It might work," my mother mumbled.

"Is there anyone we should appeal to?" I asked, hoping her connections to Elysara may prove useful.

"Prince Caspan. He has long been an advocate for reform. He believes in the sanctity of the safe haven Elysara offers. However, he also thinks the kingdom has a wider responsibility to the realm."

"That's very helpful," Silas mused. "Thank you, Your Majesty."

"Something tells me we can drop the formalities," she said with a knowing smile.

"Ah yes, about that," my father said and my stomach clenched.

"I was curious as to the nature of your, ah... relationship with my daughter," he said, directing his question towards Silas.

A wicked grin curved the corner of Silas's mouth. "You may need to ask your daughter that."

My father turned his gaze to me expectantly.

"Well, we haven't really defined it," I said.

My mouth felt dry all of a sudden. I did not want to have this conversation with my parents.

What was there to say? I love riding his cock and I'm almost certain I am in love with him, but I'm too afraid to say it out loud.

**"That could work,"** Misneach chuckled.

**"Thank you, Misneach, for that sage advice,"** I drawled.

**"You are most welcome, Fire Heart."**

"You are courting, yes?" my father pressed.

"Something like that," I mumbled.

"Can we expect a betrothal soon?"

By the gods. Would the ground just open up and swallow me?

Silas had already started calling me his wife, and this would only encourage him further.

My gaze darted to the man in question. He was the picture of self-assured as he reclined leisurely in his chair, his arm hanging over the backrest and a satisfied smirk pulling up his kissable lips as he watched me flounder.

"We have been busy focusing on the impending war, Father. We have had little time to discuss it."

My gaze returned to Silas, and he lifted a brow in challenge.

"Of course," my father said. "But it is on your mind, right?"

I blew out a breath. What was even happening here?

"I think the timing may be a little off, my love," my mother said, saving me from further scrutiny.

"All right," he grumbled. "I only wanted to ensure she was happy."

"I am Father," I said brightly, and leaned over to squeeze his hand.

Awareness prickled along my neck, and I knew Silas was looking at me. When my eyes met his, there was a swell of emotions dancing across his chocolate depths.

Pride. Love. Happiness. Need.

The last one had me glancing away before arousal could paint my cheeks.

"What about the other kingdoms?" my mother asked, reclaiming my attention.

"We need to send delegations to Zarinia and Vidyaa to determine their stance on the matter," I said. "Although Vidyaa is unlikely to be forthcoming considering..." I trailed off.

I'd already informed my parents about the attacks Vidyaa had sanctioned against me.

"They can all burn!" my father growled and Silas made a noise of agreement.

"The actions of their monarch should not condemn the people, Father," I admonished.

It felt strange to be the one chastising a parent.

"Harlowe's right," my mother added. "The people of Vidyaa are not responsible for what has been done in their name."

"If we send an emissary to Vidyaa, how can we be sure that they will not use that information to align themselves with Kieran?" my father asked.

"We can't," Silas said simply. "In fact, they may have already done so. But that shouldn't stop us from reaching out. We have nothing to lose and everything to gain by asking the question."

"I suppose you're right," my father conceded.

"We have made contingency plans in the event they align with Netheran, however," Silas added.

"How so?" my mother asked.

"When the roc attacked, we had to adapt quickly. We used our dragons to outmaneuver their attacks, and I have incorporated those tactics into our training ever since. We still need to spread this knowledge more widely among the Cathal, but we haven't had the chance."

"You could start here in Valoren," I said. "We have time to train the Cathal here before leaving for Elysara."

Silas gave me a curt nod in agreement.

"So, that's everything?" my mother asked. "We rally the kingdoms and then wait?"

"Not entirely," I admitted.

"What else?" my father asked.

"I need to travel to the Mountains of Dragonia. Misneach believes we could convince the unbonded dragons to join our fight."

My mother beamed. "I still can't believe you have a dragon. I always wanted to be a Cathal. Did I ever tell you that?"

"No, you didn't," I said, surprised.

"I did. I grew up hearing tales of the mighty Cathal and their dragons. It was all I ever wanted," her gaze flicked to my father, "until Atticus came along and swept me off my feet."

"If I recall correctly," my father chuckled, "you were not entirely receptive to my advances in the beginning."

"I had to make you work for it," my mother teased.

"That you did."

"Sounds familiar," Silas muttered.

"Maybe there's still time, Mother. If the dragons join us, there may be some willing to bond."

"Oh, I'm not sure I have what it takes to become Cathal," she said shyly.

"I disagree," Silas countered. "Anyone prepared to stand against a man like Kieran to protect their child has more courage than five Cathal combined."

My mother straightened under Silas's praise and I think I fell a little more in love with him at that moment.

"I agree," my father said as he took my mother's hand and placed a tender kiss on her palm.

"There you have it," I beamed.

"All right," my mother said. "I will begin training."

# Chapter Forty-One

We spent the next few days undertaking preparations in Valoren and providing training to the Cathal.

Misneach, though, was relentless with the new recruits, making the other dragons hesitant to train with him. He was one of the biggest dragons of the clutch, and his less-than-pleasant demeanor did not help things.

**"You could try to be a touch more friendly, Misneach,"** I sighed.

**"No,"** he snapped. **"If I am to trust these Cathal to have your back out there, they will need to prove themselves first."**

**"They won't make it into battle if we can't train them, and we can't train them if they are too terrified to face you."**

Misneach snorted. **"They should be terrified to face me. If they are not up to the task, I will eviscerate them."**

I took a calming breath, and I tried again. **"Perhaps we should get them to understand the basics before we move to evisceration."**

**"I will not expose you to risk, Fire Heart. End of discussion."**

**"I'm taking a break,"** I snapped and slid from Misneach's back.

Catching sight of Fionn, I headed in his direction. He had been training with my mother, and I wanted to see how she was doing.

Fionn stood with his arms crossed as he watched my mother move through a series of attacks with another soldier.

"How's she doing?" I asked when I reached his side.

Fionn glanced in my direction and offered me a warm smile. "Great. She's a natural. I see where you get it from."

My mother released a battle cry, pulling my attention back to her. She lunged for the soldier, gripping his shoulders as she raised her knee to his sternum, sending him to the ground. Not wasting her advantage, she straddled his waist and leveled her blade to his throat.

"Yield," she panted, and the soldier nodded in acquiescence.

"See," Fionn said with a grin. "Apple, tree," he added, pointing between us.

I couldn't help the wide smile that spread across my face.

"Woo hoo," Emmerson jeered from the sideline. "That's what I'm talking about."

My mother stood from the ground and put a hand out to help her opponent to his feet.

Stalking towards her, I called, "That was incredible! Where have you been hiding these skills?"

"Well," she said sheepishly. "Zeke may have taught me a thing or two over the years."

I barked out a laugh. "Where is Zeke anyway?"

"He has been training with Arabella, much to Illiana's annoyance," Emmerson said, joining us.

"Why would that annoy her?"

"She doesn't think Arabella needs to learn to defend herself physically," she said. "It is her belief that Arabella only needs to strengthen her magical abilities because her powers are weapon enough."

"What if someone cuts her off somehow, like what happened to me when the Prince of Vidyaa attacked?" I pressed.

"That's exactly what I said," Emmerson huffed. "Which is why Zeke is helping her."

"Good. We can't afford for anyone to be lacking if we can avoid it."

"Speaking of," Fionn said. "How is training going with Misneach?"

By the mischievous glint in his eye, he already knew the answer to that question.

"Fantastic," I grumbled.

"Still refusing to go easy on the recruits?" he asked.

"No. He thinks if we go easy on them in training, then we won't be able to rely on them to have our backs during the real thing."

"I sort of agree with him," Emmerson shrugged.

**"See, Fire Heart,"** Misneach said, and he sounded way too pleased with himself. **"Even your hellcat agrees with my methods."**

**"Stop listening in to my private conversations."**

Misneach released an exhausted sigh. **"If I have told you once, I have told you a thousand times, Fire Heart. It is not *listening in* when you are screaming your thoughts down the bond."**

**"Very true,"** Rónán chimed in.

**"Misneach does not need you backing him up Rónán. He is plenty disagreeable on his own."**

**"That is also true,"** Rónán said.

**"Watch it,"** Misneach growled.

**"Or what?"** Rónán taunted him. **"I'm one of the few dragons who is *not* terrified of you, remember."**

**"Maybe we should change that,"** Misneach snarled.

**"All right enough,"** I snapped. **"Find something else to occupy your time."**

"Harlowe," my mother said, as if it wasn't the first time she had tried to gain my attention.

"Sorry, dragons."

"Ah, that must be interesting conversing with them all."

"That's one word for it."

Rónán snickered, enjoying my irritation a little too much.

"What were you saying?"

"I was asking you how your dream walking practice was progressing."

I couldn't contain the grimace that spread across my face. I had tried to dream walk with different people, but I'd only been able to re-enter Silas's dreams.

Save for Misneach's, which was... interesting.

**"Dreaming of battle is not unusual, Fire Heart."**

**"That level of carnage, though?"** I challenged.

**"If anything, I'd say it demonstrates my dedication."**

**"I am very pleased that you are prepared to rip our enemies limb from limb, Misneach."**

**"As you should be."**

"Still the same," I said, answering my mother's question.

It hadn't escaped my notice that I had only been able to dream walk with those I shared a bond or connection.

If anything, that should have provided some comfort that I could enter Kieran's dreams.

But it only made me feel more apprehensive.

"All you can do is try," my mother encouraged.

"Have you spoken with Silas about training with the Cathal?" I asked.

"Not yet, but young Fionn here has been giving me some informal instruction," she replied.

Fionn scrunched his nose up at the reference to his youth and Emmerson cackled.

"You are one merciless woman, Emmerson," Fionn grumbled.

"You best believe it!"

"Sometimes I don't know whether to admire Cillian for going up against you or to pity the man for what he must endure," Fionn teased.

"It should definitely be the latter," she purred.

"No doubt," Fionn chuckled.

"Did I hear my name?" Cillian asked as he approached us.

"Only if you were eavesdropping," Emmerson retorted.

Cillian gave her a sidelong look. "What were you saying, Fionn?"

"Nothing," he said as he scrubbed the back of his neck.

"Very convincing," Cillian deadpanned.

"Fionn was saying how fortunate you are to have a woman like me," Emmerson said sweetly.

"Oh, really?" Cillian said with a quirked brow.

"Not exactly," Fionn muttered.

"All right, enough brooding for one day," my mother said, cutting through the tension Emmerson so effortlessly stoked. "Let's eat."

There was a chorus of agreement as we all made our way back to the palace.

"How much longer until we move on?" Emmerson asked.

"A few more days."

Even as I said it, I couldn't shake the feeling that trouble would find us before then.

# Chapter Forty-Two

Someone pounded on my door, startling me from sleep.

"Silas," Cillian called.

"What does he want at this hour?" Silas murmured.

The pounding started again.

"Answer the door before he wakes up the rest of the palace," I groaned.

Silas got out of bed and retrieved his pants. The sight of his naked ass was enough to send my thoughts spiraling as I remembered every delicious thing he had done to my body only hours earlier.

As Silas pulled the door open, I caught a glimpse of Cillian's worried face.

There was a muffled conversation, but I couldn't discern what they were saying.

Silas swore and ran his hand through his hair.

Whatever it was, it wasn't anything good.

The scene playing out before me was oddly familiar and the sinking feeling in my stomach had me praying I was wrong.

A moment later, Silas closed the door and marched toward me.

"Get dressed," he ordered.

"What's going on?"

Before he could answer, a voice floated in from the open window.

"Well, well, well, Little Bride. It seems you are just full of surprises."

Fuck. I really wished I'd been wrong.

Scrambling out of bed, I got dressed as quickly as I could while grabbing every single weapon within reach.

Just as I finished sheathing my last dagger, my parents appeared in my chambers.

"Have you alerted the soldiers?" I asked.

"They are readying themselves for battle as we speak," my father responded.

"Kieran is incredibly powerful and should not be underestimated," I warned.

My parents nodded their heads in understanding.

"You need to leave," my mother whispered. "We can hold him back long enough for you to escape."

"You crowned me queen, did you not? I will not flee at the first test of my leadership."

"It's not that Harlowe. You still need to rally more forces. The time will come when you must face Kieran, but it is not tonight."

"I cannot abandon my kingdom," I said, glancing around for someone to support my assertions.

"Your mother has a point, Little Menace," Silas said.

If either of my parents were surprised by the moniker, they didn't let it show on their faces.

"You would have me leave my people to suffer under Kieran's wrath? You would have me abandon my parents?" I said the last part quietly so only Silas would hear.

"No, I would have you protect them. Though I hate to admit it, we both know Kieran is here for you. We can lead him away and keep your people safe."

Silas's suggestion gave me pause.

That might just work.

Illiana burst into my chambers a moment later, followed by Arabella and Zeke.

"I see we have our answer regarding the Serpent King," she remarked.

"What?" I asked, confused.

"He indeed knows you survived his attempt on your life."

"Thank you, Illiana, I hadn't noticed."

A panicked scream pierced the silent night, and I hurried to the window.

Kieran stood in the courtyard as he clutched a woman by her throat. Her feet dangled above the ground and her face was ruddy as she struggled against his hold.

"We've played this game before, Bride. Come out now or I will tear your kingdom apart piece by piece," Kieran said in a saccharine tone. "Starting with this one."

"WAIT," I roared.

But Kieran didn't wait. He snapped her neck as I watched on, helpless to change the outcome.

"Oops," he said with a cruel smirk.

"I am going to fucking kill you, Kieran!" I shouted.

"Looking forward to it," he taunted.

I turned and marched towards the door, but Silas gripped my upper arm and pulled me to a stop.

"Let me go, Silas," I growled.

"He's baiting you, Little Menace. Don't fall into his trap."

"I have to do something," I hissed.

Before he could respond, Emmerson, Cillian, and Fionn entered the room. "Anyone else getting a sense of déjà vu?" Emmerson asked.

Another scream pierced the air, followed by a gurgling sound. "Where are the soldiers?" I barked.

The sound of steel scraping against steel answered my question before anyone else could.

My father rushed to the window. "He's slaughtering them," he balked.

"We have to get down there," he shouted as he raked a hand through his copper hair.

I scanned the room, taking in the collective strength of those present. Then my eyes fell on Illiana.

"Illiana, you've been teaching Arabella defensive magic, correct?"

"I have."

"What can you do?" I pressed.

"Many things," she smirked.

"Specifics, Illiana," I snapped as I tried to drown out Kieran's taunts.

"I can cast spells, either to attack or defend, and I can also manipulate nature."

"Manipulate nature?"

"Yes. I can break the earth or invoke the fury of the elements," she shrugged.

An idea started taking shape in my mind.

More shouting erupted from the courtyard, followed by the sound of screaming. The wails of the dying wrapped around my throat, suffocating me with my failure.

"Silas, I need you to lead the escape. Take the dragons and get everyone to safety."

"What will you do?" he asked as he narrowed his eyes in suspicion.

"I'll be the distraction."

"Not a chance, Little Menace," he said, folding his arms. "Where you go, I follow."

"Not this time, Silas." He opened his mouth to argue, but I raised my hand, cutting him off. "If things go awry, someone will need to lead the forces against Kieran, and that someone is you."

"She's right, Brother," Cillian said before he could argue.

"Then I'm coming with you," Emmerson said.

I shook my head. "No Emmerson. I need you safe and out of harm's way. For my plan to work, I can't have any unnecessary distractions."

Emmerson flinched, but I didn't have time to spare her feelings.

"This is one time you need to follow the chain of command, Little Viper," Cillian implored.

Emmerson searched my face and whatever she saw there must have convinced her because she lowered her head in defeat.

"What do you require of me?" Zeke asked.

"Can you get Arabella out of here?"

"I can," Zeke nodded as he stepped closer to her.

Turning to my father, I said, "I need you to continue ruling in my stead. Look after our people."

My father pulled me against his chest and hugged me tightly. "I will, Harlowe. Just make it back to take my place."

I gave a curt nod in agreement. "Get my mother to safety," I whispered.

Turning back to the others, I said, "Once Illiana and I draw Kieran away, I want you all to leave from the western entrance and fly towards Elysara. Remain out of sight. You all know what he's capable of. Don't give him a reason to remind you."

"He's breached the palace," my father said in disbelief.

"Go," I hissed, gesturing to him and my mother. "Find Samuel and get ready to step in should I fail."

My parents nodded, tears filling their eyes as they rushed from my chambers to take up their positions.

"Oh, Little Bride," Kieran taunted.

Fuck! He was close.

Emmerson rushed forward, sweeping me into a tight hug. "I don't like this."

"Neither do I, but you need to trust me."

"I do trust you. It's the only reason I am listening at all."

A small chuckle broke free of my chest without permission.

"Keep an eye on Fionn if anything happens to me, all right?"

"I will watch his back until you return to take over the babysitting duties," she said meaningfully.

She would accept no alternative outcome.

When she released me, Zeke gave me a quick hug. "Be careful out there, Harlowe."

"I will," I promised.

Next, Fionn pulled me to his side. "This feels wrong, but you're smarter than me, so I am going to trust you," he said.

"I'll see you soon," I assured him.

Silas stepped into my space and cupped my cheeks. "Promise me you'll stay safe, Little Menace," he said as his eyes searched mine intently. "You know my heart doesn't beat without you."

"I promise, Silas," I said, even though I had no way of ensuring I could keep it.

Silas brushed his lips against mine, kissing me softly. "You best make sure you keep that promise, Little Menace, or I'll be forced to bend you over my knee."

"Yes, it's all very emotional," Illiana said, waving her hand dismissively. "What exactly are you expecting from me?"

**"Misneach, do you understand the plan?"**

**"I do Fire Heart. I'm ready."**

Turning to face Illiana, I said, "I want you to bring his world down around him."

# Chapter Forty-Three

"This wasn't exactly what I had in mind," Illiana hissed beside me.

"Just take the damn stone," I growled.

Illiana glowered at me as she tore the stone from my hand.

"You're the one who is supposed to be wielding it," she muttered.

"Well, unfortunately for you, I need to keep Kieran's attention trained on me until everyone escapes."

"I don't like it."

"You don't have to like it. Just make sure you follow my lead and remain hidden." I gave her a pointed look, knowing Illiana was not fond of taking orders.

"Fine," she snapped.

I jogged down the hallway, Illiana close behind me. When I rounded the corner, the overwhelming scent of copper filled my nose and I fought to repress the bile creeping up my throat.

It was a fucking bloodbath.

The bodies of Valoren soldiers littered the lower foyer. Limbs had been torn apart and throats had been ripped wide open. Enormous pools of blood surrounded the bodies, painting the marble floor crimson. Others lay amongst the massacre untouched, as though they were merely sleeping.

I swallowed thickly at the thought of what they must have endured to leave such a scene.

Kieran had done all of this in a matter of minutes.

One man had single-handedly caused the same level of carnage you could expect from an entire regiment of soldiers.

My heart clenched and my eyes burned when I saw a familiar mop of chocolate-brown hair, soaked in blood and standing in stark contrast to the unnatural pallor of her skin.

"Louise?" I choked, as I stared down at my chambermaid, the woman who had cared for me like a mother.

"There you are," Kieran cooed. "Aww, come now. There's no need to cry."

Was I crying?

I scrubbed at my cheeks, feeling the wetness that had fallen.

My pain morphed into fury and I screamed my rage as I summoned my flames before sending a blazing ball of fire towards Kieran.

It hit him right in the middle of his chest, sending him flying backward through the air, and out the entryway of the palace.

Adrenaline coursed through my veins, and I took a deep breath to steady my trembling hands.

As I peered over my shoulder, my gaze locked with Illiana's. "Stay out of sight," I said before bounding down the stairs and crossing the threshold to follow Kieran.

I summoned my shield just as Kieran was getting to his feet. The front of his tunic was burnt and a blackened scorch mark covered the entirety of his upper chest. Yet there was no other evidence that my flames had even harmed him.

"That wasn't very nice, Bride," Kieran smirked. "That almost hurt."

Red colored my vision and I clenched my fists.

"Keep it up and you'll turn me on," he said as mirth danced in his cobalt eyes. "Or was that your intention?"

I couldn't answer him even if I wanted to. Right before my eyes, I watched in horror as the scorch mark slowly shrank, leaving perfect, unblemished skin in its wake.

"Did you like my little trick, Bride?" he asked with a grin. "Imagine all the things I could have shown you had you been willing to serve me," he said suggestively. "Now, why don't you drop that pesky little shield you have in place?"

"I don't think I will," I said, regaining my ability to speak.

"You know why I am here, Bride."

"You failed to kill me and you intend to rectify the situation, I take it?"

"That I have," he paused before adding, "I must say, you just keep surprising me. Are you sure you don't want to stand at my side? It would be such a waste to snuff out your existence."

I lowered my shield for the briefest moment as I sent a fiery projectile flying towards him. Kieran's shadows surrounded him in a reflection of my shield as he deflected the hit.

"That would be a no," I snarled.

Kieran chuckled without mirth. "You want to play, Bride. Fine, let's play."

In the next second, a torrent of shadowy tendrils assaulted me. They curved and twisted over my shield until it started closing in on itself. Just when I thought my hold would buckle under the weight of it, an icy breeze ripped through the courtyard, bringing with it jagged ice formations that created a protective circle around me, pushing Kieran back.

Kieran's eyes widened in surprise as he retreated further, taking his shadows with him. Once he was a safe distance away, the icy daggers melted against the heat of my shield.

"It looks like I'm not the only one who's been keeping secrets," he said, cocking a brow.

I shrugged my shoulders nonchalantly, keeping up the ruse.

"What else can you do?" he asked riveted.

"I'm no longer the weak woman you first encountered all those months ago, Kieran!"

"You were never weak, Harlowe. You just hadn't unlocked the power buried deep within you."

Without warning, Kieran advanced again. This time, he sent his shadows to the base of my shield as he tried to force his way inside.

Lightning rippled across the blackened night sky and Kieran whipped his head towards it. I drew my palms into fists as I fought the urge to do the same, but I had a role to play, and lives depended on me doing it well.

Fierce winds tore up the ground surrounding Kieran, and he was forced to throw his arm over his eyes to protect himself.

It was working. The plan was working.

**"Are they out?"** I asked Misneach.

**"Almost. They just need a little longer."**

Black tendrils rose before me, creeping higher and higher, until a massive wall of shadows stood in front of me. Before I could take it all in, the shadows dropped, driving the dust storm away and suffocating the last remnants of the wind.

A tiny gasp, almost indistinguishable, met my ears and I knew that whatever Kieran had just done had taken a toll on Illiana.

"You didn't think it would be that easy to defeat me, did you?" Kieran tittered.

He prowled around me and I spun in a circle, not willing to give him my back.

Lightning illuminated the sky once more and rain began beating down on us. Kieran threw his head back and soaked in the downpour, a pleasant smile splitting his face.

He looked much younger at that moment, almost carefree as he enjoyed the rain.

Then his cerulean eyes snapped back to me and whatever glimpse of humanity I had seen a moment ago dissolved, replaced by burning determination.

**"They're clear,"** Misneach said, and I released a shaky breath.

I stood at the center of my blazing shield; the flames crackling and dancing around me as I tried desperately to signal Illiana.

Kieran was too close for me to risk lowering my defenses, but if I didn't do so, I'd never be leaving this courtyard alive.

"I grow tired of this game, Bride," Kieran hissed. "Lower this fucking shield."

"Sure, I'll get right on that," I scoffed.

Right in front of my eyes, Kieran's form began to... flicker.

Then, just as abruptly, he solidified once more and resumed pacing the exterior of my barrier. He moved in slow, deliberate strides, circling me as his shadows trailed his every step, writhing in anticipation.

I heard a soft, eerie whisper coming from all around me, but when I turned to look at Kieran, I saw his lips pressed together in a tight line. A shiver of unease raced down my spine and beads of sweat began forming on the back of my neck.

It was as if the darkness of the night was alive and conspiring with him.

My breaths came in short, shallow pants. My strength was waning, and I knew I wouldn't be able to hold my shield for much longer.

I made a flicking motion with my hands, flexing all of my fingers wide before snapping them back and repeating the movement.

I should have taken the time to discuss my arguably inadequate hand signals with Illiana before stepping foot outside.

My mind raced as I tried to figure out a way to communicate what I needed without alerting Kieran to Illiana's presence.

"Fuck!" I growled.

Kieran stopped pacing and turned to look at me. "Growing weak are you, Bride? You can come out anytime."

As if to emphasize Kieran's words, my shield wavered, demonstrating its weakening state.

Desperation clawed at my throat as I frantically searched my surroundings.

I needed a distraction.

**"I could —"** Misneach began.

**"Don't even finish that sentence,"** I snapped. "**Wait for my signal, Misneach?"**

When he said nothing, I pressed for an answer. **"Misneach?"**

**"Yes, all right."**

Another soft gasp sounded from the darkness, and this time, Kieran heard it.

He snapped his head in Illiana's direction and narrowed his eyes.

For the briefest moment, my world stood still, unmoving, as I relived this exact scenario in my mind. Everly's small gasp, Kieran's wicked smile, and then the sound of Everly choking on her blood after Kieran had torn her throat out.

Fear flooded my body, threatening to drown me in my panic.

Kieran tossed his head back and laughed maniacally. His whole body shook as he basked in the turn of events.

"And here I thought you'd developed new powers. Naughty, Naughty, Little Bride," he tsked as he waggled his finger at me, a broad grin still plastered on his face.

His gaze flicked back towards Illiana. "Isn't *this* a familiar picture?" he cooed.

I was out of time.

I sent a surge of power into my shield, and my flames flared as they roared higher and brighter.

Kieran was momentarily stunned, and he stepped back.

"NOW!" I roared as I dropped my shield and sprinted towards Illiana.

The earth shook violently beneath my feet as the ground split wide open, swallowing Kieran whole and dragging him into the darkened depths of the chasm.

A deep, resonant growl caught my attention, followed by the sound of beating wings as Misneach cut through the night sky in my direction. He tipped his wings as he angled himself towards me, swooping as low as he could manage.

My heart was in my throat as I pushed against the rush of wind created by Misneach's powerful wingbeats. My feet left the ground as I leaped into the air, stretching my arm to the point of pain, as I reached for my dragon's neck.

For one agonizingly slow heartbeat, I hung in mid-air, suspended between the earth below me and the oppressive night sky as Misneach beat his wings furiously, gaining altitude. Hooking my fingers into the ridge of Misneach's scales, I pulled myself into position between Misneach's broad wings.

**"Circle back,"** I commanded as I searched the darkness for Illiana. **"There!"** I screamed when I caught sight of her.

I summoned my flames one last time and sent a fiery tendril snaking towards her. Her eyes widened in fear as it barreled in her direction.

"Use the stone," I shouted.

Illiana's face crumpled in confusion, but a moment later, understanding crossed her features, and her lips moved quickly as she murmured a spell. A tendril of ice wrapped around Illiana's waist before it darted forward to meet my fiery one, and the two elements merged.

Illiana's feet left the ground as she hung below us, dangling in the nothingness separating the rugged terrain from the heavens above.

**"Find a safe place to land so I can pull Illiana up."**

Misneach acknowledged my command with a grunt.

What felt like hours later but was nothing more than mere minutes, Misneach descended, landing carefully so as not to injure Illiana.

I let my flames subside and thrust out my hand. "Climb on," I barked, and Illiana scrambled into place behind me.

Misneach wasted no time launching himself back into the sky as we fled the only home I had ever known.

I prayed to the gods that Kieran would follow us instead of unleashing his fury on the people I had left behind.

"Well, that was rather dramatic," Illiana huffed.

A sharp laugh burst free of my chest, and my eyes widened in shock. Before I could stop myself, my laughter exploded into a full belly laugh that left my stomach aching and my shoulders shaking.

The unexpected sound cut through the silence of the night, blending with the rush of wind and the rhythmic beating of Misneach's wings.

For a moment, all the fear and tension from earlier drained away, and I basked in the unfettered joy that came with knowing we had made it.

We'd escaped.

# Chapter Forty-Four

When we caught up with the others, I was beyond exhausted. My muscles ached with a deep, unyielding burn, and it was a struggle to remain upright.

Misneach dipped his wings as he flew closer to the small camp nestled just inside the tree line. He landed with a dull *thud* and it was an effort to pull myself from my position on his back. My limbs felt heavy, as if they were weighed down, and the ground seemed to shift under my feet as I took unsteady steps.

My entire body screamed for rest, which felt so close and yet impossibly out of reach.

Large hands encircled my waist, and I slumped against the hard chest at my back.

"Easy," Silas murmured. "I've got you."

Before I was aware of what was happening, my feet had left the ground and I was being pressed against the warmth of Silas's body.

"I've got you," he repeated.

Silas carried me to the fire and set me down against a log. My eyes flicked upward as I searched for Illianna. Fionn had his arm wrapped around her as he helped her towards the fire and she looked about as good as I felt.

"Are you all right, Harlowe?" Emmerson asked as soon as Silas had released me. "Let me look you over."

"I'm fine Emmerson, just drained is all," I said, waving her off.

"You don't look so good," Zeke said from over her shoulder.

"Gods, Zeke," I scoffed. "You know how to make a girl feel good about herself."

Zeke.

Louise.

Fuck.

"Zeke, I have to tell you something," I said hesitantly as I met his gaze.

Zeke stiffened, sensing the change in my demeanor. "What's that?"

"It's Louise, Kieran killed her."

Zeke's eyes grew wide, and his face paled. Emmerson reached out to him, but he shook her off, marching away from the camp.

When she made a move to follow him, I shook my head. "Leave him be. He needs a moment."

Guilt swirled in my gut. I was so damned exhausted I couldn't even cry. I couldn't mourn the loss of a woman who was so important to me.

I was numb for the moment, but I wasn't naïve enough to believe tonight's loss wouldn't come back to haunt me.

Silas rubbed my shoulders as if sensing my inner turmoil. "It's all right, Harlowe. I've got you."

"Would you like me to make you a tea?" Arabella's soft voice came from behind Fionn. He stepped aside, allowing a head of chestnut brown hair to come into view. "It will help with the fatigue."

"That would be great, Arabella. Thank you." She nodded her head and disappeared to rummage through her pack.

"Here," Illiana said, tossing something in my direction. "If I ever see that stone again in this lifetime, it will be far too soon."

My reflexes were too sluggish and the Aurora Stone fell to the dirt beside me. The flames of the small fire danced and flickered across its surface, mixing with the iridescent colors inherent to the stone.

"You're supposed to be the keeper of the stone," I grumbled.

"Yes, well, you were supposed to be its wielder. It looks like neither one of us is going to bed satisfied tonight," she snapped.

"People would kill to get their hands on this stone," I mused as I picked it up.

"Great. Let them have at it."

I pocketed the stone as my eyelids drooped. The simple act of keeping them open seemed like a monumental task.

"Do you think Kieran will retaliate against Valoren?" I asked in a small voice.

Emmerson stiffened, a faraway look entering her eyes. I knew where her thoughts had taken her.

We left people we loved behind tonight, knowing we may never see them again. If Kieran unleashed his wrath upon my kingdom, there was no telling what we might find once we returned.

The lump forming in my throat made it difficult to swallow as a feeling of dread continued to rise within me.

Emmerson cleared her throat. "With any luck, Kieran will remain true to his obsessive, psychotic ways and follow you."

"Wow Emmerson," Cillian said. "Way to restore the mood. I feel downright jovial."

She turned in his direction, baring her teeth.

**"Is the hellcat serious?"** Misneach asked incredulously.

**"She's only trying to distract us."**

**"Wonderful job she's doing,"** he muttered.

Arabella arrived at that moment, breaking the awkward tension. "Here you go, Harlowe," she said, offering me a mug of steaming tea.

"Thank you, Arabella."

I lifted the mug to my lips and blew on the hot liquid to cool it down.

"Sip, don't gulp," Arabella instructed.

Doing as she said, I took a tentative sip of the tea. The heated liquid slid over my tongue, carrying the distinct sweetness of honey with hints of citrus and mint.

It was soothing and a slight comfort in the circumstances.

The effect of the tea was immediate. Warmth radiated throughout my body, spreading to each of my exhausted limbs. The fatigue that had gripped my muscles and weighed them down lessened before dissolving.

The world around me also sharpened, and I found I could focus once more, as though a fog had been lifted from my mind.

I glanced towards Illiana, and I saw the pink returning to her cheeks. She looked more refreshed than she had in days.

"What did you put in this tea Arabella?" I asked. "I feel fantastic."

"It's something my mother used to make for me whenever I fell ill as a child. It helps revitalize the senses and restore depleted energy stores."

As I rolled my shoulders, I couldn't help the sigh of relief that escaped between my lips. With each passing moment, the tea continued to banish the remnants of exhaustion, leaving me with a new sense of vigor.

"Better?" Silas murmured against my ear.

"Yes, much."

"Good." He pressed his lips to my temple, giving me a gentle kiss.

"How long until we need to move again?" I asked, now that I was thinking more clearly.

We couldn't remain idle and risk Kieran catching up to us.

A howl sounded nearby and a moment later, an enormous black creature broke through the tree line.

Illiana jumped to her feet as she raced forward, throwing her arms wide. The first dire wolf skidded to a stop in front of her and she curled her arms around the beast. A second wolf followed the first and then the others emerged from the forest as one.

A smile spread across my face at their reunion. Illiana continued to mutter words of affection as the five massive wolves crowded around her, slobbering all over her as they each vied for her attention.

"That's so gross," Emmerson shuddered.

"Just wait until you wake up one morning with your dragon leering down at you with drool dripping from his mouth," I said with a repulsed shiver.

**"I was not leering,"** Misneach growled.

**"No? What would you call it?"**

**"I was assessing the state of your well-being."**

**"Right,"** I drawled.

Emmerson screwed her face up further, and Silas chuckled.

"That was quite entertaining," he said, and I elbowed him in the ribs.

"Ow, Little Menace," he hissed. "You're the one who brought it up."

"We should get going," I said, my good mood slipping away. "We can't afford to let Kieran close the distance if he is, in fact, following us."

Everyone muttered in agreement as they moved to collect the small smattering of belongings they had unpacked.

I glanced in the direction Zeke had disappeared, but he was already striding towards Rónán with Arabella in tow.

I tapped the side of my pants, making sure that the stone was still buried deep in my pocket, before I climbed up Misneach's foreleg to reach my seat on his back.

Misneach crouched low to the ground before launching himself heavenward.

And then we were flying.

# Chapter Forty-Five

As we approached the tall wrought-iron gates, I couldn't help being entranced by their beauty. They had been painted a glossy white and intricate patterns had been carved into the metal, giving it a delicate, almost lacy appearance.

The palace itself sat at the end of a long cobblestone pathway, with towering columns and large arched windows that undoubtedly flooded the interior with light. Its pristine white exterior captured the rays of the sun, making the entire place appear majestic, almost ethereal.

Beautifully manicured gardens decorated the front of the palace with vibrant flowerbeds showcasing every color under the rainbow alongside perfectly trimmed hedges that gave it a regal ambiance.

A grand fountain stood at the center of the garden. Water cascaded down a series of elegant and interconnected tiers, creating a soothing rhythmic sound.

The entire palace was a masterpiece.

"Stop and announce yourselves," a burly-looking guard said as we approached.

Silas placed a fist over his heart and said, "My name is Silas, King of Pyrithia," — he turned and gestured to me — "and this is Harlowe, Queen of Valoren."

The guard's eyes widened, and he whispered something to his companion. The other guard disappeared between the gates and ran up the cobblestone path towards the palace.

"My apologies, Your Highnesses. I will need to have someone from the court verify your identities," he said with an apologetic smile.

"Of course," Silas said as he nodded his head.

A moment later, the other guard returned and advised us we could enter.

"His Majesty has asked if you could leave your dragons outside of the gates for the time being," he added.

**"You will not go inside those walls without me to protect you, Fire Heart,"** Misneach growled.

**"It's all right, Misneach. This place is a safe haven. They do not tolerate any form of trouble within their walls, so it is unlikely that they have any ill intention toward me."**

Misneach grunted, but I could tell he wasn't convinced.

**"Besides, it's only the difference of a few hundred feet. You'll still be able to burn the place down if they move to harm me,"** I added.

**"That is a given, Fire Heart."**

**"Great. We're on the same page."**

Misneach muttered something inaudible, but he didn't argue further.

"Ready?" Silas asked as he extended his hand for me to take.

I nodded and entwined my fingers with his.

My boots made a dull *thudding* sound as I walked across the cobblestone path towards the palace. The uneven surface caused subtle variations in each step, resulting in a resonant effect.

"Ah, the... hounds too," the guard said, and I glanced over my shoulder to see the dire wolves following on Illiana's heels.

"They are dire wolves," Illiana scoffed.

She turned to speak with her familiars, and they let out a soft whine.

It seemed they shared Misneach's reservations.

Whatever she said to them had them scurrying away, so she must have assuaged their concerns somehow.

The cobblestone path led to the palace's grand entrance, where a set of sweeping marble steps invited guests to ascend to the main entryway. Porcelain balustrades lined the stairwell, and they, too, were decorated with ornate engravings.

The entire palace exuded grace and opulence.

"This place is splendid," Emmerson murmured, echoing my thoughts.

At the top of the stairs, surrounded by a retinue of guards, stood a tall man with a muscular build and black hair that hung loosely past his shoulders.

He wore a well-fitted tunic and brown leather armor that appeared to be custom-made, denoting his importance.

Light stubble covered his chin and upper lip, giving him a handsome, rugged look. His tanned complexion matched the dark coloring of his eyes, which appeared almost black as they sparkled with interest.

His lips curved up in the corners as he appraised us.

His lips were irresistibly full, as if they were made for kissing.

"Prince Caspan, I assume," Silas said as we reached the top of the staircase.

"Indeed I am," he said in a rich, full tone that sent my heartbeat fluttering.

If the sounds of approval I heard coming from behind me were any indicator, I wasn't the only one who found the Prince appealing.

"Em," Cillian growled as Silas tightened his hold on my hand.

"And who might you be?" the Prince asked Silas.

"Did your guards not announce us?" Silas questioned with an arched brow and the Prince chuckled.

The sound made me want to melt into a puddle at his feet.

Silas glanced towards me as if sensing the direction of my thoughts. A flush crept up my neck as I kept my eyes trained straight ahead, refusing to meet his probing gaze.

"You would be Silas, the King of Pyrithia, I take it?" the Prince said.

Silas gave a curt nod in confirmation.

"I understood your father, Leith, held the throne?"

"He did. Until my brother murdered him and took it for himself."

"Ah," the Prince said, graciously ignoring the fact that Silas's brother was no longer crowned king.

"And who is this stunning lady?" the Prince asked, turning the full weight of his dark eyes on me.

I opened my mouth to reply, but nothing came out. My mouth was suddenly dry, and it felt as though my heart was beating in my throat.

Gods, what the hell was wrong with me?

"This is Harlowe, Queen of Valoren," Silas said when it became apparent I was incapable of answering.

The Prince smirked roguishly. "The last I heard out of Valoren, the Crown Princess, Harlowe, if I am not mistaken, had just pulled a disappearing act. Am I to take it you are one and the same?"

"Yes. The elevation to Queen was a recent occurrence."

"Like four days ago, recent," Emmerson said from behind me.

The Prince chuckled as he took my hand. "Well, it is my pleasure to meet you, Your Majesty."

The Prince drew my hand to his lips and placed a kiss atop it. His lips lingered on my skin for an inappropriately long time and my cheeks blazed with warmth.

Silas growled next to me, but the Prince kept his intense gaze locked on me. When he released my hand, he said, "I very much look forward to getting to know you, Queen Harlowe of Valoren." His voice was low and silky, and it had goosebumps erupting on my flesh.

Silas pulled me to his side as he glared at the Prince.

"Follow me if you will," the Prince said with a charming smile as he turned and marched back inside the palace.

Silas gave me an incredulous look, and I just shrugged. He ran his large, calloused hand down his face and muttered something under his breath before following the Prince. Cillian fell into step beside him, and the two of them began discussing what arrangements they would need for the dragons.

Emmerson joined me a moment later, linking her arm through mine as she grinned broadly. "The gods outdid themselves when they created that man," she said, gesturing towards the Prince. "Can you imagine what he looks like under all that leather?"

Silas and Cillian stopped dead in their tracks and turned to face us. Their mouths were slightly parted, and their eyes were blown wide as they stared at us.

"What?" Emmerson asked innocently.

"Are you serious?" Cillian hissed while Silas continued to stare at me slack-jawed.

"Jealous of a little competition?" Emmerson teased, as she waggled her eyebrows at them.

"Emmerson," Cillian growled.

"Oh, keep your pants on, Cillian. I am only teasing."

"Harlowe?" Silas asked.

"What?"

He gave me a pointed look.

"Oh, sure. What she said."

Both men exchanged uneasy glances before they continued walking.

"This is going to be so much fun," Emmerson whispered.

# Chapter Forty-Six

When we entered the throne room, my eyes immediately fell to the dais. Much like the rest of the palace, the throne was white marble and had been etched with fine lines, creating a beautifully intricate design.

Sitting in place atop the throne was a stern-looking woman with long, straight hair the same shade as the Prince's. She eyed us with interest as we approached, taking in our disheveled appearances and obvious exhaustion.

"Mother," the Prince said. "May I introduce you to King Silas of Pyrithia and Queen Harlowe of Valoren."

"It is a pleasure to meet you," I said as I dipped into a bow.

"Likewise," the Queen responded. "You look so much like your mother, Harlowe," she added with a small smile.

"You know my mother?"

"Very well. Clementine and I were childhood friends," she said wistfully. "I must admit, I may have cursed your father for taking her away from me."

"Forgive me, Your Majesty, I seemed to have forgotten your given name," I admitted as heat flared in my cheeks.

The Queen let out a delicate chuckle. "You may call me Adeline."

A moment later, she asked, "Did my son just say you are queen?"

"He did. My father passed the crown to me only a few days ago."

"How interesting," she mused before her eyes flicked to Silas. "And what about you, Silas? Did your father also abdicate?"

"No," Silas said. "My father is dead."

"I am sorry to hear that."

"Thank you," Silas replied without emotion.

"I apologize for our unannounced arrival," I said, cutting through the awkward silence. "However, I have come to discuss a rather pressing matter."

The Queen's gaze returned to me. "What matter would that be?"

I took a deep breath. I needed Elysara's support in this war, but their historical neutrality did not weigh in my favor.

"Quite simply, the King of Netheran has ambitions to conquer the realm and I am seeking alliances from those who can help thwart those plans."

Adeline's eyes widened, and her lips parted with a soft gasp. "How do you know of this?"

"Because he told me."

"I am going to need more information than that, my dear," Adeline said.

"Have you heard of a prophecy about the Daughter of War and Peace?" I asked.

Adeline eyed me keenly. "Go on," she said.

"Kieran knew of this prophecy. He believed I was the one the prophecy spoke of, so he had his witches spell the rulers of Vidyaa and Zarinia to bring on the Skirmish of Power. Once he had my father backed into a corner, he bartered for my hand in marriage."

The Queen continued to watch me but said nothing.

"He told me this when he came to my kingdom to claim me as his bride. As I am sure you have heard, I fled Valoren. What you don't know is that I sought the help of a truth-sayer."

That garnered the Queen's attention. "A truth-sayer?" she asked in surprise.

"Yes, I found the Lost Witch."

I could feel Illiana's eyes boring into the back of my head. I had no intention of revealing her identity, however. That would be her decision to make, and hers alone.

A flurry of shocked gasps filled the throne room, and the guards lining the walls shifted uncomfortably.

"She's nothing but a legend," the Prince scoffed.

I felt a smirk tug up the corner of my lips. "I used to think the same, but rest assured, she is indeed real, Your Highness."

"Please, call me Caspan," he said with a broad smile.

"And what did she tell you?" Adeline asked, interrupting her son's attempt at flirting.

"She told me it was true."

"You are the Daughter of War and Peace?"

I nodded.

"The prophecy spoke of great power," Adeline pressed.

"I have the ability to wield dragon flames," I said as I brought my hand out in front of me.

Closing my eyes, I summoned my flames.

Exposing myself like this was a risk, but I had little time and no viable alternatives. I could only hope it would be worth it in the end.

Warmth spread across my palm and more gasps filled the room, followed by murmured conversations.

"It's true."

"I can't believe this."

"But why is she here?"

"Will the King of Netheran follow her?"

"Is our home in danger?"

"Silence!" the Queen boomed and the hushed conversations died off.

Opening my eyes, I fixed my gaze on the Queen as I recalled my flames.

"Say I believe you are the prophesied Daughter of War and Peace. What does that have to do with the King of Netheran?" Adeline asked.

"If you're familiar with the prophecy, you know I'm the only one who can match his power."

"We have seen no evidence of this supposed power," Caspan challenged.

"Be thankful that is the case," Silas said, as he stepped closer to me. "The King of Netheran's powers come from dark magic, and he has spent centuries strengthening and perfecting them. He should not be underestimated."

I reached out, taking Silas's hand in my own. "Silas speaks the truth. I wish it were not the case, but it is."

"You said Kieran has ambitions for the realm," Adeline said, directing her statement at me.

"He does. He seeks to reclaim what Netheran lost during the War of Witches," I said.

"That's hardly the entire realm," the Queen remarked, and I didn't miss the hint of skepticism in her tone.

"He also seeks to punish those who were responsible for what Netheran lost following the war," I elaborated.

"The victors of the war," she clarified.

"Precisely."

The Queen studied me for the longest time. I did not know where her thoughts lay, but I knew we would be fighting a losing battle without greater support.

"Let me be abundantly clear," I said, looking around the room. "War is coming."

"Elysara has never taken a side in any of the great wars. We value our neutrality. We stand for peace. Why should we change that now?" The Queen asked and murmured agreement broke out around us.

"With all due respect, Your Majesty. The realm has never faced a threat like Kieran before. Make no mistake, he will come for you. He is coming for us all."

I let my words sink in before continuing. "What you need to decide is whether you are going to lie down and surrender your way of life, your freedom, to his tyranny. Or are you going to stand with us and fight to protect what you value the most, because war is coming for you all the same?"

I glanced towards Silas, and I saw the pride radiating from him.

"You have given us many things to discuss, Harlowe," Adeline hummed. "I can see why your father passed you the crown," she added. "Please enjoy our hospitality as we consider the news you have brought with you today."

"Thank you, Adeline," I said, inclining my head.

"Caspan, if you wouldn't mind showing our guests to their quarters," the Queen said.

"Of course, Mother," Caspan replied with a bow.

"Follow me," he said with a wink, and we all exited the throne room in his wake.

As I turned the corner, I peered back at the Queen. Her knowing gaze clashed with mine and she dipped her chin.

Even if I failed here, I would carry on with this fight until I put a stop to Kieran's oppression, or I would die trying.

# Chapter Forty-Seven

"One of our guest chambers overlooks the gardens and the fountain out front of the palace, if that interests you, Harlowe," Caspan said, flashing me a smile.

"There is also one that overlooks the training grounds which might appeal to you, Silas," he added, glancing towards the man in question.

"We'll be sharing our chambers," Silas said as he pulled me to him.

"As will we," Cillian interjected, gesturing between him and Emmerson.

"I don't know, Cillian," Emmerson said as she battered her eyelashes. "I might enjoy some time to myself."

"You are trying to kill me, woman," Cillian grumbled.

I caught Fionn and Zeke trying to hide their laughter behind their fists, and I couldn't fight the smile that spread across my own lips.

"So," Caspan said, clapping his hands together. "Which will it be? The gardens or the training grounds?"

"I want the training grounds," Emmerson said, pushing her way past everyone until she stood beside Caspan. "I need to see what other specimens this kingdom is hiding."

Cillian growled, and this time Zeke and Fionn howled with laughter.

"I think our offering will please you," Caspan said, ignoring the death glare Cillian directed at him.

Turning his attention back to me, Caspan said, "Then this one is yours."

"Ours," Silas corrected.

"Sure, sure," Caspan said, dismissing him.

"Come on, before someone starts beating their chest," I said to Silas as I dragged him towards the door.

"Thank you, Caspan," I called over my shoulder.

"You are most welcome, Harlowe." He crooked his elbow, offering it to Emmerson. "Shall we?"

Emmerson slipped her arm through his and I shook my head.

I almost felt bad for Cillian.

Almost.

Upon seeing the bed in the room, I longed to collapse on it.

But I was still filthy from my fight with Kieran and a day's worth of travel.

Sighing, I headed to the washroom.

Silas followed me and helped me undress. "Lift your arms," he said, as he removed my tunic.

I was grateful for his help. I was so tired, I barely had the energy to raise my hands over my head.

"I left my pack with Misneach," I complained.

"There are spare clothes in the chamber. We can get our packs after you've had time to rest."

Silas wet a cloth with warm water and set about cleaning the dirt and grime from my skin. "How are you feeling?" he asked softly.

"I'm exhausted," I said with a yawn.

"About Louise," he pressed.

I'd been trying to push thoughts of my friend far from my mind, and it had worked until now.

"Talk to me, Harlowe," Silas pleaded.

"I don't know how I'm feeling. I feel everything and nothing all at once."

Silas nodded his head as if any of what I said made sense. "How can I feel nothing when she's been in my life since we were young?" I asked. "She treated me as one might a daughter, but we actually grew up together. She was only one year older than me. Did you know that?"

Silas shook his head as he skimmed the wet cloth over my neck. He dropped to his haunches to remove my boots, followed by my pants.

"I'll be right back," he said.

I stood in only my undergarments, my arms wrapped around my middle, as I recalled all the small things Louise would do for me growing up.

The extra piece of chocolate cake at dinner because she knew it was my favorite.

The special shampoo that left my hair feeling silky to the touch.

How she would run interference with my tutors because she knew how much I detested my lessons.

A moment later, Silas returned with a clean tunic and pulled it over my head.

"How can I feel nothing?" I repeated.

Silas cupped my cheeks in both his palms. "Listen to me, Little Menace," he said, his eyes searching mine. "You have been through so much and you have survived, time and time again. Most people would have given up by now, but not you. You are strong. You are brave. You are resilient," he said, punctuating each word with a kiss.

On my forehead. My nose. My lips.

I listened intently, not sure I understood what he was trying to tell me.

"It's not that you don't feel, Harlowe. It's that you feel too much," he murmured as he pressed his brow to mine. "Right now, your mind is just trying to protect itself."

"What do you mean?"

"We shut off our emotions when the pain becomes too much to bear. When we can no longer cope with one more tragedy and still expect to wake up in the morning and fight another day," he murmured. "We become numb to all our suffering, just so we can draw our next breath and keep living."

Tears pricked the back of my eyes, and I reached up to clutch his forearms.

"What if it becomes too much and I can't keep going? What do I do then, Silas?"

"Then you share your pain with me, Little Menace. I'll carry it for you so you don't have to."

His words unlocked something within me.

Something buried deep within the recesses of my mind.

Something splintered.

And then I shattered.

Tears spilled down my cheeks, and painful sobs tore free of my chest. I tightened my grip on Silas's arms as I struggled to draw in enough air around the clawing sensation in my throat that threatened to suffocate me.

My back slid down the wall and Silas followed me, pulling me into his lap and clutching me close to his chest. He ran his hand over my hair as he whispered words of love and adoration in my ear.

My whole body shook with the force of the emotion I had bottled up and was only now being released.

I clawed at Silas, wanting to bury myself under his skin so I could escape the pain of every loss I had endured.

Cian.

Teller.

Everly.

Grainne.

Louise.

And even as I recalled each face, my heart continued to fracture because I knew there would be more to come before all of this was over.

"I'm here, Harlowe. I'm here," Silas soothed as he rocked me back and forth.

My tears drenched the front of his tunic. Even so, it wasn't enough. The pain continued to writhe and twist within me until all of my tears had dried up and there was nothing left behind but the pieces of my shattered soul.

Time ticked by without my permission, and I had no idea how long we sat there, huddled together on the floor, as we clung to one another.

All I knew was that the man holding me would always be there to catch me when I fell, ready to put all of my broken pieces back together again.

No matter what.

# Chapter Forty-Eight

"How long do you think we will have to wait?" Emmerson asked as we sat watching the Elysaran soldiers train.

It had been two days since we'd arrived in Elysara and the Queen had convened a meeting with her council to discuss everything we'd told them. Yet we were still no closer to finding out whether they would join our fight.

I curled my hands into fists.

I was beyond frustrated.

Kieran was out there preparing to annihilate everyone who stood in his path, and we were hiding behind the walls of a beautiful palace, twiddling our thumbs.

"I need to do something," I said as I stood, shaking out my hands.

"Like what?" Emmerson asked.

"I don't know, I just need to do... something, anything. Sitting around waiting for them to come to their senses isn't helping."

Emmerson looked pensive for a moment before her face split into a wide grin.

"Come with me," she said, taking my hand.

"Where are you taking me?" I asked as she dragged me behind her.

"You'll see."

We walked past the soldiers as they ran drills and rounded the corner to where a dirt sparring ring was set up. Men and women encircled the ring, standing with their arms folded across their chests as they watched two people who were currently grappling.

"Now this is more my speed," Emmerson said, grinning.

She pushed past the onlookers until we had a clear view of the pair. A mane of black hair caught my attention, and I watched as Caspan pinned a brawny man twice his size beneath him.

Emmerson let out a low whistle. "I must admit, I am impressed."

"Silas said they were remarkable fighters," I said, remembering our conversation at his manor house.

Caspan rose to his feet with the litheness of a dancer and extended his hand to the man panting and sweating on the ground at his feet.

"Who's next?" he asked as he pulled the man up.

Without warning, Emmerson pushed me into the ring and I stumbled as I caught myself from falling.

I glared at her, but she only grinned wider.

"My Queen could teach you a thing or two," she hollered.

Caspan returned her grin. "I bet she could," he said with a voice made of silk.

Sunlight broke through the clouds, enveloping Caspan in its warm embrace, and highlighting the contours of his handsome face. He had a slightly crooked nose like it had been broken previously, but it didn't detract from his beauty. If anything, it added to his appeal.

"Well, Your Majesty," Caspan pressed. "What's it going to be?"

"Fine," I huffed.

Caspan rubbed his hands together in anticipation.

"What are the rules?" I asked, as we began circling one another.

"How cute," Caspan said mockingly.

"No rules?" I questioned.

"No rules."

"It's your funeral," Emmerson yelled.

A slow smirk curved the corner of my mouth. I suddenly wanted to show Caspan exactly what I was capable of.

As he came within striking distance, I feigned left before lunging to my right, delivering a sharp jab to his midsection. Caspan parried the strike effortlessly, countering with a sweeping kick. My back hit the ground, but before Caspan could capitalize on his success, I rolled out of reach and sprang to my feet.

"Not bad," he grinned.

Caspan reached for the hem of his tunic and ripped it over his head before tossing it to the side. Sweat glistened on his golden skin and the female onlookers hooted in appreciation.

"Are you trying to distract me?" I asked, cocking a brow.

"Is it working?"

I darted forward, delivering a punch to his kidney, followed by a knee to his ribs. Caspan groaned, and I danced away.

"Not in the least," I hummed.

Caspan threw his head back and laughed. "I think I like you, Queen Harlowe."

"Just Harlowe," I corrected.

Caspan came at me again and our movements blurred as we tested the limits of our bodies. The sound of dull *thuds* and fists hitting flesh mixed with the scraping of sand under our boots and our heavy breathing.

I kicked my leg high, aiming for his head, but Caspan caught my leg and used the momentum to flip me. Twisting in mid-air, I kicked out with my free leg and connected with Caspan's sternum, forcing his grip on me to loosen.

I landed in a crouch and then straightened to my full height. Caspan didn't hesitate as he charged toward me, closing the distance between us. Caspan dropped his shoulder and wrapped his thick muscular arms around my waist as he drove me into the ground with enough force my breath left me in a *whoosh*.

The entire length of his body pinned mine to the earth beneath me and I sucked in a sharp breath as fire spread throughout my lungs.

That fucking hurt.

"Come on Harlowe," Emmerson jeered, and I had never wanted to prove myself more than I did in that moment.

I could feel the bulk of Caspan's weight leaning to the right, so I grabbed his left wrist, trapping it between my breasts with my hands.

His eyes widened, and I grinned up at him, letting him see the wicked determination sparkling in my gaze.

I hooked my foot around his left ankle, and I trapped his leg in place, immobilizing him. Then I drove my hips upwards in a burst of power, throwing him off balance. The muscles in my legs and stomach screamed in protest as I forced my hips higher until my back curved at an unnatural angle off the ground.

I threw all of my remaining energy into the move, as I twisted my body to the left and used the momentum to roll, pulling Caspan's trapped arm with me while pushing my leg into the ground as I flipped us.

I was breathing heavily as I stared down at Caspan, who seemed confused by the turn of events. Using my free hand, I gripped the hilt of my dagger and pressed it to the underside of his throat, careful not to cut him.

Shocked gasps rang out around us, but they were muted by the sound of my beating heart filling my ears.

"Do you yield?" I demanded, and Caspan swallowed against my blade.

When he didn't answer, I pressed my dagger further into his flesh and gritted out, "Do you yield?"

"I yield," Caspan said, and I loosened my grip on my dagger.

"Woo!" Emmerson hollered. "That's what I'm talking about!"

Caspan and I glanced at one another before we broke out into fits of laughter. Once I re-sheathed my dagger, I went to release Caspan, but I felt the weight of a heavy gaze searing my flesh.

My head darted up and my eyes clashed with chocolate-brown ones that seemed to peel back every layer of my skin, exposing the raw soul beneath.

Silas's lips curved into a sinful smirk and I could feel his pride crashing against me in waves from across the ring. He gave me a curt nod, and I grinned back at him.

Caspan cleared his throat, and I remembered I was still lying atop him, trapping him with my body. I jumped to my feet and extended my hand to help him up.

"Very impressive, Harlowe," he said.

"You weren't too bad yourself."

The next moment, Emmerson collided with me as she wrapped her arms around me in a fierce hug.

"I should have taken bets," she beamed. "I could have cleaned up with the amount of people spilling nonsense about their Prince being unbeatable."

Caspan chuckled as he bent to retrieve his tunic.

"My Prince," a guard called as he made his way over to us. "The Queen has requested your presence in the council room."

The guard's gaze flicked to me. "You too, Your Majesty."

Caspan thanked the guard and turned towards the palace.

"Maybe we're about to find out if Elysara will aid us," Emmerson whispered.

My gaze searched the training yard for Silas, but he was nowhere to be found.

"May the gods deliver good news then," I said as I trailed after the Prince.

# Chapter Forty-Nine

"You go ahead," I told Emmerson. "I need to find Silas."

She gave me a curt nod and followed Caspan.

I had no idea where Silas had headed after the training ring, but I figured I would check our chambers first.

The hallway leading to the guest wing was quiet, likely because everyone had been trying to keep themselves busy while we waited.

Zeke and Fionn had been spending more time together while Illiana continued to work with Arabella.

I had no idea what Cillian had been up to over the past few days. However, if I had to guess, it had something to do with Emmerson since they had both been scarce.

I was pulled from my musings when I was slammed against a hard chest, the smell of leather and male filling my nostrils as a large hand covered my mouth.

Instincts kicked in, and I battled my attacker, only to be tossed into a dark room. The sound of the door clicking shut and the lock sliding into place had gooseflesh rising on my skin as my eyes searched my surroundings.

The only  within the room was the sliver that crept in from under the doorframe.

On my second glance, I realized I wasn't in a room, but in a closet. If I stretched my arms out, I was sure I could touch both sides of the walls.

"Little Menace," Silas's deep, rumbling voice said from within the confines of the blackened room.

"Gods, Silas," I said as I released a relieved breath. "You couldn't just call out my name like a normal person."

Silas chuckled, and the sound reverberated around the tiny room before settling in my core.

He prowled towards me, his broad muscular frame barely visible in the faint light seeping in from under the door. "You took down a man almost twice your size out there, Little Menace," he growled. "You made it look so easy. Like it was child's play."

His hands landed on either side of my head, caging me in.

"It was so fucking hot," he whispered huskily.

"Oh, yeah?"

"Yeah. It made me rock fucking hard."

Silas grabbed my hand and placed it over the front of his pants, where the evidence of his arousal strained against the fabric. I gripped his length, squeezing roughly, and Silas groaned.

"Turn around," he commanded.

Heat pooled low in my stomach and I almost forgot why I had been searching for him.

"We can't, Silas," I breathed.

"And why not?"

"The Queen summoned us. I think we're about to find out if Elysara will aid us in the war. That's why I was searching for you."

Silas made a pained sound in the back of his throat, but he didn't move away from me. Even though I couldn't see his eyes, I could *feel* them boring into me.

A second passed. And then another.

"Fuck it," he hissed and crashed his lips against mine.

My arms snaked around his neck, and he angled his mouth, deepening the kiss.

"We'll be quick," he said, pulling my tunic up and exposing my stomach.

His large hand splayed over my belly before dipping below my waistband. A calloused finger skimmed over my folds and I shivered.

"Yes, quick," I panted.

Silas ripped my pants down my legs and spun me around. My hands landed on the wall and I arched my back, pushing my ass out.

"So needy, Little Menace," Silas taunted.

"Yes, and it's your fault, so do something about it."

Silas pressed his weight against my back as he gripped my hips. "Oh, I intend to," he murmured as he lined himself up with my entrance.

Without preamble, Silas snapped his hips forward, pushing inside me. He didn't give me time to adjust to the intrusion. Instead, he wrapped both hands around my throat and began thrusting.

I had to arch my neck, tilting my head back, just so I could breathe.

The sound of flesh slapping against flesh dominated the small space, and I clenched around Silas, making him groan.

"Fuck, Little Menace," he said roughly. "You keep clenching your cunt around me like that and this will be over quicker than either of us expected."

I repeated the action just to fuck with him.

A moment later, pain erupted on my shoulder, and I twisted my head to see Silas biting down. At the same time, he slid one hand from around my throat to stroke my clit.

I moaned as intoxicating pleasure spread throughout me.

"You like it when I mark you, don't you, Little Menace," he rasped.

"Yes," I moaned.

"You love it when I lay claim to your body."

I couldn't answer him. The pleasure building in my core had me struggling for breath.

"You're going to come for me, aren't you, Harlowe?" he growled. "You're going to shatter all over my cock as I wreck this pussy."

A cry tore from my throat as I came. My breathing was ragged, and I fought to catch my breath.

Silas continued to slam into me, chasing his own release. When he came, I felt his whole body shudder as he pressed himself against me.

We stood like that, his cock still buried inside me, our heavy breathing the only sound as we came back down from our shared euphoria.

Silas slipped out of me and I bent over to pull up my pants.

"Don't move," Silas ordered.

I froze, unsure what was wrong.

Silas's fingers grazed the inside of my thigh, collecting his come before he pushed it back inside me.

"Silas, what are you doing?" I chuckled.

"When we're sitting in that council room with every fucker ogling what's mine, I want to know your pussy will be overflowing with my come. With every movement, every press of your thighs, you'll feel me there, inside you." Silas leaned in closer, his nose grazing the side of my neck. "And that thought,

Little Menace, is fucking intoxicating."

"You're an animal, you know that?" I snorted.

"I prefer beast," he said and I could hear the grin in his voice. When he was done, Silas fixed my pants and said, "Come on, we're late."

"And whose fault is that?"

Light flooded the room when Silas opened the door.

I was right. We just had sex in a broom closet.

Silas grabbed my hand in his and pulled me towards the council room.

Just before we rounded the corner that would lead us to the entrance, Silas stopped and faced me.

He scanned me from head to toe, and I folded my arms over my chest. "What?" I demanded.

"You look freshly fucked," he murmured.

"Again, whose fault is that?"

Silas straightened my tunic and readjusted my belt before smoothing my hair.

"There," he said, giving me another once-over.

"Well?" I said, arching a brow.

"You still look freshly fucked," he grinned, and I punched him in his shoulder.

Silas's laughter followed me as I marched towards the council room. When I reached the door, the guards stationed out front pulled it open, allowing me to enter.

"Ah, so nice of you to join us," one councilman said as he eyed me up and down.

A low growl sounded behind me, and a flush crept up my neck as everyone turned in their seats and studied me expectantly.

"Sorry, something came up," I said, and I saw Emmerson grinning at me from across the table.

"I bet it did," she mouthed, and I shot her a glare, but that only made her grin wider.

Silas took my hand, and I caught the small upward curl of his lip as he led us to the two remaining seats.

"Not a word," I gritted out when we were seated.

I shifted forward in my chair and I could feel Silas's come dripping out of me and dampening my panties.

As if he knew exactly what was happening between my thighs, Silas smirked at me and winked.

"I'll get to it," Adeline said, reclaiming my attention. "Elysara will join you in this war, Harlowe. We stand with the Kingdoms of Valoren and Pyrithia."

I let out a relieved sigh. We'd done it. We'd actually done it.

"Tell us what you need."

# Chapter Fifty

By the time we'd departed the council room, the sun had dipped below the horizon, surrendering the sky to the moon.

We'd spent hours going over what needed to be prepared, and setting a rough plan in place for what would come next.

"Are they going to be ready?" I asked Caspan as he escorted us back to our chambers.

"They will be, Harlowe. I give you my word," he said with a slight bow.

"We need to return to Valoren," Silas said.

His unspoken words rang loudly in my ears. We needed to find out what remained of my kingdom.

I swallowed past the lump forming in my throat at the thought of what Kieran may have inflicted on my home and the people I'd left behind.

A wave of images assaulted me.

Bodies broken and mutilated.

Blood soaking the marble floor crimson.

Louise.

Closing my eyes, I inhaled a deep breath and shook my head, clearing my wayward thoughts from my mind.

When I opened my eyes again, dark brown ones met mine, pinning me in place. I gave Silas a brisk nod, letting him know I was all right.

I wasn't all right. Not even a little.

But I had tasks I'd yet to complete and people who were relying on me.

My grief and guilt would need to wait.

**"Misneach?"**

**"Yes, Fire Heart?"**

**"Tell me more about the unbonded dragons,"** I said.

**"About the fracture?"** he asked.

**"Yes. What are we dealing with exactly?"**

**"From what I understand, the division arose because some of my kind resented the conduct of the humans during the War of Witches."**

**"How so?"**

**"At first, the witches' uprising was seen as a betrayal to the realm. They believed the witches had an obligation to use the gifts the fates had granted them to ensure the realm prospered. When they instead used their magic for selfish gain, it caused the first crack in the relationship between humans and dragons,"** Misneach said.

**"So, what? Did they side with the monarchs during the war?"**

**"Not exactly,"** Misneach said. **"While the dragonfolk saw the need to suppress the witches' uprising, the... methods used... further strained the relationship."**

**"What do you mean?"** I asked.

This version of our history was entirely new to me, and it piqued my interest.

**"You know the monarchs banished all witches, correct?"**

**"I do."**

**"Well, that included witches who had played no part in the uprising... many were mere children."**

My steps faltered and Silas gave me a side-long look.

I waved him off and refocused on what Misneach had told me. **"They expelled children from the kingdoms. Where did they go?"**

**"Yes, Fire Heart, they did. Some kingdoms were more... brutal... in their banishment than others,"** Misneach said, causing a shiver to wrack my body as my mind conjured up all sorts of vile possibilities.

**"As to where they went... well, they only had one option."**

**"Netheran,"** I surmised.

**"No, Fire Heart,"** Misneach said, regret filling his tone.

**"Everly told me that Kieran took in witches following the war,"** I protested.

**"Adults, Fire Heart. He took in adult witches. He knew they could be of use to him, but children..."**

Misneach didn't have to finish his sentence for me to understand his meaning. Kieran did nothing out of kindness. If he perceived the children to offer no value, he would have cast them aside without a backward glance.

**"So where?"**

**"They took their chances within the Forest of Nightmares."**

**"No,"** I gasped.

**"I'm afraid so,"** Misneach said.

**"That makes little sense. They could have hidden their identities within the kingdoms, or... followed the dragons. The Forest of Nightmares..."** I trailed off, unsure what I could say.

**"That may have been possible, Fire Heart, if they hadn't captured them and kept them in captivity for the duration of the war."**

**"They imprisoned children?"** I balked.

**"Yes. They also branded them so they would be easily identified."**

My head was reeling. If all of this was true, then my grandfather was not the man I had believed.

**"Why not follow the dragons?"** I asked as I struggled to come to terms with the missing pieces of our history.

**"The Mountains of Dragonia are not what I would call hospitable,"** Misneach said. **"At least not to humans."**

**"The unbonded dragons... they retreated from the rest of the realm because of this?"**

**"Yes,"** Misneach confirmed. **"They believed that if humans could treat their own kind in such a way, then they could never trust them to act in the best interests of the realm. So, they returned to the Mountains of Dragonia, and left the fate of humankind in their own hands."**

**"But some dragons remained committed to humans. I mean, we wouldn't have the Cathal if they didn't, right?"**

**"In a way,"** Misneach mused. **"Some chose to work with humans because they believed in a greater duty to the realm and its inhabitants."**

I blew out a breath. This was so much worse than I had expected.

"You all right, Harlowe?" Silas murmured.

"I'm fine, just talking with Misneach."

Caspan furrowed his brows and looked at me as though he was concerned for my well-being. I didn't have the energy to ease his discomfort.

**"Tell me what you truly think, Misneach. Do we have any chance of convincing the unbonded dragons to join this fight, or are we wasting our time?"**

**"I wouldn't have suggested it if I didn't think we could succeed,"** he grumbled. **"You are a reflection of everything good in this realm, Fire Heart. Once they meet you, they will see it too. The unbonded will join us, you will see."**

We were silent for a time as I mulled everything over. I didn't believe I deserved Misneach's praise, but I wanted to be worthy of it all the same.

**"All right,"** I said as a plan took shape in my head. **"I'll talk it through with Silas and once we've finished our business here, we can leave for the Mountains."**

A strange sensation shot down the bond. It made me feel uneasy, almost nauseous. Then I realized the feelings weren't mine, but Misneach's.

**"Misneach,"** I growled. **"What aren't you telling me?"**

**"Considering... everything,"** he said nervously, which made me apprehensive because Misneach was never anything short of self-assured.

**"I don't think we should tell the General."**

**"What? Why?"**

**"It's been four centuries, Fire Heart. The unbonded dragons have had plenty of time for their resentment to fester,"** he said. **"I don't think bombarding them with an entire group of humans, some of whom have questionable morals, is the wisest idea."**

Ignoring his jab, I asked, **"What are you suggesting, Misneach? We go alone?"**

**"That is exactly what I'm suggesting,"** he said, sounding far too pleased with himself.

It was Drakkon all over again, only this time I would have both Emmerson and Silas pissed at me. There was no way I could slip past one of them undetected, let alone both.

I stole a glance at the man in question, but his attention was on Caspan as the pair discussed weaponry.

**"We can do this, Fire Heart,"** Misneach said. **"I promise."**

# Chapter Fifty-One

**"We can do this Fire Heart, I promise,"** I mocked.

**"Stop being so petulant and focus on the plan."**

**"The plan,"** I said derisively, **"relies on me sneaking out on a man who may very well sleep with one eye open, undetected, while his entire body is pinning me to the bed."**

**"Did not need that visual,"** Misneach grumbled.

**"Where is the *we* in this scenario, Misneach?"** I said, ignoring his comment.

**"I am waiting at the agreed extraction point, Fire Heart. We all have our parts to play."**

I wanted to scream, but couldn't risk waking Silas.

**"My part is much more complex than yours."**

I was whining. I knew that, but that didn't soothe my irritation.

When Misneach had suggested waiting until everyone was asleep to make our great escape, it seemed logical. It would be dark, there would be fewer people around to observe me roaming about, and both Silas and Emmerson would be unaware of my movements.

Sounded simple enough.

What I didn't count on was Silas deciding that tonight would be an opportune time to become clingy.

**"Just push him off you,"** Misneach growled.

**"He is twice my size and dead weight right now."**

**"What would you do in any other circumstance?"**

**"I would wake him and ask him to move,"** I said, all but rolling my eyes.

**"Right. Perhaps try to wriggle out little by little,"** Misneach suggested.

**"How do you suggest I do that without waking him up?"**

**"Carefully,"** Misneach deadpanned.

I will not fight with my dragon over trivial things.

**"That's the spirit,"** Misneach chuckled.

**"Misneach,"** I snapped.

**"What? I was being supportive."**

**"Would it be that big of an issue if Silas or Emmerson were to come?"**

**"If you want it to work, then yes."**

**"All right,"** I said, as I blew out a breath.

As gently as I could, I raised Silas's arm from around me, inching it upward, and carefully placed it beside him on the bed.

I held my breath and waited a moment to see if Silas would stir. When he didn't, I started to disentangle our legs.

Sliding my leg out from between Silas's was a feat worthy of its own ballad.

His legs coiled around mine, leaving me completely immobilized. I shifted onto my hip to create room to slide out, but all I achieved was stirring Silas enough that he locked me down even tighter.

I released a controlled breath as I gently pushed Silas's upper body from my chest.

He rolled off me, but his legs remained firmly entwined with mine. The way his body was contorted must have been extremely uncomfortable, and I was surprised he didn't wake up.

**"What is taking you so long?"** Misneach hissed.

**"I'm working on it!"** I barked.

**"Work faster."**

**"Of course, Misneach. Any other helpful tidbits?"** I asked in a saccharine tone.

**"Yes. Don't get caught."**

**"You are testing the limits of my patience,"** I muttered.

**"What a coincidence, I had the same thought about you."**

I will not fight with my dragon over trivial things.

Rising onto my elbows, I pulled at my leg again. Just like every attempt I had made before, it didn't budge. Growing desperate, I yanked my leg back, pulling it free... and careening over the side of the bed.

"Oomph!"

**"Fire Heart!"** Misneach snapped.

I held my breath as my heart thudded against my chest. It was so loud that I was certain it would pull Silas from sleep. I didn't dare respond to Misneach even though I was well aware that Silas had no way of overhearing our conversation.

**"Now would be a good time to get off the floor, Fire heart,"** Misneach growled.

**"One more minute."**

**"Move, now!"**

I scrambled away from the bed and then peeked over the mattress to find Silas still sound asleep. My heartbeat slowed, and I rose from the floor. Without realizing what I was doing, I leaned down and pulled the covers over Silas's torso.

My hand froze in the center of his chest.

**"Did you... did you just tuck the General in?"** Misneach asked, the disbelief crystal clear in his voice.

I pulled my hand back as if burned and watched as Silas's chest rose and fell in harmony with his breathing.

**"Not a word, Misneach. Do you understand?"** I gritted out.

Something crossed between a snort, and a chuckle escaped my dragon.

I ignored him as I crept towards the door and over to the velvet chaise I had hidden my pack behind earlier in the day.

I didn't stop to get dressed or pull my boots on. My hand gripped the doorknob, and I glanced over my shoulder at the man sleeping peacefully in the bed I had just vacated.

He was going to be irate.

But it was better this way. Or at least that's what I told myself.

I exhaled my doubts and twisted the doorknob. As I crossed the threshold, I was careful to shut the door as quietly as I could. The lock clicking into place sounded so loud in the silence of the night that I held my breath as I waited for Silas to wake.

When he didn't stir, I left the antechamber and crossed the hall to the unoccupied guest room opposite me.

**"What are you doing?"** Misneach hissed.

**"Getting dressed."**

**"Why are you doing it in there?"** he pressed.

**"Cover. If someone comes along, I don't want to be seen."**

**"Good point,"** Misneach conceded.

Now that I was fully clothed, I shouldered my pack and headed back into the hallway. There was no one around as I made my way down the passageway and past the library. I had spotted a servant entrance adjacent to the stairwell that led to the reading space on the second floor earlier in the day.

The entire palace was encased in darkness. The only light illuminating the space was from the moon peeking through the tall glass windows.

I was alone. Aside from the occasional guard, I hadn't seen a single soul since escaping my chambers.

And yet, I could feel unseen eyes watching me from the shadows.

*It's only your imagination,* I tried to convince myself.

I shook off my unease and darted forward, my hand wrapping around the door handle that would lead into the servant's quarters.

My palm was sweaty against the metal as I turned it. Before I opened the door, however, a large hand pressed against it, keeping it in place.

All my breath left my lungs in a *whoosh*.

Fuck. I hadn't fooled Silas after all.

"Where do you think you're sneaking off to in the dead of night?" a deep masculine voice asked from behind me.

My eyes widened in surprise and I turned around to meet chocolate-brown eyes.

"Zeke?" I shouted in a whisper.

"Harlowe," he rumbled.

Relief flooded through me, and I sagged against the door. "Why are you up so late?" I asked.

"You first," he said in his stern instructor's voice.

It had the desired effect.

I opened my mouth and stumbled my way through an explanation. "There is... ah... something I need to do and... ah... I... I mean, Misneach said... I have to... ah... do it myself," I finished, but it sounded more like a question.

**"Oh yes, blame the dragon,"** Misneach grumbled.

**"It *was* your idea,"** I seethed.

Zeke raised a brow, clearly not satisfied with my answer.

I knew Zeke well enough to realize I wasn't getting out of this palace without a proper explanation... if at all.

"I am going with Misneach to the Mountains of Dragonia to convince the unbonded dragons to join our fight," I said with a sigh.

"And you're doing this in the dead of the night without telling anyone...why?" he pressed.

"The dragons don't trust humans after..." I trailed off, not wanting to follow that thought. "The unbonded dragons don't involve themselves in human affairs. Misneach and I are going to change their minds."

"Again," Zeke said, "why alone and why in the middle of the night?"

"Because Misneach doesn't believe we will be well received if more than one of us approaches them," I huffed.

I knew Zeke was just trying to do what he thought was best for me, but I didn't have the time to explain everything. The sun would rise soon and time wasn't on my side.

"Look, Zeke," I said, pinching the bridge of my nose. "You need to trust me on this."

"I don't like it, Harlowe," he growled as he raked a hand through his hair. "What if something happens to you? Who will protect you?"

**"You tell that *Cathal* there is not a single being in this entire realm who can keep you safe as I can, and if he would like a demonstration, I am more than happy to give him one,"** Misneach snarled.

"Misneach will," I said, omitting his barely veiled threat to Zeke's life.

Zeke studied me for a long moment before his eyes softened. "Fuck, Harlowe," he sighed. "Emmerson is going to kill me."

I grinned at him before throwing my arms around his waist in a tight hug. "Thank you, Zeke."

"Don't thank me," he scoffed. "You likely just signed my death warrant."

"She won't know if you don't tell her."

Zeke muttered something unintelligible and tilted his head towards the ceiling.

When he looked back at me, I could see the worry warring behind his eyes. "Go now, before I think better of this, and drag you back to Emmerson to deal with."

"Get them to meet me in Valoren," I said, as I kissed him on his cheek.

"So much for not telling her," he muttered, and I couldn't help but grin.

As I burst through the kitchen door, Misneach was waiting for me.

**"It's about time, Fire heart,"** he huffed.

**"I made it, didn't I?"**

**"I told you, you would,"** he retorted.

Scaling Misneach's foreleg, I made my way onto his back and slid into place between his wings.

**"Let's get as far away as possible before Silas, or worse, Emmerson, finds out what we've done."**

**"You wouldn't be afraid of the hellcat, would you now, Fire Heart?"** Misneach teased.

**"Absolutely!"**

We were silent for a moment before we both exploded with laughter.

# Chapter Fifty-Two

I woke to an empty bed.

I slid my hand to the other side of the mattress where Harlowe should be, only to find it vacant and cold.

"Harlowe?" I called out, sleep thick in my voice.

Clearing my throat, I called louder, "Harlowe?"

When she didn't answer me a second time, my chest constricted painfully, and I threw the covers off as I raced to the bathing chamber.

I knew I was overreacting. She was likely absorbed in her thoughts and didn't hear me.

She was fine. There was nothing to worry about.

Nothing at all.

A cold sweat broke out over my body when I found the bathing chamber as empty as the bed.

I grabbed my discarded tunic from the floor and pulled it over my head as I scrambled to find my boots.

I would not panic. She was likely at breakfast, I reasoned.

*She does have a habit of disappearing,* my inner voice taunted me.

None of which was her fault, I argued back.

I strode from my chambers and headed toward the dining hall with purpose. The guards I encountered along the way gave me quizzical looks as I approached.

I suspected that the expression on my face was none too friendly.

Once I reached the dining hall, I yanked on the door handle, and it rattled in its frame.

I needed to calm down.

Taking a deep breath, I slowed my pace and strode into the wide room. Emmerson and Cillian were already there, and as I surveyed the rest of the room, I spotted Zeke and Caspan among the bodies, busying themselves with their preparations for the day.

My gaze narrowed in on Emmerson.

If anyone knew Harlowe's whereabouts, it would be Cillian's Little Viper.

"Emmerson," I said, trying to sound casual as I approached them. "Have you seen Harlowe this morning?"

"I assumed she was with you, seeing as she hasn't joined us for breakfast," Emmerson said, furrowing her brows.

"Fuck," I hissed.

"What's wrong?" Emmerson asked, jumping to her feet.

"Harlowe wasn't in bed when I woke this morning," I admitted. "She wasn't in the bathing chamber and I haven't been able to find her."

"All right," Emmerson drawled. "Have you checked the training grounds? She sometimes likes to watch the soldiers practice."

I arched a brow, waiting for her to elaborate.

Emmerson lifted one shoulder in a shrug. "What, you didn't think your pretty face was the only thing she ever wanted to look at, did you?"

"You think he's pretty?" Cillian asked and Emmerson rolled her eyes.

"Come on," she said as she marched towards the door.

"Where are we going?" Cillian called out as we trailed after her.

"Did you not hear what I just said?" she retorted, as she shot Cillian a pointed look over her shoulder.

Cillian glanced in my direction, and I smirked. I knew exactly what portion of the discussion he had fixated on.

It seemed I wasn't the only one who lost the ability to function when their woman was within their vicinity... or beyond it, in my case.

My last thought sobered me immediately.

As we rounded the corner of the palace that led to the training grounds, I scanned the surrounding area for my copper-haired vixen.

"She's not here," I said gruffly.

I tugged on the ends of my hair, allowing the pain to ground me before I could lose my fucking mind.

"She's not here," I repeated louder.

"We'll find her," Cillian assured me. "I'm sure she's around here somewhere. Let's go check in with the dragons."

I gave him a curt nod and followed him. Before we could get far, a chuckle rose through the air, mocking me and drawing me to an abrupt halt.

I spun around, my eyes clashing with the man responsible for stoking my ire.

"What's so fucking funny, Caspan?" I snarled.

"You," he said casually, taking another bite of his apple.

My hands clenched into fists, and I stalked toward him, closing the distance between us. "Care to elaborate?" I gritted out.

"You misplaced your woman, who is very much capable of looking after herself, by the way, and now you're losing your fucking mind. You're a gods-damned king, and here you are panicking like a wee one who can't find his favorite toy." Caspan eyed me. "And you're supposed to lead us into battle," he scoffed.

I rushed forward, pressing my forearm to the base of his throat as I slammed him against the closest wall. "If you know something, you better tell me right fucking now!" I growled.

Caspan only smirked at me.

"WHERE IS MY WIFE?" I roared, shoving him harder. "If you have done something, Caspan, I swear to the gods I will relieve you of your capacity to breathe this fucking instant!"

"You'd be sealing your own fate in the process," he said, sounding unfazed.

"Maybe," I rumbled. "But you and I both know that there isn't a single person inside this kingdom who could stop me from taking you with me."

Caspan's face split into a wide grin. "Relax Silas," he laughed. "I was only fucking with you. You're so easy to rile up. It's rather entertaining."

My eyes darted between his, and I could see the truth of his words.

"I was about to fucking murder you, Caspan," I hissed, not loosening my hold on him.

"I know," he grinned. "Fun, isn't it?"

"You're fucking crazy," I grumbled, letting him free.

"Not much happens around here," he said, waving his hand in the air. "As I'm sure you can imagine, I have longed for something, anything, to come along that might challenge me."

"For fuck's sake," I muttered as I stalked away from him.

"Did you say, wife?" Caspan called after me.

"He wishes," Emmerson snorted. "He keeps asking, and she keeps letting him down gently."

"So you're saying there's still a chance for a little competition?" Caspan said, wiggling his eyebrows.

I glared at him and bared my teeth.

The fucker just winked at me.

"We need to find her," I said, redirecting the conversation.

Zeke cleared his throat, drawing my attention to him.

"What is it?" I said, pinning him in place with my glare.

I had a bad fucking feeling I wouldn't like whatever he said next.

Zeke palmed the back of his neck, stalling.

"Spit it out," I growled.

"Harlowe had something she needed to do, and she asked us to meet her in Valoren," he said. His gaze flicked to Emmerson warily.

I stared at him for a moment before I lunged for him. Cillian anticipated my reaction and jumped in front of me to stop me from ripping Zeke to pieces.

"Easy," Cillian soothed. "Harlowe will most certainly be pissed if you kill one of her best friends."

Right now, I was willing to risk it.

But I didn't have to.

"Zeke," Emmerson growled as she rounded on him. "What did you do?"

"I didn't *do* anything," he snapped. "Harlowe said she had something she needed to do, and that she needed to do it alone."

"And you just let her go?" Emmerson asked incredulously.

"Yes, Emmerson, I did. She asked me to trust her and I do. She knows what she's doing."

Emmerson invaded Zeke's space, thumping her finger into his chest as she growled, "If anything happens to her, Zeke, I will come for you."

My spine straightened as I watched their exchange with renewed interest. Emmerson could kill Zeke without getting into trouble, I thought smugly.

Zeke's eyes softened as he peered down at her. "I'm worried too, Em. But she's the strongest of all of us. You need to trust her judgment." His gaze flicked above Emmerson's head until his eyes met mine. "You all do."

"I don't like this," Emmerson said, as her voice wavered.

Zeke pulled her into his arms and rested his chin on her head. "Neither do I, but she deserves our confidence, Em. The gods know she's earned it."

Emmerson sighed and wrapped her arms around Zeke, mumbling something unintelligible against his chest.

Fucking hell. I had hoped for a little bloodshed, at the bare minimum.

Cillian stiffened next to me and took a step in their direction. I flung my arm out to stop him and gave him a pointed look. He huffed out a breath and raked his hand through his hair.

"So, what do you suggest we do now?" I gritted out, barely looking in Zeke's direction.

"I suggest we ensure we're in Valoren when she finds her way home."

# Chapter Fifty-Three

**"Are you sure about this, Misneach?"** I asked, unable to hide my increasing anxiety.

**"Calm down, Fire Heart. They'll hear the rapid beat of your heart and think you have ill intent."**

**"Ill intent?"** I hissed. **"That's hardly a way to help me calm down, Misneach."**

**"Why not? If you are aware, you can take action and remedy the issue, no?"**

**"That's not how emotions work, Misneach,"** I growled.

I tipped my head back and glanced at the moon to soothe my mounting unease. It hung low against the backdrop of the sparkling night sky, casting a silvery glow over the rugged mountainside.

**"Won't sneaking into their territory also make them suspicious?"** I asked.

**"They don't trust easy, Fire Heart. I don't want to give them the chance to turn us away before we've even pleaded our case."**

A formation of jagged rocks with sharpened tips jutted out from the side of the mountain ahead of us. Misneach moved with surprising grace as he skirted around it to reach the narrow ledge off to the side.

His dark scales blended seamlessly with the rocky terrain, with only the tiniest hint of the indigo hues visible when he flexed his wings.

Misneach's body was long and muscular, which allowed him to advance with controlled and deliberate movements. His clawed limbs were perfect for navigating the rough surface, and with his wings folded against his body, he appeared smaller in the shadows of the night.

Misneach's serpentine eyes scanned our surroundings before returning to the path ahead.

**"Is there something out there?"** I whispered.

**"Nothing we need to be concerned about."**

Misneach made the treacherous climb look easy as he swung his tail back and forth, using it to counterbalance the weight of his body as he continued with the precarious ascent.

The mountains were alive with the sound of the nocturnal creatures dwelling nearby, and every so often, Misneach would pause, listening intently before he resumed climbing.

**"What do you think I should say when we meet them?"** I asked, to distract myself from the ever-expanding drop into nothingness beneath me.

**"I would never let you fall, Fire Heart,"** Misneach scoffed, having followed my train of thought.

**"Why do you sound surprised by that? I can sense your every thought. We've been through this too many times to count, Fire Heart,"** he said, sounding exasperated.

**"Let's get back to the topic, shall we?"**

**"Which topic? Your fear of heights or how you intend to sway the dragons?"** He asked.

**"The second one,"** I said, ignoring his attempt to rile me.

**"I guess that depends on how we are received,"** Misneach mused.

The night air was cool against my skin and I shivered as Misneach lurched forward, finding purchase in the smallest of crevices. My gaze traveled up the side of the mountain and my breath caught in my throat. My eyes locked onto a sheer cliff face with only the barest of ledges scattered across the face of the mountain haphazardly.

**"Is that the only way up?"** I gulped.

**"You forget I have wings, Fire Heart,"** he reminded me.

I nodded my head, even though I knew he couldn't see me.

With a powerful thrust of his hind legs, Misneach surged forward, launching himself upward, as his claws gripped the uneven surface. Smaller rocks crumbled under his grip and went sailing down the side of the mountain into the darkness of the night. I strained my eyes to follow their descent, but couldn't make out their forms once they slipped past me.

Misneach used his wings for balance as he expertly lunged from one ledge to the next. He barely made a sound as he crept higher and higher. As we neared the summit, Misneach paused again and scanned the area.

**"What are you looking for?"**

**"Just making sure we haven't been detected,"** he said.

Seemingly satisfied, Misneach continued his ascent. We scuttled over the edge of the cliff and Misneach crouched low, concealing himself within the shadows cast by the moonlit rocks.

**"Over there,"** Misneach said, flicking his chin upward.

**"I can't see anything,"** I said as I strained to see what he was looking at.

**"Beneath the overhang."**

Slowly, my vision cleared and I could make out a portion of the rock face that extended beyond the flat area below it.

**"That's the entrance to the cave?"** I clarified.

**"It is. Are you ready?"**

**"As ready as I'll ever be to face a clutch of human-hating dragons,"** I said.

**"It's going to be all right, Fire Heart,"** he soothed.

Misneach moved toward the entrance of the cave, slinking from shadow to shadow, until we were standing at the mouth of the cavern. I slipped from his back to stand at his side.

**"If anything goes wrong in there,"** he said, inclining his head toward the cave. **"You flee. No hesitation, understood?"**

**"Understood,"** I repeated.

I wasn't interested in getting myself killed on our little expedition.

The temperature dropped even lower as we stepped inside the expansive chamber. The faint echo of dripping water filled the space, and I scanned the area as Misneach moved further into the cave.

A series of tunnels stood before us and I studied them, unsure of what path to take.

**"This way,"** Misneach said as he moved with a confidence I did not share.

**"How do you know which way to go?"**

**"I can sense them."**

**"Does that mean they can sense you, too?"** I asked, as the hairs on the back of my neck stood to attention.

**"I think it's safe to assume they can,"** he muttered.

While I couldn't make out anything beyond the few feet in front of me, Misneach, with his keen eyesight, led us further and further into the labyrinth of the cave. His wings were tucked tight against his back so as not to scrape along the roughened walls, and when the tunnel narrowed, he lowered his body to the ground and all but slithered through the confined space.

At the end of the tunnel, Misneach froze.

**"What is it?"** I asked.

Misneach's head tilted at an unnatural angle and his nostrils flared as he sniffed the air.

**"Dragons,"** he rumbled.

# Chapter Fifty-Four

Misneach stepped from the confines of the tunnel into a massive, open chamber. Stalactites hung from the ceiling of the cave and stalagmites rose from the ground, making it feel as though you were standing in the jaws of an enormous beast.

Lichen clung to the walls, glowing brightly and illuminating the vast expanse in front of me. Misneach stood to his full height and stretched out his wings before drawing them back against his sides.

**"Misneach,"** a deep, gravelly voice snarled from across the cave.

My eyes swung toward the sound and locked on an enormous emerald dragon that rivaled Misneach in size.

**"Aodhán,"** Misneach rumbled.

The emerald dragon, Aodhán, was flanked by at least a dozen others, and even though the chamber was huge, they dominated the space, making it shrink around me.

**"Why have you come to my mountain?"** Aodhán demanded as he jutted his snout toward me. **"And with a human, no less."**

**"Take care with how you speak, Aodhán,"** Misneach warned. **"For you might not like the consequences should you choose poorly."**

Aodhán chortled. **"I see you are as pleasant as ever, Misneach."**

**"My demeanor depends on the company I find myself in,"** he retorted. **"Unfortunately, yours is lacking."**

**"It's all right, Misneach,"** I said, placing a hand on his foreleg to soothe him.

Aodhán's serpentine eyes widened before they narrowed in on me.

**"Why can I hear her?"** he snapped.

Misneach growled low in his throat and took a step towards the other dragon, shielding me from his scrutiny.

**"I warned you, Aodhán. Choose your words carefully. Your life may very well depend on it."**

Growls and snarls echoed throughout the chamber, seeming to come from every direction.

**"Misneach, please, remember why we are here,"** I murmured.

My dragon peered down at me, his eyes dancing with protective fury. I gave him a small nod and Misneach stepped aside, allowing the other dragons to see me.

Aodhán eyed me skeptically.

**"I have not come to cause you any trouble,"** I said. **"I am here to inform you of a great threat to our realm."**

**"You humans are the threat,"** Aodhán scoffed.

**"I can't disagree,"** I said. **"Yet I still need your help."**

**"Why is it we can communicate without a bond?"** Aodhán demanded.

**"Do you know of the Daughter of Fire and Flame?"** I asked.

Aodhán didn't respond, but I got the impression he knew *exactly* what I was talking about.

**"I am she."**

**"You expect us to believe that you are the foretold savior of the realm?"** Aodhán snorted.

**"Whether you believe me is up to you, but it won't change the fact that the realm is in danger."**

**"What danger?"** a female voice demanded.

Unsure of who had asked the question, I directed my answer to all of them. **"The King of Netheran seeks to conquer the realm. He has done many things to ensure he is victorious, including reaching for power that was never his to take."**

Murmuring broke out among the dragons, but I pressed on. **"If you know of the prophecy, then you know the fates created me to balance out his power,"** I said. **"I have met with Drakkon and he has confirmed that I am who I say I am."**

At the mention of Drakkon, the whispered mutterings grew louder.

**"How does she know of Drakkon?"**

**"Why would Drakkon meet with a human when he hasn't bothered with the dragon folk in centuries?"**

**"If Drakkon is involved, then the situation is likely worse than she is letting on."**

**"Quiet!"** Aodhán boomed.

**"Say you are the Daughter of Fire and Flame,"** Aodhán said, tilting his head as he studied me. **"Why should we be concerned with a war among the humans? Countless battles have been waged throughout history, yet we've remained detached."**

I thought over my answer before saying, **"That is all true. However, the upcoming war could decimate our realm. And while I acknowledge you may remain unscathed by the impending conflict, there was once a time when you stood beside the humans to protect and defend the realm. I am asking you to do that again."**

Taking a deep breath, I continued, **"What happened in the past was deplorable. I am ashamed to have been born to a line that was responsible for such atrocities. But I am not my forebears. I love this realm and the people in it. I know it might not count for much, but I am ready to lay down my life to protect it, and there was a time when you would have done the same. The realm has changed in the last four centuries. The people have changed. It's worth saving."**

**"You say the realm is worth saving,"** Aodhán mused. **"You say you are prepared to lay down your life for it."**

**"Yes,"** I said without hesitation.

**"Am I to take it you intend to rule the kingdoms within the realm?"**

**"I am the Queen of Valoren and the future Queen of Pyrithia."**

Misneach gave me a quizzical look, and my cheeks heated. It took all of my strength to keep my eyes trained on Aodhán.

**"Six kingdoms make up the realm of Aetherian, Daughter of Fire and Flame."**

**"Elysara has joined us."**

That piqued their interest.

**"Elysara has remained a neutral territory for centuries,"** Aodhán said.

**"They trust in Fire Heart,"** Misneach interjected. **"They are preparing to stand at her side as we speak."**

I could feel the pride washing over Misneach and I smiled despite myself.

**"And she is the Queen of Fire and Flame,"** he corrected. **"She is born from the same life force as all dragons. Fire Heart possesses power beyond your imagination, bestowed upon her by the fates themselves, and with the blessing of the original dragon. She leads us in the darkest days of our history, and before this is over, you *will* bow to her."**

Aodhán chuckled and the other dragons shifted uncomfortably.

**"We bow to no one, Misneach,"** he snarled.

**"You will. I promise you that."**

**"If she is as worthy as you claim, then she would have no qualms about forming a life bond,"** Aodhán challenged, his agitation mounting with every flick of this tail.

Misneach darted forward, snarling in Aodhán's face and baring his teeth. **"The entire realm is sitting on the edge of obliteration and the only thing that can stop it is the heart beating inside her chest,"** he seethed. **"I will not allow you to jeopardize that."**

**"She claims to be better than those who have come before her, then let her prove it."**

Misneach clawed at the ground as though he was preparing to attack. The situation was getting out of control, and fast.

**"What's a life bond?"** I asked.

Both dragons were too consumed with their escalating aggression to pay me any mind.

**"What's a life bond?"** I repeated, louder.

Aodhán glanced at me out of the corner of his eye, but Misneach remained rooted in place.

**"Misneach,"** I pleaded.

A moment passed before Misneach took an infinitesimal step back, giving Aodhán some room.

**"It is a bond where two beings tether their life force to one another,"** Aodhán answered.

**"What's the catch?"** I pressed.

**"One life, one death,"** he said cryptically.

**"If you share a life bond, and one of the bonded dies, then the other follows them into the afterlife,"** Misneach gritted out.

**"Oh."**

The dragons began debating among themselves once more, but I blocked them out. We needed the unbonded dragons in the upcoming fight. We were at a significant disadvantage, given Kieran's strength and experience. The life bond didn't assure my death, but it did increase the possibility.

My thoughts swirled in my mind until I settled on one undeniable fact.

We needed the unbonded dragons.

**"I'll do it,"** I murmured.

The chamber fell silent, and I straightened my spine. **"I'll do it,"** I repeated.

**"No, Fire Heart!"**

I turned to face my dragon, giving him a soft smile. **"The fates chose me to protect the realm, Misneach. I will do what is required to see it done."**

**"We can find another way,"** he pleaded.

**"Can we? Who else are we going to ask? We have done all we can. Now is the time to consolidate our resources and prepare for battle. Kieran is bringing this war to us, whether or not we are ready."**

**"Please, Fire Heart,"** he begged.

I could see the pain etched in his features and the tears welling in his eyes. **"I'm sorry, Misneach. We are out of time."**

Turning back to face Aodhán, I said, **"Do it."**

He surveyed me for a moment before he stepped forward and lowered his forehead to mine. Just like the last time, lightning scorched my skin, delving into every corner of my body before settling over me in a soothing wave.

Aodhán stepped back.

**"It is done."**

# Chapter Fifty-Five

My stomach twisted uncomfortably as we flew closer to the outer townships surrounding the palace in Valoren. I prayed to whatever gods would listen that Kieran had not unleashed his fury on my home and my people.

**"Whatever comes, we will face it together,"** Misneach said.

He was still upset about the life bond. Although, he'd conceded it was my decision to make.

**"I'm not upset,"** Misneach grumbled, following where my thoughts had wandered. **"I only seek to protect you."**

**"You can protect me from a great many things, Misneach, but not this."**

**"I can try."**

We enjoyed the silence as we traversed the clear blue skies, the warmth of the sun beating down on us, until the watch tower came into view, fracturing the serenity.

*Please let them be alive.*

**"There is a wide, open courtyard directly in front of the palace,"** I said to the dragons who had accompanied us. **"We'll land there before sorting out where to place you."**

**"We do not dance to your every whim,"** Aodhán barked. **"We will make our own arrangements."**

**"Of course, my apologies."**

**"Do not apologize to him, Fire Heart. He is being unnecessarily disagreeable. He knows you meant nothing by it,"** Misneach growled.

I ignored the rumblings coming from the dragons and focused my attention on the people milling about below us. It didn't appear like the palace was in disarray, but I couldn't be certain from this height.

My eyes scanned the grounds intently, hoping to recognize a familiar face.

**"Down there,"** I shouted, and Misneach dipped his wings as he moved to descend.

My heart was beating rapidly within the confines of my chest and sweat broke out all over my body. My hands were trembling so hard that I had difficulty maintaining my grip on Misneach's scales.

He had barely reached the ground before I flung myself from his back and raced toward the stoic-looking man I had spotted from the skies.

"Samuel," I called, and he had just enough time to turn and spread his arms wide before I was throwing myself into them.

"Harlowe?"

I gripped him tightly as I fought the burn stinging the back of my eyes.

"I was so worried," I murmured.

"It's all right, Harlowe. Your plan worked. The King of Netheran left the moment you did," he said as he smoothed my hair. "I am so proud of you, my girl."

Without warning, the ground shuddered beneath my feet, and a wave of gasps engulfed me.

I knew without looking what had captured everyone's attention.

Over three dozen dragons were landing in the courtyard behind me. And if I had to guess, they didn't appear all that friendly.

"Harlowe," a voice called out, and I snapped my head up.

Emmerson bounded down the steps of the palace as she sprinted for me, and I ran to meet her halfway. We collided with such force my knees threatened to buckle, but I didn't care.

She was here, and she was safe.

A low chuckle sounded behind us, and a moment later, corded forearms wrapped around me as Zeke joined us.

"I should murder you where you stand," Emmerson mumbled against my shoulder. "I was so scared something would happen to you."

"Wouldn't that be counterproductive?" I laughed.

"Probably," she sighed. "I'm just so relieved you're all right."

We broke apart, and I could see the relief etched into every corner of her face. My gaze flicked to Zeke, and he smiled down at me warmly.

"Thank you," I said, and he nodded his head in acknowledgment.

"Harlowe?" a soft, feminine voice called out. "Harlowe," she called again, louder this time.

My mother pushed people aside in her haste to get to me, drawing more than one shocked glance as she did so. When she reached me, she pulled me into her arms and held me so tightly it felt like she would never let me go.

Her body trembled against mine as she said, "I thought I might have lost you. When you didn't return with the others..." she trailed off as her voice cracked.

A lump formed in my throat and the tears I had been fighting slipped free. "Leaving you behind to the mercy of Kieran was one of the hardest things I have ever done in my life. I imagined every horrid scenario where he decimated our kingdom in retribution."

"Shh," my mother soothed. "It's all right, it's over now."

"Clementine?" my father's voice boomed over the murmurs of the crowd.

"Atticus! Atticus! She's home. Harlowe is home."

"Harlowe," my father breathed when he reached me.

He pulled me from my mother's embrace and crushed me to his chest as he lay his head atop mine.

"I'm sorry, Harlowe," he whispered.

"What are you sorry about?"

"For not standing between you and Kieran. It should have been me who faced him, not you."

I softened against him. "It was always meant to be me, Father."

"No. As your father, I should never have put you in a position to be harmed," he paused before continuing, "That is something I deeply regret and not only the most recent attack."

I glanced up at him. His eyes were misted and his lower lip was trembling.

"I forgive you, Father," I said, and I meant it.

I'd accepted he did what he thought was best for his people.

"I don't know if I'll ever forgive myself," he whispered, and I wasn't sure if his words were meant for my ears.

Seeming to regain his composure, my father peered over my head, his eyes widening at what I assumed were the dragons lined up behind me.

"I see you were successful in your endeavors," he said in awe.

"Somewhat," I grinned back at him. "Come on, I'll introduce you."

"You know I can't communicate with them, right?"

I lifted my shoulders and proceeded towards the clutch of dragons standing around the courtyard.

"Aodhán," I said out loud for the benefit of those around me. "This is my Father, Atticus."

Aodhán narrowed his eyes at my father and he shifted uncomfortably.

"And this is my mother, Clementine," I continued, ignoring his obvious displeasure.

After a moment, a few of the other dragons moved forward, sniffing the air around my parents. A bronze-colored dragon appeared to take a special interest in my mother, nudging her with its snout.

My mother glanced in my direction, looking for guidance, but I had none to give. I had no idea what the dragon was doing.

**"My name is Orla,"** the dragon said in a soft, melodious voice.

**"She can't understand you."**

"The dragon's name is Orla," I told my mother.

"It's lovely to meet you, Orla," my mother replied.

**"She is my Cathal,"** Orla said, nudging my mother once more.

**"What?"** Aodhán and I said in unison.

**"She is my Cathal,"** Orla repeated. **"I can already feel the bond flourishing within me the longer I am in her presence."**

My mouth dropped open, and I stared at my mother.

"What is it?" she asked, sounding slightly panicked.

Clearing my throat, I said, "Orla is offering you her bond. She wants you to be her Cathal."

My mother gasped before glancing back at Orla.

**"We are unbonded, Orla,"** Aodhán hissed.

**"We are unbonded because we haven't found humans worthy of such a gift. That is changing. This human is my Cathal. She is worthy. I feel it in every fiber of my being."**

**"Orla,"** Aodhán growled.

**"You share a bond with the Queen of Fire and Flame,"** Orla countered.

**"She is not our queen,"** Aodhán snapped.

**"She is. You just refuse to see it. In any case, it is my choice with whom I share my bond, and I choose her,"** she said, tilting her head toward my mother.

Aodhán growled again but made no move to interfere.

Orla lowered her head toward my mother expectantly.

"What am I supposed to do?" she asked frantically.

"Lower your forehead to hers. Orla will take care of the rest."

My mother did as I instructed, and a moment later, a soft gasp escaped her. The memory of the bond delving through my body and setting my flesh aflame assaulted me, and my eyes wandered until I met the serpentine gaze of my dragon.

A small smile spread over my lips, and he dipped his chin.

**"It is my honor to meet you, Clementine,"** Orla said.

My mother inhaled a sharp breath. "I can hear her."

"You'll get used to it," I chuckled.

Cheers erupted all around us, and I threw my head back and laughed, basking in the joy of the moment.

As I scanned the crowd, my eyes locked on a pair of soulful brown ones, and my body lit up in response. He was standing at the very top of the stairs, his muscled arms folded over his broad chest, and his face was set in a blank stare.

I swallowed roughly.

Silas turned on his heels and marched back inside the palace.

"Someone's in trouble," Emmerson cooed.

"Shut up," I drawled, giving her a gentle push before moving to follow him.

"Make him work for it," she called after me, and my cheeks flushed with embarrassment.

I was going to kill her.

First, it was time to face the consequences.

# Chapter Fifty-Six

I was both relieved and furious at the sight of my Little Menace.

Relieved, because she appeared unharmed. No obvious injuries and she had convinced the unbonded dragons to join the fight. I had complete faith in her ability to win them over, and she delivered. Harlowe was a beacon of light, and others couldn't help but be drawn to her.

But I was equally furious with her for deceiving me. She asked me to promise not to endanger myself and then went and faced a clutch of hostile dragons who abhorred humans all on her own.

If that wasn't reckless, then fuck if I knew what was.

I thought we'd moved past this distrust. We'd agreed to do this together, and I'd proven that I would support her and let her lead, even when I didn't want to. Did she think this was a one-sided relationship? That the rules applied to me, but she was free to do as she pleased?

She'd fled in the middle of the night like some fucking criminal. Without so much as a hint from her about where she was going or for how long. More importantly, she had gone alone. Did she think I would have stopped her? After everything we'd been through.

I'd been left behind to worry about her, imagining every horrible thing that could have happened to her, and feeling utterly despondent because I wasn't there to protect her.

I'd been going out of my fucking mind.

I was pulled from my frustrated musings when the door to my chambers swung open.

Well, Harlowe's chambers, I supposed.

"Silas." Her silken voice filtered across the room, caressing me gently.

A head of copper hair appeared around the door, and Harlowe took a tentative step inside. I stayed rooted in place, my hands clenched into fists as I waited for her to shut the door.

"Silas," she repeated. "I understand you're upset with me."

I barked out a laugh, but there was no humor in it.

"Rightly so," she continued. "However, I need you to understand —"

"Shut up!" I snapped, cutting her off. "You don't get to tell me what I *need* to do."

Her eyes widened, and I took a deep breath to calm myself down. The last thing I wanted to do was frighten her.

"Tell me why."

"Tell you why, what?" she asked, confused.

"Why didn't you trust me enough to confide in me?"

Her eyes softened, and she stepped closer. "I do trust you, Silas," she said gently. "If it were my decision, I would have."

I arched a brow and crossed my arms over my chest. "It wasn't?" I challenged.

"Well, yes and no," she answered.

"Explain," I demanded.

She let out a resigned sigh. "Misneach told me about the division between the dragons and why the unbonded dragons had decided to... separate themselves from the rest of the realm."

I knew our history well, but it surprised me that this seemed to be news to Harlowe.

"He thought it would be best if we went alone given... everything, and I agreed with him. I didn't want to go behind your back, Silas, I just... couldn't see another way."

"You could have told me, Harlowe," I growled. "We agreed to be honest with one another. If you had come and explained, I would have trusted your judgment. But you didn't. You left me to think... gods, I thought so many things, all of which ended in your bloody demise."

My throat thickened, and I choked on the last word.

A flicker of surprise crossed Harlowe's face and understanding settled over her features.

Fuck.

I hadn't meant to bare my soul like that. This woman held all the power over me and she didn't even realize it.

"I'm sorry, Silas," she whispered. "I didn't mean to hurt you, and I certainly didn't mean to worry you like that."

"What was I supposed to do, Harlowe? Carry on like the other half of my soul wasn't out there alone, facing only the gods knew what, unsure if she would make it back to me still breathing."

Fuck. There I went again. It was like I had no fucking control over the words spilling from my mouth.

Harlowe took another step closer.

"Don't," I warned, putting my hand up to stop her. "I'm still angry at you."

A coy smile pulled up the side of her mouth. "Can I make it up to you?" she purred.

The low, husky tone of her voice had my cock twitching to life in my pants.

I was so gone for this woman.

"And how do you intend to do that?" I asked, my voice full of gravel.

There was no point trying to fight it. I was pretty sure she could see the evidence of my arousal straining against my pants.

Instead of answering me, Harlowe gripped the hem of her tunic, sliding it up her porcelain frame before she pulled it over her head and discarded it on the floor.

The sight of her exposed breasts had me groaning internally. Why did she have to be bare underneath her tunic?

I moved back until my knees hit the chair beside her bed and I took a seat before the sight of her brought me to my knees.

"I'm not sure this is a good idea, Little Menace," I rumbled. "I'm in the mood to punish you."

"Maybe that's what I'm hoping for," she said, biting her lip.

"I mean it. I won't be gentle."

"I'm counting on it," she said as she slid her pants down her toned legs.

She toed off her boots and her pants quickly followed until she was completely exposed before me. When she took a step in my direction, I shook my head.

"Crawl," I demanded.

Her eyes darkened, and I saw the desire burning in her emerald depths. I bet if I dipped a finger inside her cunt, it would be dripping wet for me.

Harlowe lowered herself to her hands and knees and crawled towards me, arching her back and pushing out her breasts.

Fuck me.

I ran a hand down my face to distract myself from the blood pooling below my waistband, which was now bordering on painful.

When she reached me, Harlowe ran her hands up my thighs and gripped my belt buckle.

"What's your next command, master?" she said in a voice that had pleasure shooting up my spine.

"Careful, Harlowe," I growled. "I like how that sounds."

Harlowe unbuckled my belt, pulling it free from my waistband. Her tiny, petite hands slipped below the edge of my pants and gripped the base of my cock.

"Pull it out," I said, barely containing my aggression.

Harlowe did as instructed and my cock sprang free as she ran her fingers up and down my length.

I gave her a pointed look, and she lowered her mouth to the tip, swirling her tongue around the opening and making me see stars.

When she took me into her mouth, I groaned and tilted my head back as pleasure flooded me.

I gripped the back of her head and pushed her all the way down on my cock as I thrust up, fucking her face as she mewled around me.

"That's it, Harlowe," I gasped. "Fucking take it. Swallow me down that delicate little throat of yours."

She choked around my length, and when I peered down at her, I saw tears filling her eyes.

I could feel my balls tightening, but I wasn't ready for it to be over yet.

Pulling her off me, I wrapped my arm around Harlowe's waist and lifted her, spinning her around. I quickly shed my clothing before settling behind her. Her gorgeous ass was on full display. Mine to use as I pleased.

"Tell me if I become too much," I said, and she gave me a curt nod.

I lowered my mouth to her ass cheek and sank my teeth into the supple flesh. Harlowe cried out, but her whimper turned into a moan when I drove my finger inside her.

"So wet," I chuckled. "How badly do you need to be fucked?"

"So badly," she panted.

I reached forward and gripped both her hands in one of mine, pinning them to the base of her spine. Her body fell forward under the pressure, but she didn't complain.

"Spread your legs," I demanded, and she shuffled on her knees until I could see the pink flesh of her swollen pussy.

I watched my finger disappear inside her, only to reemerge slicker and slicker with every thrust. The sight had something primal inside me roaring to life.

I retracted my finger, and Harlowe whined at the loss. My hand came down on her bare ass and she yelped before moaning as I squeezed the reddened skin.

I pushed my thigh between her legs, and Harlowe began grinding herself against me.

"So needy, my little whore," I taunted. "You're so desperate for my cock I could do just about anything to this body and you would let me, wouldn't you?"

"Yes," she breathed without hesitation.

My hand snaked into her hair, and I wrapped it around my fist. I tugged her back until her ear was level with my mouth.

"Make yourself come on my thigh," I hissed before nipping the shell of her ear.

Harlowe whimpered again, but it was more desperate, more wanton than before. She ground herself against my leg as I held her hands captive and her hair firmly ensnared in my grip.

Her body trembled, and I knew she was about to come. I closed my mouth around her shoulder and bit down, making her cry out as her orgasm hit.

"Oh... gods," she gasped, and she struggled to suck in a breath.

I released her shoulder and pushed her forward until her cheek kissed the floor.

"Stay down," I ordered.

My fingers dipped inside her, gathering her release and drawing it up to her puckered hole.

Harlowe stiffened, and I paused, giving her time to protest.

When she didn't, I spat into my hand and rubbed it up and down my length.

I positioned myself between her ass cheeks and nudged her back hole with the tip of my cock. She let out a shaky breath and nodded her head.

Pressing my hips forward, I watched as the crown of my cock disappeared inside her. A guttural groan escaped my chest as her muscles clamped down around me, strangling my cock.

"Fuck, you're so tight," I hissed.

She whimpered, and I reached around her to tug on one of her nipples.

"Play with your pussy," I said, releasing one of her hands, and I watched as it vanished between her thighs.

When I felt her body relaxing, I let go of her nipple and fisted the hair at the base of her head.

"Don't stop fucking yourself while I lay claim to this ass," I snarled and shoved her face further into the floor.

I used the hand entangled in her hair and the one keeping her other hand captive to leverage myself as I snapped my hips forward, pressing all the way into her ass.

I sucked in a sharp breath as I remained still for a moment, allowing Harlowe to become accustomed to the intrusion.

I rocked my hips against her ass, my cock growing impossibly hard at the mewling sounds she was making as she brought herself to climax.

Picking up the pace, I pounded into her tight hole repeatedly as pleasure built inside me.

"This tight little ass of yours is taking my cock so well, Harlowe," I panted.

"More," she demanded, and I almost exploded then and there.

"My dirty girl," I praised as I increased the speed of my thrusts.

"Now be a good girl and give me one more."

Harlowe tensed beneath me, her body glistening with sweat as she trembled.

"That's it, give in to me."

She cried out, muttering unintelligibly as her pleasure washed over her.

I pulled out, releasing my hold on her hair as I pumped my cock with my fist. Ropes of my come spilled over Harlowe's back and I let go of the hand still pinned behind her as I smeared my come over her sweat-soaked skin.

"You look so beautiful covered in my come, Little Menace."

She barked out a laugh and collapsed onto the floor. "You're depraved," she teased.

"That I am."

I dragged my finger through my come, writing a single word: Mine.

"But you love it," I added before collapsing to the ground beside her.

"I do," she said breathlessly.

I pulled her into my arms and held her close. "Promise me that next time you feel the need to embark on some dangerous mission alone, you'll at least discuss it with me beforehand."

"Promise," she whispered. "I am sorry, Silas. I never intended to hurt you."

I pressed a kiss to the top of her head and inhaled.

Her scent always had a calming effect on me.

"Come on," I said, gathering her in my arms and carrying her into the bathing chamber. "Let's get you cleaned up."

# Chapter Fifty-Seven

"This is it, isn't it?" I asked Silas as we overlooked the training ground.

Men and women sparred with practice swords, others were shooting targets with a bow and arrow, while Cillian led the Cathal in a series of exercises.

"Are you asking me what comes next, Little Menace?"

I nodded my head.

"We have done everything possible to prepare. Now, we face our enemies head-on."

I spotted my mother's golden head of hair and I smiled to myself as I watched her. She was born to be a Cathal. Despite her lack of experience, she appeared as though she'd been riding dragons her entire life.

She was comfortable, at ease... free.

"She's a formidable woman, your mother," Silas said, following my line of sight.

I hummed in agreement. She was certainly that.

My thoughts drifted to the other soldiers preparing to enter a war they hadn't asked for. My father had pulled me aside shortly after I'd returned to inform me that the emissary he sent to Zarinia had returned.

The news hadn't been what I'd hoped for.

The Kingdom of Zarinia would not join us in the upcoming war, citing neutrality, but I knew better.

They feared what would happen to them if Kieran won.

I couldn't blame them for their hesitation, but that did nothing to ease my frustrations over their cowardice.

If we were victorious, they would congratulate us on our success and seek to build relations with our kingdom.

If Kieran proved victorious, no doubt they'd attempt the same.

If only they realized Kieran had no intention of seeking alliances. This time, Kieran sought total dominion over the realm.

Not surprisingly, Vidyaa had not responded to our emissary. If I was being honest with myself, I hadn't expected them to. The best I could hope for was that they abstained from joining the conflict instead of providing aid to Kieran.

Time alone would reveal their intentions.

"When do the soldiers from Pyrithia arrive?" I asked.

"By the end of the week. Eoin sent word of their impending departure."

"And Elysara?"

"I expect them any day now. We left immediately after your disappearing act, and Caspan assured me they would not be far behind."

"We'll need to make room for them all," I mused. "The unbonded dragons have returned to the nearby mountains, so the space I had set aside for them is available."

"We'll make it work, Harlowe," Silas assured me.

"Do you know how Arabella's training is progressing?"

"You should ask, Zeke," Silas said, sounding amused.

I turned to face him. "What do you mean?"

"They've been spending quite a lot of time together of late," he said, as he wiggled his brows suggestively.

"Are you insinuating that they are sleeping together?" I laughed.

Silas put his hands up in front of him, feigning innocence. "I'm not suggesting anything. It's merely an observation."

Liar.

Truthfully, I hoped they had connected on some level. Zeke deserved to have someone in his life, and Arabella was the kindest, most generous person I had ever met… aside from Everly.

I pushed away the throbbing sensation that started up inside my chest at the reminder of my friend.

"You all right?" Silas asked, having detected the change in my demeanor.

"Just thinking about Everly."

Silas pulled me against his chest and wrapped his arms around me.

"Do you think they'll be ready?" I asked nodding toward the Cathal Cillian and now Fionn were instructing.

"They'll have to be."

"I'm glad we have Illiana on our side," I added. "She was incredible against Kieran."

I had no doubt she'd be a significant asset when the last battle dawned.

Silas muttered his agreement and then mumbled something about the dire wolves that I didn't catch. A grin spread across my face as I recalled his reluctance to enter Illiana's chambers whenever they were present.

I let my gaze wander over my people engaged in various preparations as we readied ourselves to confront Kieran.

My father and Samuel were hunched over some parchment, bowing their heads as they discussed whatever was written on it.

Next, my eyes flicked to where Illiana and Arabella stood, practicing incantations and summoning spells. I noticed Zeke training nearby, his gaze returning to Arabella every so often, and for the first time, I wondered where he had been headed when he caught me in Elysara.

I saved that thought for later, then found the person I desperately wanted to share my theory with.

Emmerson stood in the center of the sparring ring, her short swords leveled in both hands, while a group of soldiers circled her. The men kept darting glances toward Samuel, unaware that the real threat stood among them.

I chuckled, unable to contain it.

"What's so funny?" Silas asked, pinching my side.

"Emmerson," I said, pointing in her direction. "They keep checking to see if Samuel is watching them. They have no idea Emmerson could tear them to shreds with her bare hands."

"She's vicious, that's for sure," Silas muttered and I elbowed him.

"That's my best friend you're talking about."

"Pretty sure she would take it as a compliment," he grumbled.

I couldn't argue with that.

In the ring, the men swiftly closed in around Emmerson. For a second I lost sight of her, but a moment later, her boot landed on the stomach of the man nearest us as she unleashed a battle cry. She swung her swords high and the sound of steel meeting steel rang out, filling the surrounding space.

Emmerson dipped her shoulder as she drove it into the center of another man's chest, sending him flying backward. Her leg connected with the shins of another man and she head-butted a fourth, sending blood pouring from his nose and coating the ground crimson.

"See," Silas said, sounding smug.

Cillian glanced in her direction, and he started to make his way over to her, but Emmerson bared her teeth at him, stopping him in his tracks.

The two remaining men shared unsure glances and were quick to concede defeat once she'd disarmed them.

"Fuck," Silas chuckled. "What the hell is wrong with Cillian?"

"What, she's fun."

"There are many words I would use to describe Emmerson, but I'm not sure *fun* makes the list."

I stomped on his foot and pushed him away.

"Ow, Little Menace. That hurt."

"Good, because that was my intention." Narrowing my eyes, I continued, "If I had to choose between you and Emmerson, you would be on your way back to Pyrithia quicker than you could say Little Viper."

Silas smirked, once against raising his hands in a placating gesture. "All right, all right, I surrender," he chuckled.

Emmerson bounded over to us, sweat coating her brow as she caught her breath. "That was exhilarating," she said with a broad grin.

Silas gave me a pointed look I ignored. "You were great, Em."

She grinned even wider, showcasing the blood covering her teeth. "You should freshen up," I suggested. "You have a little something..." I trailed off, pointing to my teeth.

"Yeah, it was the headbutt," she sighed. "Bit my fucking tongue. I'll catch up with you later."

When I turned to look at Silas, he was fighting the smile threatening to break free. "Not another word."

He nodded his head and donned a serious expression, despite his face growing redder by the minute.

My gaze instinctively drifted toward the dragons who were standing back from the Cathal Cillian was training. They seemed to be observing their progress and if the occasional tilt of their heads were any indication, they were providing feedback as they went.

When my eyes landed on Misneach, he was already looking at me.

**"We are ready, Fire Heart."**

**"How can you be sure?"**

**"Just as you stand ready to lead us, Fire Heart, we stand ready to follow."**

**"What if I make a mistake?"**

**"It's alright to falter sometimes, Fire Heart. The real challenge lies in standing up and trying once more. Don't let fear keep you down. I believe in you, they believe in you,"** he said, tilting his head towards the soldiers as they practiced. **"You just need to believe in yourself."**

"There's only one more thing we need to do," Silas said, reclaiming my attention.

"And what would that be?"

"It's time to leverage the gift Kieran gave you."

# Chapter Fifty-Eight

I paced the meadow in irritation as I waited for Kaleb to appear in the dream I had created. He was late, and I had exhausted all of my patience following my failed attempt to eliminate Harlowe.

It had been a little over a week since she had slipped through my grasp and while her escape frustrated me, I also couldn't deny her growing strength impressed me. Of course, as it turned out, not all of her capabilities had been *hers*.

A smile curved the corner of my lips at the thought of how my Bride had duped me.

I heard a sharp intake of breath behind me and stopped my pacing.

"Just when I thought you needed a reminder of who you serve, you graciously decided to bestow me with your presence," I sneered.

Kaleb shifted in place, looking uncomfortable. He ran a hand through his dirty blond hair, making it appear more disheveled than usual.

"I apologize, my Lord," Kaleb simpered. "I used a tonic to help me sleep, but it took time."

"I do not care for your excuses, Kaleb. The next time you keep me waiting in the dreamscape will be your last. Do not overestimate your value to me."

"Yes, my Lord. Of course," he whimpered.

"Tell me where our preparations are up to," I demanded, resuming my pacing.

"We have wrapped up all conscripts and your armies will arrive in

Netheran's capital in two weeks," he said.

"Only those who wield fórsa?" I clarified.

Kaleb hesitated for a moment.

"Well?" I demanded, arching a brow.

"Some conscripts were not wielders, however, they showed exceptional skill on the battlefield." Kaleb's tongue darted out, licking his lower lip. "We thought they could be useful. If not, they would at least slow down any advance."

"Did you?" I challenged.

I didn't mind the exercise of discretion on this occasion. What Kaleb said rang true. However, I wouldn't allow him to think I approved of his blatant disregard for my orders.

"I-I'm sorry, my Lord," he stuttered. "If we were wrong, I'll send them away upon their arrival."

I studied Kaleb for a long moment and he grew increasingly nervous under my scrutiny.

"I'll guess we'll see," I mused.

Kaleb visibly relaxed and continued. "Vidyaa has committed a host of roc and their riders to counteract the threat posed by the dragons."

"Interesting, considering their goal until recently was to see an end to my ambitions," I said, unable to hide my amusement.

"The death of the Prince changed things," Kaleb muttered.

"Ah, yes. My Little Bride has been a very naughty girl."

Kaleb gave a curt nod before lowering his eyes.

"Tell me about the witches," I commanded.

"There are roughly six covens, each with ten to twenty witches, depending on their location."

"All versed in dark magic?"

"Yes, my Lord. I have arranged everything precisely as you stipulated."

"Good," I growled.

"You have amassed the greatest army in the realm's history," Kaleb said, awe evident in his tone.

This fight had been a long time in the making and I'd be damned if I let anything... or anyone... get in my way.

My thoughts drifted to my father and the reckoning that was headed his way. I could almost taste my retribution on the tip of my tongue. The satisfaction that thought invoked was unparalleled.

As much as his screams and pleas soothed my soul, the thought of finally delivering what he never could, brought a potent sense of accomplishment. In my victory, he would see the utter failure he was, and when that moment came, his end would swiftly follow.

My only regret was that I would not get to enjoy the spoils of war.

My Little Bride would be the ultimate prize.

I had become addicted the first and only time I had been inside her. Being buried in her tight heat brought me more pleasure than any woman before her.

And considering the debauchery that I indulged in between the sheets, that was high praise.

As if my thoughts had conjured her, I caught a hint of Harlowe's scent on the breeze. I spun around, scanning the meadow and the tree line encircling us for any hint of her.

But there was none.

I don't know why I expected to find her in the dreamscape. Every other time she had entered, it had been at my behest.

And yet...

Turning to face the shadows, I inhaled deeply.

She smelled of roses mixed with cherries, and something that was uniquely... her. Her scent was like ambrosia. Heaven sent to enchant those around her.

It was faint, as if she was moving in the opposite direction.

But it *was* there.

A wicked grin split my face, and I set off after her.

My Little Bride was full of surprises.

I pumped my legs hard, and my heart hammered away inside my chest.

I could have moved through the shadows, but there was something extremely enticing about hunting her down like prey.

It was instinctive.

Thrilling.

Primal.

Weaving through the trees, I used the dim light of the moon peeking through the canopy to guide me. A faint rustle sounded to my left, and I crouched low to the ground and listened. The snap of a branch shattered the silence of the night, and my grin grew wider.

She was close.

I could almost taste her fear in the air.

It was intoxicating.

Spurred by my determination to *finally* catch her, I sprang to my feet, and with a sudden burst of speed, I moved like a ghost in the night as I closed the distance between us.

A short gasp had me pivoting mid-stride as I leaped over a fallen log and pushed forward, adrenaline fueling my every step. The underbrush clawed at my limbs while the skeletal branches of the overhanging trees snagged my tunic, in an effort to derail my advance.

I ignored it all.

My Little Bride was here and I wasn't letting her get away from me again.

Then suddenly, everything fell silent.

Even the rustling leaves had gone still, as if the entire forest was holding its breath.

My eyes searched wildly before landing on something snagged on a branch ahead of me. I approached slowly, and once it was within my reach, I plucked the lock of copper hair from the branch and rubbed it between my fingers.

It was soft and silky… just like I remembered it.

A growl tore up my throat as realization dawned on me.

She got away.

My Little Bride escaped my grasp once again.

Loud panting sounded behind me and I spun, catching Kaleb by the throat and pinning him against the nearest tree.

"What the fuck are you doing here?" I snarled.

He heaved in large gulps of air as he struggled under my grip.

Or at least he tried to.

His face quickly turned a mottled red as he desperately tried to suck in a breath, but failed.

I studied him closely.

His eyes were blown wide, and his pupils were dilated. Tears welled in his eyes as his body responded to his distress, and a glassy sheen washed over them as his gaze became unfocused. Tiny, red spiderwebs filled the whites of his eyes as his blood vessels bulged under the pressure.

With an annoyed sigh, I released him, and Kaleb fell to the ground, wheezing and coughing.

"Are you done?" I snapped in irritation when he failed to regain himself.

"Y-yes, my Lord," he rasped as he got to his feet on unsteady legs.

"Good, because there's one more task I need you to complete before we're ready."

Kaleb nodded his head vigorously.

"You will meet with the witches and together, you will make sure *she* is ready for what's coming."

Kaleb's eyes widened, but he said nothing. He knew exactly who I was referring to. Despite how much he reviled her, he would make the necessary arrangements in order to execute my command.

"You have one week."

# Chapter Fifty-Nine

I woke with a gasp to the sound of Silas's panicked voice as he shook me gently.

"Harlowe. Harlowe, can you hear me?" he asked.

"I'm here, Silas, I'm here."

A collective sigh reverberated around the room, and my cheeks heated as I recalled I'd had an audience while I'd slept.

"Are you all right? What happened in there?" Silas said.

"I'm fine," I reassured him. "But I'm not sure how useful the information I gathered will be," I said as I bit my lower lip.

Confused gazes met my hesitation. "I was discovered."

"He didn't hurt you did he?" Emmerson asked at the same time Silas snarled, "He better not have touched you."

"He didn't catch me," I said, the relief clear in my tone. My gaze flicked to Silas. "You woke me up right as he was about to reach me."

His shoulders sagged with relief.

"What did you find out?" Illiana asked, drawing my attention to the others spread about my chambers.

"Well, from what I gathered, he has a sizable army. He has been conscripting anyone who can wield fórsa and anyone who showed any promise on the battlefield."

"Conscription?" Arabella asked, disgusted.

"Yes, and not only soldiers. He has witches in his ranks." I gave her an apologetic smile. "It sounded like he had forced them to learn dark magic."

Arabella paled while Illiana's face grew crimson in outrage.

"How many?" she demanded.

"How many witches?" I clarified, and she gave me a curt nod.

"Ah," I wracked my brain, trying to recall what Kaleb had said. "I think Kaleb mentioned six covens with a dozen or so witches in each."

Illiana swore under her breath and mumbled something about oath-breakers.

"Who's Kaleb?" Zeke asked.

"He is one of Kieran's advisors. He accompanied Kieran on his trip to Valoren." When Zeke furrowed his brows in confusion, I pressed on. "Originally from Vidyaa, dirty blond hair, surly look permanently etched on his face..."

"Oh yes, I remember him. Riveting conversationalist," he muttered.

"So he has a sizable army and six covens of witches," Cillian said. "Anything else?"

"Yes. Vidyaa has committed a large host of roc and their riders to the war effort."

"What?" Silas snapped. "That makes little sense. After everything they put you through to keep you out of Kieran's influence, they just threw their support behind him?"

Guilt gnawed at my stomach as I recalled the reason behind their decision.

"It's because of me," I said quietly.

"What do you mean?" Silas asked.

"They committed their forces because they want retribution for the death of their Prince," I admitted.

"That's not your fault, Little Menace," Silas said to reassure me. "I'm the one who ended his miserable existence, and I'd do it again. He had it coming after what he did to you."

"All the same, it looks like they blame me for his demise."

"They're fucking cowards," Emmerson spat. "Even without the Prince's death as an excuse, they still would have allied with Netheran. They'd want to tether themselves to who they perceive as the bigger threat."

There was murmured agreement around the room, and it improved my mood somewhat.

"Why do you say the information won't be useful now?" Cillian asked, ever the strategist.

"Kieran somehow knew I was there. I don't know how he figured it out, but he chased me into the woods. He'll likely alter his plans now that he knows I was listening."

I couldn't help but feel dejected. I had entered the dreamscape to seek some sort of advantage for us as we headed into battle, and I had failed.

"Not necessarily," Silas mused.

I raised a brow as I waited for him to continue.

"For one, Kieran is an arrogant prick, so even if you heard his plans, he'll believe it doesn't matter because, in his mind, he's strong enough to crush you either way."

"Not untrue," I muttered to myself.

"Cut that out," Emmerson hissed, and my head snapped up.

"Cut what out?"

"Stop underestimating yourself," she ground out. "You are fucking incredible, Harlowe. The rest of us can only dream about doing the things you have accomplished. You are strong, resilient, and brave. I don't care how many years Kieran has on you. When the time comes, you're going to kick his ass! I have no doubt about that."

By the end of her tirade, Emmerson's chest was heaving with the emotion pouring out of her.

**"The hellcat has a point,"** Misneach chimed in.

**"Stop listening in,"** I chided.

**"It's not —"**

**"If you finish that sentence, I'm leaving you behind,"** I warned.

Deep, rumbling laughter filled my mind, and it took me a moment to realize it wasn't only Misneach's laughter.

**"You're all terrible gossips,"** I grumbled.

**"Your mind is *so* much more entertaining than mine,"** Rónán teased.

**"You're incapable of engaging thought... I'm shocked,"** Oisín deadpanned.

Ignoring the dragons, I returned my focus to Emmerson. "You're right," I said with a shaky smile. "We can do this."

**"Of course we can,"** Saoirse scoffed, and I snorted.

"What's so funny?" Silas asked, his lips curling in amusement.

"Emerson's dragon is a perfect fit for her."

"They're both brutishly stubborn," Cillian whispered, but not quietly enough.

"Fucking hell, Emmerson," he growled. "Enough with the hitting already."

"When you stop saying idiotic things," Emmerson cooed, "I'll stop trying to knock some sense into you."

The room exploded with laughter, and I struggled to contain my broad grin.

Cillian grumbled unintelligibly before sighing. "Did they mention when they would be ready?"

"Kaleb mentioned something about the conscripts being brought to the capital within two weeks, so I'd guess anytime thereafter," I mused. "How long would it take them to move a large army from Netheran to Valoren?" I asked, directing my question to Silas.

"How big are we talking?" he asked, crossing his arms over his chest.

"I don't know exactly. Kaleb only said it was the biggest army the realm had ever seen."

Silas hummed as he ran his hand along his jaw. "When are we expecting Eoin?" Silas asked Cillian.

"In three to four days."

"Elysara will arrive in two at the most," Silas muttered to himself. "Once Pyrithia's forces arrive, we'll let them rest for a day or two, then we can march out."

"March out where?" I asked, confused.

"You don't want them to bring the fight to you, Little Menace," Silas said. "Let's use the week to put as much distance between your people and the battle to come."

"But where do we go?" I asked as I chewed on my lip.

I felt stupid not having any of the answers. People expected me to lead, but I had no clue what I was doing.

"Zeke, do you still have that map?" Silas asked.

Zeke unbuckled the leather satchel at his hip and handed a piece of rolled-up parchment to Silas.

Silas walked over to the breakfast table near the window and unrolled the parchment to study it. A moment later, Cillian joined him, peering over Silas's shoulder as they both considered the options.

Silas lifted his head, and his gaze locked with mine. "Come here, Harlowe," he said, beckoning me over.

When I reached him, he pointed to a section of the map that sat between Valoren and the path we had taken to reach Drakkon's lair. "I think we should aim for here."

"That's off the path Kieran would take to reach Valoren," I said. "He could bypass us entirely and cross into my kingdom, which would be undefended and unprepared."

Silas grinned as if my response pleased him. "We could set up scouts on the path and redirect Kieran's attention," he said smugly.

"What if he didn't follow?"

"Then we'd wait until he passed and ambush him from behind," he smirked. "Either way, it puts us on a path to intercept him, but removes the threat of Vidyaa coming at us from the side and encircling us."

I studied the map closer this time, and Zeke joined me on my other side.

"Makes sense," Zeke shrugged.

"The mountains will provide added cover, especially for the dragons," Silas said, gesturing back to the map.

I exhaled a deep breath. "All right. Let's make it happen."

# Chapter Sixty

The next few days passed in a blur. First, Caspan arrived with Elysara's army, followed by the rest of the Pyrithian forces. We spent long days gathering the remaining supplies we would need and even longer nights discussing strategy and planning for every eventuality.

I was exhausted, and we hadn't even departed yet.

So as I sat astride Misneach, settled between his broad wings, I surveyed the masses who had heeded our call and felt immense gratitude for each soldier prepared to defend our realm.

The fight was far from won, but at least we would head into battle from a position of strength.

I glanced to my side and caught sight of my mother shifting nervously in her position atop Orla.

"Anxious?" I asked, and she looked my way.

"A little."

"I'm sure you've already been told this, but let Orla lead you. She knows what she's doing. All you have to do is trust that she will keep you safe."

Orla made a noise of agreement and a small smile tipped up the corner of my mother's lips.

"When did you become so wise?" she teased, but I could see the pride burning behind her eyes.

"I had a great example to follow," I grinned back.

"Flattery will get you everywhere," she said with a wink.

"Have you got the stone?" Silas asked on my other side.

I patted the pocket that was concealed on the inside of my tunic and nodded my head.

"Then we're ready," he said.

The intensity of his stare had me momentarily breathless until I realized he was waiting for my command.

The thought immediately sobered me.

Taking a deep breath, I cleared my mind and shouted, "Move out!"

Misneach crouched low to the ground and pushed off his hind legs as he hurtled towards the sky.

This was it, everything we had been preparing for.

We were headed for war.

It took an entire week for us to arrive at the spot where we would await Kieran's arrival. It had been slow-moving with the ground forces in tow, and while we had horses for transportation, we didn't have nearly enough to accommodate everyone.

So the Cathal had worked in shifts, flying ahead to ensure our path remained clear as we waited for the armies to catch up.

I took some solace in knowing that Kieran was similarly delayed as he awaited the arrival of his own forces. Although, I wasn't taking any chances where he was concerned. We set scouts in place as we made our way toward our final destination, and more would join them come morning.

By the time I dismounted Misneach, the sun was setting, and long shadows stretched across the valley from the neighboring trees.

The air was thick with anticipation, but there was also a subtle undertone of fear among the armies as they approached. It was evident in the way they shifted their weight from foot to foot, and how they moved their weapons from one hand to the other, and back again. The way they studied the surrounding tree line as they scanned the area, and the sweat that coated their brows.

They knew what was coming, and they weren't foolish enough to believe that everyone would make it out unscathed.

The more seasoned warriors took control of the organized chaos that unfolded as the soldiers set up our camp.

I was grateful for it. I had no clue about coordinating such a large mass of people.

"Here," Samuel said, thrusting a water canister toward me. "You look like you're about ready to throw up," he chuckled.

I took it with a grateful smile and drank greedily. "I have no idea what I'm doing," I confessed.

"I'll let you in on a little secret. None of the monarchs ever do. That's why they delegate." He nudged my shoulder with his much broader one and I grinned up at him, thankful for his company.

"Except maybe that boy of yours," he said, pointing in Silas's direction. "He looks like he knows how to command an army."

I glanced towards Silas and saw him barking orders as he and Cillian made arrangements for the Pyrithian soldiers.

"He does," I agreed. "I guess being a general before becoming king has served him well on this occasion."

"I guess so," Samuel chuckled.

A crashing sound caught my attention, and I glanced to my left to see a stack of wooden stakes had fallen off a wagon. The canvas tent that accompanied them lay in a haphazard pile on the ground.

Samuel sighed. "I better go give them a hand before they get lost in all that material."

"I'll come with you," I said, and Samuel gave me a quizzical look.

"You sure?" he said as he rubbed the back of his neck. "This lot can be quite unruly."

"I'm sure."

Once Samuel had sorted out the mishap with the first tent, we set to work, pulling out the remaining canvas and setting the stakes in place.

It was hard work, but I relished the burn of my muscles as I drove my hammer into the wooden rods and tugged on the rope that secured the tent in place.

We erected dozens of tents and as I looked around, I saw a sea of white canvas where the others in the camp had been busily working.

On the outskirts of the camp was the largest firepit I had ever seen, with an entire crew of cooks tending to the roaring fires in preparation for cooking the evening meal.

A massive open-sided tent stood off to the other side and several blacksmiths were part way through setting up a makeshift forge, ready to repair the army's weapons and armor.

It was incredible how quickly it all came together. The camp was bustling with energy. Everyone seemed to know their role and worked efficiently to get things done.

"What is that tent for?" I asked, pointing to a large tent that stood in the middle of the camp. Lanterns sat around the exterior and the flap was open, allowing me to see inside. A long table stood at the center, surrounded by at least a dozen chairs.

It must be the war room... or tent.

Samuel chuckled beside me and shook his head.

"That would be your tent, my Queen," he said pointedly.

"My tent?" I squealed as I stopped walking mid-stride.

"In case you forgot, you are the leader of this little group," he teased, his eyes sparkling with mirth.

"I don't need a tent that big. We should use it for meetings or something."

"We will, but it will also be where you sleep at night. It's well-protected and has enough space to accommodate those who will call on you."

When I opened my mouth to argue, Samuel raised his hand to silence me. "The soldiers need this, Harlowe. It gives them a sense of security to know there is a central point of authority."

I swallowed roughly, but nodded in acquiescence.

As we stepped inside the tent, I found my father and Zeke deep in conversation as they examined the documents scattered across the table.

"You're here, good, good," my father said, not taking his eyes off the report he was reading. "Come, take a look at this."

I strode to his side, and Samuel settled into one of the chairs at the table.

"What are they?" I asked.

"Suggested shift rotations for the scouts and the border watch."

I scanned the parchment before saying, "Add two more soldiers to each shift and extend the patrol further out. We can't afford to underestimate Kieran, and we'll need as much lead time as we can get."

When I glanced up again, Zeke, my father, and Samuel were all beaming at me.

"What?" I asked, feeling self-conscious.

"I told you," Zeke said. "She's a natural."

Heat lanced my cheeks, and I gave them a tentative smile in return.

At that moment, Silas strode inside the tent followed by Cillian, Fionn, and Emmerson.

"Where's Arabella?" Zeke asked, then hastily added, "And Illiana."

Silas gave me a knowing grin as Cillian said, “I think I saw them helping set up the healers’ tent.”

He gave a curt nod and turned to me. “Unless you need me here, I might head over and give them a hand.”

“Go ahead,” I said, waving him off.

The hours ticked by in a mix of fierce debate regarding our strategy and the more mundane tasks, such as the operational requirements to keep the camp running smoothly.

The noise outside the tent had gone quiet a couple of hours prior, as the soldiers finished their meals and retired to their beds for the night.

Honestly, I doubted I could keep my eyes open much longer.

When a yawn escaped me, Silas called an end to our planning session, ushering everyone from our tent and closing it behind them.

“Come on, Little Menace,” he said, extending his hand to me. “Let’s get you to bed.”

# Chapter Sixty-One

Silas picked me up and carried me over to the makeshift bed that was more comfortable than any bedroll we had used before. I couldn't help but feel a little guilty about the extravagance, knowing everyone else was all but sleeping on the cold, hard ground.

However, I quickly forgot my worries when Silas slowly and sensually stripped my tunic from my body. His fingers glided over the side of my ribs as he freed my breasts from their bindings, leaving gooseflesh in his wake.

Silas stared down at me, seemingly in a trance, as his hungry gaze feasted on my exposed flesh. He scrubbed a hand down his face and crouched before me so he could untie the laces of my pants. My breath hitched as he gripped the waistband and tugged.

He gave me a knowing smirk as he peeled the fabric down my legs. His fingertips grazed my inner thighs, making me shudder.

"Do you need something, Harlowe?" he asked as he pulled my boots free, followed by my pants.

"You know I do."

I crawled up the bed, spreading my legs wide to give Silas the perfect view of my current state of arousal.

He groaned and ran his hand over the front of his leathers, where the evidence of his desire was growing by the second.

"I wasn't going to fuck you tonight, Little Menace," he said, sounding pained. "You're exhausted and you need to rest."

"Then you should have thought about that before you touched me in the way you just did," I taunted him.

Silas growled and joined me on the bed, climbing over my body and caging me in. He leaned down and captured my lips in a bruising kiss, devouring me.

"You're wearing too many clothes for the occasion, don't you think?" I said when we broke apart.

Silas chuckled, but stood from the bed and shed his tunic. He toed off his boots and unbuckled his belt. As he tugged the leather free, his gaze remained fixed on me. I bit my bottom lip, my anticipation growing.

Silas dropped his belt to the floor and dragged his pants over his hips and down his muscular thighs. His hard length sprang free, a bead of moisture glistening on the tip.

"Do you like what you see, Little Menace?" he asked in a low, thick tone that turned my core molten.

I nodded my head, incapable of forming words at that moment.

Silas lowered himself back on the bed, the muscles in his forearms flexing as they held him in place above me. He searched my eyes for a long moment. I wasn't sure what he found there, but he smiled down at me, and it was so dazzling I just stared back up at him in awe.

"You're so beautiful," he murmured, and then he leaned in to kiss me.

This kiss differed from the one we'd just shared.

It was tentative. Gentle. Loving.

Silas was showing me all the ways he adored me with only his kiss.

I angled my head to deepen the kiss as I let my body tell him all the things I couldn't say.

Silas's hand snaked into my hair, and he pulled me close. He pressed our naked bodies together, so that not even a whisper of air separated us.

This time, when we broke apart, Silas lowered me onto my back and lined himself up with my entrance. His hands trailed down my arms until he reached my much smaller ones, and he interlaced our fingers. Then he pulled my hands over my head, our fists locked together as he entered me.

Silas stretched me around his pulsing erection and I cried out, the sensation both painful and pleasurable at the same time. He gave me a moment to adjust, and then he was moving inside me.

Silas rocked his hips against mine slowly, and the anticipation was excruciating.

"More," I demanded, but Silas shook his head.

"I'm going to take my time with you tonight, Harlowe."

Silas lowered his head and sucked my pulse point into his mouth, his tongue lapped at my skin in rhythm with his gentle thrusts.

He left a trail of wet kisses from my pulse point, up my throat, and all the way to the shell of my ear. He nipped at my earlobe and then soothed the bite with his tongue.

"Are you going to be a good girl and come for me, Harlowe?"

"I would if you picked up the pace."

Silas shifted his hips until he was rubbing himself against my aching clit with each thrust.

"How's that?" he asked. I didn't miss the smirk pulling up the side of his mouth.

I moaned in answer, and he chuckled. "That's what I thought."

"Please Silas," I begged, and he increased his speed.

He continued to thrust inside me, kissing, licking, and nipping at my flesh as he held my hands in his, the connection feeling more intimate than anything else we'd shared before.

When I felt my orgasm building, I closed my eyes.

"Eyes on me, Little Menace," Silas commanded. "I need to see you as you come undone."

My eyes flew open just as my release tore through me. I arched my back, Silas's name falling from my lips like a prayer.

"That's it. That's my good girl," Silas praised.

His thrusts deepened and his movement became shaky as he chased his own release.

"I love you, Harlowe. I promise to do everything in my power to keep you safe."

He rested his head between my breasts as he slammed his cock inside me.

"I'm nothing without you. It's like I've spent my whole life just waiting for you to come along. With every day I spend by your side, it feels like the sun has risen just for me."

His breathing became choppy, and I knew he was close.

"I love you," he repeated as he emptied himself inside me.

Silas collapsed on the bed next to me and rolled onto his back. He pulled me onto his chest and I rested my head over his heart as I allowed the rhythmic thudding to steady my breathing.

Silas stroked my hair as he hummed. He seemed so content, so at ease.

"What are you humming?"

"It's something my mother used to sing to me and my brother when she would put us to bed." I could hear the smile in his voice and I couldn't resist the one that spread across my lips.

"I'll hum it for you until you fall asleep," he said as he kissed the top of my head.

I settled against Silas's chest and allowed the soothing melody to sweep me into the darkness.

# Chapter Sixty-Two

The camp was abuzz with activity as I emerged from my tent. It had been almost a week since we'd arrived at the valley where we'd make our last stand, and the tension mounted every day as we waited for Kieran to make his move.

I was beginning to doubt our plan with every day he failed to show.

Maybe Kieran had figured it out and slipped by us somehow.

Uncertainty continued to plague my thoughts as I strode through the camp. Despite the early hour, soldiers milled about, polishing their armor and sharpening their weapons as they discussed battle strategies in hushed voices.

The sound of fighting caught my attention, and I diverted from my path toward the firepits where breakfast was being served. Instead, I headed to the small training ring Silas had set up on our first day in camp.

Just as I expected, Silas stood in the middle of the ring, chest bare and glistening with sweat. Cillian stood opposite him, his muscular torso on full display. My gaze dipped to the Adonis belt framing his hips and plunging below his waistband.

"Not a terrible view first thing in the morning," Emmerson purred from beside me, and I jumped.

My cheeks burned with embarrassment at being caught ogling the man she had grown close to.

"Don't worry, Harlowe. I've been enjoying every inch on display," she said, as she wiggled her eyebrows.

The sound of steel grating against steel reclaimed my focus, and I turned to watch as Silas and Cillian exchanged blows. Their movements were swift and precise, their swords glancing off one another as they each attacked and defended.

It was like a dance, and I was mesmerized by their confident strikes and agile footwork. Silas would press forward one moment and Cillian would step back. Then, with a flurry of strikes and parries, it would be Cillian who pressed an advantage while Silas retreated.

They were too evenly matched.

"You can see why they have such a lethal reputation," Emmerson said with approval.

Yes. Yes, I could.

"Whoo," Emmerson hollered, pulling them both up short.

Both men looked our way, and when Silas saw me, he grinned broadly.

"That man is so in love with you," Emmerson teased, and I couldn't help the grin I gave him in return.

Silas and Cillian exited the ring, grabbing their tunics from the ground where they had discarded them, and pulled them over their heads.

"I said whoo, not ew," Emmerson pouted.

I shook my head at her, but I secretly agreed. It should be a crime to cover such works of art.

Silas stepped into my space and wrapped his arm around my back. He dipped his head and smashed his lips against mine in a searing kiss.

When we came up for air, I felt slightly flustered.

"Good morning," I breathed.

"Good morning," Silas rumbled, and it raced through my body, settling in the juncture between my thighs.

"Why don't you greet me like that, Cillian?" Emmerson complained.

"Because the one time I did, you punched me and I had a black eye for a week," he growled.

"Oh yes, I forgot about that."

"You're incorrigible, woman," Cillian muttered.

A distinct *swishing* sound cut through the air, followed by the sound of deep resonant beats.

I turned my gaze to the sky and spotted a green and black dragon making its descent toward the valley.

"Must be time for the shift change," I mused.

"It's not," Silas replied, as he stiffened behind me. Taking my hand, he tugged me along after him. "Something's wrong."

Curious glances followed us as we made our way toward where the dragon would land. Emmerson and Cillian were on our heels, and Zeke joined us along the way.

"What's happening?" he asked.

"Not sure, but we're going to find out," I said.

The primal creature landed with a *thud,* sending a wave of vibrations through the ground. Its tail cut through the air like a whip before curling around its hind legs. Its serpentine eyes followed my advance, and it dipped its head in acknowledgment. A gesture which I returned.

The young-looking Cathal jumped from his dragon's back, his chest heaving like he had sprinted back here instead of flying.

"Your Majesty," he said, waving a hand as he rushed toward me.

Silas put out his hand to stop him from colliding with me, and he gave me an apologetic smile.

"What is it?" Silas demanded.

"It's the King of Netheran. He's coming."

An icy shiver wracked my body, and it took all of my willpower to stop myself from shuddering.

These people, this young Cathal standing in front of me, they needed me to be the picture of confidence. Someone who they could draw strength from in the battle to come.

Things were going to get worse before they got better, I reminded myself.

*If they got better,* my inner voice taunted.

"How many?" I demanded.

The Cathal swallowed before saying, "More than I could estimate. I couldn't see the back of their army."

*You have amassed the greatest army in the history of the realm.*

Kaleb's words came back to haunt me.

"How long until they reach us?" I asked.

"They'll be bearing down on us by midday."

That gave us a little over five hours to get into position.

"Thank you. You've done well," I said before I turned on my heels and headed toward my tent.

**"Misneach?"**

**"Yes, Fire Heart?"**

**"Recall all the dragons except those in position to redirect Kieran's**

**forces."**

**"On it."**

I burst through the flap of my tent and inhaled a sharp breath.

"Give us a minute." I heard Silas say before he entered behind me.

I paced the small area in front of the bed, as I interlaced my fingers and laid my palms flat on my head.

My thoughts were swimming as unease grew potent within me.

Silas stepped into my path and forced me to stop pacing. "Breathe," he said as he pulled my hands free. "Just breathe."

"I'm not sure I can do this, Silas?" I confessed, and I was ashamed by the way my lower lip trembled.

Silas's large, calloused hands framed my face as he demanded my attention.

"You can do this, Harlowe," he said, as he pressed a kiss to my forehead.

"But Kieran is so strong and every time I have faced him before, I've had to flee because I knew I couldn't beat him."

I could feel the hysteria building inside me, clawing at my throat and stealing my breaths.

"Harlowe," Silas snapped as he shook me gently.

It was a shock to my system and exactly what I needed to fend off my impending panic attack.

"Better?" he asked.

"Better."

"Every time you faced Kieran in the past, you didn't have the backing you do now. There are thousands of people just outside this tent who are ready to lay down their lives to protect this realm, and they will follow you until the very end."

Tears pricked my eyes, and I swiped at my lashes. "That's just it, Silas. What if I'm leading them to their deaths? What if I've been fooling myself all this time and I can't defeat him?"

"Would you stand by and watch as he decimated kingdom after kingdom, doing nothing?" he challenged.

"Of course not," I answered without hesitation.

"Then that's all you need to know. Win, lose, it doesn't matter, Harlowe. What matters is that you are prepared to take a stand because it's the right thing to do."

I released a shaky breath and nodded my head. He was right. There was no other option.

I'd stop Kieran, or I'd die trying.

"All right. Let's call everyone in and start moving."

Silas smirked and pulled me into a tight hug. "That's my girl."

Only five minutes passed before my tent was full of people. Emmerson and Cillian stood to the side of the table, while Fionn had claimed a seat in front of them. Zeke, Arabella, and Illiana huddled together in one corner, going over everything Arabella had learned recently.

My parents sat at the table with Samuel, Eion, and Caspan, and there were a few others I recognized from Elysara. A moment later, Maxim joined us and then all eyes turned to me.

I swallowed past the lump forming in my throat and forced myself to meet their gazes.

"I'll get straight to the point. We have a little over five hours to get into position before Kieran is upon us," I said without emotion. "We've planned for this moment down to the very last detail. Now it's time to put those plans into action."

There was worry etched into the faces of those before me, but there was determination, too.

"I —"

Emotion clogged my throat, and I paused, unable to get the words out. Silas's hand reached out to take mine, linking our fingers together. As I glanced at him, his eyes radiated with pride and unwavering belief in my ability to accomplish this.

Clearing my throat, I tried again. "I just wanted to say that you all have my deepest gratitude for putting your faith in me, and that is not something I take lightly."

I looked at them each in turn before continuing. "We stand on the brink. A moment in time where the outcome of this day will shape the future of this realm."

My words hung heavy in the air, but I pressed on. "This battle will test us. Push us to our limits, and there will be times when we won't want to continue with the fight. But we must make sure we never lose sight of what we're fighting for. We don't only fight for our lives," I said, gesturing around the room. "We fight for every life within the realm. We fight so our people can live free from the threat of tyranny. We fight so they don't have to."

Murmured agreement broke out among those gathered, and I held up my hand to silence them. I needed to get this out before I lost my nerve.

"Not everyone who steps out on that battlefield today will make it home. We can't let their sacrifice be in vain. We stand strong. We dig deep. We summon the courage of a dragon, but we *do not* give up. We fight to our last breath if necessary because that's what the people of Aetherian deserve."

Cheers erupted inside the tent, and I flushed. Emmerson rushed toward me and pulled me into a tight hug. Zeke joined her a moment later. Fionn and Cillian embraced me next, and Caspan gave me a nod of approval.

When my parents reached me, they had tears in their eyes. "I couldn't be more proud of you," my mother said, hugging me to her chest.

"You are more than I ever could have hoped for," my father beamed.

"Stay safe out there, all right," I instructed. "Don't let your dragon talk you into any heroic feats."

My mother chuckled. "Don't worry, Harlowe, there's no risk of that."

"Good," my father grunted.

"You all know what needs to be done," Silas said over the cacophony of voices, sobering the mood inside the tent. "We need to get to it."

Everyone filed out until only Silas and I remained.

He cupped my cheeks and pressed a kiss to my lips. "Well done, Little Menace. Well done."

# Chapter Sixty-Three

Sweat lined my brow as the heat of the midday sun bore down on me. The roaring sound of the war drums had been drawing closer with each passing moment, steady and relentless. Every beat bounced off the nearby trees and echoed throughout the valley, which only amplified the mounting fear of those gathered.

*Thump. Thump. Thump.*

The beats came faster and harder, a crescendo of sound that reverberated through the air, causing a tremor to break out across the armies assembled in the valley.

Silas shifted in his position on Caolán's back so he was facing the mass of soldiers standing behind us.

"Cathal," he called out. "And our brothers and sisters in arms from every corner of the kingdoms."

The valley grew eerily quiet as soldiers craned their necks to see Silas.

"Do you hear that?" he asked, pointing toward the approaching army.

*Thump. Thump. Thump.*

"That is the sound of despotism. We fight today, not just for our victory, but for the very salvation of our realm."

Cheers broke out among the soldiers, and Silas waited until they died down.

"It's all right to be afraid. Just don't let your fear hold you captive. Courage is your armor, and determination is your sword."

"He's good at that, isn't he?" Emmerson murmured with approval.

"It's not the first time he's done this," Cillian drawled, but Emmerson just shrugged her shoulders unbothered.

**"They have breached the top of the hill,"** Misneach said, and my eyes scanned the horizon.

Figures dotted the distant hill, but they were too small to distinguish.

**"Here we go,"** Rónán said, far too gleefully for the seriousness of the situation.

A shrill screeching sound pierced my ears, and my head swiveled all around as I tried to locate the source of the call.

Roc crested the top of the hillside, blackening the skies and my stomach sank at the sheer number of them.

"Remember your training," Silas shouted over the murmuring that had broken out. "Trust in each other, and let the fire of your conviction light the path to glory!"

*Thump. Thump. Thump.*

The sound of the drums beat in sync with my thundering heart.

"Let history record how we were unyielding in our resolve. For honor. For duty. For your QUEEN!" Silas roared, pumping his fist in the air.

The sound of feet pounding into the ground drowned out the beating drums as the soldiers sent out a war cry of their own.

**"Get ready, Fire Heart,"** Misneach instructed, and I watched as the first wave of soldiers descended from the top of the hill and raced toward us.

"Hold," I shouted.

The ground shook beneath us as their descent sent a ripple of vibrations in our direction. The beating of the drums added to the ominous anticipation, and my palms grew clammy.

*Thump. Thump. Thump.*

**"I hope you are as powerful as they say,"** Aodhán said as he pushed his way forward, taking the position next to me. **"We will likely need your strength before the day is done."**

**"If that's your idea of a good luck speech, Aodhán, it needs work,"** I chuckled, and the dragon rolled his eyes.

**"Just keep your eyes on the horizon, oh powerful one,"** he mocked, but I could tell I was growing on him despite his best efforts to dislike me.

**"Stay safe out there, Aodhán,"** I said, and he seemed taken aback by my sincerity. **"My life depends on it,"** I added with a wink.

Aodhán snorted, but I could see the grin tugging up the side of his mouth.

"Cathal, get into position," I called.

Misneach crouched low to the ground, waiting for my command. Movement to my left and right indicated that the other dragons had followed suit.

When the first wave of soldiers reached the bottom of the hill and started sprinting across the valley, I screamed, "Now!"

With a powerful thrust of his hind legs, Misneach pushed off the ground and soared into the sky. He beat his wings with vigorous strokes to gain altitude and quickly rose above the impending battle.

My fingertips tingled and my palms heated as I summoned my flames.

**"Remember, this is only step one of many, Fire Heart,"** Misneach warned. **"Do not burn yourself out before the real battle has begun."**

**"I've got this, Misneach. I promise."**

A flash of white light sailed through the air toward us and I pulled up my shield, extending it out until every dragon was protected.

Fórsa collided with the fiery wall in an explosion of energy that sent sparks flying in every direction. My shield shuddered, but I barely felt the impact.

More orbs of fórsa pummeled my shield as the Netheran soldiers tried in vain to bring it down.

A satisfied smirk pulled up my lips at how much I had grown into my powers. My shield vibrated under every assault, but it did not waver.

When the attack fell away, I dropped my shield and commanded the dragons to attack. Misneach opened his maw wide and a familiar rumble worked its way up his throat. The air surrounding us crackled as it shimmered with the growing heat.

Misneach's nostrils flared and his chest expanded under the taut muscles of his scales. With a deafening, guttural roar, he unleashed a torrent of blazing flames that surged forward in a powerful, unstoppable stream.

All around me, brilliant red flames burst forward, cascading toward the earth in a frenzy of fiery destruction, engulfing everything in their path.

Desperate pleas rent the air as flames melted skin from bone, the acrid smell of burning flesh making my eyes water.

As the fiery assault abated, all that was left of the first attack were the smoldering remains of the soldiers.

I could feel the heat radiating from the scorched ground, and I watched as small embers were picked up and carried away on the breeze.

Our victory was short-lived, however.

A blood-curdling scream erupted from the hillside and the next wave of warriors pushed forward, racing toward us to deliver their retribution.

This time, Kieran had learned and adapted.

Wave upon wave of fighters descended upon us. They cut a path down the hill and headed for our waiting armies.

**"We need to move closer to our soldiers and provide them with as much cover as we can. They won't be able to hold off that many on their own."**

Misneach directed the unbonded dragons to circle the ground forces before he dipped his wings and moved to position himself between our armies and the advancing horde.

An ear-splitting screech drew my attention, and I watched in horror as hundreds of roc took to the skies and headed right for us, splitting our focus.

**"Change of plans,"** I said, praying to any gods listening that the ground forces would hold.

# Chapter Sixty-Four

A clap of thunder exploded above me and the brilliant blue sky darkened into an oppressive, merciless grey, that made it difficult to see the approaching swarm of roc.

Perhaps the gods weren't listening after all.

A flash of lightning burst across my periphery and a moment later, another crack of thunder rattled the sky.

"At least it's not raining," Emmerson called out, always one to see the bright side of things, even in bloodshed.

**"Hellcat,"** Misneach growled but before he could finish his thought, thick, black clouds rolled overhead, and the sky opened up to unleash a violent stream of raindrops.

They pelted my exposed flesh so hard I could imagine them leaving tiny abrasions in their wake.

**"Don't temp the fates,"** Misneach finished with a grumble.

Rain blurred my vision, and I reached up to swipe at my eyes, only for them to be inundated a second later.

A screeching sound erupted from above me and I looked up to see the razor-tipped wings and clawed feet of a roc as it advanced on us. It was moving so fast that it appeared as though it was aiming to drop right on top of us.

A surge of adrenaline spiked in my veins and I threw my hand up, sending a blazing ball of fire directly toward it. The roc had no time to alter its course and my flames engulfed it, incinerating it in seconds.

**"Try to conserve your power for when you need it,"** Misneach reminded me.

**"It kind of felt like I needed it,"** I panted as I caught my breath.

**"We have a long way to go yet, Fire Heart, and you and I both know that the Serpent King will be playing in the shadows until he has a clear shot at you."**

**"Noted. But first, we have to survive."**

As if to prove my point, three roc broke through the clouds, their sharpened feathers spread wide as they sailed toward us.

**"Fuck! They've all got riders,"** I hissed.

**"Hold on,"** Misneach ordered as he pulled his wings in tight and we dropped with a sudden burst of speed, freefalling into the unknown beneath us.

The rapid descent sucked all the air from my lungs, and I couldn't scream, even though I very much wanted to. My fingers clutched the rough edge of Misneach's scales and I clamped my legs tight around his body as I hung on for dear life.

The roc soared right over the top of us, their lethal strikes missing the mark, leaving them with nothing to grasp except the empty air.

Misneach pulled out of the dive and sliced his long tail through the air like a blade until it collided with one of the roc, sending it flying backward and plummeting to the ground.

My chest collided with the hard planes of his back, and pain shot through my torso as I struggled to force oxygen into my lungs.

I pushed through the pain as I whipped my head around and spotted the two remaining roc who had corrected their course and were now flying straight for us. Before they reached us, however, the two rocs parted, and circled wide, coming for us on both sides.

I raised my hand, sending a torrent of flames sailing toward one roc, and the telltale rumble from Misneach's chest told me he had done the same to the other.

The roc angled its wings, gliding on its side through the small space separating us, narrowly avoiding my hit. With renewed determination, it leveled out and sped towards us.

We didn't have enough time to prepare for the collision.

The roc curved its wings in front of it, exposing its razor-sharp feathers, and raked them down Misneach's flank with deadly accuracy.

My dragon roared in pain, dipping his wings as he fought to shake the creature free. Using the momentary distraction, the roc's rider jumped from its back and landed with a thud behind me.

**"Stay seated,"** Misneach bellowed, but I was already getting to my feet.

A tall, muscular man with a hooked dagger in one hand and a heavy-looking sword in the other smirked down at me as he prowled closer.

Misneach reached around his side, his jaws clamping down on the roc's wings and tearing it from his body. I could hear the crunching of bones as Misneach shook the creature ferociously before opening his mouth and letting it careen toward the ground.

I glanced to the other side to make sure the third roc hadn't survived Misneach's attack somehow and was using the mêlée to sneak up on us again.

But all I saw was open space, completely devoid of life.

When I returned my gaze to the man advancing on me, he was standing right in front of me. He raised his sword and thrust the pommel into my face.

My eyes watered and blinding pain quickly followed as the foul taste of copper filled my mouth. Blood poured from my nose and my hands darted up to stem the flow instinctively.

Cruel laughter filled the air, and the man watched on triumphantly as I ran my sleeve under my nose.

Blood continued to stream down my face, but I ignored it as I focused on the new threat.

**"Fire Heart, drop,"** Misneach ordered, but I refused.

**"No,"** I growled. **"This asshole is mine."**

"You know, we've all been given strict instructions to take out the copper-haired witch and her black dragon," he goaded.

"I'm a witch now, am I?" I said, raising a brow. "And Misneach isn't black, he's dark grey. Oh, and you forgot the streaks of indigo."

"Doesn't matter. The point is, everyone knows exactly who to look out for, and they're all coming for you," he said, as he pointed his dagger in my direction.

"I welcome it," I purred and smiled menacingly.

The look on my face must have been nothing short of maniacal, with my battered nose and blood-coated teeth. All the while, I smiled like some deranged, unhinged idiot.

The man grimaced, and I used the moment to blast him with my flames.

Before he could react, my strike collided with the center of his chest. His eyes widened in surprise and he stared at me in disbelief. He staggered back, his boot catching on the ridge of one of Misneach's scales, and crashed to his knees.

I approached him slowly, stopping just out of his reach.

I glared down at him and held his gaze as I lifted my foot and planted my boot in his face, returning the favor for his earlier strike. His head snapped back and a moment later, his body followed. He dipped over Misneach's side, disappearing from view.

**"Fucking asshole."**

**"I suddenly understand why the General calls you Little Menace,"** Misneach said, partway between awe and incredulity.

**"Come on,"** I said, retaking my position between his wings. **"We have a war to win."**

# Chapter Sixty-Five

The rain eased, and I was thankful for it. As I wiped the last droplets from my lashes, I shook out my hand and surveyed my surroundings.

**"How are you holding up?"** I asked Misneach. **"How is your side?"**

**"I'm fine, Fire Heart. Don't worry about me."**

I gave him a curt nod he had no hope of seeing given my position on his back.

**"We need to get lower to see what's happening on the ground,"** I instructed. **"I can't see shit from this height."**

Misneach leaned into a dive and sent us shooting toward the ground, before he pulled up sharply, avoiding a collision.

I jumped from his back and glanced around the battlefield.

Everywhere I looked, skirmishes were playing out across the valley. The sound of steel meeting steel rang loudly in my ears and the ground had already been stained crimson with spilled blood.

Bodies were scattered about, some intact and some missing limbs, but they all had one thing in common.

Empty, vacant eyes.

I forced myself to search their faces to ensure none of my friends had fallen. My gaze locked on a young-faced male, and nausea churned my stomach.

It was the young Cathal who had brought us the news of Kieran's impending arrival only hours earlier.

**"Can you see any of them?"** I asked Misneach as panic clawed at my chest.

**"You can't think about any of that right now, Fire Heart. Get out of your head and focus on the battle unfolding before you."**

He was right. I was letting emotion cloud my judgment, and that never ended well.

My eyes scanned the battlefield until I locked on two petite figures standing back-to-back as they battled seasoned warriors twice their size all around them.

**"Misneach, I need you to fly over the rest of the valley and see what's happening,"** I commanded. **"And find out where Kieran is,"** I added as I sprinted towards the women.

I pulled twin daggers from the sheaths at my ribs and gripped them in my palms as I readied myself to enter the fray.

Arabella and Illiana stood locked behind a wall of thick muscle. Their lips moved endlessly as they chanted. Sweat coated their faces and their chests heaved in unison from the effort required to call upon their magic.

I watched in fascination as their hands twisted and locked at odd angles as they sent spells spiraling toward anyone who got too close. Bursts of color rained down on the attacking force and I had the peculiar thought that death wielded by their hands was objectively beautiful.

Five massive dire wolves surrounded the soldiers trying to reach the women, and a low growl from one wolf pulled me from my musings. Its hackles were raised and spittle formed in the corner of its mouth as it snapped its jaws at the warriors.

The wolf closest to me lowered itself to the ground as it prepared to attack. Its belly pressed against the dirt which coated its fur with a fine layer of dust. The wolf snarled as it launched itself into the air and rammed the chest of one soldier.

The wolf slammed him into the ground and sank its pointed canines into the man's neck. With a savage shake of its head, it ripped his throat out. Blood flooded the ground beneath him and he gurgled, unable to disperse the crimson liquid as it drowned him. But the wolf refused to relent, as it shook its head from side to side and sent blood flying in every direction as it became lost to its animalistic instincts.

The remaining wolves lunged for the soldiers, and they worked together in a coordinated attack as they sank their teeth into any exposed flesh they could find. A woman cried out as one wolf tore into her shoulder and dragged her to the ground where they wrestled in the dirt.

The woman ripped her dagger free, but the wolf sprang out of her reach. It moved swiftly as it leaped through the air and collided with another soldier, knocking him to the ground.

Vicious snarling drowned out the sounds of battle all around me and I used the soldiers' distraction to sneak up behind one fighter, running my dagger across her throat. Blood coated my hand, and I lost my grip on my dagger as the slick substance prevented me from tightening my hold.

I let her body fall to the ground and quickly wiped the blood from my hand as I flexed my fingers around the handle of my blade.

Another growl rumbled from somewhere within the scuffle, but then a pained yelp cut through the ringing in my ears, followed by a pitiful whimper.

"No!" Illiana shrieked, and the sound pierced the air with a raw, unfiltered intensity that threatened to send me to my knees.

She waved her hands around wildly as she sent out spell after spell, the myriad of colors a stark contrast to the gut-wrenching anguish filling the valley as she screamed in despair.

I charged forward, driving my blade into the kidney of the man standing in front of me. He didn't have time to acknowledge his stun as I dragged my dagger upward, tearing through muscle and tendons before retracting my blade.

He wavered on his feet for a moment before falling to the ground, where his lifeless eyes stared back at me.

My moment of reprieve was cut short when large arms encircled my waist and my feet left the ground before my body was slammed into the dirt. My head collided with the hardened earth and dark spots erupted behind my eyes. Thick, calloused fingers closed around my throat and squeezed roughly, cutting off my airflow.

I raised my hands to my attacker's face and clawed at his eye sockets. He howled in pain, but he didn't release me. I summoned my flames as I pressed my thumbs into his eyes, and I could feel the tissue melting under the intense heat.

The man jerked back, and the hands that were wrapped around my neck fell away. I rolled onto my side as bile flooded my mouth and I heaved.

My body spasmed as I tried to fill my lungs with air, but my efforts were hampered when I started coughing.

**"Fire Heart!"** Misneach shouted.

"Harlowe!" Arabella called before dropping to her knees beside me. "Just breathe," she said in a soft, melodic voice as she rubbed my back.

I felt myself calming under her touch and I inhaled sharply, the burning pain a welcome relief as my lungs expanded.

"There you go," she soothed.

A despondent wail drew our attention to Illiana, who was lying atop a prone dire wolf, her heaving sobs cutting straight through my heart like a blade.

I scrambled to my feet and rushed to her side.

**"Fire Heart, are you all right?"** Misneach demanded, the edge of panic detectable in his tone.

**"I need a minute,"** I said as I peered down at the dying beast.

Its side rose and fell with each shallow breath, and its tongue lolled to the side of its mouth as it panted through the pain. The other dire wolves whined and nudged their fallen companion with their snouts.

My gaze darted to Illiana. Tears streaked her cheeks and her whole body trembled as sobs tore free of her throat.

"Help him," she begged Arabella. "Please."

I looked at the wolf's belly, where a large dagger protruded from the mottled fur. It had been dragged along the base of its stomach, spilling the creature's entrails on the ground.

I swallowed thickly and glanced at Arabella.

"I... I," she stuttered, unable to say the words that would destroy Illiana.

I crouched down to the ground, my hand running through the mane of black fur around the wolf's ears.

"She can't help him, Illiana," I whispered. "The damage is too great."

Illiana buried her face in the wolf's coat, muffling the sounds of her unbearable sorrow.

The other wolves dropped to the ground and placed their heads on their friend's body, providing what little comfort they could as he took his final breaths.

Glowing yellow eyes met mine, and I smiled down at the wolf as I continued to stroke its fur.

"I'm sorry," I whispered as tears pricked my eyes.

The wolf let out a small whine as though it sought to comfort me in this moment.

My tears spilled over my cheeks, and the wolf blinked slowly. With one last shaky exhale, the wolf's eyes slid closed and didn't open again.

Illiana threw her head back and let loose a bone-chilling scream that sent shivers racing up my spine.

Lightning flashed in the sky and the ground rumbled beneath our feet.

"Illiana," I called, but she couldn't hear me as she surrendered to her agony.

"Illiana," I called again, this time gripping her shoulder.

She snapped her gaze to me and I gasped as I jumped back. Streaks of bright light flashed across her eyes in what could only be described as an imitation of lightning. The air buzzed with static energy and her hair lifted around her like a halo.

"Illiana, can you hear me?"

"I hear you, Queen of Fire," she gritted out. "Now tell me where to strike."

I blinked to clear the fog coating my mind and shared a worried glance with Arabella.

"Tell me," Illiana demanded. "Before I lose control of the power, I have summoned."

I scanned the battlefield, but every large target was interlocked with people of our own and I wasn't prepared to sacrifice them to annihilate our enemies.

"Make it count," Illiana said, as if reading my mind.

My gaze snagged on the ridge where Kieran's army had first appeared. "Over there," I shouted, and pointed to where their reserve army waited.

"Step back," Illiana commanded, and I moved to stand beside Arabella.

Illiana raised her hands and pointed them toward the hill. With a raw cry that was bursting with emotion, Illiana released her power, and lightning surged from her palms. It snaked across the valley and hit the ridge, causing a deep fracture in the landscape.

Illiana dropped to the ground and pressed her palms into the dirt below. She pushed her magic into the earth and the fracture widened before branching off, causing the hill to break apart. In a slow, wavelike motion, the waiting army tilted to their sides before sliding from the hillside and being buried in the open chasms.

Illiana swayed in place before collapsing to the ground.

"Illiana," I cried.

I pulled her upright and took in the pallor of her skin. Sweat coated her brow and her breathing was shallow.

"Illiana," I repeated.

"I can hear you, Queen of Fire. No need to shout," she grumbled. "Use your advantage wisely," she added.

Turning to Arabella, I asked, "Can you get her out of here?"

"I can," Arabella nodded confidently.

"Then go. Get her to safety," I said as I got to my feet.

**"Misneach?"**
**"Fire Heart,"** he breathed.
**"Come get me."**

# Chapter Sixty-Six

I'd lost sight of Harlowe early in the battle, and while I knew she could handle herself, it didn't stop me from scanning the battlefield for her every spare moment.

**"She's fine,"** Caolán soothed. **"She's over on the eastern side of the valley."**

My shoulders relaxed, and I returned my attention to the surrounding fight.

"You know," Caspan said as he thrust his sword behind him, right into the abdomen of the man trying to sneak up on him. "It's not fair that you lot keep jumping in and out of the fray on those dragons of yours."

He raised his palm and sent a blast of fórsa sailing straight for me and I ducked to avoid the hit.

"What the fuck was that, Caspan?" I growled. Then I heard the grunt that sounded from behind me.

I spun in place and saw a giant of a man attempting to hold his neck together. Fórsa had torn straight through the man's throat and erupted from the other side.

His efforts to avoid his impending death were in vain, and he toppled to the ground, unmoving.

"You're welcome," Caspan grinned.

I didn't have time to respond as another soldier came at me. He wielded a sword in one hand and a battle axe in another.

"Are you compensating for something?" I jeered as I raised a brow.

The man snarled, and he sounded more animal than human. He lunged for me and I side-stepped him with ease, as I spun my blade in my fist.

He looked around his surroundings as if confused, not understanding what had happened.

"Over here," I called, and when he turned, I planted my boot in his gut.

He fell to the ground with a *thud* that vibrated beneath my feet. I raised my blade and plunged it into his chest before he even knew what had happened.

"As I was saying," Caspan panted, his face covered with splattered blood. "It's sort of cheating."

We went back-to-back as five soldiers circled us. "What the hell are you talking about?" I asked.

The first combatant stepped forward. He raised his sword and struck hard and fast. My blade came up to meet his, and a sharp clang rang out around us. The others followed his lead, and a woman ducked low as she tried to stick me with her dagger. My palm darted out before she could land her hit, and I sent fórsa sailing toward her. It collided with her head, killing her instantly.

The man above me howled and his fingertips glowed with a brilliant white light.

"Down," I shouted, and Caspan dropped to the ground beside me.

"You do have a habit of pissing people off," he muttered.

The burst of energy that was meant for me sailed right over my head and into the sternum of another warrior as he came up behind me.

The man above me gasped. His eyes widened as he realized what he had done. Not one to waste my advantage, I jumped to my feet and pulled my dagger free from my hip. I didn't hesitate as I drove it into the man's stomach before he had the chance to recover. Blood gushed from the wound and I pushed my dagger higher for good measure.

And then there were two.

Caspan and I whirled on the remaining soldiers and advanced.

"I want the big one," Caspan called, and I shrugged.

"Suit yourself," I said, as I re-sheathed my dagger.

I stalked toward the smaller of the two fighters. With their petite frame, I was almost certain it was a woman. I couldn't be sure, however, as the cowl of their hood was pulled low over their head and obscured their face.

The warrior extended twin swords in my direction and, with a deft flick of their wrists, they executed a flourish before they charged straight for me.

Our blades clashed, and a high-pitched ringing sound followed.

"You killed my brother," the soldier hissed.

Definitely a woman.

"I don't know if you noticed this," I grunted as I pushed against her blade, forcing her to retreat. "But he tried to kill me first."

The woman ignored my jab as she spun out of range, but not before she raked her blade over my forearm. Pain exploded from the site and crimson droplets burst to the surface. Blood poured down my fingers as I tried to shake it off.

The woman smirked, pleased with her handiwork.

Well, this just got interesting.

I raised my sword and beckoned her forward.

She didn't hesitate as she rushed for me. Our blades met in a flurry of movement. The sound of steel grating against steel pierced my ears. I pulled back, and she lunged for me, feinting left. I cut off her attack as I caressed her blade with my own, and sent her stumbling back.

Pressing my advantage, I thrust my sword forward, aiming for her chest. The woman parried at the last moment and blocked my attack.

I gritted my teeth and unleashed a barrage of strikes. Her arms trembled as she struggled to push back against my blade, and I pressed my weight into my sword. I reached down and grabbed my dagger, pulling it free and sinking it into her side.

A soft gasp passed between her lips, and her eyes widened. The resistance she was trying to maintain fell away, and her swords clattered to the ground. Her gaze darted to the dagger protruding from her body. She sucked in a sharp breath as she gripped the handle and pulled it free.

Blood poured from the wound in a steady, dark stream, painting her tunic crimson. Her hand flew to the site and her fingers were quickly coated in the slick substance.

I advanced toward her and gripped the back of her head as I pulled her against me. The injury would be fatal, but it would be agony as she faded away.

"I'll make it quick," I said as I dragged my dagger across her throat.

Her body slumped against mine, and I lowered her to the ground.

"Quite the gentlemen," Caspan snorted.

"She earned it."

"Silas!" Cillian shouted from where he stood with Emmerson, both covered in blood and panting heavily.

I hoped they had been fighting Netheran soldiers and not each other.

"Fionn's in trouble."

My head tipped back as I looked in the direction Cillian was pointing. Fionn was clutching Niamh's wing as two fighters hovered over him.

**"Caolán,"** I shouted.

My boots pounded into the hardened earth beneath me as I sprinted across the battlefield, my arms pumping in sync with my legs as I leaned forward. A rush of wind passed over my head as Caolán glided over the uneven ground and I coiled my muscles tight as I pushed off the dirt, launching myself into the air.

Time seemed to slow, and everything around me faded away. With my arms outstretched for balance, I landed on the end of Caolán's tail and he flicked it upward, propelling me forward.

As I sailed through the air, I twisted to adjust my position and bent my knees as I braced for the landing. When my feet connected with the hard ridges of Caolán's spine, everything sped up again, and I was jolted forward with a burst of speed.

I rolled onto my shoulder to dissipate the force of my landing and came up in a crouch. When I straightened, I darted forward to take my place between Caolán's wings.

**"Get us to Fionn, Caolán,"** I commanded as my heart thundered inside my chest.

My dragon beat his colossal wings and gained altitude quickly. My stomach had lodged itself inside my throat and I watched on helplessly as Fionn's grip faltered.

**"Hurry Caolán!"**

Caolán thrust his wings harder as he closed the distance between us.

"FIONN," I roared. "Drop."

Without hesitation, Fionn let go of his hold on Niamh and plummeted through the air until he crashed into Caolán's back right behind me.

I released a breath I didn't realize I was holding and bunched my hands into fists to steady the trembling.

Niamh snarled with fury before tipping her wings and diving into a roll. The two combatants couldn't secure their hold in time as they slid across her spine and over the edge of her wings. They fell into open space, their arms flailing as they grasped at the empty air.

Their bodies were carried away with the wind until they slammed into the side of a nearby mountain.

I winced. That couldn't have been pleasant.

As I glanced over my shoulder, I surveyed Fionn and noted he appeared unharmed.

"Thank you, Brother," he huffed as he fought to catch his breath.

"You good?"

"Yes. I winded myself on the landing," he said sheepishly.

I gave him a curt nod and said, "Ready to jump back in?"

"Always," Fionn grinned.

I gripped his palm and pulled him in for a quick embrace. "Stay safe out there."

"You too, Silas," he said, standing to his full height. A mischievous grin spread across his face, showcasing his youthfulness. "I think Harlowe's the type of woman who would murder you if you got yourself killed."

With that, Fionn dove over Caolán's flank and landed between Niamh's wings as she soared beneath us.

I barked out a laugh and shook my head.

She absolutely would.

# Chapter Sixty-Seven

From my vantage point, I could see the roc were swarming the Cathal, dispersing the advantage the dragons had gained early in the battle by leveraging their aerial dominance.

It was a calculated move on Kieran's part to bring in the roc simultaneously as the ground forces attacked, and it was paying off.

I put my fingers in my mouth and sealed my lips around the digits as I blew forcibly, emitting a high-pitched whistling sound.

Cillian recognized the call immediately, and his head snapped in my direction.

I waved my arm in the air, signaling for him to join me. He turned and whispered something in Emmerson's ear, and she nodded.

"We could really use some help up here," I heard Zeke call, but when I scanned the skies, I couldn't see him or Rónán anywhere.

As I returned my gaze to the ground, I noticed Cillian and Emmerson had disappeared.

They were moving. That was all the confirmation I needed to shift my focus back to the roc overwhelming the Cathal.

**"We need to make as much of an impact as we can, in as little time as possible,"** I told Caolán. **"The ground forces will need help again soon enough."**

My eyes darted to Caspan, but he was happily engaged in a brawl with three other soldiers.

He was laughing. The fucking maniac.

As I surveyed the horizon, I spotted roughly a dozen roc launching from the western side of the battle, ready to join their brethren.

**"Let's intercept,"** I ordered Caolán.

**"I'm calling Rónán in to help,"** Caolán said as he adjusted his course and headed for the incoming roc.

Caolán's powerful wings sliced through the air, creating gusts of wind in his wake.

"This should be fun," Zeke said, and I shook my head at his antics.

Rónán flew beside us, his blue scales shimmering in the tiny hint of sunlight that peeked through the cloud cover.

When our gazes locked, he gave me a sly wink.

Was I the only one who didn't find war a jovial event?

Caolán let out a deafening roar, one that Rónán mimicked, pulling me from my musings.

The incoming formation screeched, their talon-tipped wings spread wide as they soared toward us.

I knew the moment Caolán drew upon his flames.

It was in the telltale rumble of power and the vibration that reverberated throughout my whole body.

He opened his mouth wide and I could visualize how he curled his tongue, embers dancing along the roof of his mouth as he prepared to unleash his fiery rage.

With another vicious roar, Caolán sent a blazing stream of flames sailing through the air headed straight for the roc.

The formation parted down the middle as the roc dipped their wings and angled away from the scorching inferno. When the fire cleared, they circled back around and came for us again.

Some flapped their wings with forceful strokes, turning their bodies heavenward, and gaining altitude. Others tucked their wings tight against their sides as they dove below the cloud cover, undoubtedly circling back to cage us in.

A light mist of rain began to fall, but it wasn't like the torrential downpour that had swept through the battlefield earlier.

It was a nuisance, but it didn't hinder my sight.

"Did you see if any of that lot had riders?" Zeke asked, pointing in the direction the roc had disappeared.

"No, they were too far away."

**"We need to go wide so when they try to corner us from above and below, all they'll find is empty space,"** Caolán said.

"You go left and we'll go right," I signaled to Zeke as Caolán leaned away from our central position.

Zeke gave a sharp nod, acknowledging the order.

We flew through the dark grey clouds before Caolán dove into a sharp turn, redirecting our path back the way we had come.

The first roc broke through the cloud cover, and its ash-colored wings glistened in the rain. Caolán shot forward, surprising the winged creature as he captured it in his jaws and bit down.

The roc hadn't stood a chance.

Caolán's razor-sharp teeth tore through the roc's neck, separating its head from its body before letting it fall to the ground with a ferocious growl.

"Look out," Zeke called, and Caolán twisted mid-air, narrowly avoiding another roc that came at us from the side. Its sharpened talons were angled toward his head, its lethal intent clear in its movements.

Caolán countered with a swipe of his claws across its middle, and the roc shrieked in pain before retreating.

Two more roc appeared, attacking in unison as they dove toward us. Caolán sent his flames spiraling in their direction while I targeted them with a blast of fórsa.

They were unable to dodge both attacks and Caolán's flames corralled them into the deadly orb of energy I'd unleashed. It struck the first roc and feathers exploded around the creature on impact, sending it plummeting to its death in a flurry of wings and plumage.

The second roc escaped the blow and let out an ear-splitting screech. It flung itself forward and, blinded by its rage, failed to detect the threat coming up behind it.

Rónán used his tail like a whip as he struck the roc hard enough to break its advance. He snapped his massive jaws, catching the creature's wing in his mouth. The crunch of bone was audible even over the sounds of battle that threatened to drown it out.

When Rónán let the roc drop from his mouth, it tried in vain to force its wing to support its weight, but the appendage refused to cooperate. With a final shriek, the roc cascaded toward the earth below where it met its end.

Five more roc appeared before we'd even caught our breath and hurtled through the sky toward us.

"Fucking hell, where are they all coming from?" Zeke muttered as Rónán tilted his massive body to face the oncoming attack.

The dragons opened their mouths wide and together, released a fiery exhale.

Zeke sent a dagger flying through the air by the hilt, and it struck one roc in the center of its chest with deadly precision.

I gaped at him, and he merely shrugged.

I didn't have time to marvel at his blade work as the roc skirted around the dragons' flames and kept coming. One roc came in close, its talons outstretched as it raked the sharpened tips over Caolán's flank, digging in deep.

My dragon roared in pain, and I summoned fórsa. The familiar tingles set my fingertips alight, and I shot the destructive orb straight into the side of the roc's head.

Its talons came away bloody and my fury intensified. The creature screamed in agony and I didn't get another chance for retribution as it fell from the sky.

Another pained roar sounded, and I whipped around until I caught sight of Rónán. He struggled against a roc that had locked its talons into his shoulder as it attempted to pull him down.

Zeke stood and raced toward the creature, but before he could eliminate it, it retracted its talons and dove out of reach.

"Fuck this," I muttered.

**"Caolán, are you all right? Can you keep going?"**

**"I'm fine a chara,"** he said.

The remaining roc circled back around and came at us for a second time.

**"You see that canyon between the two mountains?"** I asked.

**"I see it,"** Caolán answered. **"And I like where your mind has wandered."**

Caolán dove toward the narrow canyon and I peered over my shoulder to see the roc following suit. With his wings tucked tight at his sides, Caolán gained speed quickly and the roc had to push hard to keep up.

As we approached the canyon, I sent a blast of fórsa over my shoulder and the roc doubled down on their efforts to gain on us. The canyon was almost upon us and at the last moment, Caolán veered upward on a sharp incline, almost caressing the rocky terrain on his way.

The roc didn't have time to pull out of their dives and they collided with the steep, rugged wall.

I panted heavily as I pressed myself flat against Caolán's back and caught my breath.

**"We need to make sure Zeke and Rónán are all right,"** I huffed, and Caolán made a noise in agreement.

As we approached the blue dragon, I could see three more roc had appeared, and this time, they carried riders.

Zeke stood from his spot between Rónán's wings and flourished his blade as he prepared to engage.

A streak of black cut through the air behind the formation, and Zeke suddenly dropped to Rónán's back.

Red and orange flames engulfed the roc, taking them by surprise and incinerating them in seconds.

Saoirse sailed through the ashen remains of the roc and I grimaced at the thought of being covered in the remains of their riders.

"About time you showed up," I called to Emmerson, but I couldn't keep the laughter out of my tone.

"The words you are looking for are thank you," she called back, and my laughter broke free. "You're welcome, by the way," she added, raising a brow in challenge.

"I am always thankful to meet you on the battlefield, Em," Zeke beamed.

"See, Silas," she said pointedly. "Manners."

My laughter died on my tongue when I caught sight of the skirmish taking place on the ground. At least ten soldiers surrounded Caspan, and he only had two others at his back.

**"Go Caolán,"** I shouted, and my dragon dove toward the ground.

I didn't wait for him to pull up before I jumped from his back and sprinted toward the Elysaran Prince.

Pulling my blade free, I struck out at the first warrior, slicing the back of their knees and sending them to the ground. I cut, stabbed, and beat my way through the horde, spilling blood and hacking limbs until I finally breached the circle tightening around Caspan.

"We've got to stop meeting up like this, Silas," he grinned. "What would Harlowe think?"

I ignored his teasing and said, "It looked like you could use some help."

Our reunion was interrupted when one soldier grabbed the man at Caspan's back and pulled him onto his blade. I took his place, swinging my sword high and striking the side of the warrior's neck. His head left his body in a spray of crimson, which splattered across my face.

I scrubbed my forearm across my face, clearing the copper substance from my eyes.

The man to my left let out a pained groan, and I turned in time to see him topple over, a sword protruding from his back.

"Ah, finally it's just the two of us," Caspan laughed.

"You're insane, you know that, right?" I asked as I thrust my sword to meet the blade of another fighter.

"Aren't we all a little insane from time to time?" he said wistfully.

"No," I deadpanned, and he barked out a laugh.

Our blades met steel, biting and grinding as we fought our way through the horde until there was only one man left standing. He lunged for me, but I parried and struck my sword through his stomach from behind.

Panting heavily, I kicked his body off my blade and he fell to the ground, lifeless.

When my gaze locked with Caspan's, his eyes widened and he gripped my arm, pulling me toward him as he spun around behind me.

A sharp stinging sensation erupted on my hip and I glanced over my shoulder to see Caspan with his back to another soldier who had sneaked up on us.

Shoving Caspan out of the way, I thrust my palm forward and sent a rush of fórsa straight for him. He stumbled back from the hit and dropped to his knees. A moment later, he fell face-first into the dirt, exposing the bloodied hole in his back.

The pain in my hip intensified, and I swiped my palm over it. When I pulled it away, I studied the blood coating my hand in confusion.

"Silas," Caspan breathed, and my gaze darted to him.

I dropped to my knees when I took in the sight of the blade protruding from his abdomen.

"Caspan," I said, panic lacing my tone. "What the fuck happened?"

He chuckled and then winced as blood escaped his mouth.

"I thought you had eyes," he joked. "Did the sword sticking out of my body not give it away?"

I gently turned him on his side and saw the blood-stained blade had been driven in to the hilt.

"Fuck!" I hissed.

"It's all right, my friend," he said as he coughed up more blood. "Just take care of that woman you and I both know you don't deserve and we'll call it even."

"Why?" I choked out, unable to conceal the emotion clogging my throat.

"I saw the chance to save you and I took it." He coughed again, sending more blood flying across his chest.

His eyes met mine, and a serious expression crossed his face. "And I'd do it again," he wheezed.

I gripped his hand in mine and lowered my head until our brows met. "Thank you, Brother," I murmured, tears welling in my eyes.

Caspan remained quiet, and when I pulled back to look down at him, his eyes were closed.

"FUCK!" I threw my head back and screamed, purging the pain from my body.

All that was left was a red haze.

Picking up my sword, I forced myself to my feet.

They were all going to die.

Every fucking one of them.

# Chapter Sixty-Eight

"**Misneach, have you spotted Kieran?"** I asked as I took a moment to orient myself to the shift in viewpoint.

The ground battle I had been fighting just moments ago was becoming indistinguishable as Misneach gained altitude.

**"The snake is hiding in the shadows,"** he growled. **"Waiting for the perfect opportunity to strike."**

**"So you haven't been able to find him?"** I clarified.

**"No,"** Misneach gritted out.

**"What did you learn on your flyover of the valley?"**

**"The Serpent King has greater numbers than we do and he is using that advantage to overwhelm us,"** he said. **"Even so, our forces are holding strong."**

A swell of pride rushed through me with his words.

**"The roc have hindered the aerial advantage of the Cathal, but they are regaining ground,"** he continued. **"You can thank the unbonded dragons for that...and your General."** It sounded like it pained Misneach to admit the last part.

A smile tugged at the corner of my mouth. Silas was relentless in all things and for once, I was grateful for it.

**"What about the witches?"**

**"Haven't spotted them yet, but I can't imagine it's easy to conceal over six dozen witches,"** he mused. **"Maybe they fell when you had your**

**witchling open up the earth to swallow the enemy whole."**

My heart ached for Illiana, but I'd be lying if I said I wasn't thankful that her rage had transformed into something so beautifully destructive.

**"Then we need to make sure. We can't afford to be blindsided by an attack later,"** I said.

Misneach tilted his wings, leaning into the motion as he circled the battlefield, bringing us closer to the ground forces. We soared through the sky, skirting around the edges of the fighting unfolding across the heavens until an unnatural mist caught my eye.

**"What's that over there?"** I asked, pointing toward it.

**"I don't know."** Misneach tipped his wings and headed for the pale grey formation.

Mist billowed from the edge of the forest surrounding the valley, and the closer we came, the more unsettled I felt. An eerie stillness pervaded the air, and I shivered, my body signaling that something was amiss.

**"I don't like this, Fire Heart."**

Before I could answer him, a woman emerged from the mist. Her tall, slender frame and raven-black hair had me blinking rapidly.

"How can this be?" I whispered. "I watched Kieran snap her neck right in front of me."

The memories of my time in Netheran still haunted me.

Lucinda's head whirled in my direction, and her lips curled into a wicked smirk.

More women stepped through the mist and joined Lucinda, flanking her as they took up their positions.

My hand instinctively fisted the Aurora Stone beneath my tunic and some of the tension left my body when I felt its hard surface.

**"Misneach, I need you to do exactly as I ask without question."**

**"I can tell by your tone that I will not like what comes out of your mouth next,"** he growled.

**"I need you to leave me here and go find Arabella. Then I need you to bring her back to me, all right?"**

**"No, not all right,"** Misneach snapped. **"There is no way I am leaving you here with six covens of witches to fend off on your own."**

**"Misneach,"** I snarled. **"For the love of the gods, do as I say for once."** I took a deep breath and added, **"Trust me. I know what I am doing. Just bring me Arabella."**

**"Fire Heart,"** Misneach said, his tone pleading. **"Don't make me do**

**this."**

**"I can hold them off, Misneach. Just bring me my witch."**

Fear overwhelmed the bond, but there was also a hint of resignation. Misneach dipped closer to the gathering of witches, an unspoken signal that he would follow my orders.

**"You best be alive when I return for you,"** Misneach growled.

**"Promise,"** I grinned, but it fell flat.

Misneach hovered above the ground and I jumped from his back, closing the distance.

**"Hurry,"** I said before facing the witches.

**"On my life,"** Misneach replied as he beat his massive wings and headed back in the direction we had come.

"You think you can take us all on your own?" Lucinda taunted. "That's rather audacious, even for you."

"How are you alive?" I asked as I let the warmth flooding my stomach spread throughout my body.

"Oh, did I forget to mention that I am a Necromancer?" she purred. "I have died many deaths and none have stuck."

"How about I change that for you?" I offered.

"You're welcome to try," she said with a shrug. "But I bound my soul to this realm a long time ago and it would take a special kind of power to break a spell that strong. My body will continue to reanimate and there is little you can do to prevent that."

"I think I'm up for the challenge."

My fingertips grew hot and without having to look down, I knew flames licked at the digits. Lucinda's eyes grew wide and a flash of uncertainty flickered across her features, but it was gone a moment later, her characteristic smugness firmly back in place.

"You'll need to do better than that to impress me," she said, gesturing to my palms.

My hand darted up, and I sent a stream of fire toward the witch standing next to her. The Witch's dress caught ablaze as my flames danced along the material, consuming her. Terrified screams pierced the silence as the woman tried in vain to suffocate the burning inferno that sought to end her life.

The rest of the witches looked on in horror, their shock held them captive as their companion withered and burned. When the woman's cries finally died out, her ashen body slumped to the ground where she remained, unmoving.

"Something like that?" I asked.

Lucinda rounded on me, her eyes narrowing into slits as she raised her palms.

I expected her fury, and I had already locked my shield firmly in place.

A greenish hue spread across Lucinda's irises as an electric current sparked and hummed in the air surrounding us. The witches at her back stepped closer, creating a formidable line of defense as they each called upon their powers.

Their mouths moved as one, their whispered spells inaudible over the crackling flames drowning my senses. I reached into my pocket and withdrew the Aurora Stone, and my shield strengthened in response to its presence.

Lucinda's arms flew wide as she moved them in an arc before bringing them back together and sending a bolt of blinding white light at me. The coil of magic collided with my shield, and I could feel the coat of something dark, something sinister, crawling along its exterior, trying to find a way in.

I pushed against my shield, repelling the dark magic, and sent it sailing back to where it came from. Lucinda gasped and then ducked before her magic could reach her.

The witch behind her wasn't so fortunate.

As the magic found its mark, the witch began to tremble and writhe where she stood. Her body shook so violently that I could almost hear her bones cracking against one another, unable to escape the terror being unleashed.

Her skin pulled tight against her frame and it looked as though her skeleton was attempting to burst free from the flesh that contained it.

The witch groaned; the first sound she'd made since her torment began.

Foam seeped from the corners of her mouth and, with a single, bone-curdling scream, she collapsed in on herself as she fell toward the ground.

Lucinda roared in fury, and she doubled down on her efforts to break through my shield. She moved with deadly grace as she sent spell after spell at me, but none could penetrate the protective barrier I had erected.

The other witches joined her, and when I sensed their battle fatigue set in, I struck hard and fast.

As I lowered my shield, I hit one witch with an orb of fire and looped a flaming rope around the throat of another. With one hard pull, it burned through the tissue and bone in her neck until her head had been severed from her body.

The other witches launched a barrage of counter-attacks, but I deflected them with ease as I constructed a partial shield and pushed their offensive magic straight back at them.

I lost sight of Lucinda, and slammed my shield in place, not wanting to take any chances where she was concerned.

As I surveyed the ground, a knot of discomfort formed in my gut. I wondered how many of these witches had only been seeking a safe place to call home when they were forced to flee to Netheran.

Just like Everly.

"You have the Aurora Stone," Lucinda said from behind me, and I spun around to face her.

Her eyes rounded in awe, but I didn't miss the greed sparkling just as brightly.

"If you give it to me, I will leave this place and your people in peace," she said, unable to pull her gaze from the stone.

I barked out a laugh, and she jolted.

"What's so funny?"

"You thinking I would ever hand over something so powerful to the likes of you!"

Lucinda snarled and moved to lunge for me, before remembering my shield and pulling herself up short.

"I will help Kieran kill every single person you love before leaving this battlefield," she warned.

"You'll do that either way."

Lucinda raked her hands through her hair before pulling at the strands and tugging in frustration.

"You're going to regret this," she threatened as she pointed a finger at me. Lucinda turned to the other witches and said, "Do not let her leave this field."

Then she turned on her heels and disappeared back into the mist.

Unease tightened my chest, and I knew Lucinda would keep her word if I didn't stop her.

But first, I had to deal with the witches she had left behind.

I closed my eyes and let the power of the stone flow through me.

**"Fire Heart,"** Misneach called, the concern clear in his tone.

Ignoring him, I drew more power until it was all-consuming.

**"Fire Heart!"**

I opened my eyes and peered out at the witches. An audible gasp rolled through the women before me like a tidal wave.

Clenching my fists, I lowered my shield and thrust my hands forward.

When I opened my palms, a torrent of flames burst free. The witches standing directly in front of me were incinerated in mere seconds.

Then I moved my hands over the group, decimating anyone in my path. The women tried to flee, but their panic had them tripping over each other as they desperately fought to survive.

It was no use. They sealed their fates the moment they set foot on the battlefield.

It was all over in less than a minute. That's all it took to extinguish dozens of lives.

As I watched their ashes get swept away with the breeze, I faltered, and my legs trembled. My knees buckled under my weight and I fell to the ground, crying out in pain as I slammed into the hardened earth.

**"FIRE HEART!"** Misneach roared, and it was the last thing I heard before darkness swallowed me.

# Chapter Sixty-Nine

**"Fire Heart!"** I heard Misneach call, but it sounded like his voice was coming from somewhere far away.

Was I dreaming?

**"Fire Heart,"** he called again, closer this time.

Something nudged my side, and I groaned as pain pulsed at my temples with the movement.

**"Fire Heart, please,"** Misneach begged.

Please what?

Misneach breathed a sigh of relief.

**"She's coming around,"** he said, but I didn't know who he was talking to.

**"I need you to get up, Fire Heart. You're exposed out here and we need to move."**

Another nudge came at my side and I reluctantly peeled my eyes open.

A mop of chestnut brown hair was the first thing I saw, and then a face came into view.

"Arabella?" I croaked.

"Gods, Harlowe," she breathed. "You gave me quite the fright."

I tried to sit up, but I couldn't get my body to cooperate.

"What happened?" I asked as Arabella helped me into a sitting position.

"I was hoping you could tell me."

I glanced around, but my dragon's muscular frame blocked my vision.

**"Could you move back, Misneach?"**

**"No,"** he gritted out. **"I am never leaving your side again."**

Ignoring him, I returned my attention to Arabella. "Why are you here?"

Her nose wrinkled in confusion, and she glanced at Misneach. "Your dragon came for me. He was rather insistent."

Images suddenly flooded my memory.

The witches.

**"Where are they?"** Misneach asked.

**"Dead."** I swallowed thickly. **"I killed them."**

But not all of them.

I tried getting to my feet, but Arabella pushed me back down.

"I need to go. Lucinda got away, and she's going after everyone I love," I said as panic squeezed me tightly.

"You can't even stand in your state," Arabella chided.

"Then I'll crawl."

**"Misneach, help me."**

He didn't get a chance though, as Arabella thrust a vial in my face. "Drink. It'll help you recover your strength."

Without hesitation, I gripped the vial and tore the cap free. The cool liquid slid down my throat and I could feel it working to repair the fatigue in my muscles. The pain in my temples abated, and I pushed off the ground.

I wasn't at my full strength, but it would have to do.

"Come on," I said, tugging Arabella alongside me. "We have to go."

She didn't hesitate when I pulled her into place on Misneach's back.

**"Find Lucinda."**

**"What does she look like?"** Misneach asked as he pushed off the ground and launched himself into the sky.

**"She was the raven-haired woman who emerged first from the mist. Did you get a good view of her?"**

**"Yes, Fire Heart. I remember."**

The battle still raged all around us, but I blocked it all out, narrowing my focus until I found the one person I was searching for.

Lucinda.

**"Over there,"** I shouted when I caught sight of her midnight-colored strands.

"Oh gods," I breathed.

"What is it?" Arabella asked as she fidgeted in place unable to control the nervous tension.

Copper hair that was so familiar I would recognize it anywhere, swung back and forth as my father leveled his sword at each enemy that dared to come near.

His skill with the blade was honed to a masterful art, and he effortlessly cut down those seeking to bring him before the gods. He was so preoccupied with the enemies in front of him, however, that he didn't notice the danger closing in from behind.

My heart beat so fast it was almost painful, and I gripped Misneach's scales with enough force to draw blood.

I watched on in horror as Lucinda made her way toward him undetected.

**"Go Misneach!"** I shouted, as my fear threatened to be my undoing.

Misneach tipped into a dive, heading straight for the woman preparing to take my father from me.

"Please... oh gods... please," I cried.

The wind whipped against my face and stung my eyes with the pressure of our rapid descent, but I didn't care.

I just needed to reach him before Lucinda did.

**"Faster, please, Misneach,"** I begged, as moisture glistened on my cheeks.

Misneach pushed harder, closing the distance with each mighty beat of his wings.

I was almost there.

I was going to make it.

I...

Lucinda raised a blade, and my world stopped moving.

"NO!" I roared as she raked the blade across my father's throat before he even realized she was there.

My father turned, and his hand flew to his neck as he tried desperately to stem the crimson liquid gushing from the wound.

His eyes flicked to me, and they widened. He seemed to realize this was the end, and his gaze softened. With a single look, he said all the things he could not voice out loud.

I love you.

I am proud of you.

I believe in you.

I am sorry I won't be there to stand beside you at the end.

A broken sob wrenched itself free from my throat as I threw myself from Misneach's back and raced toward him.

My father sank to his knees, and I heard a strangled cry sound nearby.

My mother.

With one last glance in my direction, my father made sure I would never question his love for me again.

Then he fell, and he never got back up.

I gripped the Aurora Stone in my bloodied fist as I summoned all of its power until my very being merged with its intoxicating magic.

**"Fire Heart, no,"** Misneach cried.

But I was beyond reasoning.

Lucinda faced me with a vicious smirk on her painted lips. "I warned you," she taunted. "Now you know I do not make idle threats."

With a scream filled with agony, I thrust my palm forward and unleashed a fiery orb at her. Lucinda shifted in place, angling her torso away from the blast and letting it skim by her.

I had no idea where it landed, nor did I care.

The only thing I fixated on was my rage and my need for vengeance.

Lucinda countered as she tossed a spell at me. The green haze that trailed after it told me it wasn't something I wanted to experience.

I pulled a partial shield and deflected the blow as I sunk further into the power offered by the stone.

**"Fire Heart, you're pulling too much power,"** Misneach warned, but I barely acknowledged his words as I let a tendril of flames snake free from my palm.

It coiled and writhed as it darted for Lucinda, but she was surprisingly agile, and with quick footwork, she avoided being tangled in its grip.

I snarled as I unleashed a torrent of flames, but she let loose a searing energy of her own and the two elements collided, pressing against one another as they fought for dominance.

Leaning into my power, I pushed Lucinda's spell back, forcing her to retreat a step. Worry furrowed her brow and a bead of sweat slid down the side of her face.

I pushed harder and the first true sign of fear morphed her features.

**"Fire Heart, please,"** Misneach begged and I could feel him trying to tug me back as he anchored me.

I shoved against him, directing all my fury towards the woman, who finally realized she was outmatched.

**"Please,"** Misneach whispered, his voice cracking on the single word.

Emotion flooded the bond; fear, guilt, crushing defeat, but above all others was unconditional love.

**"I promise I will pick you up and carry you until you can bear to stand again, Fire Heart,"** Misneach said thickly. **"Just don't let our story end here. We are not done yet."**

Intense longing washed over me, and all I could think about was getting to my dragon.

With painstaking slowness, I released the power I held, and recalled my flames.

I saw Lucinda sag in relief, and unable to hold out any longer, her spell faded away as she wobbled on unsteady feet.

Sobs wracked my body, and I ran to Misneach. His large wings cradled me as I clung to his foreleg.

**"I have you, Fire Heart,"** he murmured, nuzzling my hair.

I drew strength from the comfort of my dragon and when I had regained control of my emotions, Misneach lowered his wings so I could face Lucinda once more.

I squared my shoulders and marched in her direction, but I paused as I registered the pain contorting her features. A dark stain spread across the front of her dress and I looked over her shoulder, meeting sky-blue eyes that were wet with tears.

My mother wrenched her blade free, and Lucinda let out a pained gasp before falling forward onto her hands and knees. Her labored breathing was the only sound I could hear until her body gave up its fight and she collapsed in a heap on the ground.

**"Misneach?"** I asked, and he stepped forward, taking a deep breath before he engulfed Lucinda's body in flames.

She would have a hard time reanimating a body that was nothing more than ashes.

"Are we having fun yet?" a low, menacing voice said from behind me and I spun around, my gaze clashing with cruel cerulean ones.

"Are you ready to play, Bride?"

# Chapter Seventy

My mother lunged for Kieran and he threw up a hand as tentacles of his shadows shot forward and slammed into her, sending her body sailing through the air.

"Mother!" I shouted, but she didn't respond as her body crashed against the earth.

**"Orla!"**

The dragon roared and darted toward my mother.

**"Get her out of here."**

I didn't know if she was alive, but if she had any chance of surviving this, it was with her dragon at her side.

**"I have her Queen of Fire and Flame,"** Orla said as she swooped in, wrapping her clawed feet around my mother's prone body and lifting her from the battlefield.

"Arabella, run," I ordered, and the witch hesitated, unwilling to leave me.

Kieran smirked, and I knew what his intentions were.

I didn't allow him to act on them, as I shot a hand forward, pushing him back with my flames. Angling my body toward Arabella, I threw my other palm out, sending heat licking at her heels and forcing her out of the area.

Unsurprisingly, Kieran was unharmed by my assault.

"You're no fun," he pouted.

Wisps of shadows coiled and writhed around his legs, climbing higher like snakes eager to strike. Kieran's gaze remained locked on me. The hunger in his eyes burned brightly.

But it wasn't his hunger for my submission that I saw.

It was a different kind of hunger.

A hunger for power.

And this time, he wouldn't hesitate to annihilate me to get it.

Kieran's shadows crept higher, morphing and twisting until they stood tall behind him. The air around me grew cold and Kieran's shadows lurched forward, encircling us in a dome of suffocating darkness.

"Now it's just the two of us," he grinned.

He'd mimicked my shield and trapped me inside his shadowy enclosure. I'd been too caught up in my musings to notice his plans and counter his attack.

Something crashed against the shadows containing me, and a visceral roar followed.

**"FIRE HEART!"** Misneach roared, and then he struck again and again.

"I've been watching you throughout the battle, you know," Kieran said casually, ignoring the attempts of my dragon to break through the barrier separating us.

"Enjoying a front-row seat to your prowess. I must confess I'm rather impressed," he cooed.

His gaze roamed over me in an assessing, calculative manner.

"When you obliterated my witches," he said with dark amusement. "I wasn't even upset by the magnitude of the power I'd had at my disposal that just... disappeared... lost in a single heartbeat," he said, as he snapped his fingers.

"All I could think about was what I would do with the limitless power I'd replace it with once I had you."

"I've already told you I won't side with you, Kieran, so if this is just another attempt to bring me to your side, then you're wasting your time."

Kieran's eyes lit up with mischief, and his grin stretched wide. But it wasn't friendly.

Far from it.

"Oh, I have no delusions about where your misguided loyalties lay, Harlowe," he said as he bounced on the balls of his feet.

I'd never seen him like this. He was always the picture of controlled lethality.

It was almost as if he was... excited.

Another thunderous crash sounded from outside the barrier, and the shadows shuddered under the intensity of it.

"No, I wasn't talking about you, Harlowe," he said as he licked his lips. "I was talking about the Aurora Stone."

I could feel the color draining from my face as my body broke out in sweat.

"Come now," he purred. "You're incredibly powerful, maybe as powerful as me, but even I took centuries to grow in strength."

My palm tightened around the smooth surface of the stone, as my heart beat so wildly I didn't know if I'd survive it.

I'd been careless. I'd used the stone out in the open, and now Kieran knew I possessed it.

The things he could do if he held it within his grasp.

An involuntary shiver coursed through me, flooding my veins with adrenaline, and I attacked. A battle cry passed between my lips as I raised my hands and scorched the very earth Kieran stood upon.

The heat inside the barrier grew stifling, and my arms shook, but I didn't stop the searing stream of flames.

Only when my throat burned and my breathing grew labored did I pull back. My damp tunic clung to my skin, and I bent at my waist, taking a moment to catch my breath.

I'd summoned more power in that single moment than I had when extinguishing the life force of dozens of witches.

Kieran's voice broke through the exhausted haze of my mind. "Are you done?" he mocked.

My head snapped up, and I gasped as I took in his pristine state.

I couldn't do this.

I couldn't beat Kieran.

Even with the stone, his ability to heal himself gave him an advantage that I couldn't match.

And yet, I refused to give up. I refused to accept that all of this, every tragedy, every sacrifice, every hardship, had been for nothing.

Misneach continued to attack the barrier relentlessly, but he wasn't getting inside unless Kieran allowed it.

Once again, I sank into the power of the stone. Warmth flooded every inch of my body, regenerating me and giving me strength.

No, that wasn't the stone.

It was Misneach.

He was lending me his strength in my weakest moment and I leaned into it. I drew upon the power of the stone and trusted Misneach to anchor me and build me up again.

As if he sensed my renewed determination, Kieran struck. A tendril of shadows shot toward me as it snaked around my boot and pulled me to the ground. I kicked out at the darkness that ensnared me, but my foot passed right through it.

With a snarl, I shot my own fiery rope in his direction as I jumped to my feet. My hands clamped around the shadowy tendril still holding me and it hissed, recoiling away from my touch.

Interesting.

Kieran might be able to heal himself, but I could harm his shadows.

Would that weaken him enough to gain an advantage?

There was only one way to find out.

I lunged toward Kieran, a blazing orb burning in the palm of my hand before I released it, sending it straight for him. A shadow in the shape of a sword appeared in his hands and he deflected my blow with the darkened blade.

I summoned my own fiery sword, its blade alight with flames that roared in the silence of the barrier.

I advanced on Kieran but froze when he disappeared right in front of me.

He had stepped inside his shadows and just... vanished.

I spun around, searching every darkened corner for any sign of him.

A sharp pain erupted at the back of my calf and I cried out. When I turned to peer over my shoulder, I saw Kieran retreat inside his shadows until the darkness concealed him once more.

"I've faced the darkness before and come out stronger," I murmured to myself.

Another jolt of pain exploded along my ribcage and I lowered my sword as I pressed my hand against my injured side.

The wound didn't burn with the heat of my blood.

No.

It was cold, almost freezing.

As much as I tried to fight it, fear formed a lump in my throat and I felt as if my chest was being squeezed to the point of collapsing.

"This fear is just another shadow to conquer."

A low chuckle surrounded me, making the hairs on the back of my neck stand on end before another bite of pain assaulted my forearm.

"I've faced the darkness before and come out stronger. This fear is just another shadow to conquer," I whispered into the void of oppressive shadows, willing myself to believe the words.

Another burst of pain battered me, followed by another and another.

My palms grew clammy and a violent tremble wracked my frame. Tears pricked at the back of my eyes and I cursed myself for showing any signs of weakness.

I abandoned my sword and called up my flames until they encased my entire body. The raging inferno lit up Kieran's shadowy barrier, and he fought against it. His shadows bore down on me as they attempted to smother my light.

"I've faced the darkness before and come out stronger," I chanted, as my voice grew louder. "This fear is just another shadow to conquer."

Kieran stepped out of the dim corner he'd been lurking in. The source of my fear materializing before my very eyes.

He tsked. "Do you think so, Bride?"

Then he took a step closer. "Do you really think you'll come out stronger?"

Kieran pointed his palms to the ground and thick, black shadows filled the space between us. I pulled more power to me and pushed against the darkness as I fought with everything I had left.

Kieran's shadows crept up his frame as they concealed him from my view, and he laughed. The sound was dripping with menace.

"Do you really think you can conquer me?" he boomed and his words sounded like they were coming from every direction at once.

"I've faced the darkness before and come out stronger. This fear is just another shadow to conquer."

I pressed against the cold, merciless magic, forcing my flames to invade it, smother it.

For every surge of blazing fire I unleashed, there was an answering, suffocating darkness.

"I've faced the darkness before and come out stronger. This fear is just another shadow to conquer."

My breathing became choppy as I panted against the fatigue that tried to overwhelm me. Exerting more power, I pushed against Kieran's shadows as I tried desperately to force them out.

Flames intertwined with shadows in a violent dance, and I reached out, brushing my fingertips against the murky tendrils. They hissed as they recoiled, retreating just a fraction before Kieran forced them back with an indomitable, unrelenting push.

"I'VE FACED THE DARKNESS BEFORE AND COME OUT STRONGER. THIS FEAR IS JUST ANOTHER SHADOW TO CONQUER," I roared as I snapped my hands together in front of me, and then I threw my arms out wide, gritting my teeth, as I shoved my flames against the blackness.

My hands brushed against Kieran's shadows and they tried to withdraw from my touch, but I thrust my palm out further. This time, when I reached for the dark tendrils, my fingertips gripped a solid mass and I squeezed.

I let out a tortured scream, and the sound echoed in my ears. The wall of shadows surrounding me shattered, falling to the ground where the earth consumed them, setting me free.

# Chapter Seventy-One

A thunderous humming sound pounded inside my head and I stumbled as I tried to get to my feet.

Had I fallen? Why was I on the ground?

As I surveyed my surroundings, I could see that the battle was still being fought on every front all around us. I glimpsed Cillian locked in a fierce contest, his sword clashing against the bloodied blade of a man trying to use his larger frame to force him to the ground.

Cillian's head reared back, and then he slammed his skull into the face of his opponent. Blood exploded from his nose and he retreated. Cillian followed him and swung his sword high before plunging his blade through the other man's chest.

Emmerson fought at Cillian's back. With her short swords drawn, Emmerson lunged, thrust, and parried. Saoirse flew overhead, near enough to protect Emmerson should she require it as she aided the unbonded dragons in their aerial attack against the roc.

Her jagged teeth sank into the neck of one roc and she bit down hard, its blood dripping from her massive jaws before she dropped it. Using her tail, she cut toward another roc, the pointed tip piercing its chest and eliciting a horrible shriek from the dying creature.

Niamh flew by her with Fionn nestled between her wings. He sent an orb of fórsa sailing through the sky and it collided with a rider preparing to jump from his roc in a stealth attack on another Cathal.

I swung my gaze to the other side of the valley and I spotted Zeke and Arabella. Zeke cut his sword through the air, deflecting a hit from one fighter and kicking his leg out, sending his attacker crashing to the ground. Then he thrust the pommel of his sword behind him, delivering a brutal strike to another combatant who attempted a low sweep of her leg.

Arabella wove spells around her delicate hands before she sent them hurtling toward any soldier who attempted to converge on Zeke's position.

My eyes darted around the battlefield as I searched for the one person I needed to know was alright more than I needed my next breath. The one person I needed to know was alive and fighting so I could summon up the willpower to finish this once and for all.

When I spotted the dark waves of his hair, the light bronze of his skin, and the tattoos that I knew by heart, something in my chest unlocked, easing the pressure of the vise that had been slowly crushing me.

Silas moved with a graceful fluidity; his steps were light and agile. He exuded a confidence that could only be earned through years of honing and perfecting his skills.

With precise movements, he struck at the shoulder of one warrior, then spun in a tight circle and thrust his blade through the middle of another. Silas withdrew his blood-stained sword as he parried. He then executed a controlled riposte against a third soldier who thought to take advantage of his divided attention.

He dragged a bloodied hand down his face and, as if he could sense my gaze on him, he turned in my direction. His soulful brown eyes locked with mine and he took a step forward. Silas raised his sword, and he fought with renewed determination as he cut a blood-soaked path toward me.

A shuffling noise drew my attention, and I glanced behind me.

Kieran dragged himself into a sitting position and he looked about as good as I felt.

When our eyes met, we both scrambled to our feet and Kieran sent an unrelenting wave of shadows right for me. My arms shot up and flames erupted from my outstretched palms.

The two forces collided in a cataclysmic explosion, and shock waves rippled across the blood-stained landscape.

The ground beneath my feet buckled and groaned as if it struggled to bear the weight of such immense power.

Black, snake-like shadows twisted and flickered as they danced towards me and tongues of my fire met their every move. Embers floated in the air and I could make out the haze of heat that followed them.

The opposing energies fought against one another, each vying for dominance, but neither would yield.

The ferocity of each ebb and flow cost us both.

Our slick foreheads were a reflection of the other's, the subtle tremble in our arms as we pressed against one another, and the pained inhalation of our breaths as our lungs fought to draw enough oxygen.

A sharp tugging sensation exploded behind my ribcage and my hold faltered. I stumbled back, unable to stop myself, and Kieran grinned.

Pain, the likes of which I had never experienced in my life, assaulted me, driving me to my knees as I struggled to keep my arms in place.

Black spots marred my vision, and I tried to blink them away, but more took their place.

Misneach roared in fury and he dove for Kieran.

But Kieran was ready, and he threw one hand in Misneach's direction, erecting an imposing wall of darkness in his path.

Misneach didn't have time to pull out of his dive, and he collided against the wall of shadows, falling to the ground out of sight.

**"Misneach!"** I screamed, but my dragon didn't answer.

Tears cascaded down my cheeks and I glanced around, desperately searching for anyone who could come to his aid.

My gaze fell on Zeke and I sucked in a ragged breath as I watched a blade pierce his abdomen. He fell forward, the blade still lodged in his flesh as he sank to his knees.

An anguished scream escaped Arabella, and she moved her hands rapidly, firing spells in every direction.

Another jolt of pain wracked my body and my throat closed over.

A hand flew to my neck without my permission as I clawed at my skin.

I was dying, of that I was certain. I just didn't understand how or why.

"Harlowe!" I heard Emmerson call, and I followed the sound of her voice until I met her fearful gaze. Her lips were parted and true terror contorted her features.

She was so fixated on me that she didn't notice the combatant sneaking up on her. I thrashed against the ground as I frantically tried to call out to her, to warn her, but no sound escaped me.

Emmerson gasped and sucked in a shaky breath. I fought against whatever power held me captive, but it didn't relent.

My vision blurred, and she disappeared from my line of sight.

A rough, strangled sound filled my mind and my heart pounded as I waited to hear Misneach's voice.

But it was Aodhán's deep rasp that met my ears.

**"Live and finish this fight, Queen of Fire and Flame,"** he murmured.

**"Aodhán? What's happening?"**

**"I release you from our life bond,"** he choked.

**"Aodhán?"** I called again.

Suddenly, all remnants of the crippling pain I had experienced moments ago vanished, leaving me feeling stronger and invigorated as newfound energy coursed through my veins.

I ripped my hand away from my neck and thrust it forward as I let my power surge through my shaky limbs.

I knew at that moment that Aodhán was dead.

He'd used his dying breath to save my life, and my heart clenched with his loss.

**"Misneach,"** I sobbed, needing his strength now more than ever. **"Please be all right."**

I didn't think I could carry on if I'd lost him, too.

**"You are stronger than the doubts that plague your mind and the fears that shackle you. You can overcome any obstacle that stands in your way. Now get to your feet and fight, Fire Heart!"** Misneach gritted out.

I closed my eyes and let silent tears streak down my face, thanking the gods for this one act of mercy.

Then I pushed myself to my feet and faced Kieran.

# Chapter Seventy-Two

With a guttural scream, I summoned every ounce of power the stone had left to offer me and sent it coursing down the stream of my flames that pressed against Kieran's shadows.

Kieran shifted back, but he quickly regained the ground he'd yielded.

Gritting his teeth, he pushed back, sending a violent tremor through my flames that traveled up my arms and threatened my resolve. My boots slid against the muddy ground and I stumbled, barely catching myself before I fell.

"Harlowe," Silas called, and my eyes darted to the side as I watched him sprint toward me.

Kieran snarled and pushed his power at me again with such ferocity that an involuntary cry escaped my lips.

"Forgive me."

The familiar voice drifted to me over the sounds of battle and my gaze flickered to where Silas had been standing, but the spot was now vacant. My brows furrowed in confusion as I searched for him.

"Silas, what —"

My confusion transformed into horror and I watched on helplessly, unable to stop Silas as he threw himself between me and Kieran.

The intrusion severed the connection between Kieran's power and mine, and I was flung backward. My shoulders hit the ground, but I continued to slide across the earth from the sheer intensity of the blow.

Rolling to my side, I groaned in pain, but I forced myself to press my palms against the dirt until my trembling arms held my weight. I bent my legs and slowly slid them upward until I made it onto my hands and knees.

My gaze snapped back in the direction I had come.

Silas lay on the ground, unmoving.

"Silas," I called, my voice sounding hoarse. "Silas!"

Time didn't simply slow down around me... it stopped.

I stopped.

My heart stopped beating.

My breaths stopped coming.

My world stopped moving.

All of my attention had narrowed to a single focal point as the sounds of battle faded, only to be replaced by the crippling silence now engulfing me.

Silas didn't respond.

My heart began beating with such violent intensity that I had to clutch my chest to ensure it hadn't smashed its way free.

Adrenaline flooded my veins, and I inhaled deeply, yet I couldn't suck in enough air. The tightness in my chest constricted my lungs and my breaths came in short, ragged pants.

On shaky limbs, I pushed myself to stand.

And then I was running.

As I reached Silas's prone form, my body betrayed me, and I stumbled, falling to the ground beside him.

Pain shot through my body, but I didn't care.

All I could see, all I could focus on, was the way Silas's chest remained still.

"Silas," I whispered, as I clambered over his body to touch his face.

When he didn't respond, I gripped his shoulders and shook him forcefully. "Silas!"

My fingers danced to the pulse point at his throat and I swallowed my fear as I pressed my thumb against it.

And then I waited.

And waited.

And waited.

"Si... Silas," I choked as my vision blurred and bile crept up my throat.

"Silas!" I shouted, shaking him harder.

Movement sounded behind me and I swung my head around to see Cillian, Emmerson, and Fionn standing there, looking down at me with misery and... pity.

"Get help!" I demanded, and their eyes grew wet, but they remained rooted in place. "Don't just stand there! He needs a healer."

Emmerson's features contorted in pain and she buried her face in Cillian's shoulder.

"Please, please help me," I begged.

"Harlowe," Cillian said, a tear making its way down his cheek.

But I turned away from him, refusing to hear the words that would shatter my world into tiny irreparable pieces.

"No," I gritted out as I pounded a fist against Silas's chest.

Still, his body refused to respond to my touch.

"No," I repeated, louder this time.

"Don't you dare do this to me, Silas," I growled. "You. Promised."

The tears blurring my vision spilled over and I scrubbed them away as though any acknowledgment of my pain would make this all real.

"You promised me, Silas," I said, as my voice broke. "You promised me you would never sacrifice yourself for me."

A hand landed on my shoulder and I looked up into Fionn's brown eyes, which glittered with unshed tears. "I'm so sorry, Harlowe. He's gone."

I shook off his touch and slammed my palms against Silas's chest as I begged the gods to have mercy.

"No," I whispered. "You have to follow through on your threat to make me your wife," I chuckled, but it came out sounding strangled.

"I need to see that satisfied glint in your eyes when I tell you that I love you for the very first time, even though you knew it all along."

Vibrations shook the ground all around me as the dragons converged on us, but I never took my eyes off Silas's blank ones.

"I..."

Caolán lowered his head and he nudged Silas. When he didn't respond, the dragon let out a broken cry.

"I... I..."

"Harlowe," Emmerson whispered, her voice thick with tears.

"I... this can't... I..."

I couldn't form words. This couldn't be happening. It couldn't be real.

A scream worked its way up my throat, slipping past my lips and slamming against my ears.

It was raw.

Visceral.

Etched with so much pain, I didn't think a person could experience such torment and live through it.

I pulled Silas's limp body into my lap as I threw my head back and howled.

The shattered pieces of my soul filled the sound, echoing around the valley and amplifying the anguish building inside me.

I couldn't stop it even if I wanted to. My body moved without my permission as I rocked back and forth, needing something, anything, to take away this agony.

"Please," I begged. "Please don't do this to me."

Furious sobs wracked my body, and it felt like I was splintering, being torn apart on the blood-soaked ground I had fought to protect with my life, only to find it would cost me far more than I ever envisioned.

"Why?" I shrieked, not sure what I was asking or to whom.

**"Fire Heart,"** Misneach whispered, but I ignored him.

"YOU FUCKING PROMISED!" I roared as I laid his body back on the ground and covered it with my own. "You lied to me," I whispered hoarsely.

Hands tugged at me from behind, but I resisted them.

"Don't touch me," I screamed, my throat burning from the strain. "Don't fucking touch me," I whimpered.

Despair overwhelmed me and I felt like I was drowning, my head bobbing beneath the water, unable to breach the surface no matter how close I came.

I wanted to lie down next to Silas and never get back up again.

"I love you," I sniffed, as I buried my face in Silas's neck. "I should have told you sooner."

A fresh wave of tears poured down my face, and I wondered if they'd ever stop.

I forced myself to swallow past the lump in my throat. "I love you so fucking much, but I was afraid. I was afraid that if I gave you my heart, you'd have the power to crush me with it."

At that moment, I knew my fears had been unwarranted.

"And now, I would give anything to say those words to you," I said through muffled sobs.

"Please, Silas," I whispered. "Please come back to me. I don't want to do this without you."

But Silas remained still and unmoving, his skin growing paler the longer I clung to him.

My heart refused to accept what my mind already knew.

Silas was gone, and he wasn't coming back.

# Chapter Seventy-Three

I don't know how long I stayed there, clinging to Silas's dead body as the echoes of our final battle faded into a haunting silence.

It could have been days, and I wouldn't have noticed.

When the ground vibrated underneath me again, signaling the arrival of another dragon, I didn't bother to look up.

No amount of comfort they could offer would take away the emptiness consuming me.

**"Daughter,"** a deep masculine voice called out to me.

When I didn't acknowledge him, Drakkon said again, **"Daughter, look at me."**

**"Why?"** I asked, my voice sounding strange to my own ears.

**"I can help you."**

**"Can you bring Silas back to me?"** I laughed, but there was no humor in it.

There was a long pause, and the silence stretched out between us before Drakkon replied. **"Perhaps."**

My head snapped in his direction and his soft gaze took me in, his sympathy clear in his expression.

For the first time since Silas fell, I took in my surroundings. The battle had died off, but I had no idea what had become of the Netheran or Viddyan forces.

Nor did I care.

I could see Cillian tending to a large gash on Emmerson's back and Fionn was applying some ointment to a cut along Niamh's flank.

My gaze shifted and landed on Misneach, who stood huddled with the other dragons. He watched me closely, unable to mask his concern.

I allowed my relief to flood the bond, telling him without words how grateful I was that he was all right.

He returned the feeling, and I knew he would be there for me when I was ready.

It didn't escape my attention that Zeke and Arabella were nowhere to be seen.

When my eyes finally fell on Kieran's lifeless body, I inhaled sharply.

**"Is he... is he..."** I trailed off, unable to say the words.

**"He is dead,"** Drakkon supplied.

I thought I would have felt relief knowing that the source of my nightmares was no longer a threat to me and those I cared for.

But all I felt was... sorrow.

**"It's all right to mourn him, Daughter,"** Drakkon soothed.

**"Is it? He has caused such suffering. He is the reason, Silas... he's the reason for all of this,"** I said, waving my arm over the death and destruction littering the battlefield.

**"That doesn't mean you're not entitled to your feelings."**

My feelings for Kieran were complex. He had manipulated me, harmed me, and even tried to kill me.

But the connection we'd shared was real.

**"How can you help Silas?"** I asked, shutting the door on my spiraling thoughts.

**"Come with me, Daughter."** I glanced down at Silas, unwilling to leave him unprotected despite knowing no further harm could come to him.

**"Look around you, Daughter. He is in good hands."**

I placed a kiss on Silas's forehead, my lips lingering a moment before I reluctantly stood and moved toward Drakkon.

**"Where are we going?"**

**"You will see."**

When my fingers grazed Drakkon's scales, the world tilted around me. A familiar sensation of falling plagued me and I groaned, knowing exactly where we were headed.

Unrelenting blackness greeted me, and a moment later, my back collided with the hard ground.

The battlefield was devoid of all life, only the blood-stained ground remained. Drakkon stood beside me, unperturbed by our method of arrival.

"Well, isn't this a pleasant surprise?" a woman's voice called from behind us.

I spun in place and came face to face with three women. The curly brown hair and the warm smile on Oonagh's face never failed to settle my nerves, which contrasted with Rhene's stern aura of authority that set me on edge. The third woman, Eabha, wore a roguish grin, her light grey hair hanging to her waist as she clutched her cane in her hand.

The fates.

"It has been a long time," Drakkon chuckled, and I peered at him, unsure if he had said the words out loud or if my mind was playing tricks on me.

"It is one benefit of the void," Eabha said in answer to my unspoken question. "We are all equals here."

Hardly.

Eabha's grin grew even wider, as though she had heard my inner thoughts.

Shifting uncomfortably in place, I directed my attention to Drakkon. "What are we doing here?"

Drakkon's playful tone vanished as he said, "We've come to make a trade."

The three women narrowed their eyes at him, assessing him anew.

"What kind of trade?" Rhene demanded, and I could hear the suspicion clear in her voice.

"A life was taken today," Drakkon replied and hope surged in my chest. "You must restore it."

I sucked in a breath, not willing to release it for fear if I breathed wrong, they would refuse us.

"And why should we entertain such a request?" Rhene demanded.

The pain I had experienced the moment I realized Silas was dead assaulted me once more, crushing my brief flickering of hope, and it was an effort to keep my knees from buckling.

I stepped forward as tears filled my eyes and released a shaky breath. "Because he sacrificed himself to save our realm," I said.

My hands trembled, and I clenched them into fists.

"It was supposed to be me, but he gave his life in my stead."

The moment the words left my lips, the truth of them threatened to be my undoing.

It should have been me.

It was my destiny to stop Kieran or die trying.

"He did it to save you," Rhene said, as she jutted her chin in my direction. "Not the realm."

I wanted to scream at her. Lash out and decry the unfairness of the situation. Instead, I breathed through the pain, strengthening my resolve and squaring my shoulders.

"He did it to save me, yes," I admitted. "But he also fought relentlessly to safeguard this realm and its people, knowing what was at stake if we failed. If my life had not been in danger, he still would have made the same choice."

I lifted my chin, daring her to challenge me.

I knew Silas, and I knew every word I had spoken was the truth.

Silas was flawed, but he understood duty and sacrifice better than anyone.

Rhene tilted her head to the side as she studied me, and I resisted the urge to fidget under her scrutiny. Then her gaze flicked to Drakkon.

"You understand the price of the bargain you seek?" she asked.

"I do," he confirmed. "But you will restore what has been denied to her from the beginning."

Eabha grinned again as Rhene scowled at the dragon.

"You are in no position to make further demands of us, Drakkon," she growled.

"All the same," Drakkon said as he bowed his head.

Rhene studied him for the longest moment before Oonagh interrupted. "Stop looking at him like you are willing him to combust," she chuckled. "He won't withdraw his demand."

"She is right, sister," Eabha added, her gaze landing on Drakkon and she smiled at him affectionately.

"It pleases me to know my memory has not grown dull in your mind, my friend," Drakkon said to Eabha.

"I would recall your stubbornness millennia from now," she laughed, and Drakkon smiled in agreement.

"The balance within the realm must be restored," Rhene said, interrupting their teasing.

Her gaze landed on me.

"The Serpent King no longer poses a threat to the realm," she said, and I flinched.

"You must return the powers gifted to you so the realm may once again flourish in harmony."

If that was the price for Silas's life, I would pay it without hesitation. "And Silas will be restored?" I clarified.

Her gaze flicked to Drakkon, and he inclined his head. "Yes," she confirmed.

Tears pricked my eyes and the pieces of my broken heart slowly put themselves back together again.

A profound sense of relief washed over me, and I didn't know if I wanted to laugh or cry. It felt as though I was emerging from the darkness and seeing the sun for the very first time.

"Take them," I sobbed, as I rushed toward the three women and thrust my hands out. "Take them."

"There will be a cost," Rhene said in warning, but I didn't care. Whatever it was, I'd pay it.

"I don't care," I said, and Rhene arched a brow.

"Without your powers, you will no longer be able to commune with the dragons."

A sharp burst of pain lanced my heart, but despite how much it would hurt, I'd made my choice.

"Even Misneach?" I asked in a small voice.

"No, Daughter. He is your bonded dragon. Your connection with him will survive this change."

"Then do it," I demanded.

The women converged on me, each placing a hand on my shoulders. Drakkon stepped closer and pressed his forehead against mine.

The moment the circle was complete, a tingling sensation crept up my body. It probed and explored every inch of me, before settling heavy in my chest.

Without warning, a biting pain seared my flesh and a torrent of flames burst free from my chest, forcing a cry to escape my lips.

When it was over, I sagged against Drakkon and panted heavily.

"Is it done?"

"It is," Drakkon confirmed. "Now it is time for us to return to Aetherian."

The women turned away from me and my hand shot out to grip Rhene's wrist.

"Wait," I begged, and she peered back at me with a quizzical look.

Swallowing past my unease, I asked, "Why didn't I die when the connection between my powers and Kieran's was severed?"

"Because you held the Aurora Stone."

My brows furrowed in confusion, but then I recalled something I had read in the library in Netheran.

*The stone's ability to deflect and contain negative energies made it instrumental in establishing the wards that surround the Forest of Nightmares.*

"The stone... deflected Kieran's attack?" I asked.

"It would appear so."

"I still don't understand how Kieran died. Why didn't he heal himself?"

I'd been struggling to piece together everything that happened in the moments after Silas broke our connection, but nothing was making sense.

"The Serpent King wielded tainted and mutilated magic that was never meant to exist inside your realm," Rhene said. "He could overcome many things, but his own ambition was not one of them."

I still didn't understand what Rhene was telling me. Kieran had been all but indestructible, so why had that moment been different?

Then Rhene's words replayed in my head and an idea stirred to life in the back of my mind.

"Are you saying Kieran... killed himself?" I asked.

"In a manner of speaking, yes," she confirmed. "He pulled more power than any being was ever capable of holding, and when the connection between your powers snapped, all of that malevolent energy found a home inside him. It consumed him, destroying him from within until nothing else remained except the host that could no longer survive the suffering inflicted upon it."

A shiver raced down my spine at the thought of such toxicity penetrating the very core of one's being.

Regardless of Kieran's actions, I would never wish that fate upon him.

"Thank you," I whispered, and Rhene inclined her head before the three women disappeared.

"Come Daughter," Drakkon said, and I stepped beside him.

That same sense of weightlessness crashed into me, and my stomach lurched with the sensation.

Just as quickly as it had started, it was over.

Air filled my lungs in a rush and my breaths came out in choppy pants. Then slowly, my breaths evened out, and I pushed up from the ground.

My eyes landed on Silas and I rushed to his side.

"Silas," I gasped as my hands framed his face.

He didn't respond, and fear tightened like a vise around my heart.

Why wasn't he waking up?

I'd done as the fates had demanded.

With trembling hands, I traced my way towards the pulse point at the base of his throat.

Exhaling a shaky breath, I pressed my fingers against the soft flesh.

Nothing.

There was no rhythmic pounding beneath my touch to signify any sign of life.

"Come on, Silas," I begged. "Please open your eyes."

I was vaguely aware of the murmuring around me, but I blocked it all out. All of my attention was trained on the man in front of me.

"Please."

One second passed, and then two.

Time moved excruciatingly slowly as I held my breath.

But then I felt it.

The tiniest flicker beneath my fingertips.

"Silas?" I choked, trying to suppress the sob clawing at my throat.

The flicker beneath my fingers intensified, and the sob tore its way free.

I collapsed atop Silas's broad chest and buried my face in his neck. I wailed without restraint as I purged all the grief from my body.

Something brushed against my hair, and I stilled.

"Little Menace?"

A strangled cry escaped me and I tightened my grip around Silas's body, unwilling to let him go for fear this moment would prove to be nothing more than my imagination.

"Little Menace," Silas repeated, the sound coming out rough and brittle.

As much as I wanted to look at him, I couldn't bring myself to lift my head.

"Little Menace, look at me," he demanded.

And that was all it took for my resolve to crumble.

I lifted my eyes and they locked with beautiful, rich brown ones. A flood of tears spilled down my cheeks, and Silas reached up to brush them away.

"Hey, it's all right," he soothed.

"You died, Silas," I sobbed and his brows creased in confusion.

"Well, whatever happened, I'm here now," he said, and I tried to laugh, but it came out as a broken, wretched sound.

"I love you," I whispered, and Silas's eyes widened before he surged forward, claiming my mouth with his.

# Chapter Seventy-Four

A pained growl broke through the haze of longing that drove my need to bury myself beneath Silas's skin so he'd always carry a piece of me.

Reluctantly, I pulled away from Silas and scanned my surroundings.

Drakkon stood to the side, his crimson scales glinting in the sliver of sunlight breaking through the grey clouds.

His enormous frame swayed from side to side before he collapsed to the ground, sending a shuddering vibration through the valley like a wave.

"Drakkon!" I shouted as I ran to him.

"What's wrong?" I asked, only to remember we could no longer communicate.

**"Do not worry, Daughter,"** he said, his tone soft and gentle. **"Everything is as it should be."**

**"How?"** I asked, my mouth agape. **"How can I hear you?"**

**"It was a parting gift from the fates,"** he said.

**"I don't understand what's going on."**

Drakkon smiled weakly.

**"In order for the fates to restore the life of your twin flame, a trade had to be made,"** he said.

**"Yes, and I made it. I returned the power they had given me."**

**"No, Daughter,"** he said, his voice wavering as he struggled to regulate his breathing.

Unease coiled around me like a snake, slithering and caressing me, while I remained immobile, afraid of the next strike.

**"You needed to return your powers to restore the balance within Aetherian. However, the bargain I struck with the fates was one life for another,"** he said.

I could feel Silas's presence at my back, offering comfort and protection.

**"Drakkon,"** I stammered. **"Why?"**

**"You have given enough already, Daughter. It was my turn to protect you."**

**"I never would have agreed if I knew it was your life I was trading away."**

I would have readily given my own, but I could never ask for such a sacrifice from another.

**"I know,"** Drakkon chuckled. **"That's why I didn't tell you."**

**"I don't know what to say,"** I whispered hoarsely.

**"You don't need to say anything, Daughter. Just live, and be happy."**

I threw my arms around Drakkon's neck and he rested his head on my shoulder.

**"Thank you,"** I choked, and Drakkon nuzzled my hair.

I could feel the connection between us beginning to fade away and I tightened my grip, unwilling to let a single moment escape me.

**"Fire Heart,"** Misneach said. **"He is gone. He is finally at peace."**

More tears filled my eyes, and I was surprised that I still had any left to cry.

All of that came to an abrupt stop, however, when Drakkon's body began to... disintegrate.

It was as if his body was a blazing fire and piece by piece, he was being carried away, like tiny embers on the wind.

**"How?"** I asked in disbelief.

**"He was the first dragon,"** Misneach mused. **"We never really knew the extent of his powers."**

I watched in awe as Drakkon's body left this plane, in search of the soul I was certain was still out there somewhere.

Not even death could contain a being such as Drakkon.

"Harlowe," Silas said as he placed a hand on my shoulder.

As I peered up at him, I was momentarily stunned by how radiant he looked.

How... alive.

At that moment I promised myself I would never waste another second fearing the love I had for this man.

He was here, and he was mine.

We had sacrificed too much to bring us to this moment, and I wouldn't allow it to be in vain.

I pushed against the ground as I rose onto my toes and placed a chaste kiss on Silas's lips. His arms wrapped around my waist and he pulled me flush against his chest.

I heard Misneach shake out his wings a moment before he launched into the sky, giving us some privacy.

I felt the tension in Silas's body slowly ebb, and he sighed against my hair.

"I will never let you slip through my fingers again," he whispered.

"I'll hold you to that," I promised.

We stood like that, clinging to one another for the longest time until the sound of a throat clearing nearby drew our attention.

Cillian and Emmerson stood to the side, and we broke apart. We scanned them from head to foot, searching for injuries while they did the same to us.

"I thought I'd..." Cillian's words fell away as emotion clogged his throat.

Silas pulled his friend into a firm hug and whispered something to Cillian that had him nodding in agreement.

"Harlowe," Emmerson said, her words sounding brittle.

I didn't wait a moment longer before I lunged for her, crashing into her as she pulled me into a tight embrace. Her body trembled in my arms as she worked to regain control of her emotions.

"When I saw you take that hit, I wasn't sure I would ever see you again," I confessed.

"Me," she said as she barked out a weak laugh. "What about you? When the connection between you and Kieran broke, I thought I'd lost you," she cried. "I've never felt so helpless. You're my best friend, Harlowe. We are in this life together, or not at all."

"Together," I said thickly.

When Emmerson released me, I surveyed the area in search of Misneach. "I'll be right back," I said when I spotted him.

I jogged in his direction as I closed the distance between us. He spread his wings wide, and I stepped inside his embrace as he lowered his forehead to mine. His wings snapped tight around me, giving us a moment where it was just the two of us.

**"Thank you for protecting me out there, Misneach. I wouldn't have survived this day if it wasn't for you."**

**"Our story wasn't over, Fire Heart. It still isn't,"** he said.

**"Will you tell the other dragons..."** I trailed off, unsure of how to express what I was feeling.

Sadness and loss had my throat thickening every time I thought about the fact I would never hear their voices again.

**"They already know, but I will tell them, Fire Heart."**

I gave Misneach a curt nod, unable to hide the turmoil roiling inside me.

**"You're going to be all right, Fire Heart,"** Misneach said, sensing my thoughts.

**"So long as you stand beside me, Misneach."**

**"Always."**

We worked to clear the battlefield of the dead and prepared their bodies for the funeral pyres.

"What about him?" a man called out.

When I turned around, I saw him pointing toward Kieran.

"You will treat his body in the same manner as every other," I said firmly, daring him to challenge me.

When the man made no effort to reach for him, I growled and stalked toward him. "I'll do it myself."

Before I could, however, Silas pulled me back. "I'll do it, Harlowe," he said, his gaze soft with understanding.

Cillian and Fionn joined him, and together they carried Kieran's body to the healer's tent. Following closely on their heels, I entered the tent before my footsteps faltered.

Sucking in a ragged breath, I whispered, "Zeke?"

My friend's head swung in my direction, and a broad grin split his handsome face. Tears of joy spilled down my cheeks and I rushed toward him.

"Ouch, Harlowe," he laughed when I slammed into him.

"Sorry," I mumbled and stepped back to look him over. A blood-soaked bandage was peeking out from beneath his torn tunic.

"Are you all right?" I asked, worry taking hold of me once again.

"He will be fine," Arabella's sweet voice said as she made her way over to us. "If he can learn to follow simple instructions."

"Good luck with that," Emmerson snorted, joining us on Zeke's other side.

"All right, all right," Zeke said. "If you're only here to give me grief, you can leave," he pouted.

"And miss you being babied," Emmerson chuckled. "Not on your life."

Zeke grumbled something unintelligible, and I just soaked them in, sending prayers of thanks to the gods for sparing them.

I watched as Arabella looked down at Zeke with tenderness and he returned her expression, his eyes softening as he took her in.

Emmerson grinned over at me, wiggling her eyebrows suggestively.

"How is Illiana doing?" I asked Arabella.

"Resting," she said, inclining her head toward a bed roll nearby.

Illiana was fast asleep, surrounded by her massive dire wolves, who positioned themselves around her protectively.

"Have you seen my mother?"

"She's preparing your father's body for the funeral pyres," Arabella said, sympathy flooding her tone.

I nodded my head in thanks and left in search of my mother. When I found her, I moved to her side and picked up a cloth to wipe away the grime from my father's face.

We worked in silence until it was time for his body to be moved to the funeral pyres. Hand in hand, we followed the soldiers as they carried my father to his final resting place.

Silas and Cillian followed us, carrying Kieran's body between them.

Once all the bodies were in place, the dragons stepped forward, as they formed a line in front of the endless rows of pyres.

"May the gods welcome them home," Silas murmured before dipping his chin in the dragon's direction and placing his hand in my free one.

A low rumble filled the clearing a moment before flames erupted in an endless stream, lighting up the funeral pyres.

Those gathered watched in silence as the flames hissed and crackled, consuming the bodies of the fallen until all that remained was ash.

When the final embers died out, I turned around to leave.

There was still so much that needed to be done, but at that moment, I had to acknowledge the needs of my exhausted body. I marched towards my tent with determined strides, fueled by the promise of my bed and the warm embrace of the man I loved.

# Chapter Seventy-Five

*Three months later*

"Harder," I panted, as sweat glistened over my body.

Silas chuckled darkly. "Do you need more, Little Menace," he cooed as he pushed forward.

A cry escaped between my lips, and Silas pressed harder.

"Come on, Little Menace, give in to me."

"Keep treating this like foreplay and you'll find a dagger in your side," I said as I pressed the sharpened tip into his flank.

Silas glanced between us and then barked out a laugh. "Nicely done, Little Menace."

I stepped back to create space between us, and Silas spun his sword in his hand as he beckoned me forward.

I re-sheathed my dagger and, with a flourish of my blade, advanced on him.

Steel met steel in a brutal exchange of blows and my arms trembled under the sheer intensity of Silas's hits, but I loved that he never took it easy on me.

**"You should have stabbed him when you had the chance,"** Misneach growled.

**"This is only practice, Misneach. Besides, you'd secretly miss him if he wasn't around,"** I teased.

Misneach snorted and rolled his eyes, but I caught the faintest hint of a smile that he tried to conceal.

Silas circled me, his eyes narrowed as he assessed me for any weak spots.

Adrenaline spiked in my veins as my fight-or-flight instincts kicked in.

There was something primal about the way Silas fought. It was never just training for him.

He was a predator hunting his prey.

I adjusted my footing as I moved with him, never giving him my back. I shifted my blade in my hands, feeling the weight of it as I waited. Tension coiled my muscles tight, but I was ready.

Silas lunged forward, his sword cutting through the air in a fluid and graceful move that belied his years of experience.

I parried, our blades meeting with a sharp crack that rang out loudly in the stillness of the early morning air.

Spinning out of reach, I repositioned myself before unleashing a series of rapid strikes. Silas deflected each blow before bringing his sword down in a powerful arc. I rushed to meet his attack as I brought my sword up to deflect his blow.

Silas smirked, his eyes sparkling with mischief.

"I do love a challenge, Little Menace," he murmured.

**"I could never miss that arrogance,"** Misneach grumbled. **"You know what you have to do, Fire Heart."**

**"Yes, Misneach,"** I chuckled.

**"Say it,"** he pressed.

**"Eviscerate him."**

Misneach made a sound of approval as Silas advanced.

He feinted left and then thrust his sword to my right.

I sidestepped his attack and, with a quick twist of my wrist, I countered, aiming a strike at Silas's abdomen.

His eyes widened in surprise but he parried smoothly, as a broad grin spread across his face.

**"Now Fire Heart! Take him down now!"**

"Out for blood today I see," Silas laughed and I couldn't help the grin that pulled up my lips.

"You know me, Silas, I like it rough," I said with a wink.

"Don't I know it," he growled, and his eyes darkened as he watched me.

**"That was not what I had in mind,"** Misneach muttered.

The sun climbed higher in the sky, casting a warm glow over the training yard as we continued to trade blows.

I could feel myself growing tired, my limbs straining under the exertion.

"Had enough?" Silas asked, his voice breathless but steady.

"I can keep going," I said, even as my body screamed in protest.

Silas chuckled and shook his head. "So stubborn, Little Menace."

"Shut up and fight me, Silas," I teased.

Not needing any more encouragement, Silas pressed forward, his eyes never leaving mine as he brought his sword down, clashing with my own.

We were a blur of movement, both giving our all as our blades met again and again in a dance as old as time.

Sweat trickled into my eye, and I lifted my shoulder to wipe it away.

A strange tingling sensation erupted on my palms, and I lowered my sword to inspect them.

"What is it?" Silas asked, lowering his blade.

"I don't know."

The sensation quickly spread to my fingertips, and I flexed the digits, trying to disperse the feeling, but it only intensified.

"What—" my words fell away as bright white light formed in my palm and I sucked in a sharp breath.

"Fórsa," Silas whispered, his eyes locking with mine in astonishment.

"How is that even possible?" I mumbled to myself.

Then a memory slowly resurfaced in my mind as I recalled my last meeting with the fates.

*You will restore what has been denied to her from the beginning*, Drakkon had said.

"Could it be?"

**"If there was any being who could make it happen, it would have been Drakkon,"** Misneach said.

"Could what be?" Silas asked.

"When Drakkon made the trade for your life, he demanded the fates restore what they had denied me from the beginning. I hadn't known what he meant, but now…" I trailed off, as my mind whirled.

"But now you wonder if this was what he had meant all along," Silas finished for me as he dipped his chin toward my palm.

"Yes," I whispered. "Do you think the fates withheld fórsa from me because they had already gifted me with dragon flames?"

"I don't know. But it makes as much sense as anything else."

"How do I make it go away?" I asked, shaking my hand in the hope it would disappear.

"Not like that," Silas teased.

"Helpful."

"Close your eyes, Little Menace," Silas instructed, and I complied. "Take a deep breath."

I inhaled deeply, letting oxygen saturate my lungs before releasing it.

"Good girl," Silas praised. "Now visualize drawing it back into your body."

I did as he instructed, imagining the white light being absorbed into my palm and traveling up my arm.

"You can open your eyes now," Silas whispered.

When I glanced down at my palms, the orb had disappeared, and all that remained was the sweat and grime from my training session.

"You know what this means, don't you?" Silas grinned, and my eyes narrowed in suspicion.

"What?"

"More training!"

**"Excellent,"** Misneach beamed. **"Time to put the General in his place."**

# Epilogue

Nerves coursed throughout my body, and I couldn't stop fidgeting.

A large hand landed on my shoulder, stalling my movements.

"Why are you so nervous, Brother? After everything you've been through, she's hardly going to abandon you at this point." Cillian said.

"I don't know, Cill, Harlowe still has time to accept a better offer," Fionn teased, and I glared at him.

"Watch it," I snapped.

"I think her dragon might like me more too," Fionn mused.

"Her dragon likes everyone more than Silas," Cillian muttered.

"Thanks, Cill. That's very helpful," I deadpanned, and he gave me a sheepish smile as he rubbed the back of his neck.

I glanced out at the rows of people filling my mother's garden. They sat atop thick wooden logs that had been painstakingly crafted into beautiful benches for this very occasion.

The sun shone brightly in the clear blue sky and the flowers were in full bloom. They created a breathtaking backdrop of colors and scents that danced on the gentle breeze.

I inhaled deeply, allowing the mix of aromas to calm my nervous movements.

As I glanced around, I spotted the line of dragons that stood behind the master of ceremonies. They were tall and imposing, the embodiment of regal elegance.

Misneach stood at the front of the line, Caolán and Saoirse flanking him.

When our eyes met, he dipped his head in the slightest nod and I placed a fist over my heart, bowing deeply.

"Well, that's promising," Cillian said.

Soft music began to play, filling the garden with an enticing melody that mixed with the rustle of leaves on the trees and the distant hum of bees throughout the garden.

Sweat coated my palms, and a slight tremble shook my hands.

Emmerson stepped into the aisle, and everyone stood at her approach.

Cillian's mouth dropped open, and he stared transfixed as Emmerson walked toward us.

When she reached us, she whispered, "You might want to close your mouth, Cillian."

She took her place across from us and winked at him. Cillian snapped his jaw closed, but he couldn't pull his gaze away from the woman opposite us.

Small gasps broke out among the attendees and my gaze swung back in the direction Emmerson had just come.

At the end of the aisle, wearing a white dress that sat just off her shoulders showcasing her delicate collarbone, stood Harlowe. Her copper hair was pulled atop her head in an elegant twist and her face was concealed behind a sheer veil.

She held a small bouquet, handpicked earlier in the day from my mother's garden, and her arm was threaded through her mother's elbow.

She was absolutely breathtaking.

My heart seized in my chest and I wasn't sure if I was breathing, but I couldn't look away as she walked toward me.

I felt my throat constrict and my vision blurred as I continued to stare at her, unable to believe this woman was mine.

Cillian cleared his throat awkwardly beside me. "Silas," he whispered. "Are you alright?"

It was then that I realized I was crying.

All but fucking sobbing at the mere sight of her.

I scrubbed at my eyes hastily and sucked in a ragged breath.

When she was within reach, I closed the distance between us and pulled her to me. I flung back her veil and sealed my lips to hers in a passionate kiss as I devoured her, unable to get close enough.

The crowd broke out in laughter, and I could feel Harlowe smile against my lips, but I didn't care.

Nothing would stop me from claiming this woman because, at that moment, everything else fell away, removing all doubts and leaving only the certainty that she was my destiny and the very heartbeat of my existence.

She was my home.

# *Sneak Peek...*

My eyes raked over Cillian's muscular frame and need coiled tight in my belly at the way his leather pants clung to his firm ass.

The man had no business looking that good in training garb.

"Emmerson?" Harlowe called.

From the knowing grin that tipped up the corner of her lips, she was well aware of what had captured my attention.

"Are you even listening to me?"

"I think you know the answer to that question," I smirked.

Harlowe chuckled, but she quickly regained her composure. Her expression tightened and unease washed over me at the serious look she now donned.

"I have a mission for you..."

*The adventure continues with Emmerson and Cillian in Book Four of the Fire and Flame Series. This interconnected standalone will be published in 2025.*

# Acknowledgments

I am so thankful to everyone who has followed Harlowe's journey. It has been such a rewarding experience and that comes down to you all! Your support means the world to me!

To my sister Sherrin – Words can not adequately describe how thankful I am to have you on this journey with me. Thank you for the constant pep talks, the willingness to talk with me about my books for hours on end while we iron out all the kinks, and for all the little things you do in between to make this gig easier on me. Thank you.

To my beta team: Billie, Rebecca, and Nalannah – Thank you for giving up your time to help me shape this story and for being willing to continue this journey with me, even though I broke your hearts (again). Thank you.

To my ARC readers - Thank you for taking the time to review my work. Without you, my story would struggle to find its audience and I hope you know how much I appreciate each and every one of you! Thank you.

To my mum – Thank you for your four-star review. Keeping me humble since day one. Love you.

To my fantastic narrators, Alexa Borys and E.M. Wylde – Thank you for bringing my characters to life. You've made me fall in love with them all over again! Thank you.

To my Husband Luke and our beautiful children - Thank you for inspiring me every single day. I love you.

I hope you can all join me for Emmerson's turn in the spotlight... you know it's going to get weird (but the good kind of weird).

K.J. Johnson

# About the Author

K.J. Johnson is a fantasy and romance indie author who writes about headstrong heroines and morally grey men.

K.J. Johnson's debut novel, A Heart of Fire and Flame, is book one of the Fire and Flame series.

After a lifelong obsession with reading and escaping into different worlds where anything is possible, she decided to let her imagination run wild and penned her debut novel - A Heart of Fire and Flame.

K.J. Johnson enjoys writing romance of the darker persuasion and you can expect plenty of spice, but check your morality at the door because it won't survive the ride.

In her downtime, she still enjoys getting lost in a good book and experiencing the world through the eyes of her favorite authors.

# Also by K.J. Johnson

Fire and Flame Series

A Heart of Fire and Flame, Book One of the Fire and Flame Series
A Daughter of Fire and Flame, Book Two of the Fire and Flame Series
A Queen of Fire and Flame, Book Three of the Fire and Flame Series

*Coming soon...*

Book Four of the Fire and Flame series (title to be announced).
An interconnected standalone following Emmerson and Cillian.

A dark fantasy romance duology (titles to be announced).

# Social Media Links...

Follow me on:

TikTok/Instagram/Threads: @authork.j.johnson
Facebook: Author K.J. Johnson

Or sign up for my newsletter to keep up-to-date on all new releases and receive exclusive behind-the-scenes content at, https://kjjohnsonbooks.com/newsletter.

www.ingramcontent.com/pod-product-compliance
Lightning Source LLC
Chambersburg PA
CBHW070642310726
48982CB00001B/375

* 9 7 8 1 7 6 3 6 8 2 5 4 2 *